D0309245

THE
WATERS
& THE
WILD

THE
WATERS
& THE
WILD

DeSales Harrison

ONEWORLD

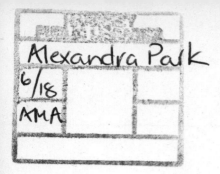
A Oneworld Book

First published in Great Britain and the Commonwealth by
Oneworld Publications, 2018

ISBN 978-1-78074-911-2 (hardback)
ISBN 978-1-78607-179-8 (trade paperback)
ISBN 978-1-78074-912-9 (ebook)

Book design by Susan Turner
Printed and bound in Great Britain by Clays Ltd, St Ives plc

Oneworld Publications
10 Bloomsbury Street
London WC1B 3SR
England

Stay up to date with the latest books,
special offers, and exclusive content from
Oneworld with our newsletter

Sign up on our website
oneworld-publications.com

MIX
Paper from
responsible sources
FSC® C018072

For Laura

THE
WATERS
&
THE
WILD

PROLOGUE
October 2008

H ad you a nightscope, or the eye of a night bird staring down from the rafters of the church, you could make him out, the priest: supine, sunk in darkness, wide-awake.

He had not seen her come in, the girl. How long ago had that been, Father Spurlock wondered, lying on the shelter cot, his gaze lost above him in the groined and vaulting shadows of the church. Three weeks, he counted, three weeks since she appeared, occupying the café table as though she had always been there, her profile still and grave as a figure cut in bas-relief. The table she had chosen in the church café was the small one beneath the Noah window, and the stained-glass eye of Noah's crow scrutinized her, or rather the sheet of paper she'd unfolded in front of her, as though the crow had perched on the gunwale of the ark for that purpose alone. That day she had approached him, shown him the paper, and abruptly departed, leaving him with nothing save the name Clementine Abend scrawled on the palm of his hand.

How long had she been sitting there, staring out at the evening rush-hour traffic? Or rather through the traffic, he thought, as one might stare through a clear stream to its streambed. Had she been there when he'd tied his apron on over his clericals and assumed the five P.M. shift behind the café counter? And at what moment had she changed, imperceptibly and without moving, from anyone into someone, from someone into that girl?

But no, she wasn't a girl anymore. Even from where he stood he could sense that. Eighteen? Possible, though she seemed older. Twenty? No, younger than that. Something in her bearing, in the unmoved abstraction of her gaze, had convinced him that she expected no one, that no one would arrive to join her. The volume of huge darkness pressed down on his chest, like a book of stone.

Yes, he remembered, she had chosen the table under the Noah window, the crow over her shoulder hunched up and pitch-black against the glassy expanse of the floodwaters. If the crow had been visible when she had come in, he thought, if the rest of the window had yet to go dark, then she had arrived before sunset. She had remained into the evening, even after Luis, the custodian, had stacked the last chairs and herded the tables together, chaining everything to an eyebolt he'd sunk in the church facade. *"Buenas noches, Padre—"* Luis had said as he always said, closing the doors on the setting sun as he left. *"Que duerma bien."* Then the girl had been alone in the closed shop.

It was Father Spurlock's custom, since the café had first opened eight months ago in what had once been the Lady Chapel, to intone a mock dismissal, filling the space with his ringing, ecclesial baritone: "Hallowed Grounds is closing now. Go in peace! We're here every day, even Sundays," before adding with hambone emphasis, *"Especially* on Sundays." Now, however, he didn't know what to say. She couldn't—she wasn't hoping to stay in the church, was she? The "overnight visitors" (as they were known with varying degrees of irony by the vestry) knew to approach the church after dark, to stash their carts behind the alley dumpsters before making their way through the service door. Surely she was not one of them. Even if there was something vagabond about her (she'd propped a worn backpack in the seat facing her), her bearing shared nothing with the unreachable, untouchable abjection of the visitors. Untying his apron, he had resolved then to revert to his pastoral approach and greet her as he would greet any tourist or passerby from the avenue. *Welcome to the Incarnation, miss,* he would say. *I'm Father Spur-*

lock. What brings you here today? He regretted now, as he never did otherwise, that he had let his beard, heavy and lion-gold, grow long enough to hide his priest's collar.

Three weeks later, staring up from his cot into the dimensionless darkness of the church, he saw it again as though she had never left, her profile against the wall beneath the Noah window. The "custodian man" (she had said) had told her to wait until the coffee shop had closed. Padre Spurlock, Luis had said, would be able to see her then.

So, Father Spurlock thought, I have Luis to thank for this as well. "We've got Luis to thank for this!" Mrs. Nickerson, his helmet-haired secretary, never tired of proclaiming, whether in amazement, or gratitude, or exasperation. Luis: whom the church payroll listed as sexton; Luis, who referred to himself—even after forty years and six rectors—as the "yanitor." With inert forbearance, Luis had taken the coffeehouse project in stride. How many "outreach initiatives" (Spurlock wondered) had Luis watched flower and die? How many hours, days, years, had he spent clearing the debris of all-volunteer projects, the pageants, the potlucks and rock operas, the water tables set up along the avenue for marathon Sunday, the much advertised yearly blessing of the animals with its attendant panoply of shit-shapes to be hustled into his dustpan? Luis responded to each new request with an undeceived and unobliging "If that's how you want it, Padre . . ." But hadn't Luis, unasked, taken to hauling chairs and tables from the sidewalk, every evening? He had Luis to thank for that, for the vigilant eyebolt, for the sidewalk hosed clean each night of sugar wrappers, lemon rinds, and coffee stirrers, for the doors opened every morning, the coffee made, and the pastries laid out for the first customers.

He had Luis to thank—and, alas, probably God too—for leaving the side door of the church unlocked. Luis had assumed this dereliction of duty not long after the coffee shop had opened for business, as though to say, "If we are going to lure the well-heeled from the avenue with cappuccino and biscotti, then *ciertamente* we could accommodate more shadowy passersby with a dry place to sleep." At first only one or two men slipped in, vague forms vaguely familiar from the church steps, where they would hunch and rock before burrowing for the night into middens of flattened cardboard, newspaper, bubble pack, and Spurlock could not bear to think what else. Later, when the weather cooled, more faces appeared at the shelter, followed shortly by a citation from the city, mounting complaints from some parishioners, enthusiasm from others, and the long, tedious debates in vestry meetings, the endless declension of earnest phrases: "the least of these," "the least we can do," "doing mission," "clarity of mission," "mission creep" . . . Holding up the citation, Mrs. Nickerson said as though for the first time, "For this, chief, we have our Luis to thank."

The visitors were men, most of them older, many of them trembling, all untalkative. God knew how long they had lived on the street or what they had experienced at Bellevue or Wards Island to drive them from the archipelago of licensed city shelters. The parish might have been more welcoming had they been battered women or gay teens expelled from suburban homes, but these shuffling mutterers shrank from all expression of sympathy or concern. To each one, sealed in his grease-caked garments and encasing stench, the merest acknowledgment seemed unbearable.

For Father Spurlock, the stench was the hardest part. At some point, in a gesture of what he'd described as solidarity, he'd begun sleeping four nights a week on a cot alongside them. He would doze briefly, overcome by the exhaustion of the day, only to wake when the smell reached him, an infiltrating mist, the sublimation of ash and tooth-rot, urine and scurf. In time (he thought at first) he might learn to give himself over to it, even to welcome it as a cleansing penance. Solidarity with the poor, the naked, the captive! O cinder-path of saintly effacements! The nobility of it! The absurdity of it! A bubble of his drowned divinity school idealism rose up in his throat, then dissipated like a sighing belch. How quickly it had happened, his transformation from freshly ordained provisional deacon— scrubbed and penny-bright, ablaze for avant-garde liturgies and boisterous youth programs—into a nail-biting, sheep-counting, budget-hobbled rector, yoked to a listless parish, or rather the remnant of one. His predecessor, Mother Janice, had departed to serve uptown as canon of the cathedral, along with her ringing laugh, her famous saxophone, and the younger half of the congregation. The senior warden still insisted on calling him Sonny the Kid in vestry meetings. He'd been in fact the youngest rector installed in the nearly two-hundred-year history of the church, but whatever remained of that youthfulness now seemed to hang from him like a dinner jacket surprised by a Sunday sunrise. The turmoil of five brief years had disgorged him onto a midlife plateau where some-where in the distance his wife, Bethany, labored grimly to make partner at her law firm because, as she put it, someone had to earn an actual living in this marriage.

Singled out among the squadron of lawyers marshaled to defend a pharmaceutical corporation in a class-action case, Bethany had been rewarded by her superiors with ever-escalating responsibilities, and the hours she spent at work had multiplied accordingly. When she'd first been assigned to the case, he'd announced with some satisfaction that he would see to it that dinner was waiting for her when she got home—whenever she got home—but this resolution had collapsed in the bone-yard of his other marital initiatives (learning bridge, couples yoga). It was more convenient for Bethany to eat with her "team" before it renewed its evening onslaught, and anyway, by the time Bethany's heels finally clacked out of the elevator, Spurlock would have long since fallen asleep on the sofa, pinned beneath the puttering bulk of Perpetua, his cat. Without consulting his wife or even himself, Spurlock had doubled, then redoubled his initial one-night-a-week commitment to the im-promptu shelter in the church.

Had he perversely come to *prefer* sleeping in the church, he asked himself, steeped in odors of sweat and destitution? Was this how the Holy Spirit bent the soul to virtue, not by persuasion but simply by revok-ing alternatives? But no: he knew he had come to spend more than half his nights in the shelter not because doing so was virtuous, but because it was plausible—plausible and easy—a path of minimal resistance, an easy slide from his upstairs office, past Mrs. Nickerson's desk, down the stair-well, and into the church. If the church was a ship—and that's what *nave* meant, he explained each year to his handful of bored confirmands—

then an imperious gravity drew him down into steerage with this skeleton crew, these ghostly stowaways. As this path hollowed its groove, he had accustomed himself to repeating that everything would be different once the pharmaceutical case was completed, or at least once Bethany made partner. If, however, that assertion had reassured him in the past, now it carried with it a whiff of dread.

In the event, it was the girl who spoke first. "Does 'Padre' mean you are the . . ." She paused and cleared her throat, as though unused to the sound of her own voice. "The head person?" Until then, her face in profile projected a severity, sharpened by the high bridge of her nose, by the ink-stroke of her eyebrow. Now that she had turned toward him, however, her face seemed younger, her lips full and pursed around an uncertainty. In his confusion at finding himself the object of that gaze, he registered somewhere in it the glint of gold, a rivet or staple piercing her septum or eyebrow, or was it the hood of her ear? Less an adornment, he thought, than a mortification of the flesh. He thought: How intolerable it is to the young, their beauty.

"Head person? I like the sound of that," he said, putting on affability. She did not smile in return, so he said, "Yes, I am the rector here, Nelson Spurlock. How can I help you?"

He would never forget what she said then: *I believe you might have something for—for a Clementine Abend. Something my father sent you.*

Her father? Whose daughter was this? Had she mistaken him for someone? Had he met her somewhere and forgotten? But that, he knew abruptly, was an impossibility. Impossible that such a face—that he could ever have forgotten it.

"I'm sorry—" he had said. "Your father? He sent you something?"

"A letter maybe. I don't know exactly. Maybe some papers."

"Your father is a parishioner?"

"No, a—he was a psychoanalyst. But I believe that a patient of his— I believe you performed the funeral for a patient of his, a person named Jessica Burke."

Jessica Burke. Of course he remembered. Hers had been the first funeral he had conducted after his "installation" as rector. Twenty-eight years old Jessica Burke had been when she died of an overdose, not much younger than Spurlock himself was at the time. He had never met her, but the sacristan had placed a photograph on a little easel by the coffin, a portrait that Jessica Burke, a struggling artist, had made of herself in a mirror, standing behind an expensive-looking box camera, a Hasselblad or Rolleiflex, her face downturned toward the viewfinder, one thin arm, heavily tattooed, crooked behind her head to keep her hair from falling down over her face. The picture had given the impression that Jessica Burke had showed up to serve as photographer at her own funeral, underdressed, uninvolved, annoyed to have to work on a Saturday morning.

"Your father knew me only because I buried a patient of his?"

The girl had spread a handwritten sheet of paper on the counter between them. "He says here—" she began, but interrupted herself. "This document," she began again, "it's a testament, a will, or at least a piece of one."

"Your father's will?"

"Yes. It's in French. I can translate if you like."

He said something about having studied a little French in high school, but she had already begun.

" 'Maître,' it begins," she said, following the line of precise cursive with her finger.

"Master?" Spurlock ventured.

"Yes," she said with a flush of what might have been impatience, "but that's just how you address a lawyer or a jurist. 'Maître,' it begins—" she said, then recommenced her fluent rendering of the French, pausing now and again, waiting for a satisfactory English expression to present itself, the legal phrases coming obediently to her (he thought afterward), as they might to one already well acquainted with the wishes of the dead.

" 'I, the undersigned,' " she read, " 'currently residing at 152 West Seventy-ninth Street, Apartment 8A, New York, New York, do hereby declare this to be the codicil to my last will and testament. As the habitation—'

"No, that's wrong," she said, "not habitation—dwelling, maybe—domicile . . .

" 'As the domicile I shared with my daughter throughout the period of her minority shall forthwith be vacated and sold, I do hereby authorize and direct that following . . .' " She paused again. " 'That pursuant to the settling of my estate all future correspondence concerning said estate be forwarded to my one child and only inheritor—'

"No, not only, not inheritor—heir, sole heir is better.

" 'To my sole heir at the following address.'

"That's this address," she said, turning the sheet toward him so that he could read it himself.

Miss Clementine Abend
c/o the Reverend Nelson Spurlock, Rector
The Church of the Incarnation
New York City, NY, USA

"Which is this church, right?"

He nodded, but she had already begun to translate the two remaining sentences on the sheet: " 'Except for the limited provision stated herewith, I confirm and republish my last will and testament duly witnessed and signed 15 August 2008, on file at the law offices of Crulwich, Labrie, and Steiner. I pray you to accept, Master, my most respectful salutations. 29 August 2008.'

"That's the end of it," she said. "He didn't even sign it."

"I am Nelson Spurlock," Spurlock heard himself say, unnerved to see his name on a page written hardly two weeks ago, snared in a stranger's handwriting, in a language he could not read.

"So, anything that would have been sent would have been sent to you."

"Is that what it says?" said Spurlock.

"You haven't received anything?"

"Received?" he repeated, as though that word too were in another language.

"In the mail, like it says, anytime in the past month or so?"

"No, although—no—perhaps my secretary—" Spurlock stammered, as though any piece of mail could possibly arrive without Mrs. Nickerson opening it immediately. "No," he said finally. "I haven't seen anything."

"No letter? No package?"

"Nothing," he said, surprised by how it pained him to say so. But why should it hurt him to disappoint her, this stranger little more than half his age?

"I am sorry, Miss Abend," he said. "But if you could write down your own address, and your phone number too, I promise I'll let you know if something appears. When something appears. Right away."

It was then, at that precise instant, that something in her countenance changed. Suddenly she was looking at him as though he were the one speaking an incomprehensible language. "I give you my word," he said. "If the address on the will, Clemen—Miss Abend—if the address written there—the one on the Upper West Side—if it's no longer good," he blundered on, "is there a better one where I can reach you?"

"What?"

"If this address—if another one is better—one way or another, Miss Abend, I promise you—" Spurlock said, forcing back the certainty that he was speaking to himself only.

"Clementine Abend—" she said, but broke off.

"Yes, Clementine, if I could," he said, unnerved by the insistence in his own voice, "all I would need—" He'd taken a pen from his pocket and, realizing he had no paper, began to write her name on the palm of his hand. "Clementine—Abend," he said, pronouncing the name slowly as he wrote it out. But after muttering something about having to go, the girl had retreated from the counter toward her table under the Noah window and in what seemed like a single swift movement had shouldered her bag and passed out onto the street. The gimlet eye of the stained-glass crow met Spurlock's. "What now, Father?" the crow seemed to ask.

✳   ✳   ✳

That had been three weeks ago. For days afterward he would find himself wondering if Clementine Abend would appear again, to inquire once more if anything had been sent to her, in his care.

In his care, Spurlock thought.

Abend, thought Spurlock. The name had meant nothing to him.

He had consulted the parish records and had found no one by the name of Abend. He had even flipped through the parish visitors' book to the day of Jessica Burke's funeral three years earlier. *Abend. Abend.* But again, nothing, and he was confident in his memory for names and faces, whether of parishioners or visitors. If something did arrive, how would he find her? She had left nothing behind. He would simply have to continue to wait for her to appear again, though there had been no sign of her. The disquiet he felt, did it stem from the sight of his name, caught in the indecipherable toil of a stranger's writing? Or was its origin—as he began to suspect—something quite different: the thought that he would not see that face, her face, ever again?

Three uneasy weeks had passed. She had not appeared. Nothing had arrived. Nothing until today. Spurlock blinked, willing himself awake. If this was sleep, he wanted none of it, this awful weight bearing down on him, cold and rigid, measuring its length to his. If he could just dislodge it, if he could rise from his cot, he could prove that the weight was not a weight. He could grope his way up to the church office, to his desk, where he would see that the package resting on it was still only a package, still was what it had been before he had, thinking of something else, torn open the seal. It was just another piece of the day's mail, just another envelope on his desk, a package like any other sent by accountants, tax attorneys, auditors, or the diocesan offices, packages Mrs. Nickerson would date-stamp and shunt to the appropriate file or vestry committee. So what if this envelope, a slick, striated paper stamped with foreign postage, proved un-shuntable, marked as it was PERSONAL AND CONFIDENTIAL in painstaking block capitals? Were he to open it again, he would see that the envelope contained just a stack of pages, each one a weightless sheet of onionskin. Maybe he would discover that he had not in fact read them through in a single, paralyzed sitting, that they too were the tatters of a dream he'd

shaken off and discarded. Maybe he would find himself once more a
stranger to the voice that those pages relayed: rapt, patient, heated, and
tempered, insistent as the bit of a rock drill drilling a rock face.

Father, you will not remember me. My name is Daniel Abend.

A cry jerked him to his senses. Had it been his, or a cry from one of
the sleepers? He tried to fasten his gaze to something, anything, in the
darkness swirling above him, but he found no purchase in it, in the particular, total blackness of stained glass at night, the panes lightless now
as the webs of lead they'd been set in, every figure as black now as Noah's
crow. He could hear, beyond the breath and rustle of the sleepers, the
restless avenue (after all, the night could not be so far gone), but the
black of the windows insisted that the church, like a cavern or coal-
gallery, had no exterior.

I believe you may have something—something my father sent you—

—she had said, her face no longer the severe, etched profile but facing him as she spoke, as it faced him now, a perfect oval, the eyes a flat-
bright nickel gray, with somewhere the glint of gold piercing her, because
(Spurlock thought) the beauty of the young was intolerable to them—

—something for a Clementine Abend.

No, it was obvious she was no longer a girl, however clear the gray of
her eye, however smooth the curve of her cheek. Something or someone
had drawn down over that face an invisible, perpetual veil of care.

I believe you have something, something my father sent you—

He'd had nothing for her when she came three weeks ago, but then
in this morning's mail it had arrived, the heavy envelope containing that
stack of weightless pages:

You will not remember me. My name is Daniel Abend.

He had read it, bent over his desk, oblivious of Mrs. Nickerson's departure, of the window's failing light at his back, the world itself falling away and with it the substance of his own body, Spurlock a mere shadow bent over the stack of lamplit pages, each sheet weightless but tight-peened with type, as though the words themselves had invested the stack with its intractable mass, the mass that now bore down upon him.

She had not returned. A certainty, at once unwarranted and undeniable, filled him: he would never see Clementine Abend again.

So sleep at last dismantled the troubled spirit of Father Spurlock, but even as that darkness without exterior closed around him, he felt the blackness shiver and crack, a network of fissures feathered out in a blizzard of fragments, flocked up and on the wing, a cloud of agitations collecting its formlessness to a shape at first spheroid and revolving, then conic, vortical, funneling itself into his chest—as when, in autumn, at nightfall, a blackout of blackbirds drains into a single tree.

ONE

Father, you will not remember me. My name is Daniel Abend. Even if you have seen my face, it was only one among the many faces gathered at the funeral of Jessica Burke, and that was three years ago, almost to the day. You do remember Jessica Burke—do you not?—dead of an overdose, the daughter, I believe, of a woman in your congregation. I had not attended your church, nor any church for that matter, in many years. No special claim to grieve had brought me there, beyond the bond between a psychoanalyst and his patient, that unequal, equivocal hold that also holds at bay.

For two years she had been my patient, my analysand, so I had seen her four times a week, five times even, at the beginning of the treatment. During those years, I had listened to Jessica Burke longer and more attentively than I listened to my daughter, Clementine, suddenly hidden from me in the maelstrom of her adolescence. I believed I knew Jessica Burke well, as well as I knew any of my patients. I believed as many at the funeral seemed also to have believed that she had come to flourish, that she had indeed found a new life. What is more, I am convinced she believed this as well and credited me with having helped her in this. After several failed attempts, Jessica had finally kicked free of the heroin. She had begun to "make art," as she put it, had reenrolled in a life-drawing class she'd stormed out of a year before. She had made an appeal to be reinstated at her college and had begun attending night school courses. She had repaired severed relations with family. I believed she was better, believed she had eluded a danger, and because I believed these things, the news of her death came as something more than a shock.

I have lost patients before, sometimes gradually, to illness or age, sometimes suddenly, and a young one more than once or twice. And I have known that deep, narrow grief any analyst knows, having peered so long into a soul freed from its contexts, unfolding and growing under the lamp of his attention—only to have the lid shut, the lamp blown out. They say psychoanalysis is a school of limits: the session must end, the treatment must end, because childhood must end, and life. Perhaps so. Even with my youngest patients, I have never felt it impossible that they could die.

And yet for Jessica I had thought it so, or felt it, even to the moment of taking my seat in a pew, alongside old Itzal, the doorman from my building, whom she had befriended. I had felt it simply, merely, impossible that she could have died—Jessica Burke!—whom I had seen as recently as the previous Friday, who remarked on her new boots as she settled herself on the couch in my office, crossing her ankles as she always did. They were motorcycle boots, the leather stiff and uncreased, so new I could smell it, tannic and fishy, as the session progressed. "I'll have to walk a million blocks," she'd said, "before they stop hurting me." It had been the first time in she didn't know how long she'd gone out and bought new shoes, and where could she walk a million blocks except in the future, a future crowded with plans and appointments, a bustling territory claimed as her own?

I said that the news of her death had come as something more than a shock. I should have said that it came as something less than one: the shock had yet to arrive. Something detained it, held it in abeyance, perhaps out of pity for me, perhaps savoring in anticipation the bitterness of comprehension once it arrived.

After the ceremony, three years ago, I had thought to write you, to send you a note. In fact, I went so far as to find your address at the church.

What would I have said? That I was grateful, for her sake, that someone intelligent and articulate and without illusion had spoken? That you had helped us to bid farewell, without falsifying the pain of her life, her perennial suffering, the frequent dissipation and final annihilation of her potential? Even now I remember with gratitude how you began your eulogy. An overdose! Too much. More than a body can handle. More than anybody can handle. We had lost our friend, our daughter, Jessica, to an overdose. Yes, and that alone was too much, but in another way, in our grief, we were all overwhelmed in the flood of death, the waters rising up to our necks. I remember thinking that you must have children. That perhaps you too have a daughter, as I do, perhaps a troubled daughter, or lost. That the death of Jessica Burke had struck you deeply as well. We were all in over our heads, you said. Everything was too much, our lives were too much. Too many temptations, allurements, false starts, false promises. Too much pain. Too much grief. And there was nothing to be said about this: some griefs, you said, outstripped all consolation.

As for explanations, we would never be satisfied. That is what I remember you saying: that the world is more full of weeping than we can understand. I had never heard at a funeral, certainly not from a priest, comfort held in such disdain, and I wanted to thank you for that. If I had written, or rather, if I had written before now, that is what I should have said.

The purpose of your sermon, you said, was to set us a challenge. The first part of the challenge was for us to make an admission: that Jessica Burke had taken with her the possibility of consolation, the possibility of satisfactory explanations, that she had abandoned us on a hard, unmarked terrain. The second part was to make a leap of faith, not faith in the providence or wisdom of God (because that would merely be another consolation), but faith that her own journey, every bit as solitary, every bit as hard, was now over. What we must begin anew each day, each one of us alone, was now for her completed. For her, something entirely new has begun. Jessica Burke is not who is lost, you said. The faith you wanted us to have that day was the faith that we were the lost.

You went on to say more, but by then my mind had withdrawn into itself, its cloud of memories, among them the memory of what a police officer had said to me afterward, after he had asked what he called "his routine slate" of questions. "It must be hard for you guys," he said, "when you lose one like this." It moved me how he had said it, his grave and serious "you guys." "Yes, it is," I had replied. He had been right, as you had been—the hard, unmarked terrain. But against that hardness, that flinty ground, something had kindled itself in me (or so I felt in the pew), something that could never go out, a grief making itself known like a dim but unkillable flame. Unkillable! Good God, how gratified I was by the thought, by the satisfactory phrase, as though the words alone could feed her unappeasable memory—or mine. And so I wept, without shame, as though it were my due. Hiding my face in my hands, old Itzal's impassive form beside me, I wept.

Had I written you, perhaps that is what I would have told you, how satisfied I had been by the funeral. I must admit it: what I felt then was a kind of happiness, as though a slaking grief, sweet and unkillable, were my compensation and inalienable right, as though that moment were not the last happiness I was to feel, the last of my life's allotment, as though the death of Jessica Burke were not for me the end of all satisfactions—all, that is, but the very last.

There: I have made a beginning to it, this confession. Will you hear it? Will you hear it even though I believe nothing, even though I cannot say whether it is a confession of guilt or a confession of sin, or whether it is a confession at all? I tell you I believe nothing. I do not offer it in hope of forgiveness, much less of absolution or redemption. What is more, when I tell you that it is I, that I am the one who caused the death of Jessica Burke, you will not believe me. You will think there is nothing to forgive, that what I need is not forgiveness but help. That is what you will believe right until the end, until my story forces its conclusion on us both. Then you will see how the man I was is beyond all forgiveness.

TWO

But know this, Father: I never laid violent hands on Jessica Burke. In fact, after shaking hands in our first consultation, I never touched her at all. I knew she lived just six blocks from my building, but I never saw her on the street or in the neighborhood. Even in all the hours she spent in my office, how fleetingly her face turned toward me. Only for an instant at the end of the session, as she rose from the couch, would she lift her eyes to meet mine, and always as though she had forced herself to do it, just as she seemed to force herself to say, *So long.*

I believed I had done my part, that without reproach I had safeguarded the integrity of the analysis, revealing nothing of myself, interpreting each instance of transference, defense, or resistance with equanimity and objectivity, as professional obligation required. I believed then that she had come to appreciate, as patients often do, this neutrality, this bland and studied featurelessness in her analyst. *Is it horrible that I don't know more about you?* she had asked once. *Is it horrible that I don't want to know more?*

"Sometimes you lose one," the police investigator had said when he interviewed me. Surely he was right. Who isn't touched, from time to time, by accident and evil luck? So I thought at her funeral, as though the story had ended, while in reality it had yet to begin.

*   *   *

After the funeral, for a few days' grace, life appeared to resume its rhythms, though I scheduled no new sessions in the daily hour that had been Jessica Burke's. I entertained vague plans of spending that freed time in observance of her disappearance, walking around the reservoir, maybe, or if my daughter, Clementine, had a free class period, meeting her for a coffee or cocoa and an elephant ear at Esmé's, a café we liked, just across the street from her high school. The plans, however, remained unrealized, and I passed Jessica Burke's empty hours staring at the tetrahedron of daylight the sun cast on the strip of wall at the foot of the couch. Over the hour it would change shape, though never so quickly that I could see the change as it happened.

That shape of light had been what Jessica Burke had looked at in her sessions over the two years she had been in my care. What was I doing, staring at it now? Waiting for that flatness to vibrate, to release a whispered echo of Jessica Burke's words? Those words had been in every way unremarkable, the runoff of everyday frets and worries, the white noise of the day-to-day muffling all cries, whether of ecstasy or terror. I had disliked her voice at first, noting my distaste as the first instance of negative countertransference, the analyst's inevitable resistance to the patient's inner turmoil. Despite her dishwater hair and thrift-store clothing, an unconcealable Brahmin croak bridled her voice's upper register, and though a tattooed word bruised the back of her knuckles, her gesticulations dispensed a blasé, patrician nonchalance. It had taken months for me to appreciate the brittle frailty in these traits, to discern in her profile the beauty she labored to obscure, to acknowledge what I must have noticed when first she appeared in my office: that her eyes were a bright lapis blue.

It seems to me now that after the funeral entire weeks must have passed like that, a score of Jessica's widowed hours dissolved in my staring at the wall. In reality, however, the interval was brief, no more than the two or three days required for a letter to make its way across town, to appear among the other bills and statements on a hall table. It was an ordinary letter, in a plain envelope, addressed to me at home. Maybe I had overlooked it or had neglected the mail for a few days. In any event, it was Clementine—no doubt looking for something else—who brought it to my attention.

"Who's sending you a key?" she asked, holding the envelope up to the light.

It was unmistakably that, a little lopsided weight in the corner of the letter, its shape shadowed on the outside of the envelope by the pressure and grime of the post office sorting belts. Inside, there was nothing else, no note, no letter, just a key affixed to a tag bearing my name, spelled out in neat capitals: ABEND, D. The key itself was stamped with the letters USPS and what looked like a serial number: a post office key. It was my own post office key, I concluded, sent to me in the mail. Like many analysts, I have always kept a post office box for patients who send checks in the mail, to preserve analytic anonymity. Clementine would tease me about this postal box, calling it my love nest, my trysting bower, but in fact I checked it only infrequently, no more than once a week. Surely I had lost the key somewhere without noticing that it was gone. Anyone could have turned it in to any post office, and the post office, identifying it from the numbers, must have sent it to me. Why not? Nor did I think to verify that my postal key had in fact gone missing. How couldn't it have, if this was it?

So that was when it began, the awareness, the first flush of it, like motion caught in the corner of the eye—an intimation prior to thought. It was there and gone even before it occurred to me to check my key chain. The awareness began as a kind of puzzled befuddlement (what is this thing? where is it from?) but turned suddenly into something else—not dread exactly, not yet, rather the solution from which dread would precipitate, a solution odorless and colorless yet permeated by an equally clear not-quite-rightness. When Clementine asked me about the key later that evening, and I reported that it was a post-box key I'd lost, that colorless, odorless wrongness was the reason I knew instantly I was lying—not just mistaken but lying. That wrongness was why I avoided checking my key chain, and why, when I finally did, I was not surprised to find my own mailbox key still there on the ring. That sense of wrong-ness must have been why I waited through the weekend until Monday, until after Clementine had left for school, to walk down to the post office to make my inquiry. That wrongness knew already that the key would not fit the lock on my box. A clerical error, I said to myself: someone has misread a column of names or numbers.

"Doesn't open your box," said the clerk.

"I've tried it in the lock—" I began to explain, but he had sighed off to retrieve a green ledger from somewhere behind the counter.

"Daniel Abend, you say? You have ID?"

"Yes, and when I tried the key—"

"That's your key. Box 5504, to be renewed—not until next year."

"But that's not my number," I began again, but he had vanished once more, only to emerge, at least a foot taller than I'd imagined, from a door giving onto the lobby.

"Box 5500, 5502, here we go—" he said, turning the key in the box directly below my own, withdrawing a large envelope. "Daniel Abend, box 5504," he said, reading the address. "You might want to write that down somewhere." It did not seem important anymore, or even possible, to say that this was not my box, not the mailbox to which my patients sent their checks, and anyway, the clerk must have sighed his way back through the lobby door because his graveled voice called, "Next!" from behind his window.

Suddenly I understood, standing there in the post office, holding the envelope the clerk had just handed me, that she had sent it, that Jessica Burke herself had addressed it to me, writing out the painstaking capitals that spelled out my name. Like the envelope in which the key had ar-rived, this larger envelope lacked a return address, and yet now I knew that both it and the key were from her. I stood there staring stupidly at the envelope, as one might stare at a car in a parking lot, a car similar to one's own and in a similar place, but not the same. Likewise this enve-lope was mine and not mine, and if it was not mine, I should hand it back as I would any letter gone astray. I would hand back the key as well. I will drop the key into the local mail slot, as one would drop a key through the slot in a door one had no intention of opening ever again. *Do it,* I said to myself. *Do it now.*

I did not do it. My hand had already opened the envelope and withdrawn from it a single sheet of graph paper torn from a notebook. On the sheet, written out in the same painstaking block characters, was—what was it?—a sort of list, an itemization? An itinerary? The steps in a sequence? No, it was none of these. It was a poem. Before I read it, I knew it, what it was, what it said. I knew how it ended.

Jessica Burke had mentioned the poem in passing, in a session. Someone had shown her a copy, or she had been assigned it in a night school class she was taking. The course had been her favorite, and she was hoping to reenroll in school, full-time if the administration would permit it. She had seemed excited, happy: if it was spring, soon it would be fall. "New pencils! New erasers! New lunch box!" she said, half ironically. Maybe it was not too late to enroll for the fall semester. If she could "throw herself on the dean's mercy," maybe it was not too late after all, not too late!

This was her plan. The very fact that she had formulated a plan at all seemed to me a sign of progress; perhaps the familiar fog had lifted from the terrain of her future. I could hear the change in her voice, in the sessions and even outside my office in the lobby if she arrived early enough to chat with Itzal, the doorman.

"You watch, Itsy," I heard her say. "I'm going to do it. I'll bet you a million dollars."

I couldn't hear Itzal's response, no doubt something about how betting tempts the devil, or perhaps he merely shrugged, his shoulders lifting somewhere in the ill-hung spaces of his doorman's coat, gaunt cheeks creased in a dry, inverted smile, as though to say: "Everything is possible."

It was the happiness of possibility, an infectious happiness, how the spring sunlight struck its frank spring shape on my office wall. Though I continued to work with her as I always had, I think now that my interpretations must have felt warmer to her: *Yes you are now able to feel a new excitement for a future, for your new course, yes you no longer want to be somewhere else, to be someone else.* For surely I felt it too, that possibility of which spring itself seemed the guarantor, the sunlit patch on the wall like a tacked-up handbill announcing a new act in town.

The poem I was holding in the post office, she had asked, in passing, *Do you know it?* It had been just so great, she'd said, just to talk about books in class again, just to talk about books. She'd just gotten her first essay assignment, to write about a poem, this poem by Yeets, no, not Yeets, Yeats. . . . Did I know it? I was obviously a literate guy, with all the books I had in my office. . . . *Do you know it?* she had asked, then without waiting for an answer, going on to say that it was a fairy poem, about how the fairies lure some child away from his familiar world, saying the world is more full of weeping that he can understand. *That poem,* she said, *do you know it?*

I had answered with natural honesty: *Yes, I know it,* I said. *I know it well.* But to have said so, to have answered her question, however truthfully, however spontaneously, was an error for an analyst, a technical misstep. Immediately I was aware of this, and of the need to regain my footing. Such a concept of error is foreign to those who have never practiced or undergone psychoanalysis, as is the idea that the analyst should disclose nothing of himself. In a well-conducted session, however, everything depends upon that abstinence. I should have said instead: *What would it mean to you if I knew it?* Or: *You want us both to know something together. You would like to have a new kind of conversation with me, about a thing we could share.* I should have said something like that, because even in her passing remark she had turned the poem into a kind of gift, and it is axiomatic to my trade that every gift conceals a squadron of vigilant desires and dissembled meanings. Here, she had in effect said, here is something I like. I want you to have it too. I want to oblige you with something in common. I want you to be obliged.

On the other hand, the lapse was minor, a hairline scratch in the reflective surface of the analysis, a surface inevitably chipped and scraped in the course of daily sessions, even while the gentle, repetitive friction of the sessions works in time to restore that surface's mirroring sheen. In any event, she had paused only briefly, and having registered my misstep, I had to turn my attention back to the stream of her speech. I never thought about it again until that moment in the glare and hubbub of the post office. At that moment, however, a conviction surged through me, not as an idea but as a jolt of current: *Jessica Burke had sent me this letter.* It was she who had sent it, and it was she who had leased the box in my name and mailed me the key. I knew then what she had meant for me to know, holding there what she had meant for me to hold. And I knew that it was not, as I had originally thought, a gift. When she had posted this letter, she had not intended it as a present. It was instead a bequest—no less so than if it had been unsealed in an attorney's office and read out to a gathering of legatees. When she had posted the letter, her death had been as inevitably fixed in her future as it was now for me irredeemably lodged in my past. In mailing it, she had as much as said: *It is my will that you should have this document. Upon the event of my death, I do desire and direct that it shall be yours.*

And yet what was it, this single sheet, torn from a notebook, this poem by Yeats you could have found in any library, any anthology? What was I meant to do with it? She had not changed it, had only copied it out by hand in blocky capital letters. Standing there, thinking none of this but knowing it, I read it through. Or rather, it read itself to me. After all, I knew it by heart, from the first stanza:

Where dips the rocky highland
Of Sleuth Wood in the lake,
There lies a leafy island
Where flapping herons wake
The drowsy water rats;
There we've hid our faery vats,
Full of berries
And of reddest stolen cherries.
Come away, O human child!
To the waters and the wild
With a faery, hand in hand,
For the world's more full of weeping than you can understand . . .

To the last:

Away with us he's going,
The solemn-eyed:
He'll hear no more the lowing
Of the calves on the warm hillside
Or the kettle on the hob
Sing peace into his breast,
Or see the brown mice bob
Round and round the oatmeal chest.
For he comes, the human child,
To the waters and the wild
With a faery, hand in hand,
For the world's more full of weeping than he can understand.

Jessica Burke would have sent me the poem no earlier than a day or at most two before her death. Her death, I knew now, was not an accidental overdose but a suicide. In sending it, she had said: *Do you remember? You admitted that you knew it. You admitted you knew it well.*

THREE

Three years ago that was, the inception of my secret. In sending the poem, Jessica Burke had entrusted me with the fact, suddenly obvious, that she had taken her own life. I was to keep this final fact as I had kept all her others, as its mute, hired guardian. That, at least, was how I understood the envelope she had sent me and the poem it contained. Or so it seems to me now, Father, now when I ask myself why I said nothing, told no one. Whatever secret Jessica Burke had confided in me, surely I was obliged to keep it. Whom, in any event, would I have told? Not her mother, who lived in Pensacola with her third husband and tormented her daughter with maudlin, alcoholic telephone calls. Should I have told the police? They had done their job and drawn their conclusions. My job was different. Was I not by trade the custodian of stories the world would not hear?

In any event, the window for disclosure snapped promptly shut. Each hour of delay would be an hour I would have to explain, and I had no explanation to offer. Thus the secret declared me its home. As for the postal box itself, I had no reason to open it again, and the key itself took its place among the other odd objects washed up in my years of practice: a Zuni fetish sent by a patient who had moved to New Mexico, a headless action figure an autistic child had named (to my amazement) the

Danger of Speculation. Surely box and key required nothing else of me, having discharged their emissary duty. Surely Jessica Burke had no more letters to send. I brought home the poem and placed it in an empty pigeonhole in my desk.

Nevertheless, I must have peered into box 5504 from time to time on my weekly trips to the post office, as though my eye sought repose in its perfect emptiness. I know I must have because one day, three years later, that emptiness had been replaced by the bend sinister of an envelope's diagonal shadow in the box.

Father, I ask you this: Why did I not assume that the letter was for someone else, that the box itself now belonged to someone else? I had never, after all, received anything else in it, had not in three years even received notice to renew its lease.

This envelope was roughly the same size as the first one, the one with the poem, though smoother than standard manila with a faint striation, a European envelope, I thought, like the ones I had used during my years in Paris. It seems to me now that when I removed it from the post box and read my address, spelled out patiently in careful block capitals, there followed a moment of stillness, a floating like the floating of a vase or glass that, having escaped the hand's grasp, turns lazily, luxuriates in air, as though no haste could trouble it before it shatters on the floor.

The letter had been sent four days earlier. It could not have been sent by Jessica Burke, dead now these three years. These were new instructions: from where, from whom? A wave of vertigo seized me and drove me out onto the sidewalk, cresting in a surge of nausea that broke in a splatter of vomit on the curb. Someone, I seem to remember, approached me to ask if I needed help, but I must have simply walked away, apparently in the direction of the park, because after a while I was sitting on a park bench, the new envelope resting beside me, still unopened. My attention had affixed itself to the ordinary, the circumstantial, the dusting of pollen that lay on the bench, the few bruised daffodils lolling at the border of the path. I needed to get home. Hadn't Clementine said something about bringing a friend by for dinner? I ought to stop by the store. I should check what time it is. The mechanical chorus of everyday obligation was urging me up from the bench. The daffodils, the face of my watch, everything nodded and whirred in a clockwork pantomime of the ordinary. But the ordinary had vanished forever the instant I took the envelope beside me from the postal box.

Yes, Father, all of that I knew even before I opened the envelope, knew so completely that opening the envelope seemed the merest formality. And in fact I was not surprised, not really, to see that the envelope contained the poem, the very poem, that Jessica Burke (I once believed) had sent me three years before. The same blocked-out, handwritten capitals, regular as architect's script, marched through the same four nearly equal stanzas, each concluding in the familiar refrain:

> Come away, O human child!
> To the waters and the wild
> With a faery, hand in hand,
> For the world's more full of weeping than you can understand.

Yes, I know it, I had said to Jessica Burke. I know it well.

It was the same poem, unaltered, as though nothing had changed at all, and yet at the same time the poem now was wholly different: the place names not just foreign but strange—Sleuth Wood, Rosses, Glen-Car—the antiquation of the phrasing not just fastidious but alien. What made it so? The strangely familiar paper of the envelope, its slick finish something I remembered from Paris, yet had never thought of again. I realized I was hearing the poem now not in Jessica Burke's voice as she might have read it to me, but in another voice entirely, a voice struggling with the poem's oddities of diction, the syllables so difficult to pronounce for someone whose first language was not English but French: heron, drowsy, furthest, faery. I heard the poem, its refractory words—eron, droassy, furdest, feery—in that other, beloved voice. What filled me then, for the briefest instant, was an inexplicable sweetness. It was as though someone had found in a closet or attic a piece of my own memory and had sent it to me, thinking I should like to have it.

Even as this tenderness flowed through me, I perceived that the sheet on which the poem was written was not, as I had thought, some unfamiliar variety of European paper, heavier and smoother, like Bristol stock, but photographic paper, thick and curled at the edges, stiffened from the fixing bath. I turned it over, and it was there, she was there, her face facing me: the image of Jessica Burke dead in her bathtub.

The image was horrid and familiar at once. In every detail the scene in the photograph was just as the officer had described it three years earlier, just as Jessica Burke had been when the building superintendent had found her. There it was: the spent needle. There were the spoon, the lighter, the pool of wax where a candle had burned down, all just as the officer had said. Her works were right by the tub, he'd said. No sign of foul play. Pretty cut-and-dried. Just due diligence. Just dotting the *i*'s. He had said that the girl's mother, unable to reach her daughter, had called the super. The super had called the police.

I say the scene was in every detail just the same as I had imagined it, just as the officer had described it, and it was the same, that is, in every detail except one—the plastic sack over Jessica Burke's head. I have read the statements, all of them, the responding patrolmen's, the super's, the medical examiner's, the young investigator's; none mentions a plastic sack over her head. But there it was in the photograph, bag drawn down over her face and gathered under her chin, where a collar of what looked like masking tape secured it against her throat. Beneath the collar, the edges of the bag formed a kind of ruffle. The sack's clear plastic did little to veil her face, her expression one of absorbed preoccupation, as though sleep had surprised her. Her head had lolled to the side, and her arm rested on the edge of the tub, hand expectantly open. A patch of sunlight had draped itself over her breasts and shoulder as though trying to cover her nakedness.

What must be obvious to you now, Father, came to me only slowly, slowly and terribly: someone besides Jessica Burke had been there. The bag meant that Jessica had died of suffocation, but there was no bag present when her body was found. Someone had to have removed it. Someone else had been there, standing a little to the side so that the sun would not lay his shadow across her body. That is what the photograph itself

meant: someone had been there, someone who had taken the photograph, someone careful to hide his shadow, someone who had removed
the plastic sack and vanished.

At first I could not accept this. After all, could not Jessica have put
the bag on her head before injecting the drug? Would not that have
made sense, for someone whose intent was not to get high but to kill
herself? I had been certain, ever since I received the first letter, that she
had taken her own life. I must admit that for a moment I even assumed
idiotically that she'd taken the bag off between overdosing and being
discovered. It took minutes for the obvious fact to become for me even a
possibility. Someone had to have been there. Someone had stood in the
bathroom and taken the photo, not the night before when it was thought
she had died, but in the morning, after the candle had burned down,
after the light of the risen sun had reached in through the window to
spread its patch of light on her nakedness. Someone had broken the tape
seal around her throat and had slid the sack off, allowing her head to loll
back to where it had been.

What struck me first was the absolute irrevocability of that nakedness, a nakedness all the starker for the sealed veil over the face. And it
was from that sense of her nakedness that everything followed. Shame
filled me to have happened upon her like this, to have happened upon
her even now, three years later, peering through the pane of the photograph, her body laid out in cold water and morning sunlight. Someone
had been there, and what they had known since that morning I knew
now too. They had wanted me to know it. The time had come. I had
been admitted into the inviolate privacy of it, and a latch had clicked
shut behind me. Only then did I notice the two words written along the
bottom margin of the photograph in the now familiar block capitals.
Only then could I read them. Or rather hear them, as though a cold
breath from a cold throat had whispered them in my ear: REMEMBER ME.

SPURLOCK
11:57 P.M.

D aniel Abend, said Spurlock aloud. No answer. Only darkness
and the shuffle of restless sleepers. Spurlock thought of the
stack of papers on his desk in the dark of his office, each sheet
a weightless onionskin, though the stack itself was heavy, like a stone.

Was this awful alertness the pressure of God's mysterious hand? To
hell with that. As for the mystery of God, Spurlock had always maintained that God's part was no mystery at all. The command was clear: to
love. But love whom? the heart objected. Everyone, God foremost. Love
how? With everything you have. A task, in short, doomed to failure, but
that was part of the plan, because fulfilling the commandment was
meant to be costly. In fact, it was meant to cost everything. Sooner or
later, everything would be taken away—success, reputation, possessions,
health, memory, mind, body—the soul at last stripped naked before
God. Love was nothing but this discipline of surrender, the practice of
relinquishment taken up each day anew. The soul would seek to avert its
gaze, to flee from the charge, but the instruction itself left no room for
doubt. The mystery was no mystery, the secret no secret at all.

How resourceful the soul was in pretending otherwise. He thought of
his wife Bethany's tireless, lucrative toil for her firm. The firm was a creature of appetite, not for justice or even riches (the money was secondary, a

means of keeping score), but for the exercise of power, perfectly adapted to the intricate wilderness of the law. This region was where Bethany lived and thrived, swooping among the mountainous contracts and filings like a hawk among everlasting alps. Faced with complexity himself, Spurlock had always trusted his impulse to stop, to sit, or to kneel, confident that in time he would hear the still, small voice of the command. What should I do? *Love.* Whom? *Everyone.* When? *Always.* If at times this imperative seemed infantile and unbelievable, well, that was how God came into the world, as an infant, cradled in the straw of an incredible story.

Now, however, as Spurlock lay on his back in the dark church, for the first time in his life he felt the weight of a new thing, and beneath the weight he felt his old confidence buckle. What was it, this new thing? He did not know, but he registered its presence as an act of justice, a chastisement for his lifelong presumption that clarity and simplicity were his due. If obedience to God's command was to cost everything, he wondered for the first time, why should it not cost his belief as well?

Father, my name is Daniel Abend. You will not remember me.

Of course he didn't. They had never met. Abend had said so himself. Nor had Spurlock ever met Jessica Burke. The only time he had seen her was in the photograph set up beside the coffin at her funeral.

Once, not long after he'd been ordained deacon, Father Spurlock had accompanied an anxious parishioner to a cardiologist's appointment for an angiography. He had watched on a video screen as the doctor steered a catheter from an incision in the parishioner's groin up into her laboring heart. Once in position, the catheter was made to release a dye, in pulses, and with each pulse, for an instant, the branching path of blood was visible, as if the body were nothing more than a mist and the mist had been blown aside. Now, thought Spurlock on his cot, he was the one who had been infiltrated. The probing voice of Daniel Abend had threaded its way into him and released its radioactive stain. Spurlock closed his eyes, but the mist kept blowing away, revealing with each gust of dye the negative image of a heart on a screen.

FOUR

Do you, Father, have children? Listening to you at Jessica Burke's funeral, I thought you must have. You said that to lose a child was to lose everything, not just a person, but hope, purpose, meaning, faith itself. There was no place to hide—not even, you said, in religion. That is why, you said, in the Passion narratives the mother *has to be there* at the Crucifixion. The Passion is the Passion because the mother is present. All of us can and will lose our friends and our illusions, as Mary Magdalene and the disciples do. All of us can and will lose our lives, as Jesus does. Losing a child, however—that is a different matter. For other people it has happened, does happen, will happen. For one's own child, however, it *cannot*. The event is not only unthinkable but, in some elemental way, impossible. One can continue to live after the death of a child, but no one, properly speaking, *survives*. After the death of a child, all life is afterlife.

I am certain you can imagine what gratitude poured into me later that day, the day I received the photograph of Jessica Burke suffocated in the bathtub, when, staring in a stupefied panic out the window of our apartment, I saw Clementine round the corner with her friend Liza. My beautiful daughter, living and breathing! Clementine was encumbered with a grocery bag and clasped the bag to her chest when Itzal came out to meet them on the sidewalk, stretching out his long arms to relieve her of her burden. You will imagine what relief I felt when she appeared with her friend in the vestibule of our apartment, kicking off her boots, dropping keys and cellphone onto the vestibule table, crinkling her nose, and asking, "What's that smell?"

I had just burned the photograph at the stove. It had arched and stiffened over the burner, the image darkened, inverting itself into a ghostly negative before igniting all at once. My regret for burning it was immediate and permanent. Those words at the lower margin, were they a command? *Remember me! Never forget!* Or did they pose a question: *Remember me?* How could it matter now, I think, then think next: Before long I shall find out.

Clementine informed me that I had met Liza already. If I had, it was in an earlier version of this young woman, without fuchsia-dyed hair and a ring piercing her nose. "Dude," said Liza to Clementine, "show me a picture of your mom."

"Dan doesn't keep any," she said. She'd taken to calling me Dan, I thought, because no one else did, because doing so was both more insolent and more intimate than calling me Daniel, as others do.

"Why not just Dad?" I had asked, saddened by the development.

"Because you're not just Dad, you're Dan," she had said.

"Dude, juices," said Clementine to Liza. Their plan was to "do some juicing," a new enthusiasm of Clementine's, before heading out again for the evening.

"Where are you going?" I asked.

"Just friends, just out," said Clementine as she snapped together the components of a juicing machine she'd persuaded me to buy. "Dan doesn't drink juice," Clementine said to Liza. "He's the only shrink in New York who doesn't believe in health."

Taking turns feeding hanks of kale and beet greens to the machine, they closed around themselves a patter of hermetic jokes and imitations, all conducted in the ironic hybrid of French and English common to students at the Lycée Français.

"*Encore de* leg-yooms," said Liza, calling for more vegetables.

"Dude," said Clementine, "cool *ton* jets."

"Aren't you girls going to eat something before you go out?" I asked in what struck me, even as I spoke, as an impersonation of parenthood.

"Aren't you going to read something," said Clementine, "before falling asleep at nine?" The girls finished off their juices and left. Where had she learned to solicit and cultivate friendship? Not from her father, I thought.

After the girls had gone out for the evening I discovered the empty vermouth bottle hidden under some carrot greens in the garbage. The pulp-clogged parts of the juicing machine, abandoned in the sink, stank of vermouth and yard waste. I put the empty bottle back in the garbage, covered it again with the carrot greens, and retreated to my room.

I was not asleep at nine, or at two thirty when Clementine's key finally turned in the door, my wakefulness unblinking, like the shutter of a camera open forever over the body of Jessica Burke. I was not asleep hours later when first light, wet and livid, dissolved the black mirror of my windowpane, replacing it with the veiled, oblique, first face of the world, an image like that of a motionless girl in her bath, fixing itself on a submerged sheet of photographic paper.

FIVE

That dawn arrived like a bailiff's summons. I had been given notice that the end awaited me. Whatever else the photograph of
Jessica Burke meant—that someone had been with her when
she had died and had removed the bag before the body was discovered—
for me it meant that the end was here. It said: See, it is over; the end is
here. It has found you at last.

The face was Jessica Burke's, of course, and yet not hers. It was also
Clementine's, as though its look alone said: Whose child is safe? Whose
child cannot be stalked and taken? What shield is your care, your worry,
when I can enter through a keyhole, the prick of a needle? That which
in her infancy you could only wonder at—what she would come to look
like, who she would become—I already knew, I who can see through
everything, through everyone. What you would ignore, what you would
deny, I know already. Whom you would keep from me, I have already
marked as my own.

And it is also another face, the one I had tried so often to describe to
Clementine when she, standing in front of a mirror, would ask me about
her mother: *Was her nose like mine? Are my eyes like her eyes?*

I had thought I could describe Miriam's face to her, just as I had
thought I could explain Miriam herself. I would invent, discard, rehearse

the sentences I would say to Clementine. I would even write them down. Should I say, *Sometimes when babies come into the world their mommies have to leave and become angels?* Or: *When you were a tiny, tiny baby your mommy got very sick and she didn't wake up?* Holy God. Could I think of nothing better?

When Clementine was a little girl, I read books, consulted colleagues, prepared myself for her inevitable curiosity, for her inevitable confusion, disbelief, grief, rage. Her questions, however, proved both simpler and more stymieing than I'd imagined.

"When you used to be Mommy did I use to be a boy?" was one of the first. Somewhat later she asked, "Was Mommy dead when you first met her?"

In the end, it was not so much her inquiries as her physical being that pushed the question of her mother out into the open. Late to develop, even her body seemed to resist this arrival, but when puberty finally overtook her, imposing upon her an arresting, unignorable beauty, the question took up residence in our apartment. It was as though an uninvited relative had come to stay. Who was this new person troubling the mirror? Where did she come from, and what does she want? It frightened me how rapidly her body took on adulthood, not only the young adult she was to become, but also, uncannily, the young adults her parents once had been and were no longer, one of them alone somewhere on the tableland of middle age, the other among the ageless dead.

Of course, I had no right to be frightened like that. She was after all a girl, a girl in a huge city, with the usual cares and the usual needs. Still, that unfamiliar face emerged from the depths of the mirror, as though to say, "Do you remember me? You must remember me."

Several years ago—before Jessica Burke died, so Clementine would have been thirteen or just fourteen—we had finished breakfast and I was washing up when she asked, "So did she look like me? Like me minus you?"

"What do you mean, 'me minus you'?" I asked.

"Like Clementine minus Dad?"

I knew what Clementine was asking: whether she could draw aside those features she attributed to my genetic contribution and look at last

on her mother's face. I do not remember my reply. Did I answer pretending that I could truly remember, as though that face that was always with
me were not also always hooded in shadow? Or did I try to dodge the
question, saying something like "She was French, of course, so she was
darker than I am, her skin more olive, her eyes brown"? Did I say, "As for
your height and eyes, you got them from me"? I confess there have been
times when I have caught a glimpse of Clementine doing her homework
at the table or reading on the sofa and the impossible notion has pierced
me: Miriam is here.

I met Miriam on the landing outside a friend's apartment in Paris. I was
thirty-one years old. My friend and I had eaten dinner, and I had taken
my leave, was on my way to the stairs, and there had been no reason to
pause, to acknowledge a stranger. The stairs were the spiral sort one sees
in Paris, the kind that wind around the caged shaft of an elevator. I could
have kept going when the elevator door clacked open on its dimly lit interior, its single passenger, her downturned face. Her eye unmet, I could
have departed by another way. I could have descended the stairs to the
unlit foyer and stepped into a different future, any of a thousand different
futures. Each time the memory resumes, each time it flickers into motion with the whir and rattle of the elevator ascending, I turn to descend
the stairs, to follow their curve around the shaft so that the elevator and
its passenger pass unnoticed. . . .

I have thought there is nothing I wouldn't give to have that chance
again, to leave those eyes unmet, the chance to step out onto the Parisian
street, out into any other future, any future other than this one. What, I
have asked, would I not give?

Well, to that question, at least, I know the answer. I know what I
would not give. I would not give my daughter.

I had been preparing my departure from Paris. I had my tickets, had
communicated to my Romanian concierge—with the aid of a calendar,

an approximate drawing of an airplane, and, finally, the advance payment of my last month's rent—that the time had come for me to return
to the States. My yearlong fellowship at the American Hospital was drawing to its close, and I had already packed up my scant possessions in
boxes I'd saved from my arrival. I had bidden my farewells to the few
colleagues I had come to know—all, that is, except for my friend Mathieu. I'd met him, also a young psychoanalyst, after a lecture at the
Collège de France. Over many coffees and with impressive patience he
had improved my French, and in return I had offered to translate an article he was hoping to submit to a prominent Anglo-American psychoanalytic review. That evening we had met to discuss the final draft, and
he'd insisted on making a farewell dinner: a roast chicken with *haricots
verts* and parsleyed new potatoes. For my contribution, I had brought a
couple of bottles of a blackish Corsican wine chosen only because I
could pronounce its name intelligibly to the wine merchant near my
apartment.

We had set aside the writing when we moved to the second bottle of
wine, discussing a journey he'd made to the States when a boy, how
some stretch of coast in New England had reminded him of his native
Brittany—did I know Brittany?—how a neighbor in his building, a graduate student in philosophy, was writing a thesis on certain English
poets—would I be willing to help her too?—about my failure to visit
more of France, more of Paris, during my stay. "And so you must come
back, then, of course!" We agreed that I would, but only on the condition that I would put him up some August in New York. How often I
have thought back over those bland exchanges, imagining a line of per-
foration between each, how easy it would have been to say, "*Bon, voilà*, I
will go now." How grateful we both would have been in the morning not
to have uncorked a third bottle of wine, and I would have stepped over
the threshold into the damp night that much earlier, would have followed the path of a different future: back to my rented room, back to the
States to establish a practice, to resume my former life, all by saying ten
or five or three minutes sooner, "*Bon, voilà*, I must let you sleep."

But no, instead I left after the third bottle, found myself on the landing in front of the elevator, which had clacked open on its dim interior and sole occupant, Mathieu's neighbor, the student of *"philo,"* her hand compact and strong shaking my own, her level gaze fixing me, the gaze from which I would never escape, her *"Enchantée"* both solemn and amused in response to my *"Je suis nommé Daniel,"* her saying then, as though answering a question I did not know how to ask, *"Miriam. Moi, je m'appelle Miriam."*

Miriam. What did she look like? What could I say to my daughter? That Miriam was beautiful no doubt to others, the plane of her cheekbones, her nose high-bridged, brow level, the lips at rest slightly open, while to me the cheek, the nose, the mouth, were beautiful because they were Miriam's alone? That in dreams even now that mouth presses itself against mine, as if starved for the air in my lungs?

And so I would lie, saying, "That's just what she looked like, Clem, like you minus me."

SIX

Mathieu had said she was a singer, *une choriste*, that she earned extra money during her studies by singing in choral ensembles. So I knew she was a graduate student in philosophy and a singer, that her name was Miriam Levaux, and that was all I had. It would have been easy enough to ask Mathieu her telephone number, but I did not. I could not, not because I was shy or ashamed, but because in some way I knew that the Miriam I would find with Mathieu's assistance, or anyone else's, would not be the Miriam I sought. The Miriam with friends, with acquaintances, at the center of her own history, would not be the Miriam I had seen in the caged interior of the elevator, not her body, knowledge of whose compact wholeness leapt like a spark from her palm to mine when she shook my hand. *Miriam. Moi, je m'appelle Miriam*, she had said, as though to say: "You will only find me if you find me alone."

And so I set to my work. Newspapers from the corner kiosk yielded a bewilderment of choral listings: Eastern Orthodox choirs, American gospel, madrigal ensembles, a "Missa Flamenca," a Palestrina festival. Attending events across the city, I slipped into back rows and pews, slipped out early when I'd determined she wasn't there. I think now how slender the odds were that I would find her. How could I be sure she was even in the city? But I was sure. I knew it was only a matter of time and in the event not very much time at all, perhaps a week, perhaps ten days.

The concert where I found her was a program of music by Tallis and Allegri, the venue a church not more than half a kilometer from my apartment. The place was more crowded than I had anticipated, and the view from my pew was partially obscured by a pillar. It was only by leaning to the side that I could make out the faces of the singers in the choir.

Was that her, small and dark, in a plain dark dress, standing in the front row? Someone behind me hissed when I leaned over farther to see. I do not remember what the first pieces were; the music seemed to pass through my person unimpeded, like radio signals. The concert concluded, however, with Allegri's *Miserere*, whose first stately notes seemed to restore to the church its extinguished purpose. I cannot describe or explain the feeling, but it was as though the music I heard was at once music no one had ever heard and music I had always loved. Was Miriam's voice among those blent in that solemn current? I was certain it was, but I could not see her. *Monsieur!* my neighbor hissed again when I tried once more to see around the pillar. I closed my eyes and listened.

Miriam, I learned later, was not one of the robed figures visible at the front of the church. Hers had been a solitary voice, separate from the choir, sequestered with two or three other singers up in a loft or gallery. Hers was the single soprano voice set apart for the ravishing upper flights of the *Miserere*'s refrain, the voice that detached itself, every other verse, to hang for a harrowing instant in the ether before swooping to a lower octave.

She did not recognize me after the performance when I approached her on the street. I repeated my name twice before she remembered where we had met. "Ah, Daniel! Excusez-moi!" she said, and it was perhaps still in a spirit of apology that she agreed to join me for a glass of wine and to humor my hobbling French. Nevertheless, she accepted a second glass, and those were followed by two more glasses, until it grew late and the café waiter began to bang chairs onto tabletops and sweep around the base of our table.

Standing by the cash register to pay (the waiter now assiduously ignoring me), I watched her smoke her cigarette, watched her reach out to stub it in the ashtray but then hesitate, lifting the cigarette again to her lips to take a final drag before stabbing it out. She had kicked off a shoe, and her foot, resting flat on the tile, looked small and sure, as though accustomed to nakedness.

Would I be in Paris a little longer? she asked, lighting another cigarette, when I returned to the table.

Not long, I said. My flight to the States would leave in a few days.

Ah, *dommage*, because maybe I could have helped her with some translations, as I had helped Mathieu. A friend of hers had composed a series of songs, settings of Irish poems that Miriam was scheduled to record. She wanted there to be good translations in the liner notes, better than the French translations she had found. Did I know much Irish poetry?

I did not.

A shame, because it was very beautiful, or so it seemed to her.

Maybe, I said, we could meet before I left.

Would it be possible? It would only be brief, and in turn she could help me with my French pronunciation. I had, she said, a lazy American mouth.

And saying that, she reached across the table as though to touch my lips but stopped just short, so close that I could smell the nicotine on her fingertips.

Yes, then, it was settled, she said, withdrawing her hand. We would meet in the next few days.

That evening, we had spoken some of the music. I remember her describing it, how her explanation of the *Miserere* grew more animated with each sip of wine. But in truth what obliterated all other recollection was the music itself, in which her voice seemed both the extracted essence of all the other voices and yet wholly detached from anything or anybody, hanging in the airless reach of that high octave, stepping down at first with deliberation, then plunging through the abrupt, descending figure that concludes the line. That single upper note seemed the point, Archimedean, illuminated, where joy and anguish converge, if only for an instant, then the voice subsides at last into silence and the cry is taken up in the cantor's stark baritone, the voice of one from whom fate has taken everything:

Ecce enim in iniquitatibus conceptus sum:
et in peccatis concepit me mater mea.

Behold, I was shapen in wickedness:
and in sin hath my mother conceived me.

Surely you know these words, Father, so often sung in Holy Week. It is through their darkness that the soprano line cuts like a beam of light. No, not like a beam: like a blade, like a torch cutting sheet iron, the cut releasing a molten shower as the figure descends, poured out, then pitched headlong into blackness. What I remember from that evening, a kind of mortal injury, a penetration not pain but deepest astonishment, a wound to instruct the wounded in one fact only: that his body can be opened, that it harbors no sanctum that cannot be breached. I do not know what I am saying, and yet I am certain that for Miriam the experience had been in its way the same—not, of course, the experience of meeting me, but of the music itself, that for her the upper reach of the *Miserere* was a clearing, an opening. No, I do not know what I am saying, but I am certain that she saw it, that opening within me, the passage the note had cut through me with the hard edge of its flame. She was in flight and saw in that opening a way out, an escape. She saw it and she took it.

So that night, after we left the café, it was inevitable that she would ask to come up to my apartment, now nearly empty, that she would accept a glass of black Corsican wine but leave it untouched beside mine, also untouched, on the floor beside the bed.

✳   ✳   ✳

When I woke the next morning, alone, I didn't know where I was or what had happened. I blinked at the wall. I thought that if I lay completely still, the taste and shadows of the previous night would reassemble themselves into a memory. Instead I heard a little shuffle, a scrape. She was there when I turned over, seated in my only chair, smoking a cigarette, her bare feet resting in a patch of sunlight on the threshold of the open *porte-fenêtre*. I remembered her bare foot on the floor of the café. I remembered, and I remember now, the odor of nicotine on her fingertips as they hovered just shy of my lips. I remembered then, and remember now, the pressure of her pubic bone against my upper lip.

She smiled and said, "Daniel."

She said, "Remember me?"

I stayed in France.

The day of my departure, printed on the airline ticket I'd tacked to the jamb of the door, came and went. The ticket itself stayed tacked to the jamb. It became a kind of joke between Miriam and me. When I left the apartment, she would say, "*Oublie pas tes billets, chéri!*"—Don't forget your tickets, sweetie!—as though I were departing on the 8:06 train to Clermont-Ferrand for an afternoon meeting. Or she would say, "Tickets, tickets!" in feigned annoyance when (for example) I had bought the wrong kind of toothpaste at the pharmacy or failed to pick up our clothes at the laundromat. "You forget, *monsieur,* that I have my tickets!"

I knew where mine were, I would say, tilting my head toward the doorjamb. But where were hers? "*Ah, monsieur,*" she would say. "*On a tous ses billets.*" We all have our tickets. And "Tickets" was our reply when one or the other would say, "*Je t'aime . . . je t'adore.*" "*Mais tu as tes billets, quand même . . .*" But you have your tickets, all the same . . .

SEVEN

And where were her tickets?

Shall I tell you? she asked, but told me nothing.

And where was she going?

Going? she said, as though we had been speaking of something else entirely.

Home? Mars? Senegal? America?

Not America! she had said. That huge Babylon.

And what was home, while we were at it? Paris?

What, Paris? I did not think she had a Parisian accent, did I?

I did not know there was a Parisian accent.

Surely I was not asking to meet her parents, to make an appearance in her hometown in the Nièvre. . . . A silent American, accompanying Levaux's daughter! What a homecoming! Could I imagine?

No, no, she said. Not where she comes from. That is not where she would take me. Not back to the past. Instead, she would take me to the place she was headed.

Or so I thought she said, though I didn't or couldn't understand what she meant. Speaking of past and future had felt suddenly wrong. I realized, in the silence that followed, how much I liked it, how much we both liked it, knowing nothing of each other's future or past. In any event, I forgot about our plan and blinked at her in confusion when she showed up one morning with a borrowed car and instructed me to pack for a week.

Even when I was driving (she had insisted I drive), she did not tell me where we were going. Eventually, after the boulevards, traffic circles, and segments of ring-road, we merged onto a highway. The plain of the Île-de-France spread out like a stilled sea, endless fields of grain, haze-hung, touching every horizon, a tundra of uninflected green.

It was not so hard to drive in Europe after all, was it? she said. I had demonstrated a basic competence, she said. Maybe I was ready to take the next step.

She kicked her sandals off, slid her seat all the way forward, and in a single, neat maneuver pivoted so that her back was pressed against the dashboard, her feet against the seatback.

Et voilà the next challenge, she said, working her skirt up above her hips and cupping her hand between her legs, drumming her fingers once or twice, as though in impatience or boredom. *T'es sûr ça te derange pas?* You're sure this won't bother you? she asked as her fingertips began to describe a slow circle.

When the drive was at last over—lengthened as it had been by Miriam's peremptory instructions, by the hunt for a shaded byway—we had switched off the ignition in the courtyard of what appeared to be some sort of monastery.

She said: So now you can see why I needed to get you out of my system.

In the office an old monk she knew by name greeted her, beaming, with a double kiss: *Miriam, ma fille, tu vas bien?* You must be exhausted from the journey. *Monsieur, enchanté,* he said, and shook my hand, beaming at me as well. Turning back toward us from time to time, as though to confirm that we were following him, he led us to our rooms.

The men's dormitory was a part of the monastic enclosure, though much newer in construction than the other buildings that comprised the cloister. Women slept in a guesthouse separated from the monastery by a narrow lane and an iron gate, long off its hinges, leaning against the gatepost in a tangle of nettles and bindweed.

After a chaste pair of kisses, Miriam disappeared into the guesthouse. The monk gestured me through the gate and said, "So Monsieur and Madame Levaux are here for a silent retreat?"

Was I supposed to say something? I said nothing.

"I wish you," he went on, "a prayerful visit."

I am certain, prior to that exchange, I had never been wished a prayerful anything, nor did I know what a silent retreat was supposed to be, but in the sheer dislocated oddness that the day had become, nothing seemed stranger than anything else. Sitting on the edge of my narrow bed, I stared out at the vast sky. The idea occurred to me that I might simply leave, even that Miriam expected me to. I could find my way back to the car without the aid of the monk, turn the key in the ignition, and vanish. Even as I formulated the thought, however, I knew I could not. What prevented me was not the desire to remain, but the sudden sense that Paris was a million miles away. What home I had had dissolved in that distance. What home I had I would never see again.

EIGHT

At the monastery, Miriam and I spent our days together and also, in spite of her sequestration, our nights, but we never spoke to each other. What was a "silent retreat"? How often had Miriam been here? And what did she believe of all this? During the daily round of services in the chapel, she sat with the monks in a chair they positioned by the choir, and she joined them in the chanting of the psalms and collects. (I, meanwhile, sat as far back in the chapel as I could, alone beneath the wooden gaze of a saint's effigy.) Was her relationship to them a musical affiliation? Perhaps she came here as some sort of choral scholar. During the offices and the daily Mass, however, in addition to singing the psalms and antiphons, she would kneel or cross herself as the monks did, and she said with them the many spoken *Amens* and *Alleluias* that punctuated the prayers. She had never suggested that she was religious, though of course I knew that as a choral singer she and her fellow musicians spent many hours rehearsing and performing in church. I imagine I would have assumed—whether from her complexion or name—that she was Jewish, or partly so, had I given it any thought at all.

Who was this person who had masturbated in the front seat of the car, her right foot jammed under my rib cage, and yet crossed herself before and *after* each meal? Had I been assigned a role in a fetish play?

Or had I been scheduled for conversion? The silence seemed almost to amuse her, as though it protected not a holiness but a depth of irony. Her greeting for me, should I encounter her under the cloister or in the library, was a bug-eyed dumb-show *Shushhhh*, index finger pressed to her lips, as though I had just unleashed a cavernous belch. I took to returning the salute: *Shushhhh*, we would gesture noiselessly at each other, especially if a sound from somewhere else—a crow's caw, a backfiring tractor—broke through the stillness. As far as I could tell, I was the sole occupant of the men's dormitory, and nothing seemed to prevent Miriam from padding through the rusted gate, across the gravel courtyard, and up to my Spartan room. There she would peel off her clothes and slip beneath the blanket, pressing her finger not to her lips this time but to mine.

When I try to assemble my memories of that week in the monastery, it is as though all voices, indeed all human sounds, have in tacit agreement withdrawn. What is left, however, is not a silence. Rather, this absence opens a vaulted space where the bells' pealing, the thud of a dropped book, or the groan of a bedspring all boom and rebound, their echoes undiminished, unable to escape.

The Gregorian plainsong of the monks was something else entirely, sound too but of a different order, of alien substance, as if silence had been compressed to a liquid state and was, at intervals, poured out smoking on the stones of the chapel floor. No, I am wrong. It was not beautiful like that, unbeautiful rather, galvanically so, as a body's nakedness is electrifying, not because it is beautiful but because it terrifies, flooding the onlooker with his unchecked hungers. It was as though those simple melodies were the product of millennia of stripping away: whoever composed them, whatever they meant to say, all dissolved, even the meaning of the texts dissipated over centuries of usage, nothing left but the starkness of a distilled longing.

Do you understand, Father, what I am trying to say? Do I understand, haunted as I am even now by the fleeting glimpse of Miriam's nakedness as she slipped beneath my sheet, or the image of her wedged against the dashboard, hand gripped behind her knee, pulling it back, knuckles white as she came? How can I explain to you what I have since come to believe—that all artifice, even the ancient artifice of the monks' plainchant, labors to hide an awful nakedness, a nakedness as of a body dumped in a ditch, the nakedness of a girl motionless in the cold water of her bathtub?

That is the nakedness I am speaking of. Who hasn't seen it some-where? Just the other day, in the subway, it was there: a lunatic woman, carapaced in parkas, overcoats, cardigans, and what looked like a pair of ski pants, wrestled her bags through the closing doors, shouting some-thing about "little machines! little machines!" She fell silent and I forgot about her, but then there was an abrupt commotion, a flailing at the far end of the car, and I saw that she was entirely naked (except for her ga-loshes), each nipple hedged in whiskery hairs, her sex hidden by the slack pouch of her belly. "Little machines!" she shrieked. "These fucking little machines!"

That is how it seemed to me, the plainchant of the monks: exposed, unbeautiful, unbearable. Of the readings in church I remember noth-ing. I remember speaking with no one. What I remember is the naked-ness of the plainchant, that volatile distillate penetrating everything. It suffused everything, along with the smell of the place, the crumbling dank of the cloister, the boxwood acrid and effluvial in the garden, all mingled with the ardor of her body, redolent under my sheet or splayed in the hot car.

On the way home after the week was over, we had driven a good hun-dred kilometers before either of us spoke, or rather, before Miriam spoke.

"So," she began, "do you see now what my ticket is?"

I didn't see.

"At the monastery. That is what I am becoming," she said.

"A celibate man?" I said. "You had me fooled."

"No," she said, "I am becoming a religious."

Still I didn't understand, thinking that by religious she meant simply a religious person. Nothing about her seemed religious. Though I had observed her precise, habituated participation in the round of worship with the monks, the idea of her belief seemed unreal, not false, just unreal. My hobbled French, however, was incapable of communicating any part of this. I said only, "You, religious?"

"But," she said, "only when I am done with you. So that is my ticket," she said. "You have yours. America. New York. Your patients. This is mine."

"But what is it?"

"You wouldn't want me," she said, "cheating on God forever, would you?" She explained that *religieuse* meant a monastic, a monk or a nun. Then she added, as an afterthought: A *religieuse* was a kind of pastry. "They are very delicious," she said with a smile. "I will make you eat one." And we were silent again, all the way up the autoroute to the *périphérique*.

And then in some way I can never explain, it was all over. Between that day years ago and this moment there is no distance. There is no distance between the crunch of gravel under the monk's foot and the beating of my typewriter against this page, no distance between Miriam's profile in the car and Clementine's as she slept on the pillowless expanse of a crib mattress, just as there is no distance between Clementine's face as it was then and as it was the day I saw her, rounding the corner with her friend, that day I received the first photograph of Jessica Burke in the mail.

Not very long after Clementine's and my return from France, a patient of mine, a woman in her sixties, announced in a session, "I cannot tell you . . . I think it is impossible for you to understand, how quickly they go, the years. It is sickening." I remember the interpretation I made because, quite frankly, I was proud of it, and I credited it (and myself) with having brought the patient to the threshold of a breakthrough. It was clear to her, I had said, it was *undeniably, irrefutably* true for her, that I would never, could never, understand her malady. In fact (I went on) that belief *was* her malady, her conviction that no one would ever or could ever understand her, that she could not be reached, touched . . .

And yet, now, I have come to believe that she was right: I could not possibly understand; I was too young. Now, however, with the past so much longer than the future, I see finally what she meant: the closer you are to the end, the shorter the distance you know you have traveled. The road does not stretch out behind you, but folds up, the point of origin gaining on you with every step.

Maybe this is a commonplace. Maybe anyone who lives long enough learns it. But I was a slow and stiff-necked learner. I thought that I had time, that we did, Clementine and I, that time was our recompense, that after all the disasters, time had been restored to us. Clementine and I had made it: we had made it to New York, to safety, to our apartment with its doorman, its sidewalk pear trees flowering in spring, her child-hood stretching into the future like a meadow sloping toward the sea.

Of course, time was not our birthright. What we had been given was the illusion of stillness, a false reprieve. That is the way they do it, chil-dren, the way they detain time. Our apartment still smelled of new paint, its interior hermetic, a satellite's self-sustaining atmosphere. That atmo-sphere was our own, that rarefied air of new paint, of the moth-breath in her sleeping mouth, of the fish-liver pungency of diaper cream. Yes, that is what it was like: a minute, habitable bubble, a satellite affixed in geo-synchronous orbit as bright as a star and seemingly as still, though in re-ality traveling at incomprehensible speed.

All the years of her childhood we spent in that capsule, all those long spring afternoons, summer afternoons, whiled away on the carpet or in the park. As I sat on a playground bench, Clementine would lie, it seemed, for hours, belly down over the seat of a swing, walking her feet around in a circle, twisting together the chains of the swing until she could twist them no further. Then she would lift her feet and begin to spin, slowly at first, then faster and faster until—*thunk*—the chains would release each other, stand separate for an instant until—clink—the swing's momentum would bend the chains around each other again but in the opposite direction, and Clementine would walk her circle once more. All the long afternoon it went—*thunk*, clink—*thunk*, clink—the pendu-lum of Clementine's chain clock.

NINE

Several days had passed since I had seen or heard from her, and I had begun to suspect that I would not see her again. Perhaps she had succeeded—as she said she would—in getting me out of her system. Perhaps the fact that I had stayed in Paris, had simply failed to get on my flight back to the States, had spooked her. Perhaps I had violated some statute in the unwritten code for affairs with foreigners, the requirement that one must be, above all, a body in motion, passing through.

Shame was what I felt, shame to have been so brusquely unhorsed by my own intoxication. I would set about shipping my things. I would find a new flight home. What I felt I did not register as grief, or longing, but as stunned disorientation. Something had happened, something to do with her voice in the upper reaches of the *Miserere*, something to do with her teeth in my shoulder as she came—something that had passed over and through me, leaving me dazed, lost, altered.

But then, abruptly, there it was again, her voice on the phone: Could we meet? Had I forgotten? I had said I would help her with some translating.

No . . . no, I had not forgotten.

I made out her face in the crowd as she approached the café on the rue de Vaugirard. She had not been late, but by then I was finishing my third pastis. "I was afraid you had left," she said.

"Maybe I ought to have."

I realized then what I had hoped for. I had hoped that the sensation of aftermath would stay with me. That she would, in appearing, reveal herself to be merely someone, anyone, a face in the crowd, a face already sinking into the past. But she was there, each gesture intensely her own even to the trembling of the match flame at the tip of her cigarette. Her proximity was something I could taste, could breathe, just as she seemed to breathe it in with the first drag of smoke. Her level gaze settled on my face as though it could rest there.

"You look well," she said.

"You are beautiful."

She said nothing, then said, "No."

"No what?"

"Not beautiful. You say so because you think you do not want to go back to New York. But you have your tickets."

"We each have our tickets," I said, "mine to New York, yours to a monastery."

"You want to escape," she said. "That's why you took me in the first place."

"You want to escape too," I said, "to become a *religieuse*."

"For me escape would be not to become one. For you, escape is Paris."

Now the persistence of her gaze seemed part of a laborious preparation, a laying up of stores for a long journey. She would take it alone. The pastis now tasted dreggy and acrid, like panic.

"You are telling me that you have gotten me out of your system," I said.

"You speak as though you will not leave before I leave," she said.

"Haven't I given you what you wanted?"

"And what was that?"

"A temporary American. A disposable one."

The gleam brimming in her eye accused me.

"You said you would help me with translation, as you did for Mathieu," she said, and unfolded a photocopied sheet on the small tabletop. The waiter, having placed my fourth pastis and her first at the table's edge, set the water carafe right on the paper with an aggrieved thump.

Was I acquainted with someone named Ronsard?

A friend of hers?

Everyone knew Ronsard; every student in France was required to memorize a Ronsard poem at one point or another. She recited a few lines in an ironic singsong cadence, like a student repeating an assigned text. In a couple of weeks, she would perform a concert of Ronsard song settings.

Some of the settings were of Ronsard's poems translated into other languages. Had I really never read him, not even translated into English? This Mr. "Yeets," one of Ronsard's translators, he was a famous English poet, no? Did I not know him either?

Yeats, I had heard of Yeats, the Irish poet.

"Yeats," she said, cautiously drawing out the vowel, "*Yayyts*. Am I saying it correctly? Ah. But read it to me, Daniel, can you?"

I read the poem printed on the sheet.

"Again, please, Daniel, so I can know how to sing it in English. Read it slowly, *doucement*."

I read it once more, slowly this time, looking up at her when I could. She was looking at me as I read, or rather, at my mouth.

When you are old and grey and full of sleep,
And nodding by the fire, take down this book,
And slowly read, and dream of the soft look
Your eyes had once, and of their shadows deep;

How many loved your moments of glad grace,
And loved your beauty with love false or true,
But one man loved the pilgrim soul in you,
And loved the sorrows of your changing face;

And bending down beside the glowing bars,
Murmur, a little sadly, how Love fled
And paced upon the mountains overhead
And hid his face amid a crowd of stars.

The last lines, she said, they are different.

Different?

From the original, from the conclusion of the original poem. She recited the French version, its cadences stately and mournful. I could follow only with difficulty the courtly, antiquated French but understood that the final lines said something about picking "the roses of life" before those roses fade.

"So what are these mountains?" she asked, pointing at the poem on the table. "There are no mountains in the French. And what is this crowd of stars?"

I had no answer for her, and she merely asked me to read it a third time, and once again, as I read it, she watched my mouth as I spoke the words.

"*Peelgreem?*" she repeated when I had finished. "*Pilgreem* is how you say it?"

"Pilgrim."

"And *eed*? Do I say it right?"

"Hid," I said.

"It is impossible!" she said, exasperated, smiling. "*Heed.*"

"Hid."

"*Hid.*" She winced slightly as she repeated it, as though the *h*-sound hurt her to make. "So you see," she said, "you cannot leave. Without you I am hopeless." At some point she had folded the paper and put it back in her bag. It had been on the table for no more than fifteen minutes, but those words had burned themselves into me with the hiss of a brand.

Not that I remembered them, not literally, not that I remembered anything from that stilted, sunstruck meeting beyond the fixity of her gaze on my mouth, when I looked up from the words on the page, while her lips moved almost imperceptibly, in complete silence.

I tell you I never thought of the poem again. But when I saw the diagonal shadow of an envelope in box 5504, Jessica Burke's post office box, and when, back at my desk, the envelope disclosed a single sheet, folded so often that the paper had begun to soften along the folds, to wear away where the folds crossed, the sheet marked with a ring where the aggrieved waiter had set a sweating carafe down on it—the same sheet Miriam had unfolded before me nineteen years ago in Paris—that sheet appeared as familiar to me as if I had unfolded and read it in faithful observance every day since that day we met on the rue de Vaugirard.

> . . . *how Love fled*
> *And paced upon the mountains overhead*
> *And hid his face amid a crowd of stars.*

"So you were each other's language teachers," Clementine said when she was old enough to say such things.

I supposed we had been.

"Will you teach me French, like Mommy taught you?" she asked.

But I was never any good at it, not as good as I should have been after a year in Paris, never good enough to feel as though I weren't speaking through a veil of static.

For Clem, however, it was different. As soon as she could make her choice known, Clementine elected to attend the Lycée Français de New York, and it was not long before she, with an amused exasperation not unlike Miriam's, was correcting my pronunciation and syntax, pointing out "*la différence évidente, non, mais vraiment évidente,*" between "*dessus*" and "*dessous,*" the difference—really, the obvious difference—between "over" and "under."

TEN

Clementine's questions became harder the older she grew. There was no more wondering whether mommies die after having babies the way bees die after they sting you. Now she was on the hunt, her curiosity piqued by each scrap she found. Even when she was a toddler her look could unnerve me, so level I could believe Miriam had bestowed it on her, to track and haunt me. When Clementine's questions beset her, however, her gaze shifted, now sidelong, now scavenging.

Did you and Mom speak to each other in French?

Do they speak French in heaven?

Do I have cousins and uncles in France?

Did you bury her, or was she cremated?

Did you take me to her funeral?

Yes, darling.

No, darling.

No, my darling; it didn't happen like that.

Perhaps so, my love. Now go to sleep.

We can talk about it later, Clem. Go back to sleep.

Her questions—weren't they what I lay awake for, alone in my watchtower? When they arrived, I told myself, I would be prepared. She would take what she needed, learn what she wanted to know. I couldn't give her

her mother, but I could give her her story. That was, as I understood it, my job. At times, sometimes for weeks at a stretch, her questions would subside, but then her curiosity would flare again like a fever I could not cure.

Did you say goodbye?

Did she know me?

Did you give me my name or did she?

Where are my grandparents?

Why don't we see them?

Eventually, the urgency abated, or so I thought. Clementine seemed, if not content, willing at least to let it rest, perhaps to let me rest. Perhaps (I began to think) she had her story now. *My mother died when I was born,* I heard her say in the playground, in the coffee shop, on the telephone. Did I detect an emerging inflection, fleeting, a hint—could it be—of pleasure in her proclamation? *My mother died in childbirth.*

One day—she must have been twelve or thirteen—she delivered the news to an inquisitive saleswoman in the corner pharmacy by saying, "Sadly, my mother perished in childbed." Had she become, without my noticing, the curator of what she had collected, the bits and pieces of what I had told her arranged like *objets* in the gaslit interiors of a fin de siècle novel? What consolation I took from that thought! If her story was part of a book, then it must have a beginning and an end. It must revolve around itself, suspended at a safe remove.

Clementine was studious, precocious at school but goofy at home and with friends, inoculated by my patient, dedicated attentions (I liked to think) against the miseries of middle school, the ennui of the only child, adrift on the slack tide of her solitary afternoons. On evenings when I saw patients, she would sprawl on the lobby floor of our building, doing her schoolwork, or reading, or chattering at Itzal in her rapidly improving French. Of course I knew (or thought I knew) that it all had to end, that the storm-front of adolescence would arrive one day and blow everything sideways. . . .

* * *

When can I get pierced ears?

Thirteen, like everyone else.

Thirteen! That's more than five months away! Other girls got their ears pierced by now.

They're probably thirteen already.

No, Dad, they aren't. I swear to God.

But when I insisted she wait, to my surprise she acquiesced and asked only if she could borrow the kitchen calendar. That night, with scissors and tape she produced what she called her "countdown machine." She had found a second calendar for the month of April and had cut it into little squares, one for each day. These she had pasted with great care on top of the days of the intact calendar, but in reverse order, counting down until her birthday or, as she labeled it, "Day Zero," marking it with a thumbtack right in the middle of the "Zero": her birthday, the day of what she insisted on calling her "puncturing."

Do you have to call it that, Clem?

I do, and anyway you're a shrink and you're supposed to be able to deal with these things.

Was I? I suppose I was.

Don't worry. You'll get over it. In time.

Nothing more than a moment's breeze, it seemed, shook the days from Clementine's reverse calendar and turned the Day Zero thumbtack into a little gold stud in each earlobe.

One morning not long after that I found her at the table with a *Merck Manual* open in front of her.

So, what was it, a rampant systemic infection? Or an ombolism? Or was it a stroke? What's an ombolism anyway?

An *em*-bolism. It's a kind of blood clot.

You couldn't save her?

The doctors couldn't save her.

But you are a doctor.

She couldn't be saved.

(Clementine was still looking down at the book.)
How do you know that?

What was she asking me? That was, I thought, all I needed to know. That was my profession, after all; if one could never know the answers, one could, at least, know the questions. There were so few to know. Among my patients, every quandary and confusion proceeded from one of the few, the elemental questions: What can I change and what must I accept? Of what, of where, of whom am I the issue? Can the past be touched? Can it be healed?

That, as I had understood it, was my task as an analyst: not to answer the unanswerable question, but to accompany my patient to the threshold of the mystery. It was not the answer that healed. Indeed (I thought), belief in answers was the root of all anguish. What healed was the articulation of desire, the act of setting it down, laying it out, offering it up. I believed that it was only in uttering its question—not in receiving the answer—that the soul came into being, released into longing, which is its native element. In such a way I believed myself to be the midwife of the new soul, a creature squalling and alive because hungry and exposed.

You see now how I have been repaid for such a belief, such a presumption. See with what new and terrible questions I have been repaid, questions demanding an answer: *Who is the killer of Jessica Burke? Where is my daughter?*

ELEVEN

Yes, Clementine has gone.
        What she must have suspected in some way all along, she
        had proved. The old article about her mother's death floated to
the floor. The door slammed, and she was gone. Is gone. For more than
a month now. For me, forever.

Forever? you say. Without hope of reconciliation? But God is merciful, you say. Like God, you say, a child is capable of more forgiveness
than we can imagine, more even than we can bear.

But she had said, *Jesus, you are sick!* when she stomped her belong-
ings into her backpack like you'd stomp garbage into a pail. She had repeated, *Sick, Daniel, sick!* and slammed out the apartment door, having
informed me how much more *viable* her life would be had you never
existed, had you, Daniel, been the one to die, you and not Miriam.

Surely then I could search for her, raise the cry! alert the authorities!
Of course in my panic, in my denial, I did so. I made my urgent plea at
the precinct house. The officer who took my statement asked me, Was I
certain she was missing? Maybe she'd just gone off with some friends?
Between *missing* and *gone*—almost no difference, yet all the difference
in the world.

Gone, then, and all for something I could have told her years ago, something like the truth. How easy to imagine her a child once again, the same child, yet with a slightly different story, announcing to a stranger that her mother "succumbed to postpartum depression, and took her own life." I can hear even now (in the ringing silence of the apartment) how she would have said it, her voice alive with the thrill of this news. One way or another, Clementine would have had to extricate herself from the tarry shadows of the primal rejection—*My mother abandoned me when I was a baby*—but who is to say that suicide must blight more deeply than ill-chance or sickness? We would have managed. I could have helped her. I could have explained (my tone sad, patient, grave, schooled) that postpartum depression is a condition no less bodily than septic infection, no less lethal than the "*om*-bolism" Clementine had discovered on her own. She was the same smart girl, the same resilient creature, my daughter, my Clementine! I could have helped her! We could have managed!

But I did not help her, and we did not manage. Instead, one evening, a conversation I had feared and rehearsed for years spun out of control until she had stomped the contents of her laundry basket into her backpack, sobbed and then choked back her sobs, and posed her obliterating question: "Daniel, has it ever occurred to you how much more *viable* my life would have been if you had been the one to kill yourself, not Mom?"

"Clementine—"

"Has it? Just once? Ever?"

"What do you know?" I said.

"What do I know? What do I *know*?"

"Clem, there is nothing—" I said.

"Nothing you wouldn't deny, Daniel. Just watch: you're about to deny this too." And she threw, or rather shoved toward me through the air, an unfolded sheet of paper. Once out of her hand, it floated in scooping arcs to the floor. In the wavering moment of the paper's descent, she had gone. An echo had already subsided, and she was gone.

I don't know where she found the article, though from the look of the gray, greasy mimeographed sheet, she had printed it from microfilm or microfiche in a library. What library in New York, I wondered, as though the question could possibly matter, subscribed to *Le Journal du Centre*, the paltry regional newspaper that had reported Miriam's death? There they were again, in my hand, the old words:

The body of Miriam Levaux . . . Pont de Loire . . . suicide the likely cause . . . no foul play suspected . . . after midnight Monday, 12 March . . . residing in Paris . . .

I had read these very paragraphs before, on a day when under a cold Parisian sun they appeared in fresh newsprint, a copy of *Le Journal du Centre* set down before me on the café table. Mathieu, my friend from the institute and Miriam's neighbor, had found me there, in the company of a single glass and an empty bottle. *The body of Miriam Levaux . . .* The little moment it took me to read the article was sufficient for the crowd to swallow him. In a clatter of chairs and breaking glass, I sprang after him in the direction I thought he'd gone, but the waiter seized my arm.

Monsieur! Monsieur! S'il vous plaît, il faut payer!

As indeed I must. Indeed, sir, I must pay.

TWELVE

Who will console me? Would you, Father? Could I not console myself, if only with falsehood? How is it possible that I, having fashioned for years such an intricate, vaulted structure of lies, could have lost, at last, my capacity to lie? Couldn't I say to myself: Clementine will come back? Today or tomorrow or the next day, a backpack will thump on the vestibule floor, keys and cellphone will clatter on the vestibule table, because she will have come home? I can almost convince myself, just as I can almost convince myself that I am not here alone in the apartment, another envelope open before me on my desk.

I waited until I got home to open the envelope from Jessica Burke's postal box. Its surface was the same smooth, striated beige of those that had come before. My fingers recognized at once the weight and gloss of the sheet it enclosed: another photograph. Would I have to look once more at the abstracted countenance of Jessica Burke, sealed in its plastic sack? Or would I see this time not Jessica Burke's face but Clementine's?

Instead, the photograph was an image of nothing at all, just a muddled blur, crowded glints and shadows, a mottle of blacks, streaks, and washed-out patches. I squinted at it, drew it up to my face, held it at arm's length. Was it even in focus? Was it even a photograph, not just a mass of smears? But no, it was a photograph after all, the image of an expanse of water, flecked, clouded, some distance away, though taken from directly above. Perhaps the photographer had suspended himself somehow over the surface. This picture, however, disclosed nothing, only the water, its surface without reflection, without limit save the rough edge where, it appeared, the top portion of the photograph had been torn away, and a smooth edge at the lower border, where the printing of the photograph had left a narrow margin of unexposed paper.

So I thought, so I continued to think, even after long minutes of staring, paralyzed by foreboding. What did it mean? The earlier picture, the picture of Jessica Burke in the bathtub, had delivered its news like a blow. Look, it had said, what you had thought was an overdose, what you had thought was an accident, was not one, but instead the accomplishment of an aim, planned and executed, recorded for your eyes alone. But here, in this image, there was no face, no story, only the gaze of nothingness itself. Look, it said: here the unmarked depth where your daughter was drowned.

Minutes passed before I could beat back the panic of this conjecture. The picture was not of Clementine, said nothing of Clementine, was of water only . . .

Who could have conceived such a torment? The image suspended the idea of my daughter drowning in an element of pure possibility. That possibility was not a threat, not a warning, but something that quite simply had either happened or not. The very indeterminacy of the photograph had delivered me into the hands of a pure and formless dread.

Finally, however, when I had marshaled the resolve to look at the photograph again, I saw that the white edge at the bottom of the photograph was not, as I had previously thought, the border of the print, but a part of the image itself. This element of the picture, a strip of foreground at the base like a sill or threshold, made little more than a pale band. I rifled my desk until I found a magnifying glass, peered through it at the pale band. Only by pulling the glass back so that the magnified section swelled up into the lens could I see that the band bore the imprint of hatch-marks or scoring—no, not hatch-marks but writing—crude, worn, almost erased, but unmistakably writing. I could not have made out the characters had I not known already what those letters spelled. I had, after all, cut them myself:

ML12III90

These characters designated with merciless precision the coordinates of my own inescapable past, incised with the name of Miriam Levaux, the day of 12 March, the year 1990, inscribed in the very place where she died.

The body of Miriam Levaux was recovered from the river 400 meters downstream from the Pont de Loire. The medical examiner's office has yet to release the autopsy report, but a source close to the police stated that suicide is the likely cause, and foul play is not suspected. It is believed that Levaux drowned sometime after midnight on Monday, 12 March. Levaux, 27, was a native of Nevers but had been residing in Paris.

And so I understood the message of the photograph. It said: This is where it happened. It said: Your lie, the lie you nurtured and refined throughout your daughter's childhood, is for all that still a lie. No less than the scene of Jessica Burke in the bathtub, the event recorded here was also the work of hands, careful, painstaking, thorough. That is what this photograph had said. It said: *Remember me.*

With that recognition, abruptly, the terror was gone. I knew then, finally and without doubt, what the photograph had wanted me to know. Though I had lost my daughter, my daughter herself was not lost—not yet. She had been granted a stay. She had been suffered to remain in this world—for now.

How did I know this? I knew it the instant my eye returned to the opposite, upper border of the photograph, the rough edge where the paper had been torn straight across. I knew it as surely as I knew what I would find when I turned the photograph over, the lines of the poem from the very first letter I had received, transcribed as before, but with a difference:

Come away, O human child!
To the waters and the wild
With a faery, hand in hand . . .

There it was, the same refrain, the same regular stanzas, copied in the same blocked-out hand, just as before, except that paper had been torn away at the top below where the first stanza of the poem would have been. What remained were the final verses. The four stanzas I'd first received were now three, and where there had been fifty-three lines, there were now forty-one.

Come away, O human child!
To the waters and the wild
With a faery, hand in hand,
For the world's more full of weeping than you can understand.

This foreshortening, I understood, meant that a clock of sorts had begun its countdown. The poem was shortened because the time remaining was shorter. I had no way to arrest the movement of this clock, but neither would the clock be hurried. This poem-clock afforded me a freehold, a shrinking freehold to be sure, but while I had it, it was absolutely mine. Just so, I thought, had Clementine fashioned her reverse calendar, the "countdown machine" that anticipated her thirteenth birthday, when she could pierce her ears. Both the poem and Clementine's calendar were machines for marking time, time that could be neither stopped nor sped up.

I had been given time, a little time. Because I had been given time, I had been given a choice. I knew this, and I knew what I would choose. I knew what I would do in time—in time, but not yet.

SPURLOCK

1:07 A.M.

One night, not long after Luis had begun opening the church to the homeless, Spurlock had approached one of the men at random. "Hi, I'm Father Spurlock," he said. "What's your name?"

"King—John," said the man as he squeezed the ash from the tip of a half-smoked cigarette and stashed the butt inside his jacket.

"Pleased to meet you, John King," said Spurlock, extending his hand.

"King John," said the man, making no move to accept the handshake. "I am King John."

"My name?" said the next man Spurlock had approached that night. "Sprinkles, they calls me. So you going to call me Sprinkles too?"

"You're welcome here," said Spurlock, adding "my friend" to avoid calling the man Sprinkles.

He had learned his lesson. From then on, he would say nothing more than "Welcome" to the visitors, though most acknowledged even that greeting with obdurate silence, a silence that Spurlock understood to combine two simultaneous and incompatible replies: "Of course I am welcome here—are you?" and "You lie, you lie, you lie."

You will not remember me. My name is Daniel Abend.

That was a name he hadn't asked for. And yet it had found him, grabbed at him, as though it were his own name cried out in a crowd so that reflexively he had turned and said, "Here I am." Finding no one, he had said, "Who is speaking? Where are you?"

Two phrases made the precious refrain of his first months with Bethany.

There you are.

Here you are.

Years before, waking together in her single bed in the law school dormitory, he would say, "There you are," and she would say, "Here you are." Back then, to be able to say that to one's beloved seemed everything one could want.

The past, he had concluded, had been nothing but run-up. Wasn't this how providence worked, how the obscure intelligence of surprise and accident gave the past its unchangeable shape? He could not have invented or imagined this Bethany, the line of her long wrists, her sharp rib cage, or how when studying she secured her hair in a bun by impaling it with a pencil, but they had met, and she had chosen him. "You're my guy," she had said, her manner affectionately matter-of-fact, but for Spurlock something had been decided. Here he was, and there she was, and so it was settled, the agreement for which their separate pasts had been the long negotiation.

"Today we come together . . . ," her father had said, lifting his glass at their wedding, "to celebrate Bethany's choice of a good man." It was as though the matter had been decided elsewhere. If Bethany had made the choice of a good man, and he was that man, then he must be good. His job was to assent.

And assent he had, but that assent felt different now: less the work of providence than of human provision against loneliness. Each passing year paused for a briefer interval, like Diogenes with his lantern looking for one good man, squinting at him, then turning away. "Here you are," he would still say to Bethany when she returned from work, and "There

you are" was still her reply, though the "there" sounded more and more
like somewhere far away.

He stared up into the darkness of the church and felt his thoughts turn
to Jessica Burke's mother, a boiled-looking woman slumped in the front
pew on the day of the funeral. He remembered how she remained seated
when the congregation rose in song or knelt to pray. She had once been,
he was told, a parishioner, a member of the altar guild, a decorator of the
church at Christmas and Easter, but he had not known her, and after her
daughter's funeral, she had never returned.

Should he try to find her now to tell her her daughter had been mur-
dered? Or so he thought. Or so someone named Daniel Abend had
maintained. Such an announcement would be a cruelty. No doubt, but
still, was he not obliged to say something, if not to her, then to the authorities?

This quandary was what they meant, he thought, when they spoke of
"the seal of the confessional." It was not like a seal on an envelope or a
diplomatic pouch, or a lozenge of wax pressed at the base of a document,
but something more like the seal he mentioned whenever he performed
the baptismal rite. After dousing the infant, he would make the sign of
the cross on its forehead with a fragrant oil, then proclaim the child to be
"sealed by the Holy Spirit and marked as Christ's own forever." Spurlock
had always understood that seal to be the mark of God's unshakable love,
the love that called each soul into being, but now he felt the weight of it
on his own forehead as though it were a brand or scar proclaiming his
guilt, his complicity in every sin for which he had presumed to offer absolution. For the first time, he felt a flicker of kinship with members of
the old unreformed priesthood, charged to bear bodily *in persona Christi*
the sins of the penitent, to carry them from the confessional to the altar,
where the priest in turn would be forgiven.

Informing Jessica Burke's mother would not remove the grip of sin,
would only drag someone else into its embrace. No, Nelson, he thought,

this knowledge is for you alone, an excruciation entrusted to you only, for keeps.

Spurlock understood then that it was the solitude that was unbearable, the solitude of his sleeplessness amid the sleepers, as though he had been sentenced to stand lookout forever, scanning the horizon, squinting into the darkness for . . . what? What was it? How would he recognize it when it appeared? Who was to say he would not wait forever? The prospect seemed to him as certain as it was unbearable, as opaque and unrevealing as the dark above him in the church. But even as the weight of this solitude threatened to crush him, he realized that what he waited for he had already encountered, and it was not a what but a who: a person, a face, her face, Clementine Abend's. That level brow, the flat-bright nickel gray of her eye, he could see them now as though she had never left, as though she had not fled at the sound of her name when he had said, "Yes, Clementine Abend, all I would need is your address. . . ."

THIRTEEN

As for the question of how Clementine has lived since her departure, I have said nothing of my daughter's money, the money she took to calling her "abundant riches."

"Hardly riches," I would say to her.

"Dan is jealous," she would say in reply. But I was not jealous; in fact, half of the money had been mine, my portion of my own father's legacy.

When my father died, three years after I returned from France with Clementine, I inherited half his estate, the other half to be held in a trust for Clementine's "education and upbringing." Any moneys remaining in the corpus would be disbursed to Clementine upon her twenty-fifth birthday. A smaller portion, however, was to be maintained in a separate account and released to Clementine when she turned eighteen, on the stipulation that it be used for "a grand voyage" the summer after her graduation from high school. I do not doubt that this private gift expressed principally my father's love for his only granddaughter, his "French Fry," his "Tiny," but I am certain also that it expressed his frustration with what he called my "womanish dithering" over Clementine's safety and health. "If you're not careful, French Fry," he would say to her when she was in grade school, "your pop will seal you up in a bell jar, just so you don't skin your knee."

"What's a bell jar, Grumpus?"

"Why, a jar for capturing tiny belles like you!"

That was how he spoke, the charmer, the great litigator, his eyes lit with guile, like a great cat's, even in the frailty of his last decline. His allure had always seemed to me to conceal a violence, but with Clementine, a joy clouded those eyes and welled in their corners whenever she had made him laugh, tears he would smear away with his fingertips, pushing his eyeglasses up on his forehead, saying, "Ah, Tiny, you kill me."

In short, I was to have no say in the matter. The money was Clementine's, all of it, to spend on her grand voyage overseas. "As for which seas, Tiny," my father had written in a letter appended to his will, "that will be up to you. Whether you go to Goa and grow conjoined dreadlocks with a Danish hippie, or hoist a prayer flag on Mount Everest with my name on it, or stopper the headwaters of the Zambezi with your boot heel, I shall be happy. Be nice to your pop, because he'll be lonely when you go. Try to remember that his brittle and high-strung nature is not his fault but mine and his mother's. So watch out! You probably inherited it too. A brittle lot, we Abends, so be easy on yourself, and remember your old Grumpus, who loved his granddaughter very much when he was aboveground, and loves her even more now that he's retired to Dirt City. Extinct though he is, he misses his Tiny like mad."

By the time Clementine reached primary school, my practice had flourished and provided more than enough money to support what was, by Manhattan standards, a modest life. We hardly left the city, and because I detested the idea of leaving her with a sitter, we ate our meals at home. The trust for her education covered tuition for the Lycée. As my salary was sufficient for all our other expenses, I decided, in lieu of taking out a life insurance policy, to transfer the money I had inherited from my father to Clementine, adding it to the larger of the two sums left for her, the one designated for her education. Substantial to start with, that fund became sufficient to fund several educations undertaken simultaneously. This plenty, however, I never discussed with her. It was only the smaller sum, the travel money, that Clementine called her "riches."

As trustee I received all statements and audits, affording me each quarter the pleasure of watching the corpus grow. This quarterly reassurance filled me with a satisfaction familiar from Clementine's earlier childhood, when she finally took to her bottle and began to fatten, zooming in a matter of weeks from the thirtieth to the eightieth percentile of the weight charts. What gratified most of all, Father, was that the money was not mine. I believed there was no life to strive for beyond the life we had, our little enclosure, for as long as it should last.

The death of Jessica Burke had punctured my complacency, but the letters left it in tatters. During her treatment, I had listened to Jessica Burke as though to a scout, a forward observer transmitting reports from a future that Clementine herself would one day occupy. Jessica wasn't all that much older than Clementine, after all. I fancied that Jessica Burke's interior world must in some way resemble Clementine's, even though Clementine hardly ever reported on her inner world, buffeted now by the forecast storms of adolescence. But then Jessica was dead, and instead of reports from a young woman's future, I received the letters from my correspondent.

Perhaps I attempted to comfort myself with the hope that such evil luck—having brushed past me to claim the life of my patient—wouldn't circle back for us. Hadn't the odds of misfortune narrowed? And yet, even the most remote and abstract impossibilities had now fleshed themselves with ominous substance. Disaster was something that had happened, to someone I knew, someone who had spent hours with me, who had told me more of her cares and aspirations than Clementine ever had, who had stared with me for hours at the same patch of office wall, where a shape of light shifted without motion as the minutes passed.

The letters had never mentioned Clementine. They had made no concrete threat. And yet, a conviction, both visceral and moral, overtook me. The letters had been addressed to me, to the postal box rented in my name, but I was certain they *pointed toward* Clementine, keeping her in crosshairs.

As soon as Clementine learned of the bequest for the "grand voyage," she declared she would go to France. It was unfair, unfair that we had never gone to Europe ourselves, that we never went anywhere, that my vacations never seemed to line up with hers, that all of her friends had already been to Paris, or Brussels, or Geneva "tons of times." And France was where she had been born!

I had informed Clementine of the bequest when she turned sixteen, having delayed the moment as long as I felt I could. Just as my refusals to take her abroad began to seem not merely resolute but perverse, this little heap of money rose on her horizon. For her it meant the promise that she would finally be able to make her trip to France, while for me it meant that she would not make it, at least not yet. There was still time. There was time for her to change her mind, for her to hand herself over to a new enthusiasm, a hobby, a sport, a crush. Why (I said to myself), practically anything might distract her from her younger intentions. Buddhism could. A passion for Indonesian shadow puppetry. The plight of sea turtles. Some boy, wounded and aloof. For the first time in my life I found myself wishing that the storms of adolescence would blow her off course.

The two years passed, however, and her intent held. Then the photograph of Jessica Burke in the bath arrived, and my sense of reprieve splintered in a needle-squall of dread. From that moment, my only preoccupation was how to prevent her from going. No doubt, I declared my motives responsible and loving. Was it not my fatherly obligation to protect her, not just from what could befall her, but from what she could learn? And so I chose blindness, willing myself to ignore what any psychoanalyst knows: that such righteousness is always proof of delusion.

After she turned eighteen, I declared that I had given the matter much thought, had taken into consideration the score of sixty-seven she'd received on her latest physics exam, the recent eruption of Franco-Arab unrest in Paris and Lyon, her as-yet-imperfect command of colloquial French. There would be time for her to travel after she had graduated from college, or even, should she choose, during a junior year abroad. She would profit more from the experience having deferred it than she would by pouncing on the opportunity just because it was there. Money wasn't for the gratification of rash schemes. And anyway I had already arranged for her to repeat her internship at my institute, working for Mr. Shettleworth, the librarian and archivist. He would be delighted to have Clementine back. Of course she knew what a favorite of his she was. . . .

This declaration was sufficient to touch off the fuse. The expression I took at first to be merely the shadow of her disappointment revealed itself to be a blotchy hash-up of disgust and fury.

She began almost inaudibly, "It would be sad—no, funny, really—"

"I'm not sure I see anything funny here, Clem," I said.

"No," she continued as though I hadn't spoken, "it would be funny if it wasn't merely sick."

"What is sick?"

"Daniel," she said. She had never in my hearing called me Daniel, only Dan. "Daniel, do your patients know that you are sick? Is there some kind of disclaimer you give them, something they could *sign?*"

"Clementine—"

"It's sick—sick but also sad, pitiful really—how you've convinced yourself this—this *ploy* could work. Is it possible? Have you even managed to convince yourself you aren't lying?"

"Clementine, I will not stand here—"

"I don't know. Maybe you just missed it. Maybe you were thinking of something else. Maybe you just didn't notice that your daughter is now an adult—"

"Eighteen may feel to you like—"

"—or that your precious daughter *fucks guys?* I see, Daniel, do your shrink thing, go ahead, do your silent listening thing, knock yourself out. It's worked for you so far. Have you convinced yourself in your twisted, shrinkish way that I'm something you get to keep? Jesus, Daniel, you suck all the air out of the room. You suck the air out of *my life!* I cannot calculate—no, I cannot *conceive*—how much more *viable* my life would have been if you had been the one to kill yourself, not Mom!"

"Clementine—" I said, but now she was waving something at me, a sheet of paper, a photocopy, shoving it toward me across the dead space between us. "It's obscene! But you know that, or you wouldn't lie about it—wouldn't have lied about it for years, Daniel, *years!*"

And so she was gone—cellphone snatched up, keys abandoned, backpack shouldered, the door slammed open, slammed shut—all, it seemed, before the mimeographed sheet of paper she had thrust at me had floated to the floor, the clipping I could never bear to read again, recounting the facts of Miriam's suicide.

FOURTEEN

S he did not return for supper, or later that night, or the next morning. I walked through a pelting rain to the precinct house to report a missing person.

"And how old is this lost daughter?" the officer asked, with all the sympathy she might have shown someone reporting a lost sense of optimism. "Eighteen? So not a minor. You sure she's missing, not just somewhere else?"

PEÑA, announced the badge on her uniform. Officer Peña cranked a form into her Selectric.

When had I last seen my daughter? Was she with anyone at the time? Was there reason to think she was in danger?

"Mr. Upend?"

"Was there reason—what?"

"Is there reason, Mr. Upend."

"For what? It's Abend."

"Do you, Mr. Upend, have any reason to suspect—"

"Ah . . . no. I mean, she didn't come home. . . ."

"Yes, I know."

She yanked the form from the Selectric and pushed it toward me to sign. She assured me I would be called.

When would I be called?

When there was something to call about.

From the police station I went directly to the bank, was referred to the trust department. The trust officer who greeted me I had not met before, but he shook my hand enthusiastically and asked after my daughter. Well, it certainly had been a pleasure, he said, to see Miss Abend yesterday. Gracious, what an exciting trip she had planned! He'd been to Paris once, on his honeymoon—

"Paris," I said.

Yes, sir. Nothing like it.

"Paris."

They did grow up, kids, didn't they?

I managed to say that I'd—uh, as it happened—I'd come to withdraw the funds for her trip.

He peered at me and shifted in his seat. My daughter (he cleared his throat) was the sole beneficiary named in the trust instrument. Having reached her majority . . . He paused and shifted again. In any event, all principal and accrued interest had been disbursed to her yesterday. She hadn't mentioned that?

Out on the street I hurried home, breaking into a jog at the intersections to make the light, certain that . . . certain what? I stopped at the door of the building, immobilized. I was certain of nothing. Itzal came out, his concerned gaze sheltered under his bushy brows. Had *Docteur Abend* lost his keys? He was well? He was not sick, was he?

"No, no, Itzal, thank you. I am fine. I just realized—"

And *la petite Clémentine* was well, yes?

"Yes, she's well. You have not seen her today, have you?"

He pursed his lips. Today? No, not today, he had not.

"When you do, just ask her to call me, okay?"

Bien sûr.

"You won't forget?"

At the suggestion, the brows lifted and a smile broke across his face in a thousand creases. *N'ayez crainte, Docteur Abend!* Have no fear!

For what, for whom, had I been speeding home? A vast aimlessness engulfed me, deposited me hours later on a park bench, another lost man, eyed sidelong by a pigeon on the pavement. Long minutes passed before I realized—without surprise—that this was the same bench where I'd opened the earlier envelope, the one that disclosed the first photograph of Jessica Burke, alone in her bathtub.

Clementine gone, the apartment is empty, a single dwelling for a solitary man.

But (you will ask, Father) why must I despair?

For all I know (you will say) she is not missing but—as the officer said—merely somewhere else.

For all I know, she may return. For all I know—

But no, it is not completely empty. For company now, I have the gray stranger who leans toward me out of the mirror. I have my typewriter. I have whoever it is I imagine you to be, Father.

And, of course I have my faithful correspondent.

Could it have been my correspondent who provided Clementine with the mimeographed clipping? I wondered. How else could she have found it? And yet, why should she not find it herself? Why shouldn't a daughter undertake to learn all she could about her mother?

Now that she had found the article, had she found what she needed? The revelation that Miriam had taken her own life, was that enough for Clementine? Or had the discovery awakened in her a desire for more, a hunger for raw detail, for the naked facts of the gendarmes' or coroner's reports, so that she too could construct and reconstruct the events, just as they have made and remade themselves in my memory?

Miriam had died without fanfare. She had not leapt from the bridge. When the divers finally found her, it was clear that she had waded into the water from the bank, downstream from the bridge, just as the picnickers do in the summer, though she had done so at night, her body weighted down with several meters of chain. The length of chain would have been heavy enough by itself, but she had secured the chain through the hub of an iron flywheel, increasing the burden by another thirty kilos at least. *"Elle ne rigolait pas,"* an old man had said in a Nevers café, standing beside me at the bar, when this update was announced on the evening news. She was not kidding around.

"Kidding?" said the proprietress of the café. "I'll tell you who wasn't joking: whoever trussed her up and chucked her in, that's who!"

The old man flicked his hand as though to swat away the suggestion. The proprietress had heard the news, just like everyone. Miriam had mailed the padlock key to the police the day before so they would know where to find her, along with a note saying what she was going to do—or, rather, what she had already done.

Again and again I imagined Miriam at a postal box, the envelope balanced for an instant on the lip of the slot before she let it fall. Did dread threaten to overtake her? Or had all misgivings departed? By then she would have purchased the chain already. The owner of a hardware store had come forward to say that a young woman had bought the remainder of her stock two days before. As for the flywheel, God knows where she found it. Had anyone remarked a young woman rolling an iron wheel along the road? Had she somehow transported it along with the chain, or had her preparations required multiple trips as she built up her little cache of iron in the bushes along the sandy banks of the Loire?

How often have I worked it out, the process, each step contemplated, weighed, the first step, the next step, what material, where to find it, how to move it, how to use it, just as she must have worked it, reworked it, figured it out, a way to thwart the body's agonal panic, limbs pinned, wrists bound, the lock shut, its key far away in a post box or mailroom, sealed in its envelope, as yet unopened. . . .

It must have been a kind of satisfaction she felt, however awful, satisfaction to know that the key was on its way to its destination, perhaps there already. Was it satisfaction, the sensation of the chains now tight around her, metal warming with the heat of her last exertions, a satisfaction to bear the weight, to carry it down to the water and out into the stream, bearing it up just a little longer, out a little into the current, the water now taking some of the weight, some of the warmth, from the chain, the chain taking some of the warmth from her body, the body from which shortly all warmth should dissipate in the cold flow of the river?

Sometimes it happens (usually when I am at the edge of sleep, but not only then) that her final image visits itself upon me. It is subdued to a flatness outside of time, her image like a saint's set in stained glass, the stiff form wreathed in chain, the wheel held against her side, as a martyr holds in expressionless triumph the weapon of her execution. Without recognition, without acknowledgment, her gaze passes through me, just as the light passes through her own body.

FIFTEEN

That Brazilian woman, what was her name? Fernanda? Ana Clara? I do not remember. She was my patient when Clementine was a baby, before we had returned to the States from Paris. She had come to analysis because she was, as she put it, "ruining her children." Her English was better than her French, so she had chosen me to be her analyst. "But you are so frustrating," she said. "I want you to take something away from me, and you keep giving it back."

And what, I asked, was that "something" she wanted to give away?

"The pain. The crazy," she said. She said there was a little shrine, somewhere in the north of Brazil. The land was dry, the town impossibly poor, but people would travel for hundreds of miles to get there, to leave candles, gifts, and ex-voto offerings thanking the saint for answered prayers, for healing, for having rescued them from distress.

"I bring you my worries. I bring you my tears. I bring you the dreams I have. I want to leave them here. I want to hang them on your wall and return home healed. But everything I give to you, you give back. You say, like you just said, 'What is this "something" you want to give away?'"

Years later I looked it up, the shrine. There were many like the one my Brazilian patient had described. One of them was a kind of cave or grotto, where pilgrims would leave little body parts carved from wood or wax: a foot, a breast, a head. From time to time the priest collected the wax objects and melted them down, making candles to be sold to other pilgrims. The walls and ceiling of the shrine were black with candle smoke and crowded with these suspended offerings.

I think now that my Brazilian patient managed at least to give that away, the conjured image of a blackened shrine, hung with a jumble of body parts. I think that in the soul of each psychoanalyst such a place must exist, in spite of what we profess about our neutrality, our professional detachment. Perhaps something of what we receive can be melted down and sold back as candlelight—our costly illuminations—but other elements remain just as they appeared, the dreams nailed to the walls, the abandoned hearts and limbs, the soot of inextinguishable longing.

Today I wonder: Could it be that you are praying for my soul?

Before now, it has never occurred to me that someone might pray for me. An odd sensation all the odder because I no longer know what a soul is. One would have thought after a lifetime of listening to them, treating them, peering into them, I would understand better. I have said it to student analysts under my supervision, and I have said it to myself: that everything Freud wrote was an attempt to accord the soul a rational form, a credible image. Did he succeed? Did anyone believe him? Did I? I no longer know. Is the soul one of those necessary fictions we cannot, in the end, do without? I have thought God to be such a fiction too, as surely you must have, Father. Sometimes it is impossible to believe what we believe.

I should confess that I have been praying, I who believe nothing. Not for Clementine, or Miriam, or myself, but for Jessica Burke. One session in particular returns to me, again and again, the sole session in which she described her artwork. Of course, she had mentioned her work often: her difficulty getting started, her inability to know when to stop, doubts about whether her work was any good. Was it good? I never saw anything she made. Had I been curious, the protocols of my profession would have prevented me from seeking it out. Now that she is dead, an obscure probity prevents me still, a desire to preserve that invisibility, as though it were a nakedness from which I must avert my eyes.

I'm no good at talking about my work, she said.

Everything about it is all so un-thought-out.

But I want to think it out, think it through, that's the thing. I just can't.

How am I going to write an artist's statement, assemble a portfolio, apply to graduate school, if I can't say what I am doing?

Perhaps (I suggested) she didn't want me to know what she was doing.

For a long moment she was silent, then said suddenly: *The thought of your appearing at a crit or an opening makes me want to run out of the room.*

This room? I asked.

The figure-of-speech room.

It sounds like you don't want me showing up at your show.

I didn't say that.

No. Those weren't your words.

And anyway, I hardly know what you look like. I never look at you. She paused. *I mean, what I'm saying is, I can't imagine it, I can't envision you actually there.*

It is painful to imagine me there. Maybe it is painful to imagine me here. You've made the very possibility run out of the room.

I don't think I would even recognize you on the street.

Am I invisible today because you want your art to be invisible?

She hesitated. She didn't think so, but there was one thing she would think about when she was high, one thing she would feel: that she was transparent, not invisible, but transparent. But this was the thing: she wasn't see-through, she wasn't transparent to light like glass or air, she was transparent *to the dark.*

She said that's what heroin did, it brought her down to the seafloor, the floor of an ocean trench. Relieved of the need to see, relieved of the need to breathe, she belonged to the darkness completely. It possessed her, moved through her unresisted, as though she herself were made of nothing more than water and darkness, as though she herself were noth-

ing more than a place, a place where the current turned on itself a little
and moved on.

Sometimes, she said, that's what she wanted her art to be—and she
gave a rueful little laugh—transparent and in the dark! Not very promising, is it? Maybe that's why she'd been doing what she called her smears,
these paintings on long strips of paper. She would load the left edge of
the strip with a charge of paint, then drag the paint out with a knife or a
block of wood or a ruler until the streak was exhausted and the line went
blank. She'd tried all kinds of straightedges, all kinds of inks and pig-
ments, some thin, some viscous, papers of varying thickness and stiff-
ness. The effect of the smear was always different, always engrossing to
her. But perhaps only to her. It was, in any event, the only thing lately she
found she could make. What she was looking for was a kind of transparency like that feeling she used to get when she was high. She found it
there, where the straightedge dragged out the pigment until it thinned to
nothing.

No, she corrected herself, she hadn't found it, but maybe that was as
close as she had gotten. Maybe that was as close as she was going to get.
Maybe you had to spend your life working up shadings with varnish and
glaze, old master style, to get that kind of light into your work. Maybe she
just needed more skill than she had.

She was quiet for a while, maybe a minute. *Or maybe it's only there,
in the junk, or at the bottom of the ocean, in a place where you can't stay.
Where you can't survive.*

I said that was it, the big question she carried around in her, the
question whether despair was the only way out, whether the only thing
she could really make was her escape.

That makes sense, she said, just as she said whenever she didn't agree
with my interpretation. *But . . . there's a frustration . . . a jealousy. What
I'm doing to the paint is what I want to have done to me.*

What do you want to have done to you?

This is not a sexual thing. . . .

Did I say it was?

I want to be smeared out like that. I want to be clear, perfectly clear.

You want to be free to stop hiding things.

God, if that's true, she said with sudden coldness, *then all of this is just a load of shit.*

I knew then that I had overstepped and had ruined something, that I had spooked her and she would make her escape into an anodyne or trivial association. To my surprise, however, she countered and pushed ahead. *You are wrong. It's not that I want to stop hiding. It's not that I want to come out and say the thing I have to say. Don't you see? I want there to be nothing. Nothing to hide, and no place to put it. No things, no places. Do you see what I am saying? Can you understand that? Jesus, how could you?*

Another long minute ticked past before she began again.

Have you seen the northern lights? Here's what I'm wondering: Are they made up of many individual threads or ribbons, each thread like a single northern light? I saw them once; I was camping in Newfoundland. At first I thought they were sheets of rain, lit from below by a city to the north. But there was no city to the north. They were like curtains in the sky, streaky curtains, made out of light but with a kind of fibrous look, like they'd been combed, like smooth threads. If they are threads, that's what I want to be—I want to be one of them, a single thread, a single northern light. . . .

I wanted to know what she meant by that, not just because I was her analyst but because I myself needed to know. But the session was over, and she was gone.

That desire has returned to me, the same question, only slightly modified. Now it is the desire to know what has become of her and whether her wish has been granted. Nonsense, I say. I say to myself that nothing has become of her, that she has become nothing. And yet— I find myself wondering—what *kind* of nothing? I want it to be the kind she described, a darkness, a depth of space, where a current passes, where a filament of solar wind hums to a glow. That is what I want for her. That is what I pray, I who believe nothing.

You believe in God. You mentioned in your eulogy for Jessica Burke "what it is to know God, to be known by Him." Is that knowledge a theory, a premise, something you believe in order to believe other things? Or is it a feeling, like hunger or sadness or fever?

The more I brood upon this, the less I understand. Certain plausible interpretations, of course, make their bids: she was expressing a desire to be open to someone, perfectly, transparently so, but because such a desire is terrifying, she needed to remain hidden, invisible, secure. Or alternatively, she was expressing a desire—primitive and archaic—for merger, the desire for resorption, to be compounded anew into a body of formlessness and dark. That, I think, is how I would have explained her remarks had I presented the case to colleagues or candidates in training. How credible these interpretations, how persuasive. How pitifully beside the point.

What has happened to me? What has happened so that I credit her words as witness to a vision? It could not happen that I, a psychoanalyst, an interpreter of desires, an anatomist of fantasy, could succumb to such a belief. And yet the belief is mine, or I am Its. It has claimed me for its own. Tell me, Father, if you can, while there is still time: Is that how God sees the soul, all at once, a streak, a smear, a ribbon, its beginning and end, future and past, flaring like a northern light, illuminated by His invisibility? Can you tell me?

SIXTEEN

Time now does not pass so much as it wears away. Spring ground down into summer. Old Itzal retired in June.

The building threw a party for him, the venue my office on the ground floor. Eight or nine residents showed up, avoided the couch, spoke among themselves. Cheese cubes sweated on a platter, and Itzal stood in the corner, hunched like a crow in his ill-fitting uniform, a plastic cup of sherry undrunk in his hand as though he were holding it for someone else.

"So, Itzal, I hear you've bought a house back in the Basque country," I said in an effort to relieve his awkwardness.

"*Oui, Monsieur Docteur.* It is the house of my family."

"Do you have much family there?"

His shrug seemed to say, at once, "Of course not," and "Years ago, maybe, I did," and "I couldn't begin to count them all."

"*Tu as de la chance, Itzal,*" Lucky man, I said, settling on the optimistic interpretation.

"As you wish, Doctor."

"I'll encourage Clementine to look you up in France," I said.

"*Comme vous voulez, Docteur,*" he repeated.

"*Pour toi, Itzal, un souvenir,*" I said, and gave him an old Baedeker guide to the Basque country I'd found in a used-book store.

"*Je vous remercie, Monsieur Docteur,*" he said with the hint of a bow as he slipped the little volume into his loose coat. Minutes later he'd vanished from the room, and I did not see him again. The new doorman is a mountainous, sweating Chechen named Bworz.

No word from Clementine. Six weeks since her graduation, four weeks since she left, going on five.

I force myself to walk the park or up and down the avenue, to keep myself from checking my answering machine, although the longer I am gone, the more I feel the hope burning within me, that in my absence Clementine will have gotten in touch.

Nothing.

After her departure, what felt like a terminal agony took hold of me. I was a hospice patient hooked up to a PCA drip, except that instead of a morphine pump, I clutched my cellphone and dosed myself with the redial button. Clementine's number would ring several times before the connection switched to her voicemail; from this I assumed that wherever she was, she was still charging her phone. Eventually, however, her voicemail started answering immediately, and her message changed from her brisk "Clem here—leave a message" to a synthesized recitation of the telephone number. And yet I continued to call. Finally, a small package arrived at the apartment building. At first, when I saw the French postmark, I thought that the package must be from my correspondent, that he had taken to tormenting me where I lived. It made sense: Why not strip me of the two-block buffer that separated my home from the postal box? Why not revoke the possibility that I could somehow, someday, simply stop checking it? But then I noticed that the handwriting on the envelope was Clementine's.

I tore open the package and a cellphone thudded onto the desk. It was her cellphone, the one I had been calling. Strapped to it with a rubber band was a note, also in her handwriting. *Get a grip, Daniel*, it said. *Actually*, it said, *get help*.

I tried to turn it on, but the battery was dead. Moving as though in someone else's dream, I walked out to buy a charger, walked home, and plugged the phone in, calling it mechanically one last time just to—just to what? To verify that it had been working? To reassure myself that she had heard the messages I had left? When I called her number that last time, however, and her own telephone leapt alive on my desk, ringing and vibrating, when the voicemail picked up and the synthesized voice repeated her number, I heard my voice saying, *This is your father, Clementine*. And again, *This is your father. This is your father. Your father.*

Clementine's telephone sat inert as a petrified egg on the hall table, and yet it seemed to throb with talismanic promise, as though for its sake she would bang back through the front door, exclaiming, *God, I'm such a dork! Forgot my phone again—*

But weeks passed. Suddenly it was July.

The phone had not rung.

How queer, the tendency of our days to flatten into a sameness, as water finds its level. I watched them pool up in the old routines of work and sleep. Each day I unlocked my office and watched my patients come and go. Each day I went to the post office, to peer into box 5504. Everything different, but everything also just as it was. As though everything were not, in fact, closing on its end, as though I had not, for example, begun to seek out new placements for my patients. My explanation? An unexpected family circumstance had required me to move from the city for at least a year.

The boy Micha, eight years old, my only child patient, was convinced I was leaving because he had thrown a tantrum and broken the Connect 4 set I keep for play therapy. When I explained to him that I was not mad at him, that there was a grown-up problem that I had to go fix, he announced that I was going to go spy on the Chinese and "steal the secret of their code writing." I asked him what he would do while I was gone. He was going to take Chinese pills so he could speak to me when I got back.

My patient Mrs. Thalmann embraced with passionate intensity the conviction that I had cancer—most likely pancreatic, considering my age.

And what did pancreatic cancer bring to mind for her?

Bring to mind? Nothing. It brings nothing to mind. Pancreatic cancer, that's curtains.

Curtains? I said.

Curtains means no mind, no mind left and nothing left to bring.

I said she was convinced I was going to die, that we would have to part for good, just as she had always been convinced that I would abandon her.

Everyone abandons everyone.

Yes. You are convinced of that.

But that is true, isn't it? One way or another that will be true, whatever I think of it, whatever I feel about it. The future's not some sort of Rorschach blot, Daniel. With that she stalked out of the session twenty minutes early.

It was the afternoon of Mrs. Thalmann's departure that the next letter from my correspondent arrived in the post office box. Again I forced myself to wait until I was home and at my desk before opening the envelope. When I saw what it contained, I picked up the phone on my desk and dialed Officer Peña at the precinct house.

"Where's your daughter now, Mr. Upend?" Officer Peña asked when the call was put through.

I said she was in danger.

"How do you know?"

I said she was still missing.

"Is she still an adult?"

I said I had a photograph of her, sent by God knows who.

"Is she in danger in the photograph?"

She was in Paris.

"Paris, Mr. Upend? Maybe she was the one who sent it—from Paris. Maybe she wanted to put you at ease."

At ease?

"Let me ask you again, Mr. Upend. Does the photograph indicate in any way that your daughter is at risk?"

But I knew the place, the exact place captured in the photograph, the street corner, the Métro station in the background, the newspaper stand.

"Is that a dangerous street corner in Paris? Is that a dangerous newspaper stand?" But she agreed that if I brought the picture into the station, she would put a copy on file. I hung up and ran the three blocks to the precinct house.

Officer Peña inspected the photograph, holding it for a moment at arm's length, then, after unhurriedly perching a pair of spectacles on her nose, drawing it closer to her round face.

"This pretty girl?" she said, looking up at me. "She doesn't look very endangered to me."

It was true: in the photograph Clementine did not appear in any way at risk. In the picture she was looking beyond the frame toward someone I could not see, her expression one of mock exasperation, as though urging someone to quit fooling around and hurry up, why don't you?

"You sure, Mr. Upend, she didn't send this to you to let you know she's okay?"

It wasn't her handwriting on the envelope.

Now I was the recipient of Officer Peña's scrutiny, as she fed her Selectric a fresh form. The typewriter flinched, *chunk chunk*, when Officer Peña jabbed with her finger.

"Name? . . .

"Clementine's a nice name.

"Phone number? . . .

"Left her phone at home, did she?" *Chunk jab flinch chunk*. "No . . . known . . . number . . .

"You say you'd quarreled with your daughter, Mr. Upend?"

Chunk.

"And when, approximately, was that?"

Flinch chunk.

"Are you sure, Mr. Upend, you aren't just feeling a little guilty?"

Now the typewriter merely whirred.

"About fighting with your daughter?"

Typing nothing, she nodded, squinting, lips pursed, as I asserted my conviction of urgency. When Officer Peña yanked on the form, the typewriter surrendered it with a squawk.

"That, Mr. Upend, is all I need to know. . . ."

"What is *who* going to do next? Your daughter and her friend? . . ."

"That's right, Mr. Upend, if something turns up, you can be sure we'll let you know."

Outside, I passed Esmé's, the café where Clementine and I had spent so many after-school hours. Surely Officer Peña could have been right. Might it not be possible that I should feel relief? Hadn't Clementine looked well, better than well, "that pretty girl," more suntanned than when I had seen her last? I strove by sheer force of will to convince myself that my dread, however asphyxiating, was misguided, the stuff of delusion. Could it not be that what afflicted me was not an external threat but the shadow of my own past, hooding the sun but for me alone, the sun that elsewhere shone with such brilliance on Clementine, in Paris?

In the photograph of the kiosk, posters above the stacks of newspapers trumpeted the news. I calculated that the headlines could be no older than what, four days? five? So the photograph was recent. The films advertised on the sides of the kiosk had yet to be released. Perhaps my correspondent wanted nothing but to instruct me that it was I and I alone who would never be free. This could be true, I insisted to myself. Just because he had found me, just because he had found her—that alone did not mean that he would do what I most dreaded. He had never said that he would take her life as payment for my own.

SEVENTEEN

I do not know how I got home. I do not know what happened between leaving the precinct house and the moment back at the apartment when my telephone rang. I frisked myself to find it—found nothing—lurched from counter to armchair to desk—nowhere—and then it stopped midring. When I finally discovered my telephone in my briefcase, I punched through the list of recent numbers to see who had called. No one had called. No one had called for days. Then it rang again, once, twice, before I realized that it was Clementine's telephone ringing, there, plugged into its charger on the vestibule table. I lunged for it, in the insane conviction that if Clementine's telephone was ringing, then surely Clementine herself must be calling.

"Clem! Clementine, is that you? It's me, it's Dad—!" But there was nothing, only silence on the line.

"Hello?" I said, this time as one might test a vacant room for an echo. Nothing . . . nothing . . . except (was it?) the sound of breathing, a fluctuation in the background hiss of the line. I held my breath, and the breathing stopped. The silence shifted. Click. Pop. "Hello," I said a final time, meaning goodbye. "Hello?" The hiss was now more insistent, now thickening to a low hubbub, as of a wide space busy with activity, telephones ringing, footfalls, scraping chairs, when abruptly a single voice cut in. *Do you hear me?* the voice said, strained, insistent. *Do you hear me?* it repeated, urgent now. *Are you listening to what I am telling you?*

A click and then the voice resumed: *I am saying it was another letter, along with a photograph, a photograph of my daughter. Do you understand what I am saying to you?*

It was my own voice, recorded, played back.

"I hear what you are saying." This was a second voice in the exchange, a woman's voice.

I am telling you, my voice continued, *that someone—and I don't know who—a stranger has mailed me a photograph of my daughter.*

"That's what you said the first time, when we took down the report. So where is your daughter now, Mr. Upend?" Just as I realized that the second speaker was Officer Peña, the line popped again with a sound something like a phonograph skipping, and her voice repeated, "So where is your daughter now, Mr. Upend?"

Click.

So where is your daughter now, Mr. Upend?

Click.

So where is your daughter now, Mr. Upend?

Click.

Then the gaping silence. Then a dead line.

What prevented me then, Father—having heard my own voice on the line, my own voice and Officer Peña's, played back through my daughter's cellphone—from raising the alarm, from speeding back to the station to make my declaration? Someone had recorded our conversation; even when I was in the police station, someone was listening. Was it not obvious then that I and my daughter had been chosen, had been *singled out*, the objects of a present and calculating malignity? The recording could not have stated the reality more starkly: I know where you are. I know you are holding her telephone, the telephone she sent back to you. I know that you have no way to reach her, whereas I, I can reach her whenever I please.

It was neither prudence nor fear that held me back. I will tell you even though you will not believe me: at the very moment, my direst apprehensions confirmed, what took possession of me was an utter stillness, an absolute coming to rest.

Do you remember how trains between Boston and New York used to stop in New Haven to switch engines, electric to diesel or diesel to electric? Do you remember how at that moment, silence upon silence would invade the train, each one deeper than the next, as the ventilation, hydraulics, generator, and engine each cut off one by one, until finally the lights themselves went out? What a total, unbreathing stillness that was. I used to think that death must be such a moment, an accelerating cascade of failures, the encroaching silences compounded as each unnoticed whir or whisper withdraws, making itself known only in its departure. As I stared at the cellphone, that was the sense I had: an arrival at a point of complete extinguishing.

During all the years of her childhood, how much I believed we belonged to each other, Clementine and I. Those were the years in which that bond stood immovable as the axis of our shared world. This must be true for all single fathers of only daughters, that link absolute and indefeasible. Nothing then was stronger, nothing more real than that conviction—real, yes, and yet I know now also utterly wrong.

It was precisely *because* she was my daughter and I her father that we belonged not to each other but to opposing dispensations: I to the past, she to the future. Her destination, her rendezvous, was ahead of us, in the future, while my rendezvous was with the past itself. Our mutual bond was nothing more than a temporary settlement. The distance between us now was a distance that had always been there. That gulf was vast, unspannable, but my terror poured out into it and vanished. And I tell you, as I stared into it for the first time, that gulf poured into me its own inhuman and absolute calm.

*   *   *

That calm held unperturbed even when, several days later, another photograph of Clementine appeared in box 5504. Like the others, this one had been printed on heavy stock, and as before, a ragged edge formed the upper border. The photograph had been taken at night, the camera even closer to her face than it had been for the picture by the kiosk. Clementine was seated with her back to the wrought-iron railing of a bridge, a bridge everyone in Paris knows, a footbridge over the Seine where the young people congregate in the evening. In the photograph, Clementine was smoking a cigarette. I had never seen her smoke, but she seemed perfectly at ease, holding the cigarette to the side as she exhaled and smiled at the same time, her mouth pursed a little as though about to speak. Her expression was unmistakably and uniquely Clementine's, one I must have seen thousands of times and yet never noticed. But there was something different about the way she held her mouth.

Yes, I knew. I knew what it was.

Her lips were pursed and tightened at the corners of her mouth not merely because she was about to speak, but because she was about to speak *in French*. Her French had been excellent since attending the Lycée Français, but it had been a slick, synthetic, private school French, polished and expensive, made in America. In the photograph, however, her mouth formed itself effortlessly around one of the impossible syllables. I knew that shape of the mouth: I knew it from Miriam, from Miriam's lips, smoky and muscular, whispering, brushing against my own.

And on the back, beneath the torn upper border of the photograph, the poem had been copied anew in the familiar, blocked-out handwriting:

Where the wandering water gushes
From the hills above Glen-Car,
In pools among the rushes
That scarce could bathe a star,
We seek for slumbering trout

And whispering in their ears
Give them unquiet dreams;
Leaning softly out
From ferns that drop their tears
Over the young streams.
Come away, O human child!
To the waters and the wild
With a faery, hand in hand,
For the world's more full of weeping than you can understand.

Away with us he's going,
The solemn-eyed:
He'll hear no more the lowing
Of the calves on the warm hillside
Or the kettle on the hob
Sing peace into his breast,
Or see the brown mice bob
Round and round the oatmeal-chest.
For he comes, the human child,
To the waters and the wild
With a faery, hand in hand,
For the world's more full of weeping than he can understand.

Where there had been four stanzas at first, now the final two alone remained. The first two had been torn away. Beneath them, my correspondent had written:

Que ce soit avec toi, que ce soit avec la fille, je serai satisfait.
Je suis (tu comprends) miséricordieux.

Whether with you or with the girl, I will be satisfied.
I am (you understand) merciful.

The sentence pronounced. The verdict handed down.

EIGHTEEN

I have this exchange with Jessica Burke recorded in my notebook.

"But what if I am meant to be a junkie? What if that's what I'm meant to be? Who's to say it's not?"

"You want me to say it. You want me to say it's not meant to be."

"I do. I want that. But you can't say it."

"I can say this—you are afraid that it might be true, also that it might not be true."

"I was right," she said after a long pause. "You can't say it."

Do you actually *hear* confessions in your church, Father, actual spoken confessions? For that matter, does any priest anymore, at least as the movies depict them, the little lattice between confessor and penitent, its delicate chiaroscuro screening the priest's profile and veiling the lips of the sinner? Surely Freud himself, when he positioned himself behind and out of sight of his recumbent patients, sought a similar partial anonymity. How we analysts must envy you, your belief in redress, in the promise of absolution and redemption. How clean the words sound compared to our own impure remedies: recollection, interpretation, speculation, suggestion. Strange, isn't it, how we have both sealed ourselves in small, half-lit chambers, both in the service of gods who share nothing but the name of Love.

That said, I hate and have always hated the word *therapist*. I detest the idea that my work, if it is work at all, is *therapeutic* work, that I am a member of what some of my colleagues call—without irony—the *helping professions*. My pride has sought always to refresh itself in the bracing chill of Freud's most merciless formulations, his statement that a cure only is a renewed acquaintance with "everyday misery," his designation of psychoanalytic work as a "school of suffering."

I reject the claim that psychotherapeutic treatment promises peace of mind, or comfort with oneself, however much these may be the happy by-products of the treatment—the accessory consolations, if you will. Rather than seeking to enhance self-esteem or contentment, the work strives for the opposite, to strip away all illusions of self-sufficiency or autonomy. At its most successful, this school of suffering is a curriculum in awe. The true object of this awe is the sheer, impossible fact of being here at all—to have precipitated like a sudden dew from lightless and dimensionless nothing. That is the horizon of the treatment, the recognition that we appear from nowhere under inscrutable stars, at a place and time we did not choose, driven by desires we do not choose, toward a death we do not choose, a death that chose us for its own even in our mother's womb.

Maybe this is only madness to you. Why shouldn't it be? Has my profession disfigured my mind, the endless hours of constant attentiveness, my ear for hire and open to all comers, my face painted with the glare of projected fantasies? The French have a term for it: *deformation professionelle*, the idea that all forms of work twist the mind away from reality. Hence a backfiring car sends the soldier diving for cover in a shrub. Litigators dart and cower in forests of imagined liabilities. For the detective and inspector, every testimony or confession is a network of lies and concealments. How could my work not have deformed me, all those long hours spent squinting into the soul's lightless recesses? How could I not have become some moon-eyed, cave-adapted creature, for whom ordinary daylight is an unendurable affliction?

You know what they say: shrinks make for the worst dinner compan-
ions. If dentists are always looking at your teeth, analysts are sniffing out
neurosis or delusion. The premise, of course, is absurd. You might as well
worry that the pulmonologist seated next to you will detect a spot on your
lung. Absurd, and yet true all the same, true that the practice of psychoanalysis can be a disfiguring labor, one's attention hung naked, irradiated
by the desires of others. Surely such exposure inflicts damage, a damage
as imperceptible as it is inevitable and irreparable, like the deafness that
creeps upon the machinist or the madness that leeches the wits from a
tanner of hides.

As a younger man, I burned with enthusiasm for my work: I was to
be a warrior, the champion of reviled or exiled passions. I would assail
the forces marshaled to enslave these passions, the tyrannies imposed in
the name of factitious moralities, the sadistic compulsions disguised as
highest law. I would be, in my silent, expensive way, the apostle of a
thrilling freedom. When did it abandon me, that faith?

How often have I heard it repeated, nearly verbatim, that commonplace of every educated, sophisticated patient: *I don't believe in judgment,
in divine judgment; I don't believe that someone is sitting up in the sky
frowning down at me.* In the past I would have thought: *Yes, you do—and
that is your problem.* In the fullness of time I would assist them in shaking
free of this secret conviction. Now, though, my calling has deserted me.
The premise wasn't wrong: most patients suffer more than they know
from obscure inner persecutions. What I did not realize, however, was
how deeply I myself believed in such a judgment, how along with my patients I embraced with inalienable fidelity that very conviction. This conviction did not presume a personified judge—bearded, severe, enthroned.
It presumed instead a law, inhuman, abstract, and implacable, the law to
which we owed our lives, the law to which we owed our reckoning.

Failure, worth, crisis, potential, fulfillment. Every patient returns to
these words again and again. They are the words from which my profession is made, and each of these words presumes a judgment, a mark attained or missed. No one enters my office who does not believe in his
very marrow that judgment, some judgment, is absolute and fixed. *The*

person I am meant to be: that mythical creature, that being whom each patient longs and dreads to become, is itself a judgment, a standard one does not devise but to which one must account.

What or who set the standard? What or who measured the body for its soul? What or who meant them to be the people they were meant to be? I am certain: belief in judgment is not what my patients reject or grow out of. The belief in judgment is what they cling to. Beneath their affections and afflictions, judgment is their one true love.

"You want me to say that you were not meant to be a junkie."

"I do. I want that. But you can't say it."

"I can say this—you are afraid that might be true, also that it might not be true."

"I was right," she said after a long pause. "You can't say it."

She was right. What could I have said? *The world's more full of weeping than you can understand*?

Somewhere in a book by Simone Weil there is a passage Miriam showed me. Weil writes that the only thing anyone truly possesses is the ability to say "I," nothing more. This *I*, our sole possession, is what we owe to God. Whatever else we think of as our own—names, bodies, languages, families, nations—all these belong to fate, to be lent or revoked as fate alone decides. Standing beside Clementine's crib, in the night-light's weak glow, had I ever remembered this passage? Had I ever thought: Fate can, fate will, take you away? I never thought: You are not mine; you never were. How could I have, listening to your breathing as you slept, or, later, making you peanut-butter-and-mayonnaise sandwiches for school?

This was my crime: having held her as my own, my crime, for which I am called to account.

Que ce soit avec toi, que ce soit avec la fille, je serai satisfait.
Whether with you or with the girl, I will be satisfied.

NINETEEN

C alled to account. My answer forms itself inside me. It is not a plan, not even a purpose, not yet. But still it forms itself: silent, intent, unmoving.

I peer into the second photograph: the one of the river and the railing above it where I had chiseled the date of Miriam's suicide. The other photographs are intolerable, as though from behind them my correspondent scans my every thought. The photograph of the river, however, conceals no such gaze. What it conceals is something no one else can see.

At first, when I noticed the inscription, I had thought it was a picture of one thing only, the one place I could not bear to see again. I thought I understood what my correspondent was saying. He said, *Look, this place remains. I have been there, just as you were once, working your hammer and chisel. You cannot revisit or repair the past, but you can return to this place.* I thought, he wants me to know that my secret is a shared secret, that the inscription is still there, a slate recording a debt unpaid and unforgiven. But though the photograph says all of that, it conceals something my correspondent cannot know. It is more than merely the picture of a place. It is also the picture of a memory—no one's but my own.

*   *   *

In the afternoons during our silent retreat at the monastery, the one Miriam took me to on our first trip outside Paris, Miriam and I would walk
out in the fields, following in single file a narrow path through the pastures and hedgerows. We took with us a hiking map we'd found in the
monastery, so detailed that even the faintest footpaths appear as thin,
broken lines. The path we found traversed the grade crossing of an abandoned rail spur, curved along a small copse of acacias, then happened
abruptly upon a stream. The stream, its banks steep and narrow, cut a
course nearly invisible from the level of the field. At a bend, however, a
herd of white cattle had trampled the bank into a mud slope where they
gathered hock-deep to drink from the stream. They shied a little as we
passed but then moved to follow us en masse like a slow-moving, rum-
bling rain cloud.

The third or fourth day we were there, the warmest yet, we walked
out farther than we had before, still refraining from speech. After a while
we came to where a dilapidated bridge spanned the stream. It had no
rails, its planks silvered and soft with rot. We sat down at the bridge's
edge, our feet swinging over the water that flashed shallow and clear over
the stones of the streambed.

Staring down into the water, Miriam seemed unaware of my presence. What I had believed to be silence, mutually elected and shared, in
fact sizzled with the shrilling of insects, urgent and indistinct at once,
like the ringing of a faceless clock, while the heat of the day bore down
like the blare of a horn. At some point Miriam had taken off her shoes as
though she were going to climb down the bank into the water, but then
she had removed her shirt also, revealing her small breasts and the faint
hair of her armpits as she pulled it over her head. Once entirely naked
she crouched beside me, her feet flat on the rotten boards, and unbuttoned my shirt, whispering something to each button as she eased it
through its buttonhole. Sweat beaded minutely on her upper lip, and the
warm, released smell of her nakedness rose from her like air tautened

before a squall. At first she crouched over me, but then she wanted to be on her back. She wanted my mouth against her, and held my head against her with one hand, spreading her labia with the fingers of her other. She couldn't come like that, she had said before, but nevertheless rocked her hips harder between my mouth and the grunting boards, her breathing straitened, both hands now knotted in my hair. Usually she pulled me slowly into her, looking, teasing herself with the tip of my penis, dipping it inside her, then rubbing it against her clitoris, always watching, mouth slack, brow knit. But this time there was no delay, only the same frantic grip now on my hips, now my buttocks, pressing me against her as though all of my weight and all of her force were not enough, nothing could be enough—her neck sinews bar-hard from jaw to collarbone, eyelids clenched—her climax no release but a wrenched, shuddering current relenting only to shift its grip and seize her again and then again as though to annihilate the very possibility of resistance and only then to let her drop.

When I withdrew she broke the thread of semen between us with her finger and said, *"Et toi, t'as joui aussi, mon ami."* She said this—You came too, my love—as a matter of fact. Nor had I been aware of coming, or of anything except the force of her embrace, a force that, in the end, had failed to obliterate her completely.

Afterward Miriam lay naked, facedown on the planks, staring through a gap between the boards. I did the same, and we lay like that for a while, looking down into the water. The bright surface of the stream beneath us reversed to transparency as it passed beneath the bridge's shadow. From time to time a fish would steer into one of the clear patches, idling slowly upstream though motionless against the stream-bed beneath it, or a leaf, dry on its upper side, would glide under the bridge. Mostly, though, the stream carried nothing but patches of sky and the shadows of our faces, which scattered and regrouped on the shifting surface of the water.

✳   ✳   ✳

That bridge must have long since rotted out and buckled or vanished in a spring flood. And though Miriam herself has vanished, the stream remains, motionless and unresting, and from its shallows her reflection still looks up at me, through me, to a future she will not inhabit, in a country she will never see, at a girl, a stranger, the Clementine she will never know.

TWENTY

We had met again at the café on the rue de Vaugirard to consider a new poem. The Yeats poem we had discussed first
had been a photocopy, but this time she appeared with a
broad book, wider than it was tall, and placed it on the table between us.
Leaning over, she kissed me and said, *I love to approach you from a distance, to see you before you see me.*

Do I look different then?

You look like the man I love.

Will you introduce me to him one day? I said.

She shrugged. *One day—maybe,* she said.

The wide book was a musical score, settings of poems by George
Herbert. I had not heard of him. A seventeenth-century English poet,
Miriam explained, an Anglican priest. She would be performing one of
the songs soon, and she had been struggling with several pronunciations,
the word *guest*, for example, and *worthy,* to say nothing of the name Herbert itself, which she pronounced *Air-bear.*

"It's 'guest,'" I said.

"*Guayst,*" she repeated, frowning. "Again once, please."

"Guest," I said again.

"*Gust. C'est 'gust,' non? Non, pas vraiment . . . Merde!*"

"Guest. The sound is *eh . . . eh*—guest."

"*Eh,*" she said. "*Guehh-st. Guehst.* Guest." The flat vowel seemed to darken the word, obscure it. She switched back into French: "*C'est un invité, n'est-ce pas?*" And just like that, once she had restored "guest" to its proper sense of "*invité,*" the poem itself seemed suddenly to recover transparency for her, as though a ray of sunlight had opened up the overcast clouds of English. She must have experienced in my own mauling French a similar wrongness, a shadowing or clouding of the medium that was for her merely the clear precipitate of thought. And yet when she suggested that we each stick to our own language, that I speak to her in English and she to me in French, I refused, saying something inept like *On est dans France donc il doit parler français.* We are at France so it must to speak French.

"*Tu es adorable,*" she said, lifting my hand and kissing it on the palm, "but when in Rome, maybe it is not always necessary to do as the French do?"

Every couple (it seems to me) adopts a story of origin, whether to testify to a great and fated love or merely to answer the question "So, how did you two meet?" But when did Miriam and I begin? Was it the moment I first saw her, in the dim light of the elevator? Or the night I first heard her sing, which was also the first night we slept together? On the trip to the monastery, perhaps on the rotting bridge, something had changed; had that been the moment? (Surely it was then, or nearly then, that Miriam conceived.) I am convinced, however, that none of those encounters was it. Still, in each of these meetings, we had yet to meet each other.

When I consider the brevity of those months, I can believe we ended before we began, that it was all over before it even started. But no: there was a time when we were wholly each other's, and it began that day, at the café on the rue de Vaugirard, a musical score unfolded on the café table. That, I believe, was our moment of beginning.

I believe this because the poem lying open on the table had marked

for her, as she put it, her point of no return. It was the crisis that sheared
her away from her prior life, and it was along the arc of that deviation
that I was to accompany her. Before we met, she had been pursuing a
doctorate, her thesis on the French philosopher Simone Weil. Weil, a
suicide or nearly one, had allowed herself to die of self-imposed starva-
tion at the age of thirty-four in the summer of 1943, having escaped from
occupied France to England. Up to the end she had nurtured a hope
that the Free French, under de Gaulle, would put her to some heroic
use, this skeletal, zealous, bluestocking fugitive. Though Jewish by birth
and violently opposed to fascism, she deplored and repudiated her Juda-
ism and converted to Christianity or, rather, to a caustic and unstable
isotope of Christianity, a system she cooked out in her writings, most
notably in her sprawling journals. These journals in particular had fasci-
nated Miriam. She had first encountered them preparing for her *bacca-
lauréat*, discovering in Weil a version of herself, a young woman of ardent
and unruly talents. Miriam's fascination both haunted and animated her
university studies and in time drove her on to pursue postgraduate work,
where she found she could eke out her modest stipend by singing in
choirs. Her doctoral thesis argued something concerning Weil's theory
of necessity. "Just 'something'?" I asked, but she replied only by saying:
Whatever I thought, it was wrong—everything, all of it, entirely wrong.
Late in her studies, she had veered off this path, the path she had followed since high school.

It had happened the moment she first encountered, somewhere in
Simone Weil's writings, this poem by George Herbert, the poem whose
setting she was preparing to sing. Simone Weil had read the poem on
retreat at the Monastery of Solesmes, and it had struck her with epi-
phanic force. For Weil, it gave utterance, with unworldly clarity, to the
soul's wondering disbelief when brought face-to-face with God's love:

> Love bade me welcome, yet my soul drew back,
>   Guilty of dust and sin.
> But quick-ey'd Love, observing me grow slack
>   From my first entrance in,

Drew nearer to me, sweetly questioning
    If I lack'd anything.

"A guest," I answer'd, "worthy to be here";
    Love said, "You shall be he."
"I, the unkind, the ungrateful? ah my dear,
    I cannot look on thee."
Love took my hand and smiling did reply,
    "Who made the eyes but I?"

"Truth, Lord, but I have marr'd them; let my shame
    Go where it doth deserve."
"And know you not," says Love, "who bore the blame?"
    "My dear, then I will serve."
"You must sit down," says Love, "and taste my meat."
    So I did sit and eat.

The poem surfaces again and again in Weil's writing, even to the last months of her life. It was as though (Miriam explained) the poem like Love itself persisted in inviting her, bidding her to take its sustenance, even as Weil's body hollowed and broke. When Miriam stumbled upon the poem in the course of her studies, knowing what she knew of Weil's final days, the encounter shook her. An instant, it seemed, had transformed the whole purpose of her studies, or rather, this new sense of purpose revealed itself to have been the motive all along. A text that had seemed at first merely a constituent part, a single step on her professional ascent, was now suddenly a door—a door through which she had already passed, a door already shut and sealed at her back.

But wasn't it strange (I asked her) that the same poem that struck Simone Weil with such force should overcome her, Miriam, as well? She wasn't claiming that it harbored magical or mystical virtue, was she? Maybe what she had experienced was merely an intoxication, a bewildering but explicable identification with the object of her study. Perhaps it was an occupational hazard for an academic, the risk of discerning in an object of scrutiny a promise of spiritual transformation, an intimation of transfiguring clarity. . . .

"Clarity?" she said with a sigh halfway between dismay and disgust. There was no clarity. All she knew was that everything she had thought, known, wanted, all of it had been entirely wrong. She had watched her dream of wisdom crumble. The path that remained to her was the path through the rubble field, the path of patience. "But in the end it was not so different a path," she said, "not so great a change. I went from being a student, a student of Simone Weil's work, to being—"

"A disciple?" I asked.

"Are you mocking me?"

"Not at all."

"No, not a disciple. A novice, if you want to know. That is the difference: I realized I was not a student but a novice, not even a novice—a postulant."

"And now you are about to become a real postulant, a real novice—"

"Nothing will have changed. I will just go to a place where people will call me what I am, a novice if you like, a beginner."

"If I like."

But, she chided, I seem to have forgotten that I had a job to do.

A job?

The translations. My job was to help her.

But why choose me? Had she confused me with some sort of authority on Renaissance English poetry? I was a shrink, not a professor. As for modern English, Paris was infested with native speakers.

But I suited her purposes, she said, then added: Most deliciously.

Had she chosen me because I had an expiration date?

"But that is what the poem says, n'est-ce pas? Doesn't it say there are things you can learn only from someone you love?"

"Is that who I am?" I asked.

"And . . . ," she said, not answering my question but adjusting the thought, completing it, "and from the one who loves you?"

TWENTY-ONE

The latest photograph arrived three days ago, unaccompanied: no note, no inscription, no sheared-off poem-fragment. The image—if you could call it that—is a patchwork, a botch-up of half-shapes, some pale, some dim, large or small. If you could see it, would you think that shape there, that grayish oblong shape, resembled a sort of dog, a dog lying on its side? Would you feel an inexplicable sadness for it, as I did? That is what I felt, an unexplained sadness, before it came to me, the name, the dog's name: Obus.

He is almost at the center, a little lower, at the feet of those other shapes. You see how Obus, lying down, is outlined in profile, because the picture is taken from above, just as the picture of the river's surface had been taken from above. It is as though the earlier picture of the river has evolved into this one, as though the water's surface has curdled, clumped into masses. But what, or who, are those other shapes, shapes that like the dog appear to be lying on their sides?

I cannot say, yet must.

I think, Father, I can no longer tell what I remember from what I have imagined. A boundary has vanished, the boundary separating my own memories and the memories I devised for Clementine: *Your eyes, they are your mother's exactly.* All I remember is how those eyes looked,

looked at me or rather through me—her long, level stare, how even when we were lying face-to-face, her gaze would shift from one of my eyes to the other, as if two different things required monitoring at the same time. She had better near-field vision than I and could focus on objects only inches away from her; when we lay together, she could see my face with perfect clarity, while for me her face swam in a blur. When we made love, her eyes were always open. When I spoke French, I would always know when she was having difficulty following what I was saying because she would look directly at my mouth, like a person reading lips. When Miriam slept her eyes would flick beneath her lids, as though scanning an invisible heaven.

What do I remember? Who are those two figures in the photograph, lying on their sides, the dog Obus at their feet? Time is short. I must tell you.

"Do I look exactly like her?" Clementine asked when she was six or seven years old.

"No, darling, not exactly. Like me a little too."

"Will I be bald like you?"

"Probably not, Clem, but you might be tall, taller than your mother."

"She was as small as me?"

"She was a grown-up like me, but not very tall. French people are not very tall," I said, and held my hand flat at the level of my collarbone to show her how tall Miriam had been. I remember how Miriam would tilt her head upward and lift her heels to kiss me, how when I clonked my head against one of the beams in her apartment, she gasped and then pressed her temples in reflexive sympathy. I remember her small hand resting on a page, index finger extended, as she followed a line we were reading together. I remember how, when she switched from French to English, her whole being changed, the suppleness of her mouth stiffened, as though checked with a bit.

How much also I must have forgotten. Would I recognize that world if I were to revisit it, her building, its front door? What was the street number, the street? Surely it has all changed, all except the smells, the linden trees flowering in the park below, the damp rising from the swept streets, combining with the odor of her bedding and the atticky exhalations of the beams, the worn parquet.

Her apartment: a wedge of steep space under the mansard roof. By her bed, Miriam had a compact disc player she used for her alarm clock. She never changed the CD, so that when the alarm went off, the song was always the same, like a Delta blues, but sung by an African voice, Malian, maybe, or Senegalese. Beneath that keening upper voice, someone tapped out an intricate beat, as though with a pencil on a gourd. But it is no use trying to describe it: the music seems now half-submerged in our dreams and like those dreams soluble in daylight, a part of the sweet, momentary confusion of not knowing where we were, or whose body we lay beside, her head hidden under the pillow against that daylight and that recurrent song.

How impossibly remote it all seems, but I think now that that distance is not one of time, though eighteen years have passed, or of the space between Paris and New York. It is instead an inner distance, as though those smells, those sounds, have retreated to the darkest interior of my body, distilled and condensed within a tiny ampoule of toxin. Though the capsule is small and impossible to detect, were it to crack open, releasing that tar-black suspension of memory, mere seconds (I am certain) would bring death.

But why lethal? you will ask, Father. For the love of God, Abend (you will ask), your story may be dark, may be bitter, but how does it outstrip the common lot of human misfortune? Your unremarkable share of fate was to fall for a girl in Paris, a girl more closely acquainted with despair than you knew. Sad, yes—but lethal? These elements are nothing but ordinary, the familiars of a thousand stories: the pregnancy, the desperation intolerable to her and paralyzing for you, your complicity, unwilled and unwitting, and yet participating in single-minded collusion in her self-annihilation. That she worked it out and accomplished it, drowning herself in the Loire, that she left a child behind, all this is sad, yes, tragic, yes, but surely the Loire (you will say) is used to this sort of thing.

How could I object, Father, were there not more to say?

What the ampoule holds is lethal because it contains a separate, distinct resin, darker and thicker, as pungent as tar. When I look at the most recent photograph, when I consider its overlapping shadows and compacted masses—alleviated only by the pale oblong that is Obus, asleep with his forepaws held straight out, like a superhero in flight—when I stare into that picture, I can taste it, that acridity in the back of my throat. The figures in the picture (you see now there are in fact figures in the picture) lie on a crude pallet on the floor, the recently paved floor of a half-built parking garage, to be exact. The air is heavy with an asphalt odor, and compounded with that odor the vinegarish reek of heroin, heroin cooked in a spoon before injection, or heroin torched from below on a sheet of foil, the smoke inhaled through a glass tube. And there is the odor of stale garments, hair, and bodies, and the inexpungible odor of blood.

This darkest smudge here is the hair of a girl. The paler patch is her face in profile, turned away. She too is lying down, the dog asleep at her feet, her knees pulled up and arms folded around a shadow in the hollow between her knees and chest. Who took this picture, its grain coarse, the camera's perspective elevated, its shutter staring a long moment to draw in what little light it could? Who is the girl, hugging the shadow? And that other form, curled like a question mark behind her back, who is that whose face, also in profile, faces the same direction? Would you recognize it? In the picture it is so much younger—eighteen years younger— you could not possibly have placed it, even if you could recall now its later, gaunter appearance, the face of a stranger, of a solitary man seated in the back of your church: that face—my face.

Do you see it now, how even then, even all those years ago, the dark, dilated eye of my correspondent's lens hung open over me, watching me, tracking me, as vigilant and invisible as a new moon?

SPURLOCK

3:41 A.M.

A darkness like tar has filled the church. Someone has even let the eight-day sanctuary candle burn down. In the grip of his dream, Spurlock gropes his way up the aisle, feeling for the edges of the pews with one hand while holding Abend's testament in the other. He shoves off from the front pew and sweeps the darkness with his free hand until his foot strikes the first step leading up to the choir. Finally he makes it past the choir stalls to the altar rail, where, clutching the document to his chest, he begins the climb up to the altar, the stairs in darkness so much steeper and more numerous than he remembered. How easy it would be to fall, how impossible to arrest that fall. Finally, however, he makes it to the top, where he discovers that the sanctuary candle is in fact still lit, though weak and guttering on the lampstand. In the morning he would have to contact Mrs. Burke, the sacristan, Jessica's mother, so that she could replace it.

Clinging to the altar edge with his free hand, his heels hanging over the lip of the narrow step that holds him, Spurlock can finally accomplish what he has come to accomplish: placing Daniel Abend's testament on the altar. When, however, Spurlock attempts to set his burden down on the marble surface, something objects with a desiccated crunch, seems to push back against the weight of the pages. What is this? Has

Mrs. Burke left a bundle of straw or branches on the altar, to be included in this Sunday's flower arrangements? Surely she knows the altar is not a work surface, much less a storage space. He had never known Mrs. Burke to be so careless. But then again, she had reason to be distracted, he thought, probing the bundle to see if he could move it. Her daughter Jessica had been having difficulties again. Suddenly, detecting beneath the coarse fabric of the bundle a knee or elbow, Spurlock recognizes with horror that the bundle is in fact a person, a person hunched or squatting on the altar. This person is no doubt one of the visitors, the homeless, in the crouched posture of one accustomed to sleeping sitting up, on subway cars, or on park benches divided by cast-iron armrests whose express purpose is to prevent vagrants from lying down.

"Sir," Spurlock hisses, startled by his own vehemence. "This is the altar of God! You cannot sleep here." There was no response. "Sir!" Spurlock hisses again, this time lifting the eight-day candle from the lampstand toward where he thought the face would be.

The man's hair hangs down in front of his face. With a crackle and a frizzing of acrid smoke, the candle singes a few strands.

"Oh, I am sorry!" Spurlock says, all his anger turning at once to consternation. He sees in the candlelight that the lock is perfectly black, not gray or matted, and has been braided with meticulous labor into fine plaits, sleek and lustrous. Smoke billows around the man's head. Is the hair still burning? Is the man not aware of this? Spurlock realizes that what he'd thought was smoke is in fact the cloud of his frozen breath. How terribly cold it is all of a sudden: he sees how the knuckles of the man's small hands had gone pale as marble from the exertion of clutching his knees to his chest.

"You must come with me," Spurlock says. "We must get you a blanket. We must get you a proper bed. Luis will be here, and he will bring hot coffee . . ." But Spurlock knows as he says these things that the person cannot understand him. "¿Café? ¿Café caliente?" he says, venturing one of the few words he knows in Spanish. Or is Spanish the wrong language? Spurlock knows no words in Quechua, which is unfortunate, because Spurlock understands now that the person on the altar is not a man but an Incan child, a girl, barely in her teens, a virgin surely, else she would not have been brought here to die. Bearing her on its shoulders, a winding procession has delivered her to the lip of this stony precipice and abandoned her, here, where the cold obliged her to clutch her knees to her chest, to breathe down under her cloak to conserve what little heat remained in her body. Such a cold place to die in, Spurlock thinks, and she had died such a long time ago, so many hundreds of years. So very cold, he thinks, and yet had not the cold itself kept her body intact, protecting her in its steadfast embrace? Spurlock pushes aside the curtain of her hair, careful this time not to singe another of the braids when he brings the candle closer to her face, that face, he sees now, still full with childhood, heavy with slumber. He sees how deep, how serious, it is, this slumber: the furrow on her brow, the girl's lips pushed forward in a swollen pout, her head tilted a little to one side.

With a gasp, Spurlock jerked upright in his cot, heart hammering his rib cage. A sweat chilled his skin even while a rage surged inside him: "Jesus motherfucking God, Abend!" he said out loud. "Are you satisfied?" One of the sleepers grunted as though in reply. Spurlock swung his feet onto the floor from his cot and tried to breathe as his eyes adjusted to the dimness of the church, the low light cast by the exit signs over the doors, and, yes, from the steady flame of the eight-day candle burning in the sanctuary. He was awake, but his heart still hammered, and the stench of scorched hair lingered in his nostrils. He could still feel the weight of that heavy hair, minutely braided, falling over the back of his hand as he pushed it to the side.

"Well, Abend, are you?" he asked again, more gently this time.

It had been Spurlock's idea to see the exhibit together, *Mummies of the Andes*, at the Museum of Natural History, maybe two years ago now. "You mean the hair-clump museum?" Bethany had said when Spurlock informed her of his plan.

"The what—what museum?"

"Hair-clump. Everything in that museum is either a gigantic beetle or a clump of hair."

But when he saw Bethany's reflection in the glass of the display case, her hand pressed to her mouth, he regretted his insistence. The case was a refrigerated vitrine housing the huddled body of a girl. Her hair, a sleek black, plaited in a thousand fine braids, obscured most of her face, but if you stood to the side, you could see the curve of her full cheek, the pout of the lips, her brow creased by a little furrow.

"They just left her there?" said Bethany.

"She was drugged," said Spurlock, summarizing the explanatory plaque he'd just read. "She was a sacrifice. They let her freeze to death on the mountainside."

But Bethany had turned away and was heading toward the exit. By the time he caught up with her, she was already on Central Park West.

"Jesus, Nelson, are you satisfied?"

"What's going on?"

"Why do you make me look at those things?"

"What do you mean, 'make you'?"

"It's a beautiful Saturday, and you have to fill it with freeze-dried corpses."

"Beth, it's an exhibit—"

"And you're a ghoul. You say you're a minister but you are a ghoul," she said, but smiled and took his arm as she said it, and Spurlock was filled with relief that she had not embarked on one of her litanies of discontent. "Am I taking you to brunch or not, Mr. Ghoul?"

That had been at least two years ago, possibly three, and yet the Incan child had chosen this night to appear in his dream. Knowing he would not sleep again, Spurlock had mounted the stairs to his office. The light from the avenue was sufficient to reassure him that the stack of sheets, Abend's testament, was in fact still there on his desk, undisturbed, just where he had left it.

What would Daniel Abend, psychoanalyst, have said about his dream? Would he have listened in resolute silence? Or would he have simply inquired what the dream brought to mind? What the dream brought to mind was Abend's voice itself, filling Spurlock's head like a trapped echo. Yes, that's what the dream brought to mind, a well or shaft sunk into the depths of a remote past, overflowing with echoes, flooding Spurlock's head even though that past was not his own. That past had belonged entirely to others and had remained private and sealed until the moment Spurlock slid his pocketknife under the flap of that heavy envelope and started reading.

Father, you will not remember me. My name is Daniel Abend.

"Are you happy now, Abend? Are you satisfied?" Spurlock said aloud, as though to chase the echo out of his head. His own voice, however, merely joined with the other voices, Abend's, Clementine's, Jessica Burke's. Beneath these others the voice of Abend's correspondent repeated its refrain:

Que ce soit avec toi, que ce soit avec la fille, je serai satisfait.
Whether with you or with the girl, I will be satisfied.

What Spurlock felt, to his chagrin, was envy. He envied Abend, and he envied Abend's correspondent. He envied them their shared belief that an account could be settled, a debt paid, an obligation satisfied. Was not the document itself, there on his desk, a testament first and foremost to that fact? (Spurlock had pulled his chair to the window overlooking the avenue, and he sat with his forehead against the cool pane, watching the traffic light cycle from yellow to red to green over the empty intersection.) He envied them all, Abend, his correspondent, even Bethany. After all, Bethany's job afforded her the pleasure of thumping her hand with a conclusive *thwack* on a stack of tab-indexed binders codifying the terms of a corporate merger. Months of negotiations concluded, the agreement at last drawn up and signed. "How satisfying," she would say, dropping the stack into a file carton with a thud. "Document storage will swing by to pick this up tomorrow." Spurlock envied her authority to dispatch her work for good, her power to banish it to a warehouse canyoned with obsolete documents.

What satisfaction was there for him? Spurlock recalled the time Father Babbet, his first spiritual director, had said to him, "If you're hot for worldly goods, Nelson, you won't find them in the priesthood, and Lord knows the body of Christ is replete with assholes. If you ask me, though, the job satisfaction can't be beat," and he had been right. Spurlock thought so then and had thought so many times since, and he'd made a point of repeating Father Babbet's formulation to any new seminarian posted to the Incarnation. Whatever those unbeatable satisfactions were, however, they never involved *thwack*ing a stack of binders into a box and dispatching it to document storage.

Was this a crisis of faith? Had he come to doubt that God's love was the satisfaction to be preferred above all others? It was just that his work was so . . . was so unlike work. He suspected that somewhere priests thought of their job as the salvage and restoration of souls, in preparation for eternal life. That would simplify matters. But for Spurlock this view carried the whiff of death with it: souls laid out in uniform ranks, like bodies in a morgue or pelts drying in the sun. He tried to reassure himself that the product of his labors was in fact a kind of antiproduct, a good that could not be swapped or sold and for that reason remained invisible to the eyes of the world.

Spurlock had met Father Babbet when Spurlock was still in divinity school, serving as seminarian at St. Dunstan's, an Anglo-Catholic parish in Boston. In that church's sacristy, a small room smelling of mothballs and incense, there was a special basin called a sacrarium, installed when the church had been built, its sole purpose the disposal of the consecrated remains of communion elements: the crumbs of the host, the dregs of the wine. Some altar jockey had practically tackled him when he made to pour his coffee into it and had declared to him that the

sacrarium drained directly into the earth, so that the body and blood of
Christ should not be made to suffer the indignity of the common sewer.
But wasn't mortality itself the common sewer, Spurlock wanted to ask,
into which God had already lowered Himself? He checked the impulse;
it was his first day at St. Dunstan's.

The parish's ornate observances disturbed Spurlock's idealism, but
he loved the music programming (on which the church spent an extravagant portion of its budget) and even came to appreciate something
frail and not quite absurd in the high-wire theatricality of Sunday's "Solemn Mass." When he put away the vestments after the service, he mar-
veled at the fragility of the fabrics, each cope and chasuble lovingly
preserved since the church's establishment in the heyday of nineteenth-
century Anglo-Catholicism. The lace and brocade had by now grown
brittle and beneath his fingers seemed more like museum pieces from a
lost civilization, like ceremonial costumes made from moth's wings or
from the feathers of birds long extinct.

Father Babbet, Spurlock's spiritual director and the rector of that parish, was a dried-out alcoholic whose translucent hands still shook when
he lifted the chalice during the consecration. He bypassed the customary off-quaffing of any undrunk communion wine and instead waited
until after the service, when he would tip the chalice into the porcelain
bowl of the sacrarium.

"The ecstasy of protocol," Spurlock said out loud, observing him,
because the phrase was one that Babbet himself liked to use.

"Protocol, Child Spurlock?" said Babbet, who also liked to call Nelson "Child Spurlock." "This is not a display of protocol. This sink is the
ground conductor of the church."

Spurlock admitted that he did not know what Father Babbet was
talking about.

"The ground conductor, Child Spurlock, the lightning rod. Keeps us
from getting electrocuted!"

"Please tell me that's not another thing I have to believe."

"Why not? But if you're having a heretical day, think how the Greeks
poured out their libations on the earth. Why buck tradition?"

"Well, if the tradition is crazy . . ."

"Crazier than you or I?" said Babbet, his eyebrow arching again like a cat's back. "It's better off down the drain than down my gullet, I can tell you that. And who am I to begrudge it, a little sop for the bloodthirsty earth?"

Maybe that's what his confessor's ear was: a sacrarium, a ground conductor, a pipe driven into the ground, through which something dangerous and unregulated could be discharged. A part of him revolted against the thought that something had been poured into or routed through him, as though he were nothing but an outfall pipe. Surely that wasn't what he'd signed up for at ordination.

Or had it been? Perhaps he had signed up to turn the other cheek, to walk the extra mile—but even so, Abend was wrong, he thought, culpably wrong to have put Spurlock in this position. Abend was wrong to have encumbered him with this stack of pages, this confession, unable to do anything except what he had been instructed, to hold on to them, to keep them on his desk, his attention a conduit obliged to take what it was offered. It was then that Spurlock remembered how Abend had described his own role in the same way, as a kind of prostitute, his ear open to all comers. Strange kinship, thought Spurlock, picking up the pages, this brotherhood of strangers.

TWENTY-TWO

The monastic order Miriam intended to join had been founded fewer than thirty years ago and described itself as a "new expression of monastic commitments." At the time I had been surprised to learn that the monks and nuns lived together in the same community; the average age, unlike that of most other orders Miriam knew of, was under forty. New vocations were plentiful enough to allow for the seeding of new houses in provincial cities. Members of the community dwelled and worshipped together in a traditional monastic setting; their work involved them in the outside world, aiding the homeless, immigrants, refugees, and street prostitutes. All this I have learned in the intervening years, having received from the order ever since my return to New York a quarterly newsletter and an annual appeal for money, to which I respond with a donation of five hundred dollars. Every few years, in one or another of the newsletter's photographs, I find the face of a nun taller than the others, her face round and smooth, the eyes a weatherless blue. The face is the face of Sœur Béatrice, who though English by birth has lately been elected the prioress of her monastic house, the house attached to the church of St. Julien in the medieval hill town of Leuvray. Sometimes Sœur Béatrice includes in the newsletter brief notices about the goings-on in the community. I read these notices with care, wondering if this time she will mention a small organic farm in a neighboring village, established twenty years ago. She does not. I learn instead that Sœur Thérèse has taken up stone carving, Frère Loïc will return to Rwanda in May, two new postulants have joined the community, or Bisou the cat has had kittens.

One day, not very long after we had returned from our own silent retreat, Miriam and I had taken a somewhat longer journey from Paris down into the Burgundy region. Once we'd left the autoroute, we followed narrow roads set in seams between billowing expanses of wheat or pasture, until Leuvray floated into view. Miriam wanted to show me the place where she would begin her postulancy and to introduce me to Sœur Béatrice, a young nun who would serve as Miriam's guide and helper before Miriam made her final move from Paris to Leuvray.

"And who am I supposed to be today?" I asked as we climbed the cobbled main street of Leuvray on foot. The church, at one time a basilica, seemed to ride above the town, like a ship breasting a swell.

"Supposed to be?"

"Your last-ditch, terminal fuck?" I said in English.

"*Comprends pas, enfin, sauf* 'fuck,'" she said, having understood nothing except *fuck*.

"Am I supposed to be your friend?" I said, returning to French.

She replied, however, in English. "So you say I am not your friend, only your fuck friend?"

"Maybe I should just be your silent friend. You people seem to like silence," I said, and we climbed the remainder of the hill without speaking.

Sœur Béatrice was waiting for us in the small café on the square at the foot of the church, and she greeted me with a handshake and a clipped "How do you do." I said I was Miriam's friend from the United States, joining her for a day in Leuvray, as though that were the description Miriam and I had agreed upon. Béatrice met my eyes for a long second and said, "You are welcome," as though I had thanked her for something. She greeted Miriam with a double kiss and throughout the interview spoke almost exclusively to her, in a French as rapid and fluid as it was heavily accented, marked everywhere with the British inversion of emphasis: *mais*-on, *ba*-teau, *châ*-teau. I realized Béatrice was in habit only when in the distance another nun mounted the steps to the church, wearing the same long dress of blue linen or chambray, the same white kerchief meant to cover the hair. In Béatrice's case it failed spectacularly; her hair, long and copper blond, peeked out around her ears and forehead and lay over her shoulder in a heavy braid, the length of which she stroked as though it were the tail of a great cat.

"Miriam has told me that you will be returning shortly to America. Have you enjoyed your vacation?"

I explained that I had not been on vacation, but that I'd come to Paris on a medical fellowship.

"Will you leave with what you hoped to leave with?"

I said I had never asked myself the question.

"We seldom do," said Béatrice, and shifted back into French, inquiring if Miriam had received some books she had sent. My attention strayed when a trio of hot-air balloons floated into view from behind the hulking eminence of the church. They passed, it seemed, at eye level, though still high over the valley. Periodically, someone in one or another of the balloons would pull a cord and a tongue of flame would shoot up into the balloon with a coughing roar. "*Les touristes américains, hélas,*" said Béatrice, following my gaze.

"American tourists like me, alas," I said.

"Ah," said Béatrice, "it appears you understand some French."

I said it would have been difficult, even for an American tourist, to avoid learning a little French over the course of a year.

"Miriam sings beautifully in English, don't you think?"

"She is a beautiful singer," I said.

"A voice such as hers is a gift from God."

"You do have a beautiful voice," I said to Miriam.

"It is only the voice of a little boy," she replied.

"You wouldn't agree, Daniel," Béatrice went on, "that Miriam's voice is a gift from God?"

I said I wasn't in the habit of thinking in those terms.

"Are 'those terms' not compatible with your philosophy?"

"Am I required to have a philosophy?"

"But your work is a form of practical philosophy, isn't it?"

"I'm used to thinking of it as a branch of medicine."

The conversation reverted to French, and I do not remember what else Miriam and Béatrice discussed. That afternoon, before returning to Paris, we attended Mass in the church. Miriam sat beside me this time. The towering spaces of the church blotted up the monks' prayers and consecrations, but during the chants Miriam's treble, closer to me than it had ever been, seemed to open a clearing around us, as a shaft of sunlight might open a sudden chamber in the woods. Miriam seemed merely the occupant of this space, not its source. It was a place she had brought me to, this clearing she had happened upon.

At the passing of the peace, before communion, the monastics left the choir and mingled among the sparse congregation, greeting each person with a sort of double handclasp. *May the peace of the Christ be with you*, each would say, solemnly, slowly, before moving on to the next person. A young nun with black eyes and a whiskery fuzz above her lip took Miriam's hands and addressed her by name, kissing her on each cheek. By the time she took my hands in hers, my palms had grown moist with apprehension.

"You must forgive Béatrice," Miriam said as we drove home.

"What reason would she have to like me?"

"It is only that she has known me for a long time. I am sure she feels protective, responsible for my vocation."

"Isn't the vocation supposed to be your responsibility?"

"God's, in fact," said Miriam.

Did I find it as unthinkable then as I do now, the prospect of her *becoming* one of those blue, beatific, sandaled shapes? Did I think, or hope, that she would renege when the appointed moment finally arrived? And when was the moment supposed to arrive? Would she pack up her things in her apartment? Her futon? Her CD player and her disc of African blues? Where would she put them? Would she hand over her street clothes, her *carte d'identité*, to a wardress behind a high counter? Would she take a name-in-religion, as Béatrice had? Béatrice had been named something like Fiona Burwell or Beryl Ferris before becoming Béatrice; who would Miriam Levaux become? Would a whiskery shadow gather on her upper lip once all mortal vanity had been buried in Christ's side?

"Do you think Béatrice is a lesbian?" I asked. The autoroute was dark now and the night clear, though in the distance the glow of Paris had swallowed the stars.

"No more than you are," she said, giving my earlobe a little tug, then resting her hand on my thigh. *"T'inquiète pas, mon ami,"* she said. "And anyway," she added after a pause, "we both have our tickets."

TWENTY-THREE

With absolute conviction we declare we recognize someone. The ethologists and developmental psychologists say the gift is innate, the ability to pick out one face among hundreds, among thousands. An adaptive trait, they call it, survival depending upon the parent's capacity to recognize the face of the child, the child's to recognize the face of the parent. Yet when we try to describe a face, even the most beloved, it could be any face at all.

In this new photograph from my correspondent she is seated at a café, a map open on her lap. The image flashes with captive sunlight, but the map itself hides in the shadow of the table. Clementine is the only figure in the frame, but there are two cigarette packets on the table, and alongside the coffee cup is a tall glass nearly empty, a pastis by the look of it, dilute and milky green. The café bill has been placed beside Clementine's hand. A little clip secures the slip to its tray, where a breeze lifts its corner. To her left on an empty chair rests a well-thumbed French–English dictionary alongside a glossy fashion magazine. The photograph, taken from behind, asks me to read over her shoulder, to examine the map held open on her knees. At my desk I take out my magnifying glass, lifting and lowering it with care over the image, as though I were trying to snare with a string something fallen through the grate of a storm drain.

Unlike the others, this photograph is in color, and the corner panel of the map is a bright blue, somewhere between turquoise and ultramarine, the blue that in France denotes a topological map of the most precise sort, as detailed as those issued here by the U.S. Geological Survey. I recognize the blue because Miriam and I had one with us at the monastery we visited together for the silent retreat; we had taken it with us on our walk down to the dilapidated bridge. Such a map was a hiking map, one not serviceable in Paris. There would be no reason for Clementine to have such a map now unless she were planning to leave Paris, to go on a trip.

Of course: because now one of her strongest motivations for being in France at all is to visit the place where Miriam was born, to meet, if possible, Miriam's parents, her French grandparents. Her friend at the café, whoever this friend might be, would help her locate them, their town, their address, on the appropriate map. Miriam had been born not in Paris but in Nevers, in the provincial department of the Nièvre.

In theory, the map Clementine is reading could be a map of any part of France, perhaps of some other place entirely. Are there no blue-clad maps in Spain, in Austria? This idea is present to me but insubstantial in the face of a dreadful possibility. If she goes to Nevers, if she goes to acquaint herself with the small, tattered city where her mother went to school, to locate and walk out on the bridge over the Loire, the river rapid and troubled in summertime, to look down at the place where Miriam died, if she finds where Miriam's parents still live . . . well, what then? What will happen?

I cannot say, and yet, even as I write this, I hear my own voice, my clinician's voice: "You cannot say, Mr. Abend? Or is it that you would prefer not to say? Or perhaps, Mr. Abend, you feel that for some reason you must not say?"

Someone must have calculated the average age when patients begin psychoanalytic treatment, the average age they encounter some major disruption in life or find themselves in the midst of intractable difficulties.

Whenever that moment arrives, the future grows suddenly steep, whether by dropping off precipitously and requiring a terrifying leap or by rearing up like a cliff face against the sky. One way or another, the way forward has vanished.

As a young analyst, like so many other practitioners, I quickly and without design acquired an expertise in the paralytic afflictions of afflu-ent graduate students, in the torpor of stalled writers, in the obscure tor-ments and metastatic dissatisfactions of corporate lawyers and investment bankers. However debilitating these passages were for my patients, how-ever dizzyingly steep the future had become, their predicaments pre-sumed that a future was *possible*, a future that could be, at least in principle, better than the past. This of course was my presumption as well, perhaps the presumption of every analyst. Nothing, therefore, pre-pared me for the appearance in my office of Arnold Ullman, a man in his mid-sixties who referred himself to me a number of years ago, after reading an article I had published called "The Metapsychology of Death-Anxiety in Patients with End-Stage Organic Disease."

In my writing and in my clinical work, I had been drawn by the theoretical question of what happens when anxious or psychotic patients are confronted with a real and inescapable threat. My conclusions were wholly inconclusive, but Mr. Ullman in his first session proclaimed him-self glad to have found someone who had thought about the things that he, Arnold Ullman, needed to think about, and fast. After asking me my hourly rate, without saying anything further, he wrote out a check and handed it to me. When I said that I didn't understand, he smiled a mul-ish smile.

"Look at the amount!" said Arnold Ullman.

I said I had seen it and that unless we decided to work together, he owed me nothing, let alone the enormous sum on the check.

"So look at the date, Doctor!" The date was six months in the future. "That's my expiration date. That's what my doctor calls a 'reasonable es-timate' for how long I have to live. Focuses the mind! Thanks to him I've recently discovered the joys of getting squared up."

"Squared up?"

"In advance! Because something could happen. What they tell me is that one way or another, maybe sooner, maybe later, something will happen. Hard to disagree with that, isn't it, Doctor?"

Five or six years earlier he had been treated for cancer of the colon. After a partial liver resection, his scans came back clear for several years. "Was I cured? I never knew. I can tell you I was relieved after the scans, and that I dreaded each one like my execution day. And I can tell you I wasn't surprised when finally one lit up, nodes, lungs, spine, lit up like a Christmas tree." It was then that a strange thing happened, he said. Of course he hadn't forgotten how to panic, but the dread of the CT scans vanished, and when it appeared that the palliative chemotherapy was slowing the progress of the metastases more than expected, he felt a strange restlessness. The irony, the "colossal irony," he said, spreading his arms wide, was that the cancer itself wasn't what was going to kill him—at least not directly. One of the recent scans had picked up an enlargement of the aorta, an enlargement that proved upon closer investigation to be an advanced aneurysm, the result of metastatic infiltration of the artery. Because of the location and the nature of the vascular involvement, surgery was out of the question. "I had to learn how to do nothing," he said.

"So you are waiting," I said.

"That I am," he replied. "But you doctors, you never say what you think, do you? I had the dickens of a time getting my guy to tell me what to expect."

"What did he tell you?"

"Well, finally, he admitted that I was likely to die of what he called a 'CB.'"

"What is a CB?"

"That's what I asked. It's a catastrophic bleed."

"A catastrophic bleed."

"A couple of minutes. Maybe five. And that will be that."

After a pause I asked, "And what is 'that'?" though I immediately regretted saying anything. He smiled his mulish smile, as though with no other intention than to alleviate my regret.

"That?" he said. "It! That will be it!"

"It—" I said again in spite of myself.

"So I've paid you in advance, in case I go early."

"But then you will have overpaid me," I said.

"Who will have overpaid you? Not me! Just some guy named Arnold Ullman nobody sees around much anymore."

This time I managed to say nothing.

"And anyway, you can buy something nice for your kids. You have kids, right?"

I said I would cash the check only after we had completed six months of treatment.

As for treatment itself, from the beginning Arnold Ullman referred to it as "polishing the car." He had lived upstate for many years with his partner, Raymond, where they owned and managed an antiques store in Rhinebeck. At a furniture show, he'd gotten a lead on an old Mercedes 220 in reasonable condition, so he'd bought and restored it, completing most of the work himself. He and Raymond drove it nearly a hundred thousand miles through the back roads and byways of New York and New England, before Raymond's death and his own illness required him to move back to the city. He had no more use for the car, and he'd need the money for his medical bills, so he sold the car to a collector.

"Goodness sakes I made money on that car," he said. "Eight times what I paid for it, though God knows what I poured into it in the meantime . . ." Arnold Ullman spent the weekend before the collector took delivery detailing the Mercedes, shampooing the floor mats, massaging lotions into the leather, buff-waxing the exterior to a high gleam. "The happiest I ever was with that car—and believe me I loved that car—was that weekend. I was like a country kid getting his prize heifer ready for the fair." The collector who had bought it had been so delighted with the condition of the car that he'd sent Arnold a bottle of champagne. "I won't say I didn't drink it because I did; summer evenings, Raymond and I had always had champagne in the gazebo, but I was a little disappointed. Don't get me wrong! That was one beautiful bottle of bubbly. It was just that the buyer had put a little ding in my new acquaintance with disinterested pleasure."

Since then, he had wanted to speak to someone, to talk with someone, so that he could attend to his life as he had attended to his car, preparing it for a journey without him. "The old carcass is about to change hands!" he exclaimed, evidently pleased with the phrase. "And anyway," he went on, "where I'm going, you won't be able to send me champagne."

In this way our sessions proceeded, serendipitous, breezy, anecdotal. "Ain't dead yet," he would say, swinging his legs up onto the couch. "Last I checked, at least!" His stories centered mostly around Raymond, who had died of AIDS some years before. Mr. Ullman had bought a gazebo at an estate sale and had it set up in the backyard; they spent Raymond's last weeks together there, reading the paper out loud to each other or listening to the radio. All summer long that lasted and into the fall, at least until it was too cold to stay outside, and by that time Raymond needed a hospital bed anyway. "I don't have anyone to find me a gazebo, and where would they put it anyway? In the lobby of my building? So I'm hoping you don't mind if I use your office as a gazebo. I promise I won't start reading you the newspaper."

One day, almost exactly on the six-month anniversary of his appearance, he failed to show for his morning session. Of course I knew instantly what had happened; he had never missed an appointment before. Wondrous, it struck me, that he or his doctors had counted out with such exactitude how many days remained to him. You can, then, imagine my surprise when I played back my telephone messages later that week and heard his voice. "So that was six months, Doc," he said. "You can go ahead and cash that check you've been sitting on!" He'd decided, he said, that if he had any extra time, there were some friends he should visit. He wanted me to know how grateful he was for my help. Maybe he would see me around. "Except probably I won't. But if you ever think of it, think of Arnold Ullman, will you? He'd appreciate it." Like some sort of late-night disk jockey, he signed off with a "Thanks for listening."

That was the last I heard from him. I could search for him in the telephone book or in the obituaries, but I never have. I think: You were a sort of friend, Arnold Ullman. Or could have been, had you not been my patient, had I permitted myself to have friends.

As for the check, it is still in my desk.

It was Arnold Ullman I thought of last night as I lay awake. I must have slept because when I arose I knew precisely what the photograph of Clementine had meant to communicate and how simple a statement it was. When I sit down at my desk to look at it again, I do not pick up my magnifying glass, whose bulging eye looks up stupidly from the blotter. Instead, I open the envelope and remove what I had neglected to remove at first: the Yeats poem, or rather what remains of it, copied out on a sheet of paper and torn off, just above the end of the penultimate stanza:

Come away, O human child!
To the waters and the wild
With a faery, hand in hand,
For the world's more full of weeping than you can understand.

Away with us he's going,
The solemn-eyed:
He'll hear no more the lowing
Of the calves on the warm hillside
Or the kettle on the hob
Sing peace into his breast,
Or see the brown mice bob
Round and round the oatmeal-chest.
For he comes, the human child,
To the waters and the wild
With a faery, hand in hand,
For the world's more full of weeping than he can understand.

I am aware once again, more starkly now, how the poem is a clock ticking down, not hour by hour or minute by minute, but marking its own time in other intervals: letter by letter, photograph by photograph, line by line. What time remains is short, it says, short but soon to be shorter, passing faster and faster. But some time still remains. That is what the poem also says.

My earlier obtuseness mortifies me. (*Is it, Mr. Abend, that you did not know, or rather that you did not let yourself know?*) After all, the photograph is not badly focused, or out of focus at all, for that matter. It is only that the photographer has bracketed carefully, in the picture's narrow depth of field, not the map but the cover of the magazine, the magazine resting on the chair to Clementine's left. The magazine (I can read the cover with ease) is a copy of *Elle*. The cover model stares upward, eyes violet, skin chalked arsenic white, eyes blackened with a band of kohl applied from temple to temple.

By the time I reach the international news seller on Broadway, I already know what I will find there: the same face staring out at me from the racks, that issue of *Elle* the most recent issue, the date on its cover in fact still in the future. Yes, says the clerk, it has just arrived. I stare at the face as though it might blink in recognition, but those arsenic eyes fix me from a future held ever so briefly at bay, and reveal nothing.

TWENTY-FOUR

Do we have to wake up?" Miriam asked.

With a clatter of back-paddling wing-beats, the bird had landed on the sill and set to howling.

Through the hot night we had slept with the windows open. The bird on the sill resembled an American pigeon, though more formal in its markings, neck starkly collared, wings sporting sharp bands, its call—half cry, half howl—startlingly loud. Miriam lifted the sheet from between us and pressed herself against me, adjusting my arm to serve as a pillow for her cheek. "*Chéri*, do we have to wake up?"

We had made no plans. It was a Saturday.

"No plans?" she said. "That's not what I mean. When must we wake from our little dream?"

We'd have to wake now, if the pigeon had anything to say about it.

"No, not now," she said, nuzzling her head into my armpit. "And it is not a pigeon."

Our little dream. Is that what this was? When did she think it would end?

"Not now," she said. "The end of August. Not now."

When I awoke again the bird was gone, and Miriam was folding clothes into a small suitcase. She had to leave for a few days. Back to

Leuvray, the convent, to meet with Sœur Béatrice, her spiritual advisor. The visit would be her last retreat before she was to arrive as a postulant. It was important this time that she go alone, so they would know she was serious. "Yes, *mon ami*. This time I go alone. But you must stay here. Promise me you will stay." And besides, I hadn't finished the translations I had promised her. I could work in her apartment; she would be gone only a week. This could be your scriptorium, she said.

A what?

"A place to write, a place to think and write. Heaven, as the Jews sometimes imagine it, is a place where a person can study in peace."

With a click the door shut behind her, and there I was, deposited in a sudden solitude. The week gaped, suddenly vast. What had been confusion at her abrupt departure changed to anger: to be made to play monk, while Miriam was off playing nun! And here I was still undressed, sitting at the edge of the bed. The remnants of last night's supper lay in disarray on the little table, some books and papers shoved aside, the wine half-finished, the cheese hardened and cracked at the edges. The objects looked dazed, as though stunned by a flashbulb or abandoned in haste.

It took a long time to rouse myself to make coffee, to shower and dress, but by the time I had fed myself (the bread not entirely stale, the cheese edible if dry), the sourness had departed from me. The bird had returned and scrutinized the crumbs, from first one side of his head, then the other. I swept them onto the ledge and the bird pecked them up, eyeing me with suspicion.

I picked up Miriam's volume of Herbert translations and began to read the French versions alongside the English, the originals gathered in a loose sheaf of photocopies. Words and phrases had been underlined throughout, and question marks dotted the margin. As for the French translations, they appeared reasonable enough, at least from what I could make out, though prone to archaism and ornament. In English, however, the poems spoke with disarming frankness:

> *Sweet day, so cool, so calm, so bright,*
> *The bridal of the earth and sky,*

The dew shall weep thy fall tonight
   For thou must die.

I recognized the tone from the poem Miriam had shown me at the café, its candor a kind of nakedness, communicating an invitation simultaneously seductive and disconcerting:

Love bade me welcome, yet my soul drew back,
   Guilty of dust and sin.
But quick-ey'd Love, observing me grow slack
   From my first entrance in,
Drew nearer to me, sweetly questioning
   If I lack'd anything.

The cheese and the bread had now disappeared, and the patterned sunlight on the parquet had slid into shadow. Without thinking, I had poured myself a glass of wine and then another; in fact, I had emptied the bottle before noticing I had begun to drink. The wine had warmed the poems to incandescence, as though they themselves produced the light by which I read. That light, it seemed to me, was visible only when I was reading the French translations and comparing them with the originals, pondering what the original English had refused to give up. This light (I thought) was like the corona of an eclipse, visible through the smoked glass of my contemplations. Yes, I thought, uncorking a new bottle of wine, that is what I was doing: contemplating.

I began to take notes, both in the margin of the book and on the photocopied pages, eventually spilling over into the pages of a notebook I found in Miriam's bedside table. It occurred to me that I must be hungry, and yet I had no desire to leave the table where my papers had spread out around me like the petals of a huge flower.

When I finally dislodged myself to go out, I did so expressly to lay up provisions so that I could continue this new work. I purchased tins of sardines, two bricks of coffee, and a log of goat cheese from the corner *épicerie* and from the baker next door a round loaf of some dense, brownish bread, thinking it would last longer than the usual slender baguettes. At the wine store, the wine that had made up our now depleted supply was still on sale, so I bought a case, or rather two cases, once I learned that a French case contained only six bottles.

In the shadow of the intervening years, I have come to think of the weeks I spent with Miriam in Paris as the one time I was to know love, a love, that is, other than that compelled in parents by their children. As for those few days I spent alone, with my notebook, the book of translations, and the photocopied poems, I think of them as the only time in which I knew solitude. Of course I have been alone for many years since then, alone as only a single parent can be, alone in spite of Clementine. But that is not solitude. I cannot describe the sweetness, in memory, of knowing that I had been afforded a little wedge of time and a task that fit into it. I would fulfill my obligation, and I would taste fulfillment in turn. This fulfillment depended not on Miriam's absence, but on the anticipation of her return: she would come back and there would be much to discuss.

The expanse of time that had yawned so cavernously upon Miriam's departure now seemed a tidy hermitage. How unused my hand had grown to writing; how sullenly my crabbed letters crept from margin to margin. But this was my task and I would fulfill it, and Love would see to it that I would be fulfilled in return.

It had to end, but it wasn't over yet.

In an analytic session, the impersonal constraint of the therapeutic hour is a necessary precondition for successful work. The clock moves like a cog on a cog rail. Whatever else the patient feels, he is aware of this inexorable shortening; what is to be said must be said before the end of the hour. The natural impulse to delay inhabits both patient and analyst alike, but the pressure of the hour opposes this impulse with a silent and invisible violence. Breaking off the session at precisely the appointed time is one of the hardest things a young analyst must learn, though even for the experienced the moment never passes without a flutter of appre-

hension. "That is all the time we have today—" we say, resorting to the
worn formula, or "Perhaps we shall return to this topic on Monday."
When that moment arrives for the child patient, how fascinating the letter opener or white-noise machine becomes. What bitter commotion
overwhelms the borderline patient if the end of the session surprises him
unawares. Nevertheless, it is this stark perimeter that protects the patient's session from intrusions, even as it protects the patient afterward
from whatever menace or fury or grief has been cast upon the analyst's
blank attentiveness. The session is an invention of absolute artifice, as
contrary to nature as a diving bell or vacuum chamber.

It wasn't over yet, but it had to end.

That period of solitude in my scriptorium, at first it had felt like a
sentence, but the sentence changed from solitude to the love of solitude,
a predilection discovered and claimed, a longing instilled for good. I did
not know what I was waiting for, only that I was to wait, attentive, bent
over the pages Miriam had asked me to translate. Just as the efficacy of
the analytic session depends on the session's fixed limits, the power of
this reverie derived from the fact that it had to end. My task was approaching completion, and Miriam would be back in a few days. I had
scribbled a commentary for each of the poems, and the commentaries
had filled the notebook. The notebook's weight satisfied me, each side of
each sheet dense with words and each sheet now somehow more substantial, textured with the impress of my pen, so that the notebook took
on a new thickness, as if the book had been left out in the rain and then
carefully dried, its pages now puckered and curling at the edges.

As for the fact that such happiness was possible only in the strict condition of solitude—will you charge this to my affliction, Father? Have you
diagnosed in me a malady of the soul by then, no doubt, already advanced? Surely I knew that this fever dream had to end, not only the
dream of studious solitude, but the dream of Miriam's and my affair. Had
we not called it a dream, and in the very act of calling it that, hadn't we
acknowledged that the dream had already ended? At times this regret

has consumed me, even though regret is in its own way a kind of wishful thinking: there was in fact no choice to make. What was to happen had already begun to happen. What had been stored up had to spend itself. It had already begun to spend itself, had already begun to spend the lives it was to spend.

Even then I must have known it. Had I not spent those days staring at the pages themselves? Had I never comprehended them?

Sweet spring, full of sweet days and roses,
A box where sweets compacted lie;
My music shows ye have your closes,
     And all must die.

TWENTY-FIVE

S hit shit shit shit shit *putain* fuck shit!" said the American girl behind the cash register as I stepped over the threshold of the tall, narrow bookshop. Her hair was short, a shock of shorn flax, her tone more amused than enraged. A loop of harness bells had been hung on the door, and they jangled as the door closed behind me. *"Merde de la* fucking *merde!"*

When I was a boy, no more than seven or eight years old, I saw my first movie. I remember nothing of the circumstances, neither who took me nor where the theater was. All I recall is the plot, a kid's feature, the story of a girl growing up amid snowy mountains. The girl was a skier, a tomboy, and had a big dog, a St. Bernard, maybe, or a Newfoundland. There was something about saving for new skis and bashing open her piggy bank when she had enough money to buy them. Alone on her new skis, she ventured off-trail, against the admonitions of her father, in spite of her dog's yelping protest. In the inevitable avalanche that followed, she was trapped, though not entirely buried. Someone, probably the dog, summoned aid. A search party, led by the father, arrived and pulled the girl from the snow.

A simple formula, briskly executed, but it drove into me a kind of barb that snapped off in the bone. For days afterward that girl's face visited me, at school, in daydreams, in sleep, renewing each time that strange ache. Absurd to think a wound could be sustained from such a story, less a story than a frieze-flat arrangement of customary forms, the girl's face, for all its freshness, stamped from the die of ironbound convention. One kid, spunky—check. One dad, kindly—check. One dog, fearless and cautious—check. One calamity, fearsome and toothless—check. Surely, even as a boy, I knew how it would end.

But ah, you will say, you had fallen in love! The wound was only that sweetest wound, the wound of first love!

Was it?

I believe it was not.

When I think of that girl as she is today—a woman more or less my age, pinched by the frosts of midlife—even now that broken-off bone-pang emits its pulse, and I know that it is not the wound of love, but the wound of—I have no word for it except an encounter. Yes, that is the word, however unsatisfactory, though I am certain now that the encounter was not with a person, or even with desire, but with the impossible itself. The ache inside me knew that she was unreal. The object of my longing was a figment, not of my imagination but of *what was not*. I did not know this, but the ache knew it. The ache knew that her face was the mask that nothingness itself had chosen.

Of course I had no words for that then. Even now I cannot say what I mean. Yet throughout my life, that ache has accompanied me like a companion animal, or a friend.

When Jessica Burke died, the wound opened again. For her it remains open, and toward her the ache drifts for reasons known only to itself. In my dreams, the ache guides my hand toward her. It is through her solid form that my hand passes, ghostly and insubstantial. Sometimes in the dream she turns into Miriam. We are underwater, together at last, but in my embrace her body goes rigid and crumbles, a statue of salt. Galled, enraged, my longing convokes the body of another girl: an American girl in Paris who called herself Reggie. Her arms, her legs, wrap around me, hungry and muscular, my grip seeks purchase in her short-sheared hair, and it is into her body that my longing voids its smoke.

Have I not spoken of her? Reggie Short? Why should I have? She was nothing to me.

"*Merde* fuck *merde* fuck *merde!*" said the American girl behind the bookstore counter as the loop of harness bells jangled at my back. I had gone first to Shakespeare and Company on the rue de la Bûcherie, seeking a recent English edition of George Herbert's poems. "Ah, yes, gentle Herbert," said the bespectacled man as he tapped out the name on his computer. "I believe we have— No, we sold that copy. Shall I place the order for you?"

I said I would check the library first.

"Yes," he said. "If there's a used copy in Paris, it will be there." I must have looked at him strangely because he said, "You mean the bookshop called 'the Library,' not the actual library, the *bibliothèque?*"

"In fact," I said, "I was referring to the *bibliothèque*, the actual library."

"Ah, my apologies! I thought you meant the bookshop! There's one called the Library. Clever for an English bookshop in Paris, no? La Librairie. Ha."

"Ha," I said.

He said they specialized in translations from the French but had a good back-stock of English originals as well. "You should try them," he said, sketching out a map on the back of a receipt.

Hearing the harness bell ring, the girl behind the counter of the Library interrupted her cursing with a cheery American "Hello!" then just as cheerily resumed, "Fuckadoodle donkey*schlong!*" She appeared to be on the phone, the receiver held between her shoulder and cheek. "I'm on hold, don't worry," she said. "Of course I'm on hold. This is France." With that she began whistling—was it "La Marseillaise"?—waving an imaginary flag or conducting baton. After a while she hung up and said, as though continuing a conversation, "Yes, I believe I hate them. I believe I hate them all. I divorce them, one and all. . . . Don't you just hate them?"

"Every last one," I said. "Who are we talking about?"

"The French. You've probably seen them. They're everywhere."

"Ah," I said. "I'd suspected as much."

"You think I'm kidding. Have you ever tried dealing with the phone company? Ever tried to get your service restored? Because I am fucking ready to shoot myself in the face." I said I had not. "Well, don't start now," she said. "Get out while you can, while you are still young"—she paused as though seeing me for the first time, then added—"ish. . . .

"I don't suppose you came in here to escape. Anyway, you're not safe. The French are liable to come here too, especially the professors, especially the really disgusting professors. Are you secretly disgusting because if you are I'm divorcing you too."

I asked if she had a copy of Herbert's work.

"Herbert like *Dune* Herbert? Sand-for-breakfast, I-respectfully-spit-on-your-shoes Herbert?"

"Herbert the poet. English. Seventeenth century."

"Whoa, *recherché*!" she said, dragging the word out in a campy drawl: *ray-share-shay*. "Did George Lucas steal all his ideas too?" She found a newish Penguin paperback copy. "Good thing you came in today," she said, blowing off the dust that had collected on its upper edge. "These things go like hotcakes.

"Not," she went on, ringing up the book, "that I've ever had a hot-cake. But wouldn't you kill for one? Wouldn't you just kill for a hot-cake?"

"Maim, maybe, but kill—"

"Or a Budweiser? Wouldn't you kill for a Bud?"

I observed that you could in fact get a Budweiser in France. "*En fait,*" I said, aping a Parisian nonchalance, "*c'est très branché.*"

"That, Mister American Man, is exactly the problem. I want a Bud that is not *très branché*, not *très* cool. Fuck it, there's no charge for the book."

"No charge?"

"Not for the book."

"Much obliged," I said.

"Yes, you are, Professor," she said. "I like mine tall and cold." She ran her hand over her brush of pale hair.

The whole duration of Clementine's childhood occupies what feels like a stilled instant. That span of years was (I now believe) a sort of monasticism in its own right, where the seasons, the years, turned around a single, motionless point.

This is not to say that my solitude weathered no assault. Sometimes it was an advance made by one or another of the mothers I'd met in the school yard, the divorcées lean and illusionless and, God knew, some of them beautiful. The fiercest battering, however, came from my own desire for another's body, for the sheer banality of shared life, for a companion to wake beside at three in morning because she has turned on the light to read, glasses perched on her nose, because she wakes often at this time of night and cannot get back to sleep, because we both wake easily now, because neither of us is young any longer or even, as Reggie had said, youngish.

Such companionship, however, never seemed even remotely possible, though Clementine herself, by the time she was thirteen or fourteen, took to enumerating possible wives: Ms. Strang, the vice principal; or the mother of Clem's friend Dylan, a woman who was, according to Clem, "not only smoking hot but an architect." Not now, I would say to myself. Later. When Clementine is older, we will see. But now it is later, and the solitude has become a kind of hunger in its own right. Now it is not only easy but in some way *irresistible* to retreat from the warmth of a flirtatious exchange, from the shudder of possibility. "Daniel, it's Denise again. Really, think about it. It is only Hadlyme, and only for a weekend. I don't bite. Er, unless asked. Joking. So call me." I did not call Denise. Or Ms. Strang. Or Dylan's mother. "Jesus, doesn't Dan ever get lonely?" Clementine asked. "Maybe when I go to France you'll become one of those swinging empty nesters, the hot tubs, the key parties, the sleaze-wad medallion nestled in the chest hair. I can see it. Dan can't see it, but I can."

"Reggie!" she called out after me, when with a jangle of harness bells I opened the door to leave the store.

Turning, I said, "Reggie? I'm Daniel. My name is Daniel."

"Good to know," she said, "but Reggie's my name. Reggie Short. As in Reggie-short-for-Regina. Impossible to forget, right? Like me."

She had somehow inserted herself between me and the door and was holding it open with her back.

"Reggie," I said. "*Enchanté.*"

"Well, *on-shan-tay,* Professor," she said, again in her camp drawl, clasping her hand over the top of mine and dipping in a mock curtsy.

"Until next time," I said, not knowing what to say.

"Remember, Professor. Tall and cold."

The harness bells jangled again as the door shut behind me.

TWENTY-SIX

Miriam had said she would return the following evening. Walking back to her apartment from the bookstore with my new copy of Herbert, I decided I would prepare a dinner to celebrate her return and the completion of my notes on the Herbert poems. First thing in the morning I set out to gather provisions. A roast chicken I could manage, I decided, though the one the butcher wrapped up for me still had its lower legs and feet attached, the shanks black-scaled and reptilian. The feet were folded up like squash flowers, and a tuft of feathers made a garter on one of the legs. In a *boulangerie-pâtisserie* I purchased two baguettes and a tart of apricots and raspberries shellacked with glaze. At the *épicerie* I decided we would have green beans steamed with tiny carrots. From the cheesemonger I requested a Saint-Félicien because I recognized the name. He presented me with one so ripe, it appeared to have deflated in its little box. Resting on the counter under a towel, the cheese filled the apartment with a funk partly of silage and partly of fresh manure. I laid down two bottles of champagne on the floor of the refrigerator and girded my resolve to amputate the bird's squash-flower feet.

After the chicken was safely in the oven, I attempted to wrap the notebook of my commentaries. I wanted to set it out on the little table as a present for her, but I botched the job, tearing the improvised paper

wrapping as I tried to tape it. I decided instead to inscribe the cover. I
wrote, "For his Nightingale, Miriam, from Daniel, her Friend and Ad-
mirer, with Respect and Love," but when I read over my inscription, I
tore off the cover and threw it away.

I considered meeting her at the train, but not knowing what train she
would arrive on, I decided just to wait in the apartment for the crunch of
her key in the door. An hour passed and I decided to open a bottle of wine.
A second hour passed; the chicken had collapsed, the apartment fogged
with the oven's meaty breath, the wine bottle empty. By the time I had
finished the second bottle, I knew she would not arrive. In the morning, I
woke in the little bed, greased with sweat; the visitor bird, whose howling
had disrupted my shallow sleep, eyed me from the sill. I must have dozed
again because now the phone was ringing. Miriam's voice came through
metallic and fractured, as though relayed by radio on a stray frequency.

I told her I had made dinner for her.

She was very sorry and should have called.

Was she on her way home now?

That was why she had called.

What was why had she called?

To ask if we could change our plans.

Seemed we'd already changed our plans.

Could I come and meet her?

Where? At the monastery in Leuvray?

She was not at the monastery. A place nearby. I could come and
meet her there?

Was everything all right?

Take the train to Auxerre, she said. Someone will pick you up there.
I don't know who yet, but they'll find you.

I said again, Was everything all right?

No, of course, everything was all right. I was sure I did not mind?

Was she well?

No, she was very well. Please, Daniel.

*   *   *

In Auxerre, outside the train station, I waited on a bench by a telephone booth, for whom I didn't know. Someone would find me, Miriam had said. Something would happen. How strange to be a stranger in a strange city, waiting to be recognized by another stranger. I had arrived in Paris a stranger. Over the year of my fellowship, I had continued a stranger, making few friends, even up to the day of my departure. But something had happened. Just as I was preparing to leave, a young woman, for reasons of her own, had taken me for her friend and lover. A girl from a provincial town. A singer, her voice bodiless, weightless, her body for my body less a thing than a force, whether smiling at me over her coffee cup or astride my hips or arched beneath me, her upper lip beaded with sweat, her mouth tasting of salt and cigarettes, her cunt of seawater.

She had fixed me in the steady level of her gaze. She had called me her friend, as though *mon ami* were the name by which I am known to the angels. She had guided my tongue, my lips, toward rudimentary competence in her language. And through this, word by word, she came into focus, as though her level gaze had somehow steadied mine as well, imbued it with a clarity that in turn flowed outward everywhere like daylight. Paris had altered imperceptibly from the place of my foreign sojourn, the place I would visit and leave, to the place where we simply were. Entirely by accident, I had met a foreign girl in a foreign town. She had healed me by feeding me, bit by bit, the mysteries of her language, of her body, as one might feed an invalid, adapting me to the strange taste, acquainting me with the knowledge that I was, at the center of my being, not only a stranger, not only a foreigner, but a guest—invited, welcomed, received. The words of Herbert's poem repeated themselves to me:

> Love bade me welcome, yet my soul drew back,
> > Guilty of dust and sin.
> But quick-ey'd Love, observing me grow slack
> > From my first entrance in,
> Drew nearer to me, sweetly questioning
> > If I lack'd anything.

> "A guest," I answer'd, "worthy to be here";
> Love said, "You shall be he."
> "I, the unkind, the ungrateful? ah my dear,
> I cannot look on thee."
> Love took my hand and smiling did reply,
> "Who made the eyes but I?"

I would like to believe, Father, that those were my thoughts as I waited at the Gare d'Auxerre for someone to recognize me, but they could not have been. They are my thoughts now, thoughts I would dispatch if I could to that young American doctor marooned on his bench— a warning, an antidote, a last-minute reprieve—the pay phone before him jolting awake with a jangle of bells.

TWENTY-SEVEN

*M*onsieur? he said for the second time and, again, *Monsieur?* The speaker was a young man, weedily bearded, long hair restrained by a cyclist's cap. *Vous êtes le Docteur Abend?*

I was.

"*Très bien!* Me, I'm called Jean-Marie," he said, lifting my bag. "I will bring you to the community."

The community seemed not to have a name. Jean-Marie, as his Renault *camionnette* coughed its way out of Auxerre, referred to it only as the community—*la communauté*—as did (I would shortly learn) anyone who worked there or lived nearby. I have often wondered what name they settled on, though, of course, it may never have had a name. Maybe nothing came of it. Maybe it folded. Maybe it didn't even last the year. Though the monastery at Leuvray was one of its primary sponsors, the monastery newsletters make no mention of it. I have never tried to find out more.

In any event, Father, it was from this place that Miriam had called me, not from the monastery at Leuvray, where she had first said she would be spending the week. When I asked her where she had gone, she said only, "You will see, *mon ami*. It will just be for a few days."

*   *   *

The community (Jean-Marie explained) had been conceived as an extension of the monastery. A local aristocrat, a count, had deeded the order an old mill on a tributary of the Yonne. The mill had fallen into disuse in recent decades but had been in operation as late as the 1930s. Private donations and government funds had been secured to repair and restore as much of the original machinery as could be salvaged. A small co-op was established. Other buildings from the former mill had been leased at favorable rates to a stonecutter, a cabinetmaker, and a sawyer. A potter, a Scotsman named McGarvy or MacGarry, had occupied another of the agglomerated buildings, where he manufactured floor and roof tiles using traditional techniques. The cooperative hoped eventually to rely more on the income from beekeeping, the cultivation of vegetables, and a small herd of Charolais cattle, along with some sheep. The plan, in short, had been to reproduce in microcosm the industries that constituted the local economy of small rural communities before the Third Republic, a period when moderate industrialization had lifted such communities from misery but before rural populations had collapsed in the wake of unchecked urbanization and the devastation of the great wars.

Jean-Marie explained how the order envisioned an expansion of its ministry to include the small farmers of the region and to offer a retreat site less imposing and "hyper-*catholique*" than the monastery and basilica at Leuvray. The plan was to staff the operation with a small group of lay brothers and sisters, either single or married, affiliated with the order but governed autonomously, on the model of earlier Christian collectives. As the Leuvray church was several kilometers away, the order had built a small chapel alongside the river.

So Jean-Marie had instructed me as we clattered along. He had asked me if I minded leaning just "*un petit peu*" to the left during our drive, so that a bundle of copper and PVC pipe might be permitted to extend from the bed of the *camionnette*, over my shoulder and out the side window. This arrangement required that I incline my head and upper body toward Jean-Marie as if I were straining to listen, a posture, I feared, that only egged him on.

"*T'es le copain de Miriam?*" he asked.

Was Jean-Marie asking if I was Miriam's friend or her boyfriend? "Yes," I said.

"*Donc, t'as de la chance, alors.*"

He had declared me lucky. Not knowing what to say in reply, I said nothing.

Fields of oats. Fields of rapeseed. We had passed through a region of smaller, newer houses, into a rolling countryside pieced from expanses of greenish grain spreading on either side. In time these swelling distances contracted and the terrain, paned now by hedgerows into small and irregular pastures, disclosed here a troop of whitish cows and calves, there a bull, immense and solitary, an alp of brawn. In other pastures tidy cylinders of hay dotted the stubble, each pinning to the ground a lozenge of eastward-tending shadow. As the inclines grew more pronounced and frequent, the hedgerows expanded at intervals to small patches of woodland. Soon long kilometers of road passed canopied beneath roofs of vaulted branches. On either side the forest appeared to have been stripped of all underbrush. Filled with blue-green shadow and columned by tree trunks or intermittent shafts of sunlight, the woods seemed an undersea garden of towering kelps and coral-heads.

After cresting a ridge, the road stepped in switchbacks down a series of terraced slopes. Eventually it leveled and wound its way alongside a narrow river, so that the canopy of trees made a single bower for river and road together. In the spaces where sunlight broke through, the shallows of the riverbed shone clear and stony except where tresses of weed trailed out downstream. Abruptly the river opened to a broad pond, on the far bank of which ranged a line of low stone buildings, steep-gabled, roofed in what must have been tile but looked instead like slopes of moss.

"*Voilà,*" said Jean-Marie, turning his truck over a single-lane bridge toward the buildings, "we're here."

*   *   *

I got out of the car and Jean-Marie drove off in a cloud of diesel exhaust, leaving me alone. The moss-furred tiles on one of the roofs had been removed and four workers in blue coveralls were replacing them with newer, more regular tiles. I had no idea where to go. Should I ask the roofers? What would I ask them? Pardon me, *messieurs*, but can you tell me where my *copine* is? By the way, does *copine* mean friend or girl-friend?

I was about to enter a building at random when I saw that Miriam was already walking toward me, her bare feet silent on the gravel, her gait hesitant and unsteady across the sharp stones.

She looked smaller than I'd remembered, her skin a darker bronze, and when she lifted herself on tiptoes to kiss me, I saw for the first time a constellation of freckles faint on the bridge of her nose. Taking my hand with a smile though saying nothing, Miriam led me past the largest structure in the line of conjoined buildings, the old mill itself, toward a separate structure, a stone barn converted into a house, with new-glazed dormers set in the roof.

Inside, once my eyes adjusted to the dimness, I saw that the first floor had been opened out to make an enormous kitchen. Modern stainless stoves and sinks lined two walls, while the original hearth, broad and shallow, dominated a third. An immense smoke-blackened beam served as the mantelpiece. The hearth itself was empty, swept bare of both ember and ash, though behind the grate a sooty outline stood out as though some fire had taken care to leave a record of itself, printing its image in negative on the brick. A trestle table stood on the other side of the room, flanked by benches, separated from the kitchen by a flight of stairs newly constructed and as yet without paint, nailheads bright in the raw lumber. These steps Miriam mounted, and I followed her up into a long hallway running the length of the building, air close with odors of paint and turpentine. On either side of the corridor, between expanses of fresh drywall, doorframes opened on small rooms, each unoccupied and furnished with nothing more than a single bedstead and mattress.

Miriam led me to the room on the end where she was staying, slightly larger than the others, two single beds instead of one, each neatly made up and separated by a desk and a single lamp. From a nail in a doorjamb hung a shirt of hers I recognized; a crucifix hung from a nail above her bed.

"At last you are here," she said.

"And where is that?" When I spoke, my voice, too loud, reverberated from the bare walls.

With a smile shy or frail, she said, "I was lonely without you."

"I would be lonely too, in a place like this."

"With you I am able to think."

"Think what?"

"*Eh bien,* if I knew that . . . ," she began, the smile still fragile, but then she was kissing me again, unbuttoning my shirt, easing the tine of my belt buckle from its belt hole. "You don't mind me dirty?" she asked, but it wasn't a question.

Afterward we lay side by side, naked on the narrow bed. The view from the bed foreshortened the crucifix nailed above us to a cubist abstraction of wood, gill-sharp ribs, feet.

"You do not mind staying here with me?" she said, turning to face me and lowering her voice to a whisper.

"Are you worried the crucifix will hear?"

"You think He hasn't heard it all before?"

"Was sex from behind mentioned in the Rule of St. Benedict?"

No, she said, but the room had been envisioned for couples. The hope was that the community would attract single people and couples alike.

"The community," I said.

"A religious community, yes," she went on. But a lay community, women and men alike. There would be the possibility of minor vows, but nothing would be required. People could come for a summer, a season, a year. Abruptly I was aware of the difference between this place and the first monastery Miriam had brought me to. There, the bare spaces, the silence, seemed to form an eddy outside of time. Here, however, the ambition of the community seemed nothing more than to give itself over to time, the hours, the seasons, the years, the unhurried, unstoppable clock of the earth.

"Why did you ask me here?"

"You are angry," she said.

A shame washed over me. Miriam, evidently injured, had begun to dress. "I wanted to come," I said, trying to make good. "And here—look—I finished my notes on the Herbert poems." I removed the notebook from my bag and set it down on the desk. She sat beside me and took the notebook onto her lap.

"It is finished? Already?"

"I wanted to give it to you when you got back to Paris, over champagne and a chicken."

"But we could still have champagne with a chicken. . . ."

"I drank the bottle of champagne."

"*Et le poulet?*"

"When you didn't show up, he drank the second bottle and I released him."

"Ah, he was a drunkard—like you," she said. I heard a wounded note lingering in her voice, but she took my face in her hands and said, "Thank you."

"For being a drunkard?"

"No," she said, her seriousness alone conveying reproach. "Daniel. I thank you. I thank you coming here for me. And," she added, pressing the notebook to her chest, "for writing this for me."

Side by side at the counter, Miriam and I scrubbed the potatoes in a mud-clouded tub, then dropped them into a bucket of clear water. There were beans to be snapped, the table set, and a loud bell rung to call the workers in from field or mill. At dinner, there was hardly any conversation at the long table, not, it seemed to me, by monastic protocol but simply out of awkwardness. Jean-Marie had returned from wherever he had gone with his carload of pipes. He sat down beside a young auburn-haired woman Miriam had been working with in the garden. Jean-Marie undertook to engage her in small talk, but the woman appeared to ignore him. The roofers from the mill, men from Auxerre who had been invited to stay for dinner, made a couple of remarks about the dry weather, about the effect of moss on older tiles, then fell into silence themselves. Miriam kept her hand on my knee. I kept waiting for someone to pour more wine.

How many days was I there? A few? Several? We would wake early to help prepare breakfast for the workers, for the monks and nuns who would be on site that day, and for any other visitors. Mornings Miriam worked in the garden with the auburn-headed woman; for my part I was content to take over cleaning duties in the house. It was cooler inside, and when I was finished I could retreat upstairs to the Bernanos novel I'd found. Furthermore, after lunch and dinner, nothing prevented me from polishing off what wine remained in carafes and glasses. I did not know why I was here, but my impatience with what felt like aimlessness yielded to an odd sense of acceptance, less the sense of having accepted something than of having been accepted: I could stay as long as I liked.

My second day at the community, a meeting had been scheduled with the prior of the monastery at Leuvray, several of the monastics, and a young couple who had just spent three years in Burkina Faso. The woman had given birth in Africa, and because there had been concerns about the baby's health, they were contemplating a return to France, where they would take up residence with the community. Motoring into the court in an ancient Morris, the count himself arrived, the benefactor who had deeded the property in the first place. A small, round man in a Tyrolean hunting jacket, he addressed me in colloquial English perfected (he explained) in Alberta, where he had ranched cattle for a decade.

"New York?" he said to me, dumping sugar into his coffee until it flowed like syrup from his spoon. "I prefer Texas. The really big spaces!" His Americanized accent glowed like Technicolor. "Have you visited the King Ranch? . . . Never? When I arrived, the foreman who met me at the airstrip was wearing a pistol! A real Colt revolver!"

"You have joined the community here?" the husband from Burkina Faso had asked. (Through the window behind him, I could see the auburn-headed young woman from the day before. She had not gathered with the others for coffee but had set to work tying the tendrils of a vine to a trellis.)

I repeated that I lived in New York.

"Ah! Perhaps the order has a similar community in America?"

Perhaps it did. I said I had never heard of the order before I'd met Miriam.

"*En principe*—in principle it is a beautiful idea," he said, "but to convince people to pool resources, to take on each other's problems, that's quite a different matter, no?"

After lunch, Miriam, the auburn-headed woman, and the others gathered in an adjoining room. What were they discussing? Operating budgets? Schemes of governance? From my post in the kitchen, from time to time I heard the baby squall, then smack wetly as the mother affixed it once more to her breast.

The meeting concluded, the count puttered off in his Morris. The Burkina Faso couple conversed with auburn-head, who held the baby against her shoulder.

Sunday, the parish priest, a chain-smoking Belgian called Père Albert, arrived on a motor scooter and everyone gathered for Mass in the chapel.

The windows had been opened, so an intermittent breeze ruffled the altar cloth, weighed down only by an earthenware cup and dish. The rusticity of the vessels, set off against the new cinder block of the chapel, vaunted (I thought) an ostentatious simplicity, no less falsifying than opulence or pomposity would have been. The wife and husband from Burkina Faso each read from the Bible, and Père Albert coughed and mumbled his way through the invocation and prayers.

Miriam led the chanting of the psalm, and in the open chapel, in the breeze, her voice took on a glassy fragility. When she had concluded, however, the wife from Burkina Faso directed toward me a wide-eyed nod and a gesture of pantomimed ravishment. By the end of the service, a heavy heat had killed the breeze, and an algal odor pressed in from the millpond.

Afterward, Miriam and I followed Jean-Marie past the millpond up a wooded slope, through a gate in a hedgerow, and into a pasture where a clutch of cattle turned toward us in wary expectation. One cow hoisted her front hooves up onto the hindquarters of another, who lurched forward as though piloted by the cow behind. Thwacking haunches with a stick, Jean-Marie coaxed the little herd into motion, sending Miriam and me off to the left and right, our arms spread, to discourage the herd from moving in the wrong direction. Each calf kept close to its mother's flank and, should she pause, butted her udder and nuzzled up to a teat. After the last cow and calf had been prodded into their new pasture, we set about dragging a great translucent tank in behind them. Flipping a stopcock, Jean-Marie sent a gush of water down the length of a trough. Some of the cows stood around as though waiting to be told what to do next; some began to drink.

At night, Miriam and I made love on the floor, though surely the song of the frogs in the millpond would have been loud enough to drown out the creak of bedsprings.

TWENTY-EIGHT

The following evening, Monday, Miriam had gone to bed early, exhausted from her work in the garden. A couple of hours after she had gone upstairs, I was just putting away the last of the dishes when I heard her footsteps descending the stairs. I turned to ask Miriam if she had been unable to sleep, only to encounter the auburn-haired girl instead.

"Daniel," she said. I had not heard her speak in the days since I had arrived. "You don't remember me?" she asked, her English clear, the accent British, and still a second passed before I recognized her.

"Ba—Bernadette?"

"Béatrice. Sister Béatrice. From Leuvray. We met the day you and Miriam drove down from Paris."

"How stupid of me—" I said.

"I am not in habit. Most people see only the habit."

"No, but—" How could this face—so evidently the same one I had instantly disliked at Leuvray—still appear so different? Here in soiled overalls, without kerchief or her order's blue garments, she could have passed as a graduate student, smoking in a coffee shop on a Sunday morning or grading essays on a rented porch.

"Do you like it here?" she asked. Taking a seat astride a bench at the long table, she motioned for me to sit down beside her.

"It is very scenic."

"I no longer notice the countryside," she said. She said she had been here a long time, as though she were twice as old as she was—which I took to be her late twenties or early thirties. "When I was a postulant, I thought I was signing on to spend the rest of my life in heaven."

"And you were wrong about that?"

"We are who we are, Daniel, even in Burgundy. And God knows why we choose what we choose." I felt my former dislike click back into position.

"Do you have regrets?" I asked.

"Are you asking if I am human? Is it so hard to see a nun as a human being?"

"I've never known any nuns."

"We say that you come to this life for one reason, and stay, if you stay, for another. Have you discussed Miriam's plans with her?"

Had I? Suddenly it seemed I had not.

"So she has not told you what she is considering?" There was a pause. From across the millpond, frogs chirruped in ragged counterpoint.

"Ah," said Béatrice.

"New York," I heard myself say, as though I were answering a question. "I am from New York."

"Is New York where you came from, or where you live?"

"It is where I live."

"Ah," she said again.

"And what does 'ah' mean?"

"It is where you live," she repeated. "And you are returning soon?"

"I've already postponed my departure for a month."

"Are you a believer?" she asked. "In God."

"I am a psychoanalyst."

"And a psychoanalyst cannot believe in God?"

"Needn't believe."

"Except in psychoanalysis."

"Anything can be imagined," I said.

"Imagined," she repeated. A crispness had spread over her voice, like a feathering of frost. "Can a New York psychoanalyst imagine living in a community such as this?"

"What?" The question hit me square in the solar plexus. So was this what my summons had been about? "I don't even know what this community is."

"Certainly, it may have no future," Béatrice said.

"Does any utopia have a future?"

"There's nothing utopian about the Nièvre. It is one of the poorest regions in France. There is great need."

"For backup nuns?"

"The countryside is short on doctors."

"Is that why Miriam asked me here? To sell me on a life in some kind of imaginary settlement, an unreal—"

"Unreal?" she said abruptly, as though arrested by a thought. "The need is real, whether or not we are."

"A need for American shrinks? In rural France?"

"You are also a physician."

"I don't understand."

"Forget this, Daniel. I should not be speaking to you."

"But you are speaking anyway."

"Because you must know it already. . . ."

"Must know what?"

"You must know . . ." She paused again. Finally she drew a breath and said, "You are telling me you do not envision a future with Miriam."

"I was under the impression that her future had already been thoroughly envisioned. By your order."

"Let me say only that she is considering a change of plans"—another pause—"and that the order supports that decision."

"You are saying she will not be accepted, as a novice, or postulant, or whatever you call it?"

"I cannot speak for Miriam. It may be that she has chosen another path. She is considering life in the lay community—"

"This community, you mean."

"A community composed of members under minor vows, single people and married people. Perhaps there will be children here."

"Béatrice, what are you saying?"

"Only that Miriam is happy here. And she is happy that you are here."

"Why are you telling me this?"

"Because she cannot. She will not," she said with a sudden vehemence. "Fine, Daniel, you are not a religious man. But do you feel no obligation to her?"

"Do only religious people feel obligation?"

Her fine nostrils flared. "Daniel," she said, and her gaze for the first time fixed mine, her eyes a metal blue, set like rivets. "Is it not possible that a bond has developed between you, a bond you have not noticed? You must believe me that I am not speaking on her behalf. Is it not possible that your plans—your plan to return to the States, her plan to join the order—is it not possible that they have become a means of avoiding that bond?"

"Those plans predate us. They predate our . . ."

"Relationship. Love affair. Why can't you call it what it is?"

"Our *time*. Our *borrowed* time. It has always been borrowed."

"My intention has not been to provoke you."

"I am not provoked. I am curious."

"I am not speaking to you as a religious. It is true she is my spiritual charge and my confidante, but she is also my friend. I am only asking you—" She broke off.

"What are you asking me?"

"I suppose I am asking if you love her."

"You are saying we should break off or get married."

"I am saying only that she is happy here, happy now."

"Is there anywhere else one can be happy?"

"Do you love her?"

"Yes, I believe I do, even if you—"

"You believe?"

"*That*. I believe *that*. I do not believe *in*."

"My belief, Daniel—my belief is that love is indistinguishable from obligation."

"What about the obligation to fact, to how things are?"

"Daniel, you are a psychologist, or psychiatrist—whatever you are, you cannot be entirely blind. Is it not a problem for you, does it not trouble you that you are the one she chose, you of all people?"

"I happened—"

"You did not happen. You did *not just happen*. That you, a *shrink* of all people, could believe, could choose to believe you were just anyone, passing through, some love affair—sweet borrowed time! You did not happen. You were already a psychologist, an analyst, call it what you like. That you could think—after what she has been through—that you could think for even a minute—"

"I do not follow."

"Daniel, aren't there rules, regulations, professional standards?"

"Miriam is not my patient—"

"Not yours, Daniel. Of course she was not yours. But after what happened you cannot think you are a neutral choice for her."

"What do you mean—after what happened?" Her gaze fixed me again. "Béatrice, I don't understand."

As though in pain, she pinched the bridge of her nose and held a deep breath. "I thought—I assumed you knew. I would not have— I oughtn't have mentioned it."

"You are saying there is something I should have known. And that you cannot tell me what it is."

"But now I have to, don't I? Anyway it is not a secret."

"Except, it seems, to me."

"She never told you that she spent a year in hospital?"

"What kind of hospital? What for?" But in that moment, before Béatrice said a word, I already knew what kind. I already knew what for.

Béatrice said it had happened three years ago, before they had met. Miriam had returned home to Nevers for the winter holidays. Shortly before she would have returned to Paris to resume her studies, she had tried to kill herself. Or rather, she *had* killed herself, having taken every precaution to ensure she would not fail. She had even notified the police where to find her body, by calling a non-emergency line at night and leaving a recorded message at the station. After writing to her parents and posting the letter, she bicycled into the countryside, then down a logging road, abandoned and unmarked. At the end of the road she hid her bicycle and walked a distance into the woods. In a clearing Miriam had zipped herself into a sleeping bag and swallowed a quantity of Seconal, three or four times the fatal dose, carefully stirring the drug in a cup of yogurt until it dissolved, ingesting it all, then chasing it down with a half liter of vodka. The mixture would have been sufficient to drop a bull.

"There was no reason," Béatrice said, "no reason at all why she should not have died. She ought to have. There was no reason."

What had happened, Béatrice said, was either vanishingly improbable or frankly miraculous and remained, at least to her, unexplained. Miriam would have quickly lost consciousness. Barbiturates work fast and are capable of halting respiration within minutes. But then she threw up, which should not have happened, because Seconal suppresses the vomit reflex. Though she was still rapidly dying, vomiting would have mitigated the dosage somewhat and slowed its effect. She was saved only because a dog, attracted by the odor of vomit, drew the attention of its master to the small human form on the forest floor, zipped in its bag. The dog's master managed to drag Miriam, still in the sleeping bag, up the logging road to his car on the main route. At the hospital her stomach was pumped and her condition stabilized, though she remained comatose for nearly a week.

When Miriam had recovered bodily, she was moved to a psychiatric facility, where she met daily with a doctor she referred to only as Monsieur le Médecin. While she credited the dog's master with having saved her from death, it was Monsieur le Médecin she believed had saved her life. What they discussed, however, Béatrice did not know; Béatrice and Miriam had met only afterward, once Miriam had moved to a residential facility where Béatrice was serving as chaplain. Their friendship flourished, and with it Miriam's renewed interest in the church, so that after she was released, she spent an additional two months at Béatrice's monastery in Leuvray. Together they reread Miriam's beloved Simone Weil, and Miriam came to the belief that her suicide attempt and subsequent survival had been in some sense providentially willed, that these events were the first, agonized stages of a true religious vocation.

"And that is what you believed too," I said.

"I did not know what to believe. I did not know Miriam before the suicide, her attempt, I mean. But what struck me then—as it strikes me now—is the clarity of her resolve. I do not know why she tried to kill herself; she will not discuss that with me. But I wonder at the resolve it took to accomplish her plan, just as I wonder now at her resolve to take her preliminary vows. There is an absence of doubt, and normally we believe that vocation without doubt cannot be true vocation. Still I cannot help but sense in her—no, I cannot help but *envy* in her—that absolute conviction, and I want to believe that such a conviction is possible, and not just possible, but rare, precious."

It was late now. Outside, a stillness brooded over the millpond. As she spoke, Béatrice had pressed a short groove into the tabletop with her thumbnail. By the end of her story, more grooves had accumulated at right angles, the pattern expanding outward in a rectilinear spiral, as symmetrical and regular as a Greek motif.

TWENTY-NINE

Over the course of my practice, I have listened to my patients grapple with an array of astonishing disclosures. One patient, an analyst-in-training, was informed in his early thirties that he was the son not of his father but of his uncle. Another patient, in her late twenties, discovered that she was not an only child, as she had always been told, but had an older brother, profoundly retarded, institutionalized upstate since childhood. An older woman discovered that her husband of twenty-nine years had maintained for the last thirty-five an apartment for his male lover.

As stupefying as these revelations are in the moment, most startling is how little they alter the fabric of a patient's life. It is as though such a disclosure plunges the recipient into a maze of clichés, bewildering and dark, but with a single issue, inevitably depositing him right back where he started in his ordinary life. Once articulated, the familiar phrases ("blindsided!" "out of the blue!") dissipate their power, and the "world turned upside down" reveals itself to be nothing other than the same old world. Even when cataclysms ensue (divorce, abandonment, flight), they blaze and flare out against the background of a world impassive and unchanged. Every patient, without exception, says, "I am certain that somehow, on some level, I always knew."

In the early weeks of a treatment, the period when I take extensive notes on the sessions at the end of the working day, how difficult it is to recall the substance and sequence of what a patient has so recently said, in some cases only an hour or two before. The story Béatrice told, however, repeats itself to me unbidden, in perfect faithfulness. What had I learned then, speaking with her? What accounted for the sense I had, as Béatrice was speaking, that the details of her story had only given substance to something already there, a shape or shadow hovering always at the edge of sight? Béatrice had merely directed my gaze toward it, that motionless figure in a clearing, bundled in its sleeping bag.

Miriam was asleep when I finally climbed the stairs that night, so I undressed in the dark. In my narrow bed, I waited for my eyes to adjust, but the room retained its perfect blackness, though the chirring of insects and the song of a night bird filled our little room. After some hours, Miriam got up and groped out into the hallway. Through the wall separating our room from the WC, I could hear a little torrent of urine, followed by the toilet's gush. Returning, she kicked the foot of the bed, and with a sleepy *"Putain!"* she climbed back in. Almost immediately after she settled herself back under the sheet, her breathing roughened and grew regular, and she was asleep again.

What did I think then? That some new knowledge, some new understanding, beckoned to me, pleading its case? Surely I had grasped at once the import of Béatrice's account: I was not merely someone Miriam had encountered, a dalliance, a summer's love. Whoever I had been in Miriam's eyes or against her skin, in the shadows of her soul I must have been a faceless doctor or, rather, a composite of many doctors, the doctors who had the ambiguous honor of having restored her to life. I was for her not myself but a compound ghost: at once an avatar of her past and the doorkeeper to a future—a future she had taken painstaking and unflinching steps to decline.

I listened to Miriam's breathing. Had this person, had this body asleep beside me, changed? Was it marked now with the seal of some inescapable obligation? If she believed another doctor, or other doctors, had saved her life, was I required to take up that role? Or was that obligation, as Béatrice had suggested, nothing more than the sweet constraint of love itself? Perhaps I thought that whatever obligation may have existed had now been dissolved by Béatrice's very revelation. Or if not by Béatrice's revelation, by Miriam's decision to keep her past hidden. Her religious vocation, if that was the word for it, had not been a revelation, not a fateful encounter with the Love whereof Herbert spoke. It was a bid for rescue, a salvage operation, incomplete and uncertain. What if my unwitting participation had endangered us both?

But I do not know what thoughts troubled that darkness, otherwise filled with the hush of wings, the singular voice of the night bird. How unwilling the mind is to make an account of itself. What I remember: only the bird's solitary voice, and in the bed beside mine, the regular, roughened breathing.

In time a gray glow filled the window. There would be no more sleep for me. I rose and slipped from the room, pulling on my clothes and shoes in the hallway to keep from waking Miriam. Outside, the little walkway brought me over the milldam, and I climbed the far slope up to the pastures. Finding at last the lane Jean-Marie had led us down when we were moving the cattle, I set out between the hedgerows, traversing the fields.

I did not believe I had walked very far, certainly not the nine kilometers separating the mill from the town of Leuvray, but there it was, the Leuvray church perched on the brow of its hill under a blue sky, buttresses slender as rigging, the bell tower leaning against the racing clouds, the building's silhouette as lumbering and weightless as a lightship riding at anchor. At the hill's skirt, among the newish outlying houses, the lane turned into a road. I crossed an athletic field and climbed toward the center of town. On the main street, a solitary, aproned man was cranking down a café awning. The café looked to be the only establishment open in town.

✳   ✳   ✳

"Someone is up early," said the proprietor of the café. The awning's scalloped edges snapped in the wind.

I was passing through? he asked, drying cups on his apron.

A double coffee? Coming right up.

Ah, yes, the mill. Oh, the count, he liked his projects. And when he gets an idea in his head—*ooh là!*

Sugar?

But not a bad man, for an aristo. He had raised money for the church's new roof. His wife had been very devout. Yes, he was *un peu bizarre*, the count, but generous.

As for the, er, *communauté*, of course the café owner had his doubts about it, to say nothing of the kinds of people who would be showing up at the mill. But, *bon, enfin,* as long as they weren't Dutch. I wasn't Dutch, was I?

Another coffee? No? Perhaps something to eat? Nothing? *Eh ben, merci beaucoup alors.* And if I ever needed a ride back to Auxerre, I should just call. He and his wife operated a taxi. Of course, that is, if the *garçon* from the community, Jean-Marie, couldn't take me. A good kid, that Jean-Marie.

I said I would be grateful for a ride.

Bien! If I could wait just two seconds, he would find a card somewhere here behind the counter.

No, I said. I would be grateful if I could get a ride this morning. To Paris.

This morning? To Paris?

Yes, this morning, if the taxi was available.

Comme ça? Just like that? With nothing? No baggage? *Rien du tout? Eh ben alors*, he'll call his wife to take over the café, and we'll be off.

THIRTY

That is how I left, Father: a morning walk, a coffee, a little small talk, and the long gray road to Paris. The road had sought me out, I thought, like a penetrator cable hoisting a downed pilot up through jungle canopy. All through the long drive, the café owner smoked without ceasing, lifting his hands from the steering wheel to light another cigarette, filling the tiny Peugeot with a cloud of smoke and furious gesticulation, railing against *"ces foutus arabes," "ces socialos pourris,"* the bloody Arabs, the rotten Socialists. You will say, Father, that I had sold myself to the first trader. You will say that no one was hauling me to safety, that I had hitched a ride instead to the kingdom of shame. And yet (I am certain of this) what I felt in the moment was only relief, not the transient relief of retreat, but the shuddering, bone-deep release of moral acquittal. Nothing could be clearer. I had had no choice, no choice whatsoever, but to withdraw myself.

Béatrice had been precisely right with respect to the facts in question. Miriam had what my colleagues would call a history, a history of suicidal depression, probably with psychotic features. How many times had I myself written out the *DSM* code for it, 296.34, on bills or insurance forms? And Miriam had known from the beginning that I was a psychoanalyst. Her friend Mathieu had introduced me as one. With those givens, I would have been for her, inevitably, a figure, an iteration of earlier professionals: the psychologists, the group therapists, the social workers, the prescribing psychiatrists, the unnamed Monsieur le Méde-cin. I would have signified for Miriam a component in that great ma-chine that had lifted her up and shaken her free from oblivion. The machine had thrust its tube down her esophagus, voided her stomach, then pumped it full of activated charcoal. The machine had netted her in tubes and wires and bladders, easing her upward like a salvaged ship until she broke, streaming, from the depths of her coma. It had peered into her eyes as they fluttered open to the fluorescent glare of a world she had done everything possible never to see again.

Béatrice had been precisely right: I was a citizen of that fluorescent, treacherous world, but she had been wrong—just as precisely—about what this meant. For her the fact of love meant that I should stay with Miriam, and because Béatrice was a religious, under vows herself, stay-ing certainly meant the formalization of love's obligation. How could it not? For her it was a given that love should seek a home for itself, a dwell-ing. As for the type of dwelling, that was only of secondary concern. It could be marriage, hermitage, church, monastery, or a lay community established on the banks of the Yonne. But here was the problem: The order could not accept a postulant so recently rescued from hopeless-ness. How could it be certain that such a postulant's embrace of monas-tic life was not on a hidden level another attempt to escape existence? The order must be vigilant against those who would confuse it for an afterlife or underworld. In Miriam's case the order's moral obligation was to restore her to the world, not lead her into withdrawal from it. The fledgling lay community on the Yonne could be such a restored world. While it would be ordered on Benedictine principles and dedicated to the work of God, it would remain independent, governed by its members and ventilated with the liberties of the secular world: the freedom to come and go, to marry, to raise children. This would have been the case that Béatrice had made to Miriam as her spiritual advisor.

And how did I fit? The possible roles I could occupy seemed at once various and elusive. My presence wasn't in any real way required, was it?

Had I been a stipulation of Miriam's? Had she said she would not consider joining the community unless I could be persuaded to join too? I would not believe it, could not believe that the sweet transience of our time together had transformed itself into the vision of an unlimited future. How could she and Béatrice share the fantasy that I too was not only free but willing to embark on such an uncertain project? Was the Miriam I knew even capable of such a thought? But then again, hadn't Béatrice informed me that the Miriam I knew was in fact a Miriam I had invented? Was this new Miriam, the real Miriam, capable of imagining that I—not a believer, not a Christian—would willingly surrender myself to the impetuous utopianism of the community, that mirage shimmering between the count's grief-stricken eccentricity and the church's dream of communal Christian life, a dream that history had ground to rubble, then to silt?

Nevertheless, its absurdity made a kind of sense. The proposition was clear enough, clear enough to elicit in me an unambiguous obligation to resist. I was not free. In fact, I was bound to remove myself from a position at once compromised and compromising. I could no more continue with Miriam than I could have continued with someone revealed to be my half-sister.

I wonder now, Father, in the car with the café owner, did I permit myself the indulgence of indignation? I had been willfully deprived of understanding. How could I continue with something begun under false pretenses—or if not false, then at least partial? I had been manipulated, perhaps unwittingly but manipulated nonetheless. I had been cast in a role wholly different from the one I understood myself to have been playing. (I thought of our trip to the first monastery, where I had suddenly found myself thrust into the role of silent retreatant. That silence did not care if I was a devout pilgrim or Miriam's leash boy.) Surely I had earned the righteous satisfactions of outrage.

These weeks, these months, together had been a dream, shared in part, but in essence solitary for each of us. In our cells, adjacent but isolated, each of us had painted and gilded the other person into an icon of our own desires. Miriam's desire, I believed, had been to strip away the tar of death that clung to her after her suicide, to consume it with her own hunger, as a mare craves to lick the caul from her new foal. I was merely the instrument of this instinct, used to nudge her awake, lick her upright, fuck her out of her black bag. She in turn had fucked it into me, the tar of death, filling my hollows with it. Freighted with her unbearable burden, I was to be dispatched, driven out from the city, and Miriam, spent and naked at last, could consign herself to the spent, naked enclosure of the monastery.

In my own reverie I had fashioned from her person a solitary companion for my own solitude. Certainly I had known or had at least sensed her desolation. I must have sensed from the very beginning that the mere fact of her living, of her breathing, was the accomplishment of a great labor: the perfectly simple, perfectly impossible task of staying alive. No doubt this intuition had flattered my pride, pride that she had elected me to receive the full weight of her body, to hold her up, to prevent her from sinking. She would remember me as one who had saved her from drowning, while I in turn would hold the note of an unpayable debt. How my pride, in secret, must have feasted on that.

The entirety of this secret revelation had been encoded in the strange thrill of being (as she called me) "her last lover." The first, she had said, is special only in theory, the experience is unforgettable because it is so forgettable. The last, though, she went on, tracing her finger along my eyebrow, the last was something else entirely.

In the fullness of time, having been employed in Miriam's great labor, I would return to my world, to my own city and my work. I would go back to being a doctor, an expensive New York doctor, the doctor into which I had been so expensively made. Wasn't that what New York meant, expense? When I returned, everything would be expensive. Rent for my private office would be expensive. My hourly rate would be high. And however dizzying, the fee for my patients was only the beginning of the cost, the analytic undertaking promising neither comfort nor relief. It is instead a severe curriculum, Freud's school of suffering: the universal conviction of shame, the pain of disclosure and of the resistance to disclosure, the awful vertigo of free association, the torment of encountering one's hungers, hatreds, lusts, avowing them, claiming them as one's own. I would become, anew, the minister of that suffering. In my costliness I would be a temple prostitute set apart and ceremonially dressed (in cardigan, gray flannels, polished cap-toe oxfords). My patients would pay me, not for something that they received from me, but instead for me to neutralize the account of whatever they had inserted or discharged into my person.

That was the world for which I was destined. And like Miriam's world, mine was founded on a kind of trust: the belief that the life of the body—its desires and hungers, its suffering—made for a kind of currency, valid and negotiable, a living tender to be traded for wisdom. I would place myself in the hands of this belief the day I returned to New York and reported to the clinic I was to direct. This belief, this scandalous idea (I was only now aware of this), had terrified me at least as early as the first year of medical school, when in gross anatomy my scalpel first trembled over the solar plexus of the cadaver assigned to me, the body I was to excavate for the entirety of that term. The dissection itself provoked in me neither disgust nor dread. On the contrary, from that first medial incision, it elicited a steady thrill. The work had combined, in exquisite symmetry, both violence and delicacy, one day requiring me to bear down through the squeal of the cranial saw, another demanding I hold my breath as I teased free the minute bones of the inner ear. What did appall me (I know now looking back) was the ease with which the body opened and unfolded itself, as though in life it had been as densely and tightly closed as a bud, a bud whose destiny was to unfurl itself in perfect shamelessness. Each organ repeated the desire of the body itself, to lay itself out as a single layer of cells on a glass slide, a patterned abstraction offered up to the microscope's eye. That was what terrified: to be witness to and recipient of that offering, to acknowledge that my own interior spaces were of the same sort, pulsing with a living energy, to be sure, but pulsing as well with the beat of that darker desire, the desire to be spread to that thinness, to be laid open and smeared out beneath a stranger's eye—a desire, in short, incompatible with life.

✳   ✳   ✳

With what care, what diligence, one nourishes a hatred for an earlier self. At times I feel that I am pressing the intervening years into that earlier self as one might lean with all one's weight on an oar, pinning a person underwater until his struggling ceases. But his struggle never ceases; in fact, he hardly seems to struggle at all. Look at him where he sits, impassive and preoccupied behind the flashing windscreen of a Peugeot on the A6 autoroute, while the café owner talks and smokes and talks. See how the road appears to vanish into him, as though he were swallowing a string, like a spider eating its web. At the end of the line is Paris, is New York, is the future, and he will make it to the end. He is on his way.

After all, he was convinced, certain, he was in the right. It is I, on the other hand, the man typing these words, who was wrong—intricately, extravagantly, unforgivably wrong. The truth, by contrast, could not have been simpler. Miriam was pregnant. She was carrying our child. Digging weeds from the garden, peeing in the middle of the night, fumbling back to bed, at every instant she had been carrying our child. Some people conceive children. She was one of those people. And why not? We had never been particularly careful.

Miriam had known it. Béatrice had known it. And Béatrice would have told me outright, I am certain, if Miriam had not extracted a vow of confidence. Miriam would keep the child; an abortion was out of the question. So, therefore, was the novitiate. Everything had changed. When the phone had rung in Miriam's apartment, when I had stepped off the train in Auxerre, everything had already changed. The question had never been whether or not I was obligated to Miriam. As the father of our child, I was already bound. The question for Béatrice was merely whether or not I would keep faith with that obligation once Miriam informed me of it. There were no choices but those.

I had thought Béatrice was inviting me to consider a new possibility, a new life. But the new possibility and the new life were already real, a new world brought into being by us and through us, a world that a new person would inhabit, a new person who in time would outlive us, whose world would absorb our own once we were nothing but memories. That I had turned heel on that world and fled made no difference. It was to follow me regardless. I might as well have tried to flee the moon overhead, shadowing me in dogged and silent pursuit through the branches.

THIRTY-ONE

I must have leapt from the bed at the first ring of the phone, crashing into the doorjamb on my way to the hall. I must have managed to get to the phone anyway, to pick it up and answer it. But it must have happened before I was awake because all I remember was the song and the pain in my head and the awareness that I was not standing but lying down, the phone pressed to my ear and the song, really just the refrain of the song, playing over and over, punctuated with a faint click:

> *Il y a longtemps que je t'aime, jamais je ne t'oublierai.*
> Click.
> *Il y a longtemps que je t'aime, jamais je ne t'oublierai.*
> Click.
> *Il y a longtemps que je t'aime, jamais je ne t'oublierai.*
> Click.

The voices were children's voices, distant, nearly submerged under echoing scrapes, coughs, whispers, as though the recording had been made in the hubbub of a school auditorium. The only distinct sound was the unmistakable *"chhhut"* of a French speaker commanding silence.

So long have I loved you, I will never forget you.
Click.
Then nothing.

When Clementine was six or seven, she took to asking me about "her sisters." "Her sisters" were the nuns who looked after her in the hospital during the months after Miriam's death. She never asked how she got there, content, it seemed, to assume that all babies spent some time—a few months, give or take—in the hospital after they were born. It was the sisters' job to make sure that she was healthy and happy, I had said.

And did they play games with her, and sing her songs?

They did, I said.

Which song?

She knew perfectly well which song, I said.

Would I sing it again?

And I would sing it again, as best I could, having looked up the words in the public library and memorized them:

Chante, rossignol, chante,
Toi qui as le cœur gai,
Tu as le cœur à rire,
Moi, je l'ai à pleurer.

Il y a longtemps que je t'aime,
Jamais je ne t'oublierai.

The words felt alien in my mouth (*Sing, joyful nightingale*) as I rehearsed them under my breath (*Your heart is full of laughter, mine of tears*).

And did sisters tell her stories?

She knew perfectly well they did, I said.

But those stories I could not memorize in the library, because they had to change each time. She knew too well how I had told them before, making them up as I went along; she knew even better how she had wanted them to end. They were stories about a mommy who had gone away—sometimes to become an angel, sometimes because she had been transformed into a swan, sometimes because it was revealed she had been a fairy all along. One way or another, she left her baby with the good sisters because she knew that Prince Daddy, on his gray horse, would one day find his way to the good sisters, and when he appeared, he would be leading a little pony, with a little saddle, by the halter. When she was old enough to ride a pony, they would go on a journey together to the sea.

And didn't the good sisters get to come along?

Of course they came along, riding the wind, their great robes spread like sails or wings. How brave they were, jostling and tumbling over the treetops, or swooping so low that their hems skimmed the water of the pond!

At the seaside they would embark on a boat and sail across the ocean, having many adventures along the way. However various, these adventures adhered to the strictest of conventions. The sisters were to stay in the crow's nest, all of them except Sister Cook, who labored in the kitchen making meringues. All major discoveries and solutions must necessarily be the work of the little girl, figuring things out By Herself, though By Herself did not exclude the participation of Lloyd, her thoughtful pony.

Sometimes, however, Prince Daddy would never arrive and Clementine would have to stay with the sisters.

Why did he not appear?

He had been locked inside a boulder.

Who had locked him inside the boulder?

Mr. Boulder.

Why had Mr. Boulder locked Prince Daddy inside a boulder?

Because the Swan Fairy had turned Mr. Boulder into a boulder in the first place, so this was Mr. Boulder's revenge.

Ah. But couldn't Mr. Boulder be persuaded to let Prince Daddy go?

No. Yes. Only if the Swan Fairy went away forever. So the Swan Fairy agreed to go away forever because she loved Prince Daddy very much and anyway she needed someone to take care of the little baby she had left with the sisters and who else was going to do that?

These stories were important for her, I told myself, part of her great effort to illuminate her past. They were her way of making things make sense. I told myself that I could help her. I could be the sisters she didn't have. I could be her pony, Lloyd. I could be Prince Daddy. But then, when she was seven or eight, the swan stories stopped. Once on a train trip I had started reading an actual book to her, something about a spaceship stuck in an apple tree. I remember nothing else about the book, only that from then on, for Clementine, it was as though the world of the Swan Fairy had never existed. From the spaceship in the apple tree until long after she could read fluently on her own, she sat on my lap through thousands of pages, caring less about the books themselves than the state she entered, twisting the ends of her hair or picking at her toenails while I read. Should I try to engage her in elaborations, in speculations about what had happened before or after, she objected curtly, as though I had sought to pierce the bubble of the story out of sheer malice or perversion. She especially hated my attempts to endow characters with different voices. "Just read it," she would say. "Just read it normal."

It was not until some years had passed, until she was on the verge of adolescence, that she asked me outright why she had spent those months with the nuns. We were in the library, the branch library near the apartment; we went there together most weekends. She had gone off by herself, browsing the shelves; I was at a table, correcting proofs for a forthcoming article. She appeared at my elbow and pronounced the word *hammer-hedge*.

"Pardon me?"

"Catastrophic postpartum cerebral hammer-hedge."

"I think you mean *hemorrhage*, darling," I said.

"Hemorrhage," she repeated. "Cerebral hemorrhage. Is that like a stroke?"

"It is, a brain bleed."

"Is *hemorrhage* French?"

"It's regular English."

"But didn't Mommy die in French?"

"She died in France."

"Of a cerebral hammer—*hem*orrhage."

"Who told you that?"

"Nobody. I looked it up in the encyclopedia. That's what it was, wasn't it?"

"You looked it up?"

"Wasn't it?"

What was I going to say? She did not seem upset, standing there balanced on one foot, her other foot braced against her inner calf to make a figure four.

"Well?" she said.

"That's right. It was. A cerebral hemorrhage. There was nothing anyone could do."

It was in this way that Clementine managed to inform herself of what she wanted to know. One day she would display a fascination with medical details (how do strokes work? can you have a stroke in your knee? in your butt?), while at other times she would ask about the events themselves. What had the doctors done to try to save her? Had the doctors asked me to sit down before they gave me the news?

In time her fascination with medical details eased its hold on Clementine, as though she had learned at last what she had wanted to know. Her curiosity shifted toward what she called "the big argument."

"After the big argument, Mommy's parents wanted to take me home with them, right?"

"That's right."

"That's stupid. You're my dad."

"Doesn't Oren at school live with his grandparents? Is that stupid?"

"That's different. They adopted him. He calls them Mom and Pop-ster."

"That's what Mommy's parents wanted too, to adopt you."

"So you had to wait for the police to tell them no."

"Yes, but it wasn't the police. It was someone called a magistrate. Anyway, the doctors and the sisters had to make sure you were healthy and happy. And I had to practice changing diapers and making bottles!"

Il y a longtemps que je t'aime, jamais je ne t'oublierai.
Click.
So long have I loved you, I will never forget you.
Click.
Then nothing.

I tried to reverse-dial the number. Nothing. I called Clementine's voice-mail, my own. Nothing. Shouting at the operator, I made demands, en-treaties, threats, was disconnected: nothing but silence on the line. It did not matter that the song was common, that every schoolchild in France learned it sooner or later. What mattered was that it was my song, our song, the bedtime song I would sing to Clementine. My correspondent knew that.

THIRTY-TWO

T he café owner from Leuvray had dropped me off somewhere in the 17th arrondissement. I squinted at the Métro map but decided to walk instead. Never had Paris felt more strange, even when I had first arrived. I couldn't shake the sense that people on the sidewalk did not see me, that I was invisible and insubstantial, so that people walked through me unawares. I stopped into a place called Le Bar Honcho and ordered a Pernod. Mounted on the wall, a video monitor displayed numbers for some kind of lottery. The barman had a special machine for placing bets. Every so often the numbers on the screen would change. I had another Pernod. The numbers changed. At the next traffic circle the bar had no lottery machine; after bringing me my Pernod, the bartender returned to his copy of *L'Équipe*, picking a scab on his bald pate while he read. A few traffic circles and several Pernods later, my surroundings seemed almost familiar, but still I did not know where I was.

Did I even know my destination? My destination, I was surprised to discover, was Miriam's apartment building. I had punched in the code and begun climbing the stairs before I realized where I was. I sat for a moment on the landing and went down again. By the time I reached my own apartment, the fumes of the Pernod had boiled up in my throat like gases of putrefaction. I had not been to my own apartment in weeks. I had simply abandoned it when the affair with Miriam began. I discovered when I arrived there that I had not locked the door when I'd last left. A stale odor greeted me when I walked in, and the droppings of some creature dotted the countertop. Two oranges on the table had dried out, hard and light now as Christmas ornaments. The window protested when I tried to open it, then burst open as the blare of traffic shouldered into the room.

I lay down on the bed. I would think.

When I woke a hulking, brass-plumed creature, hissing like a jet of flame, had grasped the sill in its talons. I tried to roll away from its heat, but I could not move. When I truly woke I understood that the creature had been the sun, a sun now mollified, half-sunk under the horizon. Thirst gripped me, but all I found in the refrigerator was a carton of spoiled milk.

I returned to our café, the café Miriam and I frequented on the rue de Vaugirard. It had not changed, the waiters, the clientele, all the same, even, it seemed to me, the river of pedestrians flowing by. There was no reason why I should not stop and have a glass of wine, a bottle of *eau gazeuse*, a cigarette. The waiter greeted me with a nod of dry recognition and took my order.

Sipping my wine, I stared at the feet of the passersby, not their faces. The faces were too human. My gaze steadied on the pavement beneath the blur of shoes, sandals, and stroller wheels. After my second glass of wine, I thought that staring at the pavement was like standing at the edge of the sea, where the spent waves slide back into the surf. As a child, I liked to stand where the surf, sheeting up, loosened the sand beneath my feet and opened it. With each wave my feet sank a little deeper, and the sand settled in around my ankles as though pulling me into it. If I waited long enough, the sand would have locked me fast, however lightly it seemed to grasp my calves. Only by jerking each foot up with all my strength could I free myself. That's what it felt like, staring at a single

spot on the sidewalk, as though beneath the weight of my gaze the pavement would soften, would welcome me in. After my fourth glass, the
waiter had begun to ignore me. I paid what I thought I owed and left. It
was getting dark.

The *épicerie* at the corner was out of my Corsican wine, and the grocer
pretended not to know what I was asking for, thrusting at me a different,
costlier bottle. "*Vin de Corse, monsieur. Voulez pas?* You don't want it?
Well, it's what you asked for." I left with a case of cheap rosé from the
Languedoc. Sitting at my window, my head against the railing, I poured
the orangish wine into a tumbler, the kind mustard comes in, the kind
you're meant to wash and keep. The first glass tasted a little like mustard,
then like a berry bubblegum I used to buy with my allowance. The last
glass tasted like nothing at all.

How long did this go on? Two days, four days, five? At some point, I resolved to go out and get something to eat. After rising from my chair in
the morning (having failed once again to leave it for my bed), I passed
out while standing at the toilet. When my vision swam back into place, I
was slouched on my back in the tub and warm water was dripping from
the showerhead into my mouth and nose. Only when I had grasped the
sink and hauled myself upright did I understand that the dripping had
not been water but blood flowing from a cut over my eye. The room
began to spin again. I managed to step into the bath again before vomiting; a coil of pinkish phlegm swirled in the water and refused to pass
down the drain.

My only clean clothes consisted of the suit I had brought from the
States and had never worn and a shirt, pressed but stale, hanging inside
the suit on the same hanger. I got dressed and lay down on the bed again
to avoid another spell of dizziness. I must have slept, waking up on my
face, the pressed shirt soaked with sweat, the pillow mottled with blood.

I was so thirsty that I closed my mouth around the kitchen tap and drank until my stomach swelled and I vomited again.

Out on the street, it was as though I had emerged tattered and blinded from a manhole after a year in the sewers. But at the café it was the same severe waiter who brought me, unasked, a *tartine au beurre* and coffee, the same flow of strangers washed by, surging down into the Métro station or up from it like waves in a rock cleft. I couldn't drink the coffee or touch the *tartine*, and a bottle of mineral water did nothing to settle my stomach. A half carafe of red was not enough to stop my hands from trembling. "Night shift at the factory?" the waiter asked, or rather said, setting a second carafe on the table and turning his back before I could invent an answer.

Was I waiting for someone, she asked, or was the waiter just protecting the dignity of the establishment when he set out two wineglasses?

Reggie, remember? Reggie Short, Reggie-short-for-Regina. From the bookstore.

Oh no, no Budweiser for her. That was just her line with American guys. She'd have what I was having.

Did I live near here?

What was I doing in France anyway?

A psycho*analyst*, for real? That's heavy. I didn't look like a shrink.

Shrinks she knew looked more . . . she didn't know . . . air-conditioned, maybe. Anyway, she was done with shrinks, especially psycho*analysts*.

Also: She was done with France. Had she mentioned that? She believed she had, on a previous occasion. As for her, she lived with her mother.

Of course her mother was American. Her father too, though he was in Tunisia.

Oil wells. He was an oil guy. The company had sent him to Tunisia three years ago, so his stint would be over soon. The first year, she'd stayed here, then gone back for college. Austin. UT. Hook 'em Horns. She was almost done, only had a few credits to finish, but her mother had made her come back to Paris. Her mother was helpless, hopeless, a lush, and yet had somehow managed to shop Paris blind. To get out of the house, Reggie had taken a job in a bookstore. That was the only place the mom wasn't likely to show up.

Cigarette?

Obviously, she was done with her mother too. She should add she was done with French boys. She divorced them one and all.

Her friends, though, her *potes*, those she would miss.

Was I always this quiet? Was I feeling all right?

Well, then I should order us another vat of wine.

Dad had started out as a roughneck—didn't I just love the word? Fuck if she knew. Something complicated, new oil from old wells. It made a killing. At least her mother acted like it did.

No, no thanks, she had to work tomorrow.

Oh fuck it, why not?

She was done not just with French guys, she was done with the French *tout court*. She'd divorce every last one of them. Of course, it was easy to be done with them while she was still in Paris, with someone pouring free wine into her head. The minute some Texan sorority twat tried to evangelize her she would probably run screaming back to Paris.

Would I be here then?

What did I mean I didn't know?

Who cared anyway? *En tout cas*, we should draft a prenup. Before we divorce each other for good, we should agree that her complications were hers and mine were mine. Her recommendation was to go ahead and label everything ahead of time.

No, really, she had to open the shop in the morning. It was time to scoot, to skedaddle.

No, she hated the Métro. She would walk.

Goodness, what sudden gallantry. Why, of course, Doctor, if it was no trouble.

Was this where I lived? Here?

Was it as depressing on the inside as it was on the outside?

Well?

Well, apparently I needed some help.

If we were actually going to get divorced, weren't we missing some preliminaries?

Such as, jeez, she didn't know, didn't I have some tropical fish?

Okay, no fish then, what about etchings?

Etchings like etchings, etchings of whatever, of Mount Vesuvius, of tropical fish for fuck's sake—didn't I have some etchings I wanted to show her?

THIRTY-THREE

As Clementine grew into adolescence, her curiosity subsided for long stretches. Then it would return abruptly, as though the narrative she had assembled to her satisfaction had suddenly broken down like a machine in need of a new part. One evening when she was fourteen or fifteen, she broke a long silence at the supper table: "So what's in that box in the back of the hall closet?"

"Which box? Probably process notes from my sessions," I said, and it was true that regulations required me to keep all notes for five years. "Could be drafts for articles, tax forms, bank statements, that sort of thing. Why?"

"But there's a box from France too. Is it Mom's stuff?"

"Since when did you start snooping around in my closet?"

"Since when was it your closet? Is Dan hiding something? And for your information I was looking for an empty shoebox for flash cards, if you have to know."

One of the boxes in the closet had come over with us from France, and like the others, it was heavy with files. I had been advised to keep those papers too: the deposition transcripts, affidavits and disclosures, the copious correspondence with lawyers and *notaires*, as well as the final decrees. I had planned to get rid of it all as soon as possible once I got to the States, but Clementine was still in diapers and I was scrambling to build my practice. When I thought of the box at night, or unbidden as I listened to a patient in my office, I told myself there would be time. Process notes, however, had piled up along with article drafts, and soon enough the box was just one among many.

The day after Clementine asked about the papers, I waited until she was at school and then hauled out the box. How queer the passage of time flowing around this box, like a stream around an islet, so that as I leafed at random through the papers, the legal language for all its formality seemed uncannily fresh and urgent. It was as though an alternate universe had been folded up and filed in the box, a universe where the whole process still continued, where in an alternate courtroom in an alternate Nevers, a bailiff had just closed the door and a robed prosecutor had just arisen to address the magistrate.

Clementine could have found them, could have cut the packing tape and lifted the lid just as easily as I had done. She could have read through the documents just as easily, in fact more easily, than I had, her French now fluent. The papers had always been here, never more than fifteen or twenty feet away. Stunned, sickened that chance alone had spared me, I waited for relief to break over me, to wash away the terror of what had not, in fact, happened. The relief, however, did not come, and what might have been seemed to press against me, a cold counterfactual. The possibility remained simultaneously present and entirely abstract, as an asymptomatic aneurysm must seem to a patient once it has been removed, at once lethal and unreal.

A couple of hours later, a document disposal truck arrived. Apparently the driver, a Russian, had mangled my name beyond recognition when announcing himself to Itzal, and Itzal had sent him away. Beaten back by Itzal but not defeated, the Russian had summoned me by cellphone from the cab of his truck.

"It's okay, Itzal. He's here for me," I said, arriving in the lobby, the box in my arms.

The Russian hoisted us to the level of the truck bed on the hydraulic tailgate. "We shred right in truck, so people witness," he explained, dumping out the box into a sort of broad hopper. In less than half a minute, the machine had devoured the box's contents and then the box itself. "Maximum efficiency!" said the Russian. "I call shredder Cookie Monster. You know Cookie Monster? My wife she says to me, Dmitri, Cookie Monster teached you English!"

I paid the Russian's fee in cash and watched as the truck disappeared around the corner.

A few days later, at dinner, Clementine announced, "I sold your French box to the Russians for a million dollars and one of those cool hats they wear. I figured you didn't need it anymore." I blinked at my plate. Clementine had made beets. She went on. "Actually, Itzal told me you had it ground up."

"He told you?"

"What was in it?"

"Nothing was in it, Clem. Just what I told you. Papers. Drafts. Statements."

"Then why'd you have it shredded?"

"I had several boxes shredded," I said, lying. "Most of that stuff in the closet needs shredding. I would have done it all at once, but there was only so much I could carry down." She looked at me, weighing what I had said. I took her hesitation as an opportunity to press home my explanation.

"You still think there was something in there from your mother, Clem. Am I right?"

"The box was from France, with the movers' label still on it. It looked like it had never been opened."

"You know I would never throw away anything you wanted."

"How would you know what I wanted?" she said, suddenly flushed.

"Anything that had to do with your mother," I said, correcting course.

After several endless seconds, she blinked and said: "I want to ask you a question."

Those words would have chilled me any other time, but now, after her silence, they conveyed a reassurance, the pledge that she would be satisfied with what I had to tell her.

"You know you can ask me anything, Clementine," I said.

"What I want to know is: Why wouldn't I have stayed with either you or Mom's parents during the hearings? I was going to end up with one or the other of you in the long run, right?"

I swallowed my last wedge of beet. "Miriam's—your mother's parents had alleged that I was an unfit father."

"Okay, then, why didn't I stay with them?"

I explained how I had been advised to file a countersuit claiming that they themselves were unfit. My chances of prevailing would be greater, my lawyers had said, even though in the short term the child was likely to be remanded to state care.

"Remanded?"

"Handed over."

"Wow. Parked in state care. So was it like a showdown? Was it like one of those movies where two Chinese guys each jam a gun in the other guy's eye and start screaming at each other?"

"Not quite."

"So that's how I was shipped off to the nuns," she said, as though she'd been the one recounting the events.

I said that where she was there were lots of nurses, and only some of those nurses were nuns.

"So all you had to do was prove you weren't some sort of satanic goon."

"Easier said than done," I said, trying a joke, but she was quiet again.

"But what did they say you had done to me?" she pressed.

"Done to you? What could I have done to you? You were hardly visible to the naked eye."

"No," she said, and repeated her question: "What did they say you had done to me?"

I explained that it had just been a strategy, an aggressive one, pursued by Miriam's parents and their lawyer. "They simply hated the idea that you would end up with me, back in the States. Your mother and I had been having a difficult time. A very difficult time. Her parents had taken her side. That happens. If you were having a difficult time, I would take your side."

"Okay, you were separated when I was born—" This was a statement and not a question. "That doesn't mean you weren't my parent."

"They weren't arguing that I wasn't your parent. They were arguing that I was unsuitable."

"But they hadn't even met you."

"They wanted to prove that I had already abandoned her, and you too."

"What do you mean, already? You never abandoned us."

"Clem," I said. I said it was true that I had not been in the hospital when she was born.

With the tine of her fork, Clementine was drawing beet-juice curlicues on her plate.

"So she died alone?"

"Not alone alone. There were doctors, of course, and nurses, trying to save her."

"But Mom's parents were trying to say that she died alone. Shouldn't the judge—the magistrate—have just laughed at them? I mean, didn't women use to pretty much die all the time in childbirth? Nobody sued their husbands for custody."

"It made it more complicated that Miriam and I weren't married."

"It still doesn't seem fair," she said.

"No," I said. "It didn't seem fair to me either."

"What kind of difficult time had you been having? Had you like socked her or something?" Clementine pantomimed an uppercut.

"No, Clem. Never."

"But Dan must have done something. Perhaps Dan was spending too much time at work?"

"Hardly. I had become—how to put it . . ."

"Insensitive?"

"More like involved."

"Self-involved?"

"No, Clem, I had become involved with someone else."

"Like *involved* involved?"

"Involved enough. Involved enough for her parents to say—to argue that I wasn't a fit parent."

"Involved with who?"

"And for good measure they said I was a drunk."

"A drunk! You never drink."

"Before I never drank, I drank."

"Like drunk drank?"

"Drunk drank. In short, they wanted to convince the judge I was a bum."

"I still think the judge should have laughed at them."

"A magistrate has to listen to both sides."

"He could have listened and then laughed."

"It was a she. Everybody gets to make an argument and rebut the other guy's argument, and then there's all the technical maneuvering and bureaucratic business. Your mother's parents were hoping I would just give up."

"Instead you won and punished them by turning their precious granddaughter into an American."

"Is that what you are?"

"God, why can't I have normal grandparents, the kind you can visit in Yonkers? Did they stay angry with you after the trial?"

"I don't know how they felt. We never communicated."

"Never ever?"

"No, Clem," I said. "It had all been too hard."

When Clementine was still a baby, I took on a supplemental position in the laboratory of a Dr. Tauer, a well-known developmental analyst. Parents would bring their children, between six months and eighteen months old, to what Dr. Tauer referred to as "the play-space." In an airless closet, seated behind a one-way mirror, I would watch the parents and their children, recording their interactions with a series of numeric codes. Normally this would have been the job of a research assistant or even a college intern, but I had volunteered for my own education. The job, I thought, would teach me how to be a father. With Clementine, nothing felt instinctual, nothing felt natural, while every one of these parents possessed an innate ease and confidence, even those who clearly found child rearing boring or disquieting.

I have never been able to find a suitable word to describe what I saw in those exchanges, however dutifully I applied the appropriate code: *Giving an object*; *Hiding an object*; *Eye contact (questioning)*; *Eye contact (anxious)*; *Eye contact (delighted)*; *Parental intervention (requested)*; *Parental intervention (volunteered)*; *Distress*; *Agitation*; *Acknowledgment*. . . .

Acknowledgment—is that what pierced me as I stared secretly at those parents and children? It was like a field, invisible, existing nowhere except in the space between parent and child. The parents I observed—whether sweet or severe, harried or amused—they were *there*, there with their children and there for them. Whether eager or hesitant, each did what the day, the hour, the minute, required. I felt that I had been visited by an epiphany, without knowing what it was that had been revealed. Was it a vision of openness and intimacy I despaired of ever providing for Clementine? Was it the obscenity of my learning to parent by sealing myself in a closet behind a one-way mirror? (But surely I was no more or less Clementine's parent in the booth than when I was sponging oatmeal from the crease in her neck or rocking her to sleep!) Finally, I understood. What had pierced me was a fact as immediate and unmistakable as Clementine's own face turned toward me: that I was hers, that her claim had been made. She had claimed me for her own.

In session, in supervision, in case presentations, how often it recurs, the threadbare truism: you cannot choose your parents. But as I think back, Father, to those suffocating days, watching the children and their parents, I am convinced now there is something exactly and precisely wrong about that statement. Nothing more fateful—nothing, I tell you—has befallen me than the moment Clementine's newborn gaze, solemn and slate-eyed, fixed me for her own. And today I believe I understand how mythical Love takes the form of a baby, staring down the shaft of his drawn dart, his intentions unsearchable but his aim unerringly true.

"*Oh,*" the nuns would say when I went to visit Clementine, "*regarde comme elle tend ses bras! Quelqu'un connaît son papa!*"

See how she opens her arms!

Somebody knows her daddy!

THIRTY-FOUR

How long do you have? Reggie had asked.

Days had passed since my return from the *communauté*. She had just returned to my apartment after going out for soda and another bottle of whiskey. With two packs of cigarettes this time (she added), so that I didn't smoke all of hers. I had met her at the bookstore that afternoon, and we had returned to my apartment.

Before I go back?

No, dork, before you die.

Eight days, I said, though it was a lie. I had done nothing to reserve a flight back to the States.

Oh! she said. She would have divorced me long before *that*. I was cute enough, even though I was like, what, ten years older? And anyway, shrinks were bad news. Everyone knew that. Common knowledge. Which wasn't to say she didn't like that fuck-you-awake thing I did in the mornings.

Was it weird to be in France banging a German chick? American German, that is, from-Texas Germans, brewers, polka dancers, tuba players all. Some French dude told her sleeping with her was like sleeping with a man. Could I believe it? She should have told him he was like fucking a Gauloise Bleu.

Anyway, if she was going to get fat and depressive before our divorce and I was going to get morose and cruel, we'd better get cracking. I was already morose, so she was going out to get food and more whiskey so she could catch up. I was to stay in bed. She liked me best in bed.

Fucking cow! (She had called her mother but in two minutes had slammed down the receiver.) Did the cow think she was going to spend her evenings at home listening to a drunk fucking cow? With nothing to do but get drunk with a cow or lock herself in the bathroom and masturbate in the Jacuzzi?

See, see, I liked my little pervert, my punky little dirty smart-ass Texas pervert, admit it. Admit it! Hah! Proof! Corroboration! Hard evidence!

Motherfucker if we hadn't been indoors for three days, or was it four? (she said). We were going to go for a walk. We were going to acknowledge that we were making each other miserable and that we had no future. We would pretend it was fall. We would pretend we were in a French movie from the sixties. Goddard or Truffaut, I could pick. She would be succulent and pouty. Chain-smoking, I was to be ill-tempered, silent, and unreadable. Like I was already. Pure *cinéma vérité.*

Get up, Dr. Slampiece (she said, whipping the sheet back). I could put my clothes back on now. In any event, we had run out of whiskey.

It was late, but still with a little light, the evening warm and cloudless. In a bistro we had split an omelet and a carafe. Reggie was trying to teach me how to roll a cigarette. God, she hoped I wasn't a surgeon. Did my hands always shake like that? That one was better. That one she could smoke. Maybe I wasn't a lost cause. Maybe her de-dorkification and re-

integration program was not doomed to complete failure. With luck I
might survive the transition back to the wild.

That night, after midnight. We had found a bench under a linden tree
in a dark little cul-de-sac just off my street. Almost dark: a white bead
burned glassily in Reggie's eye. She'd taken a slug from the bottle, swung
her leg over my lap, straddling me. Opening my lips with her tongue, she
let the wine flow from her mouth into my mouth. See, she said, that's
how baby birds learn how to drink wine. Was I worried that we would
scandalize the bourgeoisie? she asked with a little squirm. See, see, I
liked this kind of thing. Or at least somebody liked this kind of thing.
Couldn't we give him a little fresh air? Couldn't we let him have a little
look around?

See, he liked it when she just pulled her panties over to the side.
Didn't I see how he appreciated that?

See that.

Didn't I like to watch that—

Didn't I think—

See, like this. Nobody. Nobody could see us. Knew.

(Astride me, she pressed the meat of her palm between my teeth for
me to bite it.)

Like that. See how quick. See, nobody—

See, nobody knew that she was going to, fuck, nobody knew that she
was *fuck motherfucker coming fuck.*

Shit. Gah.

And then she had me in her hand and she was saying, Whoops, hey,
there we go, oh gosh, Doctor, sorry about your shirt, but that was better
now, wasn't it? Wasn't everything better now?

How long did she stay astride me like that? Her face was pressed against
my neck, and as her breath slowed and eased, the pressure of her body
against mine was like nothing so much as (how soon I was to learn) the

heaviness of a child in my arms, having surrendered her whole exhausted weight. Her breath was now regular, yeasty with wine. Now and again, a tremor fluttered through her.

I couldn't have slept, but time had somehow passed, or skipped.

How long had we been there, Reggie's face buried in my neck, astride me still, the heat of her long body close and heavy against me?

How long had *she* been there, on the sidewalk in front of us, small, motionless, her arms at her side?

Miriam.

How long until she said, her voice without tone or inflection: *"J'ai eu raison, Daniel: c'est toi"*? I was right, Daniel: it is you.

Light from the streetlamp somewhere hollowed her face with shadow. It laid across her face a blaze lead white like greasepaint: that face a mask, a moon, my moon, my Miriam.

And how long did she stand there, motionless, after speaking? How long did it take for that face, blank behind its grille of shadow, to brand itself on my retina, to pierce through the prospect of all future days to my very last, like an arrow through mist, like a telegram homing in on its addressee, like a pellet of white phosphorus burning through a book of hours?

THIRTY-FIVE

At that moment, everything stopped. And nothing did. The streets filled and emptied as always. The sun went down and the sun went up; commuters went back and forth. Up went the grates over the storefronts, and awnings fluttered down. At night, newspapers accumulated in piles at the kiosks; in sunlight the piles melted away. The hands of the clocks wheeled in circles. Leaves fell from trees; days flaked from the calendar. Do I remember nothing? No, I remember that time passed. How much? Seconds. Years. Weeks. Weeks like years like seconds.

Miriam is there under the linden tree, where the streetlamp lays its blaze of white over the hollows of her face. She says, *I was right, Daniel: it is you.* And then there is a gap, a break.

I remembered Mr. Michaels, my epileptic patient, how he experienced a seizure as a gap in time. Emerging from a seizure was not like waking up or coming to. It was merely the sense that time had snapped forward, had leapt from its groove into a different groove, as though into a parallel life. But there was no different life. Miriam had said it herself: *I was right, Daniel: it is you.* It is not that I remember nothing. I remember time passing, the flicker of day and night. Time was passing, moving, but around me. I was not moving with it. Or if I was moving, it was as a bridge pylon moves upriver by standing still.

Reggie must have gone back to the States, because I was standing at the counter in my apartment, watching a letter with a Texas postmark burn unopened in the sink. I must have left my apartment for provisions: bottles emptied of Corsican wine reproduced themselves on the kitchen counter, by the bed. I must have gone to the *maison de la presse* for tobacco and rolling papers, because at times, alongside the bowl I used for an ashtray, twenty or thirty cigarettes lay in a row. (I had learned to roll them, steadying my hands against the table edge.) Sometimes the bowl held thirty or forty stubbed-out butts. I must have gone out because I must have gone to the café, Miriam's and my café on the rue de Vaugirard. That was where he found me. His shadow had fallen across my table, and he said my name deliberately, first name and last, as though his purpose were to serve a subpoena. When I looked up, the sun was directly behind his head, and I had to squint to see his face.

"Mathieu," I said, as though informing myself of a name I had forgotten. Miriam's neighbor. I had not seen him since the night I met Miriam. When he said nothing, I said, "Sit, please. A glass of wine? A pastis?"

He would not have a glass of wine. He would not sit. He said, "You have not heard from Miriam." I thought he was asking a question.

"It's been several—"

"You have not," he said. "Take this," he said, placing a newspaper on the table in front of me. "It's yours. Keep it."

The article, short, unsigned, had been printed below the fold.

NEVERS: DIVERS RETRIEVE WOMAN'S BODY FROM THE LOIRE

In the photograph, people in wetsuits stood in waist-deep water beside an inflatable boat. Behind them, a sandbar. In the distance, scattered on the bank, clumps of spectators. *An autopsy would be performed, though police stated that the death was presumed a suicide. The deceased had been identified as Miriam Levaux of Paris, 27 years old. Police stated that Levaux had informed the police by letter where her body could be located.* A quotation from an officer concluded the little article: "*Of course*

we had hoped that the letter would prove a hoax, but in the end she was
exactly where she said she would be." How tender the expression seems to
me now: *"Finalement, elle était exactement là où elle nous avait indiqué"*—
just where she had said. Were I to live long enough to lose every other
memory, to recognize no human face—the image of that article will remain with me, as an arrowhead might repose in the hollow of a collapsed
rib cage a thousand years after the heart it pierced has returned to dust.

And yet it was a surprise to receive in the post office box yesterday—or
was it the day before?—a clipping of the article itself, yellowed and brittle
now, taped carefully to a square of Bristol stock and sealed in a glassine
sheath, frail as a moth's wing.

When I can no longer bear to look at it, I will turn it over. On the
back of the Bristol board I will find written (in the familiar block print)
the last stanza of the poem—the clock counting down—and once again
the words will read themselves to me, in Miriam's voice.

Away with us he's going,
The solemn-eyed:
He'll hear no more the lowing
Of the calves on the warm hillside
Or the kettle on the hob
Sing peace into his breast,
Or see the brown mice bob
Round and round the oatmeal-chest.
For he comes, the human child,
To the waters and the wild
With a faery, hand in hand,
For the world's more full of weeping than he can understand.

THIRTY-SIX

The last stanza. The clock that my correspondent has made ticks down. At times, when I think of Clementine, when I wake in the darkest, smallest hours, panic sets around me like cement. At other times, a different stillness enfolds me, the stillness of absolute conviction, conviction that when the end comes I will know what I am to do.

For days nothing arrived in the post office box. Today, again, I thought it was empty, until I opened it and discovered one little buff slip indicating a package to claim. The package was a cardboard tube, perhaps twenty inches long, capped and taped at either end and addressed in block capitals. *Please, please,* I thought without knowing what I was pleading for.

At the end of her junior year in high school, Clementine won a prize for an essay she had written. Her name as well as the title, "A Certain Slant of Light," had been engraved on a plaque Clementine refused to let me hang in the apartment. ("If you put it up," she said, "I'm hiding it the next time you leave for work.") The title was a quotation from one of Emily Dickinson's poems.

There's a certain Slant of light,
Winter Afternoons —
That oppresses, like the Heft
Of Cathedral Tunes —

Heavenly Hurt, it gives us —
We can find no scar,
But internal difference —
Where the Meanings, are —

None may teach it — Any —
'Tis the seal Despair —
An imperial affliction
Sent us of the Air —

When it comes, the Landscape listens —
Shadows — hold their breath —
When it goes, 'tis like the Distance
On the look of Death —

When I looked up the poem, I was convinced that whatever Clementine had written, she had written about Miriam, even though she had never let me read it. But whom did Clementine imagine when she imagined her mother? I had no photographs to show her. The only one I had ever seen of Miriam had been in Miriam's apartment, tacked to the wall by her bed. It was a snapshot of Miriam as a toddler, her father crouching down behind her to tie her shoes, only the top of his head visible, and his fingers, knotting the laces. Whoever had cleared out Miriam's apartment must have taken it. Had it found its way back to her parents? Had it been pressed among the pages of a photograph album no one could bear to open?

I had thought that my own halting descriptions and Clementine's imagination had provided for her a familiar, companionate image of

Miriam. ("Did Mom look like me, minus you?") Did it never occur to me that she would also harbor a darker image, the image of Miriam after she had died? Her curiosity had always had a forensic edge. She had asked me, and I had described to her the events following a catastrophic cerebral hemorrhage: the accelerating cascade of pain, double vision, nausea, disorientation, loss of consciousness, seizures, coma, death. She'd asked me what Miriam had looked like afterward. Here my professional knowledge would be no help to me. Tired, I said she looked very tired, but also somehow relieved. Clementine said nothing. I tried to change the subject. The nurses told me (I said) how overjoyed Miriam had been, just an hour earlier, when the doctor had finally lifted a beautiful, healthy baby girl up onto her chest! Labor, after all, had been long and more difficult than expected.

Had Clementine wondered how, precisely, Miriam's head had looked on the pillow, how, precisely, someone had withdrawn the intravenous lines from her veins, sponged the crust of froth from around her lips, or lifted her onto a gurney to take her away? Had she imagined Miriam's eyes closed, or open, fixed now on an impossible distance? Had Clementine wondered what Miriam beheld then, no longer blinking? Had she imagined that Miriam watched, somewhere in that impossible distance, her beautiful newborn grown now to a gangly girl, now to a young woman? Did Clementine imagine that she could feel that look, had perhaps felt it often, had known it perhaps forever? Perhaps she had encountered it in a certain slant of light, in a particular oblique melancholy, a heavenly hurt dispatched to her as a kind of communication   not as an intelligible message, but as a signal nonetheless, sustained and unignorable, a wail, a keening. . . .

At home I place the tube on my desk, this desk I have cleared of all distractions. I unroll a black-and-white print, enlarged so that the face it reveals appears exactly life-size. It is in that face that I see it, know it, the look of death that Clementine must have so often contemplated: lips slightly parted, brow not furrowed but drawn, eyes open but hooded, as though in concentration, as though straining to peer through the camera's lens.

Were it not for the moonstone pallor of the skin, you would think Miriam was about to speak. The way her lips are parted, tip of her tongue just visible, you would think she was waiting for the right moment, letting someone else have his say before saying what she has been waiting to say. She has been waiting in the cold, with her shoulders bare, her damp hair smoothed back from her forehead. She seems not to have noticed the cold, or not to care. Neither does she seem troubled by the contusion darkening the right side of her neck, nor by the two descending incisions, beginning at each collarbone, passing at an angle above her nipples to converge midsternum, incisions closed up now with an even whipstitch. You would think she looks straight at you, or rather, straight through you. She knows what she has to say, and she knows she will say it, however long she must wait. Eyes hooded, slightly open, lips parted, she has waited now for eighteen years. In eighteen years Miriam has grown expert in waiting.

On the back of the photograph, in the same block print, the final stanza has been pared down to six lines:

> *Away with us he's going.*
> *Sing peace into his breast,*
> *For he comes, the human child,*
> *To the waters and the wild*
> *With a faery, hand in hand,*
> *For the world's more full of weeping than he can understand.*

THIRTY-SEVEN

I wonder today, as I have before: Do you pray for me? What prayers are to be offered up for such a man as I? And such a man as I, who is that? An addled man, no doubt, a tormented man. How mistaken you must think me to believe that I caused a death, Miriam's death, that her death was not a suicide but my crime. You will think it no crime at all—a disaster certainly, a tragedy, and not least for me and Clementine, but certainly not a crime. Do you pray that I come to accept a judgment more merciful than my own?

Do you pray that such a man might be made to see how life has been given back to him, not only his own life but also his daughter's? If it is true that he betrayed his pregnant lover, surely he was not the first to do such a thing. He had not even known she was pregnant. And should that woman return home, to the city of Nevers, to give birth there, doomed by an old despair, surely he had not been the one to acquaint her with that despair in the first place. He was not her executioner, but merely a stand-in, a stay. Before he had met her, she had made her rendezvous.

Knowing what I have told you, you will say that from the moment of her birth, the infant's needs should have trumped all other considerations. What need was more peremptory than for a parent's love and care, and to Clementine only one parent remained. My duty was clear, and I dispatched it with honor: the child acknowledged and fought for, custody wrested from the vindictive grief of Miriam's parents, Clementine visited, hugged, and sung to throughout the long slog of the litigation, Clementine at last fastened in a car seat, a cab, an airplane, Clementine introduced to her new life in New York City. It would be wrong and vain to deny the hard-won stability, the prosperity attained, and the daughter flourishing. When the balances are weighed, you will say, such a man has no debt but that of gratitude.

How mad I must be, you will think. You have no choice. Is this not your obligation? Are you not obliged to believe that no one, no adulterer, thief, demoniac, or murderer, is beyond the reach of grace? And would it not be madness itself to withhold oneself from grace?

I concede: to withhold oneself, to elect to cut oneself off from grace, that would be madness. But to *know* that one has cut oneself off, has done so *already*, to know and avow what one has done—is that madness or the simple acknowledgment of fact?

What I have yet to tell you must be told. It is what is required.

THIRTY-EIGHT

After Mathieu found me at the café and set the article in front of me, I took the next train to Nevers. The train seemed at first to drift from the Gare de Lyon, gathering speed only imperceptibly but then faster and faster. I felt as though we were falling. Once in my seat I opened the half liter of vodka I'd bought near the station, swallowing its clear flame as a man across the aisle shot me puckered glances.

The vodka dissolved all sensation of movement. I did not feel that I was leaving Paris but that Paris was being hauled out of me, in clumps and slabs, in snarls of swerving rail, knots of roadway and wire. For a long hour a stupor enfolded me until a river—the Loire itself, I realized—veered suddenly into view, hammered with sunlight. Appearing and re appearing through the bare trees, the river seemed in its languor to sap the train's speed, dragging it first to a crawl, then at last to a stop alongside the station platform in Nevers. Nevers, where Miriam was born and where she had chosen to die.

The bottle had vanished, and I was standing in the shadow of the station's concrete facade, when a hand fastened to my arm. From a derelict's mouth, an incomprehensible request reeked forth and repeated itself several times until I understood. *"Monnaie, monnaie,"* he was saying: Change, change.

I jerked my sleeve free. Others like him sprawled around. Two junkies slouched behind a concrete planter, hugging their knees to their chests. Alongside them, curled on a patch of cardboard, a mongrel shivered, connected by a length of string to a girl pierced and dreadlocked, no more than sixteen or seventeen but heavily pregnant, her coat unbuttoned where her belly pushed through. A fine rain stung my face. The derelict pulled my sleeve again. *"Quelques sous, monsieur . . ."* A couple of coins.

I reached into my pocket and withdrew a stack of coins. *"Quincaillerie,"* I said to him—hardware store—showing him the money in my palm but snatching it away when he reached for it. "First you bring me there," I said. "Then I give you the money."

Without releasing my arm, he dragged me across a roadway into an upsloping tangle of cobbled streets. Abruptly he stopped at a storefront. The hand that had grasped my arm closed over the coins, and the man reeled away.

It was a small storefront, in an old building. Had this been the place Miriam had found? Inside, the gloom smelled of rust and turpentine. A shopkeeper in a flowered housecoat emerged from a back room.

Was there anything *monsieur* needed? *Eh ben*, nothing at all? Chain? What kind of chain? *Monsieur* would find chain on the far wall. On spools, by the rope. What gauge did *monsieur* require? How heavy? This one, obviously, was the heaviest. She had no idea: perhaps two kilos per meter. What length did *monsieur* require?

I stared at the chain. The links swam and divided, and I had to cover one eye with my hand to keep the room from spinning. Had Miriam stood here herself? Had this shopkeeper asked what *madame* required? Had the shopkeeper asked what *madame* planned to do with such a quantity of chain?

Monsieur . . . ? Monsieur is not ill, I hope.

Such a quantity of chain. The weight of it. How had she brought it down to the river? And the heavy flywheel, where had she found that?

"Ah! No chain after all? Very well, *monsieur*. A chisel instead? A chisel and hammer?" With exasperation she turned from the spools and gestured toward a different aisle. She made no further attempt at conversation, and I paid for my hammer and chisel. When I asked her to direct me to the nearest liquor store, with a snort she vanished into the back office.

And then it was night, and I was in a park, almost like a fairground, some sort of bandstand or carousel in the distance. I must have found a liquor store because I was aware that there was a half-empty bottle cached in the ivy behind my bench. The night was cold, but I was not, warmed by the vodka burning off in my lungs. In my hand was a paper bag, rumpled, weighted. Inside the bag I found a hammer and chisel and only then remembered the store. After pocketing the tools, I put the bottle in the bag and set out, allowing the slope of the streets to guide me down to the river, to the bridge.

It must have been very late, or very early in the morning. Neither car nor passerby interrupted my work, and the mist blotted up the ringing of my chisel as it cut into the stone of the parapet. My fingers warmed to the chisel and the figures took on their crude form, rough like a homemade tattoo:

ML12III90

There it was, my blunt little epitaph, crude but clear enough, recording that name, this place. Miriam Levaux, 12 March 1990.

And there it remains, even now, as my correspondent has made plain.

When I was finished, I dropped the tools and the bottle, now empty, over the parapet. Did I think then, standing there empty-handed over the river, that I had accomplished what I had come for? Did I believe that something was over and done with?

If such an illusion flitted at the corner of my sight, it lived only long enough to be crushed and swallowed by a paralyzing awareness: She was gone. There was no place to go. She was infinitely distant from everywhere. So I did not return to the train station. I did not leave Nevers that day, or that night. From the transit maps posted at the bus stops I had learned that there was a camping ground on the opposite bank of the Loire, just over the bridge. In a sporting goods store, I purchased a tent and sleeping bag. At the campground, a few RVs and camper vans with Dutch and German plates had docked themselves near the water hook-ups and canteen, but down in a grassy expanse along the river, none of the spaces were occupied, and I pitched my tent there. The sleeping bag, I discovered, had been made for a child, so I pulled it on top of me and drew up my legs. The sun made a cold white disk in the orange fabric of the tent. All that day and the following, a restless sleep came and went. Another day passed, and then another. A fifth day: it occurred to me that I had no intention of leaving this place.

In the evenings, I would make my way back up into the old town, threading my way up the ramparts above the Loire: Fountain Street, Break-Neck Street. The *épicerie* where I bought my vodka was on a cobbled pedestrian street between a pharmacy and a horse butcher. Each day, with neither salutation nor thanks, the grocer counted my money and handed me my bottle. Each night, the darkness found me seated on the parapet of the bridge, my feet hanging over the downstream side. Beneath the bridge the river shoaled and sheeted, composing itself again downstream, where the channel deepened. When the bottle was empty, I dropped it over the edge, just as I had done with the hammer and chisel. The roar of the water canceled any splash or sound of breakage, as though the bottle were falling and falling in endless space.

Why did I stay? Had I sentenced myself to a sort of purgatory, in the campground on the other side of the river? All I knew was that I was to wait, to stay where I was and await instruction. When it came, it would know to find me on the bridge.

And come it did, three or four days later, not in the evening but at noon. I had not slept the night before. Perhaps, I had thought, if I walked into town and around the park, by the time I'd returned I could sleep. Crossing the bridge, toward the city, I passed a group of teenagers loitering by the downstream parapet. A couple of kids tossed pebbles over the edge. One spat. A stray remark stopped me, and I leaned against the parapet at a distance but within earshot. One of the teenagers, a girl, barefoot in spite of the cold, had climbed up on the parapet, lifting her foot and pointing her toe, as a ballerina might.

"Was this where it happened?" someone asked.

"It was down there," said the girl on the parapet.

"They pulled her out onto Tern Island."

"No, they didn't, shit-for-brains, they pulled her onto the bank."

The girl said, "The water doesn't look that deep."

"Why don't you dive down there and tell us?" said a boy.

"Why don't you suck my dick?" said the girl.

"She would have died from the fall," someone said.

"Especially chained to all that scrap iron."

"She didn't jump," said the girl standing on the parapet. "She walked in from the bank. She drowned herself."

"No way," someone countered. "Everyone knows she jumped, or was pushed."

"Oh, they do? The autopsy said she drowned," said the balancing girl. "It was in the *Journal du Centre* today."

"Oh, the *Journal*! Then it must be true."

"It's what the autopsy said."

"It's obvious," said a boy. "Somebody threw her in."

"She was knocked up and she drowned herself," said the girl on the parapet. "My cousin said so. He works at the hospital."

"Of course she was knocked up," said the boy again. "All the more reason for someone to throw her into the river."

It was in the Journal du Centre *today.* That was what the girl had said.

Noon: the kiosk at the corner of the park shut tight. Above it, the sun had stopped in the sky. The park was empty. I sat on a bench. Something in my brain had shut as well. I could not think. There was no thought. Just the silhouette of the barefoot girl, toe pointed, balanced on the parapet.

"It's true she was pregnant," the silhouette was saying.

It's true she was pregnant. No thoughts, just the words, the silhouette. But then the kiosk had snapped open, and the air moved a little, lifting the corner of a newspaper under its paperweight.

"Help yourself," the woman in the kiosk had said when I placed my coin on the tray. "It is sad, *monsieur*, this story of the drowned girl," she said as the coin vanished into her hand. "And pregnant too, they are saying. *La pauvre. Enfin, les pauvres.* It is there inside the paper. Everything."

Poor girl. Or rather: poor both of them.

Following the drowning of Miriam Levaux, reported in these pages last Monday . . .

Was *monsieur* not feeling well?

Was he sure?

Without doubt, *monsieur*, it is the fluctuations in temperature.

The inquest, concluded yesterday, confirmed suicide as the cause of death.

The fluctuations have been terrible.

Levaux, who had notified the police where her body could be located, had been six months pregnant.

One must pay attention with such fluctuations!

The fetus had died with the mother.

But *monsieur*, you have paid for it. It is yours! Take it! It is paid for! *Monsieur*, it is yours!

Had I not known it all along, since the day she had called me in Paris, from *la communauté*, from the day she had called to ask me to come see her? Had I not known it from the beginning, even when I had persuaded myself it wasn't so? Had I not known it ever since the day Miriam and I lay down together on the rotting boards over the stream, ever since she broke with her fingertip the thread of semen suspended between us? I had known it because it was true. It had always been true. Of all the things that could have happened, this one had happened. Miriam and I had conceived a child.

And yet for all that, it was still impossible. Can you not see, Father, that if Miriam had been pregnant when she drowned herself, if she had been six months pregnant when she died, and if her baby, our child, had died with her, then that child—our daughter, our Clementine—must have died before she was born?

THIRTY-NINE

Time gave way to arrhythmic oscillations: sometimes day—close and hot, a sheet of plastic sealed over the face—sometimes night—clamped down and ground in a circle, stars studding the haze like nails in a boot heel. At some point, a fringe of restless creatures, fluttering and papery, crowded the borders of my vision. They would leave me alone, I believed, if only I could manage to sleep, but they knew what I thought. *Sleep? For you?* they seemed to be saying. *Never again!*

Their agitation spread to my own limbs in the form of an unrelenting tremor that movement alone could subdue. So throughout those days in Nevers, I walked and walked, up and down the rue de la Blanchisserie, the overgrown towpaths, the crest of the levee above the south bank. I walked down past the sad *espace de loisirs*, the "leisure park" with its shuttered puppet theater, its ice-cream stand and muddy, man-made beach. Through the underbrush, I followed a dubious path out to an isolated sand spit in the river. Wherever I went, my feet would always take me back toward town, toward the *épicerie* and another pint of vodka.

When walking no longer worked to suppress the tremor, I remembered the pharmacy across from the *épicerie*. A pharmacy would have something to make me sleep, to disperse the fringe of chattering figures.

My feet were already taking me there. With a sigh, an automatic door received me into an interior bewilderingly bright and neat.

I felt suddenly how long it had been since I had bathed, shaved, or changed clothes. To anyone in that spotless interior I would seem a spectacle of neglect. The pharmacist, however, did not seem to notice. His attention was absorbed by a scrawny, dreadlocked young woman standing at the counter. Waving a soiled sheet of paper, she shouted at the pharmacist in a lurching approximation of French. A scabby dog had flattened itself on the cool tile at her feet, taking cover from her harangue.

"*Un vrai, vois-vous, c'est vrai ordonnance. Signé par médecin. Vrai médecin. Tu faut le préparer, monsieur.*" It was real prescription, signed by real doctor. *Monsieur* have to make it.

"Once more," said the pharmacist, slowly, as though speaking to a lip-reader. "I will fill no prescription if the prescription cannot be verified."

"You has to! I am much pain!"

"No 'real' doctor would authorize opiates for someone in your condition."

But he had to fill it! A tear had loosened the grime at the corner of her eye and she smeared it away. "*Alors, then. Monsieur* was accepting to take responsibility?"

The pharmacist rolled his eyes. Why, could *mademoiselle* doubt that he was willing? He would be more than happy to call the *gendarmes* for her, for her or any of her vagrant friends.

She spun around and, jerking the dog after her, shoved past me toward the door. It was only at that moment that I noticed her belly. From behind she had seemed frail, even emaciated, but I knew now that this was the girl I had seen at the train station, the pregnant girl. The olive skin of her neck and collarbone were speckled with purulent sores, and an odor of scalp and sweat lingered after the door sighed shut at her back.

The pharmacist muttered something about *toxicomanes* and *tsiganes dégueulasses*. "Addicts! Disgusting Gypsies," he said. "And you? What do you want?"

*   *   *

On my way back toward the river, I noticed the dog first. It was whimpering behind a bench at the far end of the place de la République, where a switchback path descends the face of the old city walls. The girl was lying on her side, without cover, on the bare ground. The dog would approach her and paw at her chest, then back away, tugging at the limit of the string. The other end of the string must have been tied around the girl's wrist, because when the dog pulled, her hand jerked a little before flopping back, inert on her hip. Her complexion, olive in the light of the pharmacy, had turned an ashy, congealed hue, tallowed with sweat. When I lifted her other wrist to take her pulse, she attempted to pull away, but with a nerveless gesture. Her eyes drifted, irises gray, flecked with gold, sclera bloodshot and tinged with jaundice, pupils constricted to pinpoints.

"*Vous êtes très malade,*" I said.

"*Enculé donne pas médicament.*"

"*Vous êtes en état de manque,*" I said, uncertain of the word for "withdrawal."

A pinpoint pupil shifted past me as she repeated, "Motherfucker doesn't give medicine."

I asked her where she lived and said I could help her get home. Another limp gesture past my shoulder and then a struggle to lift herself. I managed at last to balance her on her feet, then with a jerk of surprising force she tried to twist free. She staggered and would have fallen if I hadn't clasped her in a kind of upright tackle. Her belly pressed against my side, as hard as a knee. I tried to steer her toward the bench, but she commenced a slow walk. She allowed me to hold her arm, but she was leading me, working her way through the little streets, up to the Porte de Paris and past it, the dog wheezing alongside on his string. When we passed a *bar-tabac,* I made her sit down and ordered her a Coke, but she drank a single sip before heaving herself up again. "I go," she said, and so we continued on. We had long since left behind any neighborhood I recognized, passing into a district of public housing towers, shuttered and featureless save where limp flags of laundry hung from a sill. We crossed a roadway into what appeared to be a half-built or abandoned development. Several foundation slabs stared upward into the rain, cracked where last year's weed and thistle had pushed through the concrete. Where a temporary wall of board and netting enclosed a construction site, she stopped and braced herself against a sheet of plywood, and I welcomed a chance to catch my breath as well. The dog paced to the end of its string and back, then sat down to pound at a flea behind its ear. This site, it seemed, had been abandoned in its development later than some of the others, its pilings sunk, foundation set, and the first and second levels already poured. Above the second floor, where tendons of rebar jutted from the unfinished pillars, streaks of rust streamed downward in orange veils.

"You go," she said.

"I cannot leave you here," I said. "I will bring you home."

"*Chez moi.*"

"*Chez vous.*" I said. "I will bring you there."

"*Chez moi.* Here," she said.

"Your home where?"

"Bring me just down," said the girl. "You go then."

And with that she grasped the edge of the board and worked it open until the gap was wide enough to pass through. The opening gave onto a broad ramp leading down into the darkness of the unbuilt building. As we descended, a bird, disturbed, burst into flight above us, the slap of its wing-beats twanging off the foundation walls. At its base the ramp leveled out, opening into a broad, flat space. We stood in some sort of underground garage or warehouse.

"*Attends,*" said the girl, and moved off with the dog into the obscurity. At the cough of a match, with a sudden hiss, a kerosene lantern drove hard shadows toward the corners of the room.

"You go," she said again. "*Chez moi.*"

Along the wall, beside the lantern, cardboard sheets had been stacked to form a pallet; a muddle of blankets lay on top. Without looking to see if I was still there, the girl lowered herself onto the pallet and unknotted the string from her wrist. "*Vas-y, Obus, tu bois,*" she said, and the dog, checking once to see if the length of string had agreed to follow him, drifted toward two enamel bowls laid out, in surprising tidiness, on a pink bath mat. The dog lapped water from one bowl, sniffed the other, then sighed downward between splayed legs, belly and muzzle resting on the concrete floor.

Crouching by the pallet, I asked the girl if she knew when she was supposed to give birth. "Baby," I repeated. "Baby soon. One month? Two weeks? When? *Bébé quand?*"

"Yes," was all she said. "Medicine."

"You need to be on methadone," I said, not knowing if the word existed in French. "You need to see a doctor."

"Need medicine," she said.

"Yes," I said. "A doctor, to help you."

"No, medicine only," she said.

"I am a doctor, me, *un vrai médecin*," I said, tapping my sternum, and the pinprick of her pupil shifted toward me. "If you need me, you can find me. I am staying at the campground. *Le camping, vous comprenez?* Do you know where it is? Just by the bridge, across the river."

Her lips parted as though to speak, but a voice called out from above, and footsteps descended the ramp, growing louder. The voice, in a torrent of profanity, was saying something about luck or chance, but when the owner of the voice reached the bottom of the ramp and saw me, he broke off abruptly.

A gaunt man looked rapidly between me and the girl. Who was I? And what the fuck was I doing here? The voice sounded young, but the face was drawn and creased in the lamplight, lips thin, teeth prominent. His French, though rapid, seemed to have been assembled from guttural, alien sounds.

"Doctor—" the girl started.

"Speak up!" he snapped, but didn't wait for her to continue. "You," he said to me, "you get the fuck out now."

She needed help, I was trying to say, she would soon be in labor.

"And remember," he said, pressing the tip of his index finger between my eyes, his voice now a whisper, "you were never here."

"Never where?" I asked, with the unformed notion that I could find my way back to this place if required.

"That's the idea," he said. "This is nowhere and you were never here. Vas-t'en."

I felt his stare on my back as I mounted the ramp and passed back out into the cold, the rain falling heavier now.

FORTY

id I think—and *with satisfaction*—that I was discharging a Samaritan's obligation, helping a girl, sick and pregnant, make her way home? Did I harbor the notion that something in me was capable of redemption, or if not of redemption, then reprieve? Did I imagine that in time I would be delivered, that messengers would be sent, disguised as the poor, the needy, the sick, even a wheezing dog on a string, to lead me out of the wilderness I'd wandered in since Miriam's death? Was it within such notions, Father, that my pride and self-aggrandizement concealed themselves?

The walk with the girl out to the abandoned construction site had been an ascent, a precarious tottering, but the way back was a plummet, a headlong drop. Something had caught up to me, seized and hauled me back to my campsite, as though to say: "You cannot leave, you can never leave." But what was it that had ensnared me? The fact both simple and impossible that Miriam had killed herself, had killed herself and her child, our child. Here. Yes, that was the implacable fact that had tracked me down and seized me, saying, *On n'est nulle part, et toi, tu n'étais jamais là.* This is nowhere and you were never here. You were never here, but you can never leave. Wherever I went, whatever I did, I could never leave. I had said to the girl, *If you need me, you can find me,* as though I had appointed myself her physician on call. But I wasn't on call. I was in a kind of custody, held not by professional obligation but by whatever it was—the desert, the wilderness—I knew I could never escape. I had found myself in a kind of limitless detention, a version of what French law calls *garde-à-vue,* the state of being kept in sight, without refuge.

That night in my tent, I could make myself drink only enough to keep off the shakes. Did I think if I lay very still and waited in the darkness, the fact would pass me by? Did I think that by some inscrutable mercy I would be released, uncoupled from it? But suddenly there was a voice calling out in the campground. Then the voice was nearby. Someone was beating on the tent fly with his hand and shouting, *Docteur! Docteur! Vous êtes là? Putain, il est où, le foutu médecin, le médecin américain?*

Yes, the fucking American doctor was here if he would shine that fucking flashlight somewhere else.

The beam flashed up before he flicked it off, illuminating the gaunt face of the man who had expelled me from the squatters' basement— though now he seemed a mere boy, gangly and rawboned. Panic cracked in his voice as he spoke. "*Viens, Docteur, tout de suite!* The girl, you must come, she is in trouble—"

"She is in labor," I said.

"She is dying," cracked the voice.

"Then get her to a hospital, like you should have before." I turned.

"*Pas d'hôpital!* No time." He clasped my arm and jerked me around. "She is dying. You come. *Ma moto.*" And then we were flying, my hands gripping his bony waist, the motorbike wailing over the bridge and up past the Porte de Paris, ricocheting through the twisted streets and then out through the housing projects, bumping over a curb into the unbuilt development, through the flung-open plywood door, and down the ramp, brakes shuddering, skidding to a stop in the abandoned basement.

"She is dying. You see how she is dying," he said, lifting the kerosene lantern over her body.

"She is in labor," I said. But the cast of her skin in the lantern's glare looked livid and greased. Naked, she lay on her side, a lake of dark fluid pooled beneath her hip. A groan surfaced from the depths of her body. When I turned her onto her back, her head lolled to the side. Respiration labored, eyes half-open, carotid pulse weak and thready. The young man had been speaking. They'd thought her pains were just withdrawal cramps, so he'd gone out to cop. That had taken a couple of hours. When he came back, she was worse. She had shat or pissed or something all over the bed, and she was screaming. He hadn't wanted to shoot her up, but she'd made him. She had stopped screaming then, maybe because of the hit, but she wasn't better, she was worse. She'd turned a color. He'd had no idea what to do; maybe he shot her up again . . . But she was saying something, something about getting the doctor, the American doctor. Was she dying? She wasn't going to die, was she?

"She will surely die if you don't get her to a hospital."

"But you can do something, no?"

During his explanation, I had knelt and examined her. Though the cervix was effaced and fully dilated, her labor appeared to have ceased, with the baby's head canted at a bad angle in the birth canal. I stood up.

"You see she is not dying," the young man repeated, shifting from foot to foot like a child needing to urinate.

"No," I said. "*She* is not dying. They are *both* dying, together, she and your baby. If you do not leave now, if you do not get an ambulance here now, they will die. Do you understand? *Toutes les deux.* Both of them."

Then, as though shot from a sling, he was gone, the echo of shrieking tires vibrating from the walls. An odor of scorched rubber and exhaust lingered, mingled with the odor of effluvia, ferric and excremental, pooled on the cardboard beneath her hips. I could neither look at the girl nor look away. The lantern hissed. Beside it in an ashtray, balanced across the bowl of a spoon, a loaded syringe rested, the needle-tip beaded with a clear droplet. The lantern light glowed scarlet in the needle's chamber, suffused through the mixture of heroin and blood. The young man must have stopped or been stopped after he had found the vein.

Another groan, weaker this time, rose from the girl. I had examined her at first without compunction, but now the thought of touching her appalled me. Standing there above her, I held my hands up, palms inward, as though I had just pushed my way through scrub-room doors into an operating room. My hands, however, were ungloved, and dark not with Betadine but with blood.

What—I tried to make myself think—*what what what* were the likely complications? What was most urgent and what could be ignored? What could wait until the ambulance arrived? The heroin must have retarded or interrupted labor. It would have if he had given her enough. But something else could have interfered as well. There must be a dozen, a hundred possibilities. How long could it take for the young man to find a phone, flag down a policeman, summon the EMTs? I held my breath, listening for a siren, a motor . . . Nothing, only the hiss of the lantern and the girl's breathing, irregular and stertorous.

"*Vous me permettez?*" I asked absurdly, kneeling beside her. Perhaps if I shifted her hips, I could expand the pelvic basin, but when I lifted her thigh to push it up toward her chest, a horrid gasp leapt through her. The paroxysm seemed more a convulsion than a contraction. While it lasted the crumpled crown of the baby's head emerged slightly from the birth canal, feathered with blood-matted hair, scalp waxen, blue black, and hypoxic. Leaning forward, my chin pressed into the back of her knee, I managed to pin her thigh against her chest, hoping to push the baby far enough back up the birth canal to turn it. It was during this blind and futile effort that I felt, at my fingertips, the hard, vein-ridged umbilical cord coiled in a double loop around the child's neck, while the child's shoulder remained wedged behind the cervical rim.

Shoulder dystocia. Delivery arrested by shoulder dystocia. That would account for the bad angle of the head. Yes, there could be no doubt. But why was I so sure? Because shoulder dystocia was one of the few labor complications I could remember from my obstetrics rotation? During one of those deliveries, the attending physician, with a jerk of a forceps, had snapped a baby's collarbone to deliver it, and for days I could not expel that sickening crunch from my head.

If there was a name for that maneuver—the breaking of the clavicle to extract a distressed fetus—I didn't remember it, and in any event I had no forceps but my ungloved hands. I struggled for a better purchase on the baby while cries surged through the girl with convulsive force. It was only after my hands had grown slick with vernix and blood, only after I had contrived a way to brace my elbows against my stomach while leaning over the girl, that I managed to force the baby back up enough to get a proper grip on its shoulders. At first the body felt like a greased piglet, but as I grasped harder, the tiny thorax seemed less slippery and more brittle, as though the pressure of my hands had melted away all insulating layers of fat and muscle, leaving only the frail cage of rib and collarbone. For an instant I hung paralyzed between the fear of losing my grip and the fear of killing the baby outright. I compressed the shoulder yoke with a desperate force: either the clavicle would refuse to break and the child would strangle in the canal or I would crush its thorax entirely. I was certain now I should give up, wait for someone to arrive, but the lantern hissed, I leaned harder, and it broke, the clavicle alone, with a wet snap.

With the shoulder collapsed against its neck, the baby shot out, propelled on a wet gush, not of amniotic fluid but of blood, frank and opaque. I tilted the head back and with my mouth tried to suck the mucus plugs from its nose, the slurry of phlegm and meconium from its throat. I lifted the little body up by its ankles—as though whatever blackness had filled it, had darkened its face to bruise-bronze, would rush out of it. Only a brownish froth, however, no more than a teaspoon, drained down the cheek toward the sealed eye. Nothing happened. The child did not breathe.

At last I replaced the small form alongside its mother, its rumpled feet bowed inward, the buttocks narrow. No afterbirth had followed the delivery, so the umbilical cord still disappeared in the mother's vagina. Blundering through the shadows, I found an empty wine bottle and a plastic bag. I bit off the two handles of the bag, then knotted them to ligate the umbilicus. The bottle broken, a large shard served to cut or rather crush through the gristled tissues, releasing a single spurt of blood when it breached the artery.

It was then, for the first time, that I noticed: the child was a girl. The baby was a girl. But she had neither breathed nor cried, and she lay motionless where I had set her down, beside the mother now motionless too. An immense longing overcame me to leave them alone, to leave them in whatever impenetrable silence had claimed them for itself.

I decided to place the child on the plateau of her mother's sternum, near to the heart, but when I turned the baby so that she would not slide off, the clavicle ground and gave. It must have been the pain then that did it, stiffening the little body with a galvanic jolt. In a single spasm, it kicked and arched and spewed a plume of filth, followed by a squad of cries enraged but orderly, separated by short whooping gasps. The cries drove outward in every direction and echoed off the concrete walls, and the mother's body heaved with an answering half rasp, half wail. Her eye, rolling to the side, caught mine and held it in blind, desperate appeal.

If infection had taken hold, she could be disoriented, even delirious. Perhaps she had never been aware that I was there. The face, still waxen, tensed anew, but only briefly, as a final contraction ejected the afterbirth into the slick of effluent, and along with the afterbirth another surge of blood. I had put her hand up on the baby's back, and for a moment she struggled to raise her head and look. The effort seemed to crush her and her head fell back, an enormous tear quivering in the hollow beside her nose.

"Voilà votre enfant," I said. "Une belle petite fille."

Had she heard me?

"A girl," I said again. "A beautiful baby girl."

But she said nothing. Her body shook, teeth chattering. Her lips had gone pewter blue. When I touched her, her skin scorched my fingers. The shaking had turned to shuddering, and the baby had begun to choke on its cries. I lay down on the pallet beside the mother and eased her onto her side, curling my legs beneath her backside to spoon myself around her. With my arm around them both, the baby resting in the hollow of her mother's body, I could support the child against her mother's breast. She had found the nipple herself and on her own had managed a shallow latch. Sucking, she was silent save for a little piping hoot released from time to time. How long we lay there like that, I cannot tell you. I cannot tell you because we slept.

But who could believe such a thing? I myself cannot. And yet I swear to you, the three of us, together, sank into a dreamless, obliterating slumber. When I woke, everything was different. The surroundings had not changed. Every object was exactly as it had been, only a total clarity had descended, purifying the airless space, sharpening the edges of the lamplight. The mother's breathing was regular and steady. The night, I knew, was far gone. I knew that no one would come to help us: no gendarmes, no police, no paramedics jogging down the ramp with trauma kits and stretcher boards. The young man had spurred his bike and fled. Our solitude, though shared, was absolute.

Had you been there, Father, had you stood, say, at the top of the ramp, what would you have seen, looking down? The baby, sleeping, had fallen from the girl's breast, the breast blue-veined, hard and pale in the hard glare of the lantern. Behind them both, the doctor: his eyes open now. The scene would seem frozen, fixed, a tableau, until you remarked the trembling of the doctor's hand on the mother's naked hip. At first you understand this to be a natural response, a discharge of adrenal tension after his urgent exertions. But then you see how the hand is not in fact trembling, not any longer, but shaking, and you understand that it is not the hand that is moving but the hip beneath it. The hand jerks as the mother's body jerks, and you see now that her mouth has filled with a bloody spume. Her eyes rolling, erratically at first but then back in the direction of the doctor beside her, but they do not meet his own. He does not move to clear her throat, or to turn her so that she does not aspirate her own vomit. He only holds his hand against her hip, as though the hand were an instrument whose sole purpose was to register each twitch, each throe, within his own person, recording each spasm heaving now through her in waves, each one closer on the heels of the last until they have fused into a single convulsion, driving her chest forward, her spine arched. You would think this compounding paroxysm had lasted for many minutes, realizing only afterward that mere seconds had passed before it released her, a faint tremor flickering through her extremities, followed by a hoarse, scraping exhalation. The doctor's hand is immobile now, as incapable of movement as the mother's body, now perfectly still. So absolute is that stillness that when at last the doctor rises, slowly, as though taking all pains not to wake them, you think he must have risen out of his own body. You think when he bends over the baby and wraps it in his shirt, he has lifted the baby from out of its body as well, so that even after he has departed with his tiny burden, the three of them—the doctor, the mother, the child—would remain forever in that darkness, as though carved on a tomb lid or frozen in the shadows of a near-black photograph.

FORTY-ONE

During my rounds at the hospital, I must have fallen asleep in the chair at a patient's bedside, next to the IV tree. Did no nurse think to wake me? I try to rise, but exhaustion like a great weight presses me down. And where is the patient? I wonder, aware now that I am the only person in the room—the only person, and yet not alone. Certain thoughts wait for me to regain consciousness. One, barely audibly, suggests that the chair I am sleeping in is not in fact a chair. Another indicates that I'm not sitting but lying in a bed. A third whispers that I have not been making rounds, that I have not made rounds in many years, not since I was a medical student. Another says, Listen: the voices in the hallway speak a foreign language. But it is not foreign; it is French. You have awakened in France. You took a wrong turn somewhere in the hospital, got out on the wrong floor, and now you are in France.

Why was I there? How did I get there?

If I shifted, the IV rack shook as though startled. The bags hanging on the rack drained into a converging tube, and the tube to an in-line catheter, the catheter to a needle, and the needle in a vein in the back of a hand. These elements hung together like segments of a syllogism. The hospital bed was my bed, the drip stood at my bedside, the hand was my hand. Nevers. Somehow I knew I was in Nevers. The reason, like a visiting bedside relative, had gone away but would come back later.

There had been voices in the corridor, but the voices had disappeared. I thought: So this is what it feels like, the standard combination, Haldol and a benzodiazepine, lorazepam most likely. I'd ordered it often for my patients. The sedatives corralled my thoughts away from me, as though in a tank, submerged and distorted behind walls of heavy glass. They swam like huge fish, vanishing for a while and then bulging once more into view, their flat eyes tilting toward me slightly as they pass.

At some point a nurse came in, took my temperature and blood pressure, looked at me but said nothing, and departed.

It was only when the wall of sedation ruptured and my recollections flooded over me, all at once—the abandoned basement, the hissing lantern, the mother's pinprick pupils, the baby's orderly cries, the lake of blood—when I jerked upright, or tried to, only then did I discover I had been restrained, padded cuffs Velcroed around wrists and ankles, straps anchored to the bars of the bed.

The nurse returned and a doctor followed. "He's awake now," she said. The doctor, young, put on a pair of fuchsia-rimmed spectacles and a bland smile. "Dr. Abend," he said, "I trust you are feeling somewhat better now?" Without waiting for a response, he offered an apology for the restraints, his English betraying the slightest accent, almost British, barely French at all. "You understand they are only a precaution." He spoke as though we had already met: surely I could understand, a doctor myself and a psychiatrist—in cases of agitation—

"The girl," I said.

"Yes," said the smile, blank as a surgical mask.

"The girl," I said again. "How is the girl?" Even as I asked this question, I knew I had asked it before, more than once, many times.

"Beautiful. She continues beautifully. Excellent progress, excellent vitals. She has gained another fifty grams."

"No—" I said.

"I assure you, she tolerates the methadone well," continued the smile, "though of course it is still early in the protocol. I believe I already mentioned she has begun to take the bottle."

"Not the girl," I said. "The mother. How is the mother?"

The doctor said nothing. He was taking my pulse. His lips moved as he counted the beats. The smile had disappeared. "I will be back, Dr. Abend," he said, and left the room.

As for what had happened between the birth in the abandoned garage and the moment I woke in the hospital, my memories are, you could say, secondhand recollections, furnished to me only later in the denatured French of the police reports.

At approximately 4h15 an adult subject had approached a road crew for assistance, holding a newborn infant wrapped in a shirt. Police were notified and an ambulance dispatched 4h36. Subject informed responding officers of the location of the infant's mother. Officers determined location to be a construction site at 19, rue Saint-Saturnin, and a second ambulance was dispatched. (See attached report, CZ090102.) Ambulance with subject and newborn arrived 5h11 at Hôpital Colbert, and both were taken in charge by hospital staff.

Interviewed by police at the hospital at approximately 7h00, the adult subject identified himself as Daniel Abend, a physician practicing in New York (United States). Temporary resident of Paris since last May, subject stated he had been vacationing in Nevers, staying in the campground (27, rue de la Blanchisserie). Subject stated that while in the campground, he

*had been approached by a younger male. Subject did not know the name
of the man but had met him several days earlier. The man at that time was
in the company of a young woman, whom subject described as "heavily
pregnant and probably approaching term." The young man, believing that
the young woman had fallen ill in the course of premature labor, had gone
to the campground to request assistance from subject, whom he knew to be
an American doctor. Subject stated his belief that he was approached because the mother was of foreign nationality and consequently reluctant to
involve French authorities. Subject and the young man then proceeded to
the construction site on the young man's motorbike. There they found the
child delivered and alive but the woman unresponsive. At this point or
shortly thereafter, subject believes the young man fled the scene. Unable to
revive the woman, the doctor left the construction site in order to alert the
authorities and seek medical help for the infant and mother.*

*Report CZ090102 corroborates Abend's account. At an abandoned
construction site (19, rue Saint-Saturnin) responding officers and paramedics found a female subject approximately twenty years of age, in car-
diac arrest, with nonreactive pupils. Efforts at resuscitation, including
administration of naloxone and atropine, were unsuccessful. Patient was
transported to Hôpital Colbert, where after further interventions patient
was declared dead at 6h02.*

*At 19, rue Saint-Saturnin, officers collected drug paraphernalia and a
small quantity of what appeared to be a controlled substance. Pending the
coroner's report, it is suspected that the female subject's death was brought
about or accelerated by opiate overdose. There were no indications of foul
play. As of this writing, the identity of the deceased has yet to be established, and the young man mentioned in Abend's statement (see report
CZ090097) has not been located.*

When I read these accounts the first time, in the office of my lawyer,
I adopted them and claimed them as my own. The memories they sup-
plied have sustained me, a stolen cache of fact. While it is true that the
events they record elicit in me no sense of active recollection, these secondhand memories are as vivid as any others. Who should be surprised

by this? What parent does not remember the moment his child came into the world?

My correspondent, on the other hand, has taken no chances. With what care he attends to the slightest detail. In his latest communication, today's letter, he is, once again, thorough beyond reproach. Photocopies of these same police reports arrived in the post office box, collated and stapled in sequence. Appended to these are additional statements made by one ABEND (Daniel) along with the hospital records from Nevers, including admission papers for a newborn girl. On each of these documents, in the space marked "Guardian," I see the twitchy ghost of my own signature. This same signature, sturdier now, appears with several others at the bottom of another police document, a release stating that the death of the as-yet-unidentified mother has been ruled an accidental overdose, and that the presence of Monsieur Abend (Daniel) is no longer required in Nevers. Altogether, these papers made for a thick envelope, one that had fit only with difficulty in the postal box. It was only in flipping through them the second time that I discovered two other documents I had not encountered during the hearings eighteen years ago. The first group consisted of a work order and an invoice from a private ambulance firm, for the transportation of a female infant, in the company of two medics and a pediatrician, from Hôpital Colbert in Nevers to the neonatal care unit at Hôpital Necker in Paris. The bill, for an astounding sum, had been marked *payé en totalité*. Paid in full.

The last item, a stub for a train ticket issued to "Abend D" on the date of the ambulance transfer, one way, Nevers to Paris. They were on the reverse side of the ticket stub, the last four lines of the poem, the words written out longhand in painstaking block capitals:

> *For he comes, the human child,*
> *To the waters and the wild*
> *With a faery, hand in hand,*
> *For the world's more full of weeping than he can understand.*

FORTY-TWO

You have your ticket, I have mine. That is what Miriam had said.
I can hear her saying it. I can see her lips move, can feel, as she
speaks, her breath on my own lips.
À chacun son billet.

It is what each of us said, and yet each of us made the same mistake:
we believed we knew our respective destinations. Miriam believed her
destination was the monastery. For my part, I believed that my ticket was
an airplane ticket back to New York. It would be in my jacket pocket,
nested inside my passport, when I handed my apartment keys to the
concierge and walked my single suitcase two blocks to the taxi stand.
When I passed through U.S. Customs, the stub of my ticket would still
be in my passport, the passport agent would glance at it and return it to
me with a brusque "Welcome home, Mr. Abend." After I retrieved my
bag, I would drop the stub into the trash, along with the newspaper and
a *roman policier* I'd read on the plane.

But of course Miriam's ticket was not for the monastery. It was, instead, her token to cross the last river, the river without an opposite bank.
And as for me, I was not to leave France that month, or the next. Two
years would pass before I finally handed over my apartment keys to the
concierge. I would hand in another key as well, the one to the office I'd

leased in a *cabinet de psychiatrie*, a practice maintained by colleagues
from my year at the American Hospital. There, in a small consultation
room, I would see patients in the morning and evening, American or
British citizens ineligible for reimbursement by French health services,
professionals and diplomats wealthy enough to pay my full fee. In fact it
was in Paris, as a temporary partner in that *cabinet*, that I established a
pattern of work I have maintained throughout my professional life: two
blocks of appointments, early and late, with the midday held open. Midday in Paris, I would make my way across the city to the Maison Nôtre
Dame, where a community of Ursuline sisters, assisted by a staff of therapists and social workers, cared for a dozen or so orphans and other wards
of the state.

Before Clementine took occupancy of her bassinet at the Maison
Nôtre Dame, however, she spent the first nine weeks of her life in a neonatal unit in l'Hôpital Necker, the chief pediatric hospital in Paris, where
the private ambulance had brought her. Whether she had in fact been
born eight weeks before term, as her measurements indicated, or whether
her low birth weight, liver enzyme irregularities, and respiratory difficulties were complications from the opiate addiction she had inherited from
her mother, her doctors never specified. Although I was not one of her
physicians, it was assumed from the beginning that I should attend all
meetings concerning her care. I had saved her. I had arranged and paid
for her costly private transfer to l'Hôpital Necker. And even after weeks
had passed, I could always be found in the waiting room, reading a book
about infant care or detaining the nurses with premeditated experiments
in small talk.

One day, one of these nurses, the shift supervisor, looked up from
some paperwork she was completing and remarked that such a lovely,
scrappy little girl needed a proper name.

"Jeanne DuPont seems to suit her well," I said. This was the name on
her file, the name on the little card affixed to her bassinet.

"*Ah, surtout pas!*" said the shift supervisor, laughing. "That is the
name for anybody without a name. Her mother, I am sure she was registered as Jeanne DuPont too."

In my confusion I heard myself asking if she had any suggestions.

"*Vous demandez ça à moi, Docteur?*" she said. "*Ça c'est au papa de décider! Enfin, ou au résponsable légal—*" That's for the dad to decide— I mean, the responsible party—

"Ah, *oui*, the responsible party—" I said.

"Otherwise, a social worker will provide one," she said, indicating with a gesture that nothing would be more foolish than letting a social worker think up a name.

So why did I say "Clementine" then? Had I ever known a Clementine? Had I overheard the name somewhere? These questions occurred to me only later, but there, when the shift supervisor asked me, I said it as though Clementine had been Clementine from the beginning, as though her name had been my secret.

"*Ah, Clémentine! J'adore!*" said the nurse. "A French name, for a French little girl!"

Months would pass before a magistrate, satisfied that no parent or other ascendant had come forward, would name me Clementine's legal guardian, on the grounds of my involvement in her care since her birth. Long before that, the nurses on the neonatal unit at Necker had taken to addressing me as Meester Ze Godfazzer. Once the hearings were under way and Clementine had been moved to the Maison Nôtre Dame, the sisters there addressed me simply as Papa.

"And will she return to the States with her papa?" asked portly Sister Yvonne from Cameroon, in sloping sub-Saharan cadence.

I said I supposed that would depend very heavily on who the adoptive parents were.

"*Non, mais, Monsieur Daniel*, it must be you!" Sister Yvonne said. "Nothing else would be fair." This, at least, was the opinion of Sister Yvonne—and evidently that of the other sisters. Each day when I arrived at the Maison Nôtre Dame, they greeted me with a hearty "*Bonjour, Papa!*" and presented me with Clementine, still groggy, her cheek flushed and creased from her morning nap. It was not, however, the opinion of French law. It was one thing to be awarded guardianship of an abandoned child, quite another to win full legal parenthood. From the first day I made my inquiries, I was informed—and frequently—that the likelihood of an American adopting a French baby in good health was infinitesimal at best.

"But you must fight for it, then!" said Sister Yvonne. "Do you think God brought her out of a disgusting basement to put her in foster care all her life?" Whatever I might have replied, Sister Yvonne in her indignation stampeded ahead. "What good are lawyers, what good are the courts, if they cannot keep you and your daughter together! I ask you that! *Franchement, on se demande!*"

My daughter! At times, in the years after our return to New York, I would lie awake at night wondering when it was that Clementine became, definitively, my daughter. Was it when the shift supervisor had asked me in that impromptu ceremony to pick a name? Was it when the nuns decided, spontaneously, to declare me Papa? Was it when Clementine herself, a little more than a year old and fattening rapidly in the bustle of the Maison Nôtre Dame, addressed me for the first time as "Pa-po-pa" to the clucking delight of the nuns? Or was it when at the nuns' insistence she was baptized, the priest taking her from my arms and pouring water from a silver dish over her head? After the service, Yvonne crushed me in her colossal embrace: "Now she is truly yours." Would you, Father, have agreed with her? Would you maintain that in the brief sacrament, a power of some sort had gone forth and made us each other's? Would you say, further, that such a power accounted for the surge of joy I felt when Clementine, drenched and wide-eyed, was returned to my arms?

But enough. Let it be enough that when the priest said, "Name this child," he looked to me. Let it be enough that I was the one who replied, "Clementine Levaux Abend."

After I was declared the guardian, anxious weeks passed, then anxious months, before I received another favorable ruling. Clementine had just celebrated her first birthday. The magistrate let it be known that the court affirmed the statutory particularity of Clementine's case, ruling in effect that I had assumed the role of Clementine's guardian prior to the intervention of the state. This august decree in fact concluded nothing, but once made, it meant that all procedural and bureaucratic delays could only work in my favor. With each passing month my case strengthened; no relative had appeared, and my participation in Clementine's care continued as it always had, "faithfully and devotedly," as the nuns attested in their affidavits.

On the day of the decisive ruling, the magistrate pronounced that enforcement of customary procedure would obstruct the state's primary obligation to seek the child's best interest and that the court acknowledged Daniel Abend of New York, États-Unis, as legitimate claimant for full adoptive custody of Clementine Abend, née Jeanne DuPont and formerly ward of the state, should the said Daniel Abend pursue such custody.

In the end, after twenty-eight months, when all orders and releases had been drafted, signed, and entered, I was awarded adoption of Clementine Levaux Abend on the exceptional grounds that the adoption had, in all but name, already occurred. Clementine was now mine because I had always been hers.

Her first passport picture was taken in the American embassy. By then Clementine was a rangy two-year-old with a tousle of black hair. The young clerk with the camera lent us a rubber band to tie her hair back from her face. "You better tell Mommy," said the clerk, "it's time for a haircut." Clementine's response—"My mommy is him"—earned me a look of confusion from the clerk.

The clinic directorship I'd planned to assume upon my return two years earlier had long before been assigned to someone else, but because so many of my patients in Paris had been not only American but from New

York, once back in the States I had little trouble building a full practice, stacking my morning hours with brief, lucrative medication consultations, reserving my evenings for analytic sessions. Sometime during Clementine's seventh or eighth year, it occurred to me that my practice was now indistinguishable from the practice I would have developed had I returned from Paris when I'd originally intended—indeed, had I never left New York in the first place. At times I could even believe—or almost believe—that we had always been here. After all, over the intervening years, had I not disguised myself perfectly as myself?

FORTY-THREE

À *chacun son billet.*

Even now, I can hear her, feel her say it, her breath on my lips.

My ticket has found me, or rather, my tickets, one for a flight, another for a train, and a photograph of the final destination. In the envelope, each is separated from the other by a little square of tissue paper. Having looked at the times of departure, I note that I will have a day, or the better part of a day, in Paris. Time enough for a walk over the Pont de Bercy, perhaps through the Jardin des Plantes and into the Quartier Latin. If the café is still there on the rue de Vaugirard, I will stop and order a drink, a pastis, I think, after all these years. Perhaps the same waiter will be there, grizzled now and weary. I will watch the passersby, the *commerçants* and the tourists, the students, no doubt some of them Clementine's age, just eighteen. Will I think for an agonized instant that I glimpse Clementine in the crowd? The waiter will accept my payment with a nod, and I will leave.

There will be time to step inside a little nondescript church where a stranger once heard a weightless voice suspend itself in ether, then pour itself down through the difficult descending figures of Allegri's *Miserere*. Perhaps I shall walk past an art gallery, long ago an English-language bookstore, where an American girl—now nearing forty, maybe divorced, maybe with teenage kids, living in Austin or Cincinnati or Portland—once took a part-time job. And there will be time to rest along the way, beneath a linden tree, in the shadow of its broad leaves, in the odor of its greenish flowers.

The train will not leave until nine, so there will be time to find my way back by another route, the longer way along the Seine. (I won't, after all, have luggage. All I will carry is a single, heavy envelope.) In Nevers, at midnight, the streets will be empty or nearly so. I will follow the rue de la Gare down to the river. Even an unhurried walk from the station to the Pont de Loire will take no more than half an hour. On the bridge, I will run my fingers over the softened contours of my crude inscription, perhaps leaning against the parapet, watching the current shoal up and break over the dike. From then it will take no more than ten minutes to cross to the opposite bank. I will descend the embankment road to the riverside downstream of the bridge, the sandy stretch of shore where trees and shrubbery press up to the river's edge and the fishermen's paths disperse through the underbrush. It will not matter which path I take. They divide and meet and divide around the hummocks of willow and locust, and in the end all lead to the curved spit of sand hooked out where the river runs deepest.

Will I recognize my correspondent when I arrive? Will his face be familiar from my years in Paris? From all my years in New York? Will I know it as the face reflected in Jessica Burke's face in the bathtub, in the still-pensive expression she wears in the photograph? No matter. He will recognize me.

He will know how to fasten the chain, around my wrists first and then through the spokes of the flywheel. He will have thought it through, many times, how to secure my wrists so that the hands do not pull free when the body is betrayed to panic. When the lock clicks shut, the key will already be on its way—folded in a note and posted to the *commissariat de police*. The note (in anonymous, block capitals) will state where I, Daniel Abend, the undersigned, may be found, down past the Île aux Sternes, in the deeper current off the curving spit.

And soon enough, another envelope, containing her ticket to the

United States, will be in the mail to my daughter, Clementine, wherever she may be. I will ask my correspondent to inform my lawyer of her whereabouts. Because I will have discharged my debt to my correspondent, he will do what I request. He is, above all, a man of honor. As for the expense of the ticket, my daughter will be directed to give no thought to the cost. Everything will have been paid in full.

What will she return to? The violets and the little pepper plant on her windowsill I have watered for the last time, perhaps excessively, in hopes they will survive long enough to greet her when she returns. When she emerges from customs at JFK, she will recognize, with puzzlement, her name inked on a placard, held by my attorney, a Mr. Albert Hale, to whom I have entrusted these instructions: He is to bring her to his offices for the unsealing of the will, and when she is ready he will explain the disposition of the estate. I have expressed my wish that he do so with utmost gentleness, and with utmost gentleness accompany her to the apartment, which she will enter for the last time.

She will find there that I have given nearly everything away. My room, always stark, is as I write this completely bare, without books, without pictures, without a radio even to receive the long sleepless broadcasts. My desk alone remains. As for her own things, they have been packed away in storage, where they await her. (I will not attempt to describe what it was to wrap each object, each garment, each book and photograph, and lay it in a box.) The sale of the apartment alone will net her a small fortune, to which shall be added the larger fortune of her inheritance.

On this desk, beside the violets and the pepper plant, she will find my last letter to her. It is brief, only the words necessary to express an infinite love and an infinite sorrow. I do not ask forgiveness. The only consolation I seek is release, at last, from the desire for consolation.

Unforgivable. What other word?

And this story I have told you, which is her story too, does she not deserve to know it? Does she not deserve to know the circumstances of her birth, who her parents were, that the man who has claimed her as his daughter is not her father? She does—it is her birthright—and yet she cannot know. I have burned the letters and the photographs, one by one. The only version of her story is the one you hold in your hand. You have read it, have heard me out, and for that you have my solemn thanks, but I ask you to burn these pages too.

I am told the seal of the confessional prevents you from seeking her out, even should you conclude she is in immediate danger. But I can assure you she is in no danger. My correspondent has given me his quitclaim: her safety and her freedom have been paid in full. Whether with me or with the girl, he wrote, he will be satisfied. I will be that satisfaction, as he has known all along. Should some impulse, however, goad you to seek her out, I have made certain that you will not find her. From the beginning of my confession I have dissembled her name. It is not Clementine Abend. I pray, Father, that you let this be the end of Clementine's story, and of mine. As for the man who wrote you these pages, his name makes no appearance here either. He is not—was not—Daniel Abend. Of your charity, remember him.

April 2016

The cough of a crow in the distance brought Spurlock to his
senses, although day had yet to break.

It was as though she had appeared to him in a dream: "I'm
going to go now," she had said, holding the package he had given her.
Except he had not been dreaming. She had led him to this stone bench,
she had accepted the package, and although she had said only "I'm going
to go now," something careful, almost pained, in her inflection acknowledged how long he had waited, how patiently he had kept the package,
and the fact that they would not meet again. He watched her receding
form until a bend in the cinder path took her from his view.

Come daylight, Nelson Spurlock would begin his journey home, the
job done, his purpose accomplished. He would wait for the sky to lighten,
he would rise from the stone bench and return to the hotel. There he
would hire a taxi for the two-hour trip to the airport, the road straight
through the flat midwestern fields. Until day broke, however, he would
wait here. Though the crow coughed again, night held.

The stone bench was cold and seemed to drink the heat from Spurlock's body, but the earth breathed the odor of a deep thaw, and all night
a sleepless wind had tossed in the treetops. Spurlock had not slept either.
Last night, when he'd lain down on the hotel bed, he'd felt such fatigue

that he'd wondered if he would sleep through his midday flight the next day. Might he even sleep through the onrushing onslaught of Holy Week back at the Incarnation? As tired as he was, though, his eyes had not closed, and all night the sleepless wind had paced back and forth outside his window, scrabbling at it, as though pleading to be let in.

Finally, avoiding the gaze of the clock's red eye, Nelson Spurlock had risen from the bed and walked out through the town, under the solitary streetlight swinging over its intersection and across the tree-lined expanse of the town green, passing two students smoking on the steps of a monument. "I salute you, Night Walker," said one slurrily, plunging his hand into a bag of chips held by his friend. Spurlock made his way along the streets of the college town, past slumbering nineteenth-century houses, sensing even in darkness the affably un-kempt spaciousness of the Midwest.

He had not been aware of heading anywhere in particular, but he found himself at the split-rail gate of the arboretum. Beyond it lay the cinder path they had walked down the day before. "Why not?" he said to himself, and set off down the path through what he remembered was a sort of hummocky meadow to the stand of evergreens and the curved stone bench they enclosed. This was where they had sat side by side, the heavy envelope he had just given her resting on her lap, her hand palm-down on top of it. For a moment they had said nothing. A crow spoke in the distance, and she had said, as though in response, "I am going to go now."

So it was over, he thought, the stone bench beneath him colder now than it had been yesterday, his brief mission concluded. Hardly brief, though, he thought, if you counted the eight years since she had ap-peared in his church. "Well, Nelson, I guess you should go now too," he said to himself. But it was still night, and he would wait here, as good a place as any, for day to break over the state of Ohio.

Ohio, as the last letter had informed him. He had found it without looking for it. On sabbatical from his congregation, he had not stopped by the office for eighteen days. He'd tried, in an exertion of will, to make it for twenty-one days, three whole weeks, to find something else to do with his time, but one of his aimless walks through the city had conducted him to the church unawares. He'd hesitated only briefly. *Oh, fuck it*, he'd said, and gone in.

"Couldn't quite manage, could you, chief?" said Mrs. Nickerson when he walked into the parish office.

"Any fresh horrors in the mail today?" he asked with strained jocularity.

"Nothing much, chief. The bishop called, wants you to nominate yourself for the Standing Committee. Mail's on your desk. Nothing from the law firm. What happened to 'you won't see me for a month'?"

He'd asked Mrs. Nickerson to call him if anything had arrived from his wife's attorney. The attorney referred to his client as "Ms. Pierce," declaring that "her preference henceforth was to be known by her maiden name." Maiden! thought Spurlock, but without bitterness. He supposed he should no longer refer to the lawyer as his wife's attorney, if only because Bethany was no longer his wife. Soon enough, he'd been informed, the official decree of divorce would arrive in the mail "for his records." Records of what? he wondered. There had been no conflict, no scenes in the lobby, no solitary sobbing embrace of a shower curtain. In fact there had been practically no discussion at all, just an acknowledgment, incremental and unspoken, that whatever had been was no more and quite possibly had never existed in the first place. Let the record show, thought Spurlock, still without bitterness, the nothing that was never there. His one demand had been to keep Perpetua, the cat, but in the end he had let her go as well.

Absorbed in his thoughts, Spurlock had thrown out the message from the bishop and picked up the next item in the stack on his desk, an old-style airmail envelope, the light paper a pale blue, the words *Par Avion* in the corner. Across the envelope's face, a crabbed, arthritic hand had spelled out in blocky capitals a strange name and a familiar address:

MLLE. OPPEN

CHURCH OF THE INCARNATION

NEW YORK, NY

He called out to Mrs. Nickerson, "Do we have a Millie—no, a Mademoiselle Oppen in the parish records?"

There was a brief clatter of keystrokes before she said, "Not a one. Did someone send you a mail-order bride, chief?"

Who was this Mademoiselle Oppen, and what had he to do with her? Even as he phrased the question to himself, he was aware of not wanting to know the answer. Nevertheless, he peered once more at the envelope. In the lower corner the same crabbed block capitals spelled out:

AUX BONS SOINS DU PÈRE NELSON SPURLOCK

EXÉCUTEUR TESTIMENTAIRE DU DÉFUNT, M. DAVID EVERETT OPPEN

He did not know what *aux bons soins* meant, and he was executor of no one's estate, certainly not this David Everett Oppen. Surely someone had erred. He would hand the letter back to Mrs. Nickerson. But he did not move. He stared at the envelope. For an instant it was as though the years had not passed at all, as though he'd awakened from a seven-year dream to find himself still staring at the sheet of paper that the girl Clementine Abend had first unfolded the day she appeared in the church. But she was not here, and the hands the paper trembled in were his own. And of course, the name was different. A pulse of relief spread through him, only to vanish as abruptly as it had arrived. The girl had found Spurlock because Spurlock's name had appeared on a will, or rather a fragment of a will, that sheet of paper she had received in the mail, from her father. The fragment had said that any future correspondence would be addressed to Spurlock, at the church. And so it had been. Within weeks, Daniel Abend's testament had arrived in its envelope. But Spurlock remembered Abend's closing words: *From the beginning of my confession I have dissembled her name. It is not Clementine Abend. I pray, Father, that*

you let this be the end of Clementine's story, and of mine. As for the man
who wrote you these pages, his name makes no appearance here either. He
is not—was not—Daniel Abend.

Deliberately, Nelson Spurlock set the envelope on his desk, sealed, addressed to a Mlle. Oppen, the daughter of one David Everett Oppen.

As though to test its reality, Spurlock said the name aloud: *Oppen*.

Not Abend, but Oppen. That was his name.

David Oppen.

Daniel Abend (who was not—is not—Daniel Abend) is instead David
Oppen.

For a moment, Spurlock shut his eyes. Behind his closed eyelids he
looked out over a great congregation, pews occupied to capacity all the
way to the back of his church, packed as they would be only for the funeral of a young person. They formed a receding trapezoid of faces up-
turned toward him in the pulpit, faces indistinct and backlit, the blare of
sunlight from the avenue flooding in through the west doors. Over his
shoulder, in the chancel, he sensed it, the body of Jessica Burke, shut in
its coffin, the coffin covered with a white linen pall. Daniel Abend would
have been among the congregation. Yes, on the day of Jessica Burke's
funeral, Daniel Abend would have been somewhere in the congregation, seated beside the doorman Itzal—Daniel Abend, who was instead
David Oppen.

Oppen would be the last name of the daughter too. The sealed envelope on his desk made this plain.

"Are you feeling all right, chief?" Mrs. Nickerson asked when he opened
the door to his office.

"Can you find a death notice or obituary for a David Oppen, in
2008?"

Another brief squall of keystrokes. "Oppen . . . Oppen . . . David Oppen, psychoanalyst, age fifty. A drowning. In France. Did you know him?"

"Children?"

"No children—hold it—yes: one child, a daughter, an Em Oppen."

"Em Oppen . . . Can you find her?"

The keys clattered again.

"Oppen . . . Oppen. There are several: Em Oppen, M. Oppen, Emma Oppen, E. Moppen. An Oppen Emilie. Wait, no—it looks like they are all the same person, all twenty to twenty-five years old, all in the same place, somewhere in Ohio. A town called Sidon."

"Twenty-five," he said.

"I beg your pardon?"

"She would be twenty-five. Just."

"You know this Em Oppen?"

"I've never heard her name in my life."

Mrs. Nickerson cocked her eyebrow. "Do I get to know what this is about?"

"Not if I don't," he said. "I'll be back in a few days."

Of your charity, remember him.

As Spurlock read again the last pages of Daniel Abend's confession, the plane had begun to shed altitude. They would touch down in seventeen minutes (the pilot had announced) at the Akron-Canton Airport, two hours east of the town of Sidon and Sidon College, whose library website listed on its staff roster an Em Oppen, librarian and archivist, assistant curator of Special Collections. How rapidly, suddenly even, his itinerary had snapped into place. In his satchel, alongside a change of clothes and the airmail letter addressed to "MLLE. OPPEN," Spurlock carried David Oppen's written testament, the pages he'd read seven years ago and kept in his office ever since.

*   *   *

For the long taxi ride from Akron-Canton Airport to the campus of Sidon College, Spurlock stared across the landscape's bleak expanse, the secondary roads sweeping past the highway at long, regular intervals, straight as oars. Could this be Clementine's world? Not Clementine's—Em's, Em Oppen's. What did Em stand for? Em for Emily? for Emma? for Emmanuelle? Or did her students call her Ms. Oppen? Yes, thought Spurlock, this was her world and had been for years now. A Sidon graduate herself (as the library website had proudly proclaimed), she was now an employee, having departed for no longer than necessary to complete a library degree, and no farther away than the University of Illinois, Urbana-Champaign.

Since he had read the crabbed, blocky capitals of her name on the airmail envelope, the sealed envelope with its unknown contents, an urgency had propelled him forward, out of his office, toward the airport, toward Ohio. But now, however, all haste abandoned him, replaced by a dread and a longing to abort his journey. The taxi seemed suddenly to hurtle forward at alarming speed, now past flashing fields and silos, now into the leafy purlieus of the college town.

The feeling of wanting to turn back stayed with him, even after he had checked into the Sidon Inn. Though the afternoon was not far gone, his plan to deliver his letter this evening seemed to him suddenly impracticable. He needed to get his bearings. He should figure out where he could get something to eat. He would wait until morning to find the library where she worked.

He realized in the morning that he could hardly have missed it, the immense white marble cube standing out amid the earnest brick and stone of the other college buildings, like a spaceship in a used-car lot. Inside, he approached the circulation desk to ask for Archives and Special Collections. A student crowned in dirty-blond dreadlocks, neck tattooed with what looked like a morning glory vine, directed him to the fourth floor, then added with disarming chipperness, "I was just heading up there for my shift. I can take you there if you like."

"Um, first I have to—" said Spurlock, overcome by the desire to flee. But flee where? There was nothing to the town except for a ramshackle main street, where leather-necked farmers docked their pickups outside the diner, and little swarms of college students, trailing cigarette smoke and patchouli, hovered around the lanterned patio of a coffee shop called Torrify! There was a used-book store and an old art deco movie theater operated by the college's Film Studies Department. He didn't know what he had imagined for her, but it wasn't this earnest, threadbare place. "Actually," he said, "that would be very kind."

As they climbed the stairs to the Department of Archives and Special Collections, the student introduced herself as Cat and asked his name. "Nelson's a cool name," she announced, as though to reassure him. She explained that he'd have to leave his bag in a cubby outside the reading room, though he could keep his laptop. Nelson Spurlock did not have a laptop and blinked twice when Cat pointed to the stack of claim slips, "for when you want us to retrieve a title." Spurlock muttered something about needing to get settled and to "check the holdings," then felt himself blushing at the falsehood, but Cat merely buzzed him through a door into the small reading area, saying she'd be back to check on him in a little while. Spurlock found himself alone now, seated at a long table, in a book-musted stillness he had neither remembered nor missed since divinity school.

"Not a lot of business today," Spurlock ventured to Cat twenty minutes later when she returned.

"There never is. Unless one of the profs brings a class."

"Is Miss . . . Oppen in today?"

The name as he uttered it sounded like one he'd made up, but Cat replied, "Emmy? She should be. No requests?"

"No requests," said Spurlock, adding, "Not just yet," when he detected a quizzical edge in Cat's expression. He could ask to see her, but he knew he would be unable to state a reason for his visit and resolved to wait, laying out the envelopes down beside him, where they suggested with plausible fraudulence documents for a research project. After what must have been two hours, Cat poked her head into the reading room. "I'll be knocking off soon," she said. "You sure there's nothing I can call up for you?"

Spurlock surprised himself by saying, "Yes, in fact—Herbert. George Herbert, um, the Anglican divine, priest, I mean—his poems. You seem to have here—you appear to have a copy of— Just one minute and I'll have the slip made out."

Blundering around the computer catalog, Spurlock found the title, wrote out *"The Temple: Sacred Poems and Private Ejaculations"* on a call slip, and handed it to Cat. Spurlock braced himself for a quip about private ejaculations, but all she said was "Got it. Herbert, George. Back in a sec."

When Cat returned, the white gloves on her hands and the old volume they held stood out in sharp contrast with her dreadlocks and tattoos. She eased the book open on a pair of angled foam blocks she'd placed in front of Spurlock. "When you are done with it, just leave it on the blocks and let us know. We'll take care of it." The volume she'd presented was smaller than Spurlock imagined, re-bound in buckram, and the pages, when he opened them, displayed a hectic, almost childish disorder, with their *f*-shaped S's, the irregular spellings. Surely at one time, he thought, the text had seemed as transparent as daylight. For Spurlock, however, the pages appeared to busy themselves even as he watched—like an ant colony he'd kicked by accident—with the task of restoring and repairing their ruptured privacy. Abruptly, he realized he was reading lines he had encountered before.

> *Sweet day, so cool, so calm, so bright,*
> *The bridal of the earth and sky,*
> *The dew shall weep thy fall tonight*
>   *For thou must die.*

He recognized the tone, at once weightless and grave, before he recognized the words. Of course, it had been in Abend's confession. Not Abend's, Oppen's.

> *Sweet spring, full of sweet days and roses,*
> *A box where sweets compacted lie;*

My music shows ye have your closes,
*   And all must die.*

"*The Temple*," a voice said. "Cat told me you're working on *The Temple*." There she stood. The voice had been her voice. However much the intervening years had altered her, she was so undeniably herself that Spurlock was certain she too must recognize him, though he had long since shaved his beard. But of course she did not.

"Do you have a favorite?" she asked.

"A what?" he stammered. Her face was so plainly the same, yet just as surely changed, its lines not harsher with age but clearer, as though the years had brought her into focus.

"A favorite poem," she said.

"No," he said, then, "I mean, they are all my favorite. Favorites."

"May I?" she asked, lifting the book from the foam blocks in front of him. "I've been meaning to look through this since I first found it in the holdings."

She hummed under her breath as she flipped the pages.

"My father used to sing me one of these. Not that he could really sing," she said, smiling. "But we had a song, at bedtime. Herbert wrote the words; someone else set it to music." She began to hum again, this time a tentative tune. "Gak!" she said, and laughed. "I shouldn't have even tried!"

He could see how easily she had secured the job, her youth falling in her favor, an alumna of the college, friendly but poised, at ease in her surroundings. A sweet life it must be, he thought, to inhabit this quiet, the only sound the tap of rain on the glass. When had he known such silence in New York? When had the wash and jostle of the avenues not pressed in on him, even in his prayers, even in his long nights with the homeless in the impromptu shelter? Never, that's when. And why should the young not choose quiet, if they were moved to? So many had teemed to New York, it had never occurred to him others might set out in an opposite direction. Was this what she had sought, the leveling horizon, the quiet of rain on glass, where a stranger's arrival was something to notice? It occurred to Spurlock that his very presence (to say nothing of the envelope he'd brought) would breach the sanctuary she had sought out and painstakingly maintained.

"You'll let us know if you need something," she said.

"I promise I will let you know," Spurlock said, and she disappeared through the door marked *Stacks*.

What he needed, he thought, was to leave this place, to leave his envelopes on the table, tagged with a note saying nothing more than "For Em Oppen." Yes, a note. That was the way to do it. He would write it on the back of a call slip.

Spurlock lifted his pencil over the little slip and then stopped. He had assumed all along that she was entitled to her father's testament, that whatever madness or torment had claimed him, whatever privilege of secrecy her father had unilaterally invoked, the story was not his but hers. The testament had been detained in his possession, but now that Spurlock knew who she was, he could and should hand it over. But hadn't Spurlock—by reading it, by keeping it, by brooding on it, by refraining from seeking her out for seven years—had he not agreed implicitly to the terms that Oppen had laid out? Had Spurlock not consented to tell no one but God? Had he not afterward, in prayer, imagined even placing the envelope in Christ's pierced hands? And yet now he would merely abandon it, leave it, and leave her alone with it.

Perhaps there was a simpler option, a kinder one. Why not leave just the smaller airmail envelope, the one forwarded from the lawyers? That was the only one addressed to her. Yes, that was what he should do, he thought, but even then he could not move. Cat had left the reading room. Spurlock was alone.

During an interview for his job at the Church of the Incarnation, he'd said to his interviewers that he had sensed "a reservoir of prayer" held within the church's walls. The grandiloquence of the phrase had surprised him; what had he even meant by it? Maybe he had felt—or wanted to feel—that the church was a sort of cistern or catchment basin, a pool into which the halt and the lame, himself included, could immerse themselves and be healed. Or maybe he had just repeated, unwittingly, an orotund locution he'd heard or read somewhere before. He realized, abashed, that he'd had no idea what he had meant then, but now this unvisited room seemed such a reservoir to him. The silence over which the nearly forgotten books presided seemed to him a holy silence, the silence of things that had come to an end.

Likewise his long journey had come to an end. Having done obediently what had been asked of him, he could lay his burden down, hallelujah. Something, however, hounded him still. He knew it had to do with that other, deeper desire to affix a name to her face, the face of the girl-no-longer who had appeared seven years ago in his church—to affix not just a name, but his own wondering gaze. But in this silence of things that had come to an end, Spurlock saw at last that underneath the obedience and longing, a darker motive lay: to pry free once and for all a foreign body, a hook, a barb set in the bone. Yes, that was the way David Oppen himself had described it. It had lodged in him seven years ago, that longing, that question—Who are you, Clementine?—and only one person could allay that ache. His heart knocked in his chest.

"I've got it now," she was saying. "I know what it was."

She had pushed through the door and had rested a stack of books she was carrying on the edge of his table. "I won't try to sing it," she had said. "Lucky you."

"Sing what?"

" 'Come, My Way,' that hymn I told you about. That's what it's called. You must know it."

Did she know he was a priest? Spurlock wondered, his heart knocking louder. Had she recognized him? But then he remembered the book he'd requested. Surely an expert on Herbert would know the words.

"Yes, I do know it," he said, hearing the tune in his head, a common hymn, frequently sung in his church. He'd not known the words had been written by George Herbert, but then again, he'd not known of

George Herbert until he'd read Oppen's testament. "'Come, My Way,'" he said, "I know it well. Your father sang it to you?"

"Before bed," she said. "One of those childhood memories." She had lifted the stack of books to take them to wherever she was taking them.

Spurlock, however, had stood up and was facing her.

"Miss Abend . . . ," he said, "if I may call you that."

She stopped and stiffened. A long second passed before he grasped what he had just said. "Miss Oppen, I should say."

"May I help you?" she said, her face ticking a half degree to one side.

"I must tell you—" he said. "I must tell you the real reason I've come here. I have something to deliver to you."

"To me?"

"You are Miss Em Oppen, no?"

"And you, you are . . . ?"

"My name is Spurlock, Father Nelson Spurlock, rector of the Church of the Incarnation in New York. We met some years ago, when you came to my church. You wanted to know then whether your father had sent you something, in my care."

"Spurlock—" she said.

"I had a beard then," he said, adding inanely, "I was younger then." He was now holding the envelopes, holding them out to her, both of them, the smaller airmail envelope and the larger bulk of Oppen's testament. When she saw the packets, her face took on a gray sheen.

"Maybe—" she said, "maybe we'd better go outside."

The rain had turned to a tight mist that beaded minutely, he noticed, on her hair as they walked. They had passed from the library through the quadrangle. A sort of converted golf cart, bristling with gardening tools, was parked to one side of the path where a groundskeeper on all fours troweled up a flower bed. "Afternoon, Emmy," he said as they walked by.

"Hey there, Ray," she said. "Is the arboretum open this time of year?"

"The arb?" he said. "Don't know how we'd close it. . . ."

✳   ✳   ✳

The hinges sang when she swung open the arboretum gate, and together they walked along a broad cinder path that crunched beneath their feet. The path wound past clumps of sumac and blackthorn, between swaths of long brown grass flattened by winter, disturbed here and there by first green. Although the fine rain had not quite let up, the clouds had broken up in chunks, pried apart, it seemed to Spurlock, by the late light leaning in oblique beams. Bare branches vibrated in the freshened chill. "Cold front," she said, "looks like.

"Welcome to my office," she said, pointing to a U-shaped stone bench beneath a stand of evergreens overlooking a swale of new-mown grass.

"You came here from New York just to give me these?" She had taken both envelopes, hefting their weight.

"You should have them," he said.

"But what are they?"

He felt she had had to force herself to ask the question.

"They are for you."

"But the big one isn't even addressed to me. It's addressed to you."

"They are both for you."

"Who sent them?"

Spurlock hesitated, then said, "I don't know," moved by the sense that his response was both dishonest and true.

"You are going back to New York now," she said. It was a statement, not a question.

"My flight leaves tomorrow."

"So it wasn't really our extensively unremarkable George Herbert holdings that brought you here," she said with something not quite a smile.

"I'll look up that hymn when I get back."

"You should know it. You're a priest."

"So they insist."

"I could tell you to come back and visit, but people never do."

"Do you ever get back to New York?" he asked.

"One day I'll go back. See what it's been up to."

"Pretty here," he said, imagining how in the warmth of the coming months, students would gather on this slope to sun themselves.

For a while she did not speak but at last stood up from the bench. "I'm going to go now," she said. "I'm going to find a place where I can read these things." Spurlock, awkwardly, stood up too. "Do you need directions back to the hotel? If you get lost you'll be the first in town history." She gave a little laugh. "I don't want to seem ungrateful. I just don't know what to say. You made the trip, which I cannot believe. Thank you. That's what I should say, all I should say."

"I don't know if you should thank me," said Spurlock. "And I don't know if I should say you're welcome. But I hope you will be in touch if the spirit moves."

Somewhere beyond the field's edge, a crow's percussive cry dislodged a series of echoes. Another crow answered, and for a moment the overlapping echoes contended in free air. She was gone.

Later that night, having returned to the bench where she had led him, Spurlock sensed that daybreak was not far off. The last darkness had settled now into the trees like a sediment cast from the sky, the sky not lighter now but clarified. Spurlock felt the tug of the old summons. Now, he thought, now would be the moment to pray, to tap into the silence and stillness hidden under the surface of his being, like the dome of a water table beneath an irregular terrain. Now would be the moment, but this unfamiliar landscape pressed upon him the weight of an absolute solitude. His task accomplished, he had expected a wave of relief, the satisfaction of release after long suffering: that old knot finally loosened, that barb at last freed from the bone. But there was no sense of ease, no restoration. Instead, he felt sacked, used up, spent in a service neither chosen nor understood.

*   *   *

"Nelson," she said.

He had not heard her approach. He turned and squinted: her face was indistinct, her hair loose and heavy, hazed with a coppery border against a sky red at her back. As she walked toward him, her feet had marked a green track in the dew. "I was afraid you'd already gone," she said. "There was no answer in your room." She sat down beside him on the bench.

"I didn't sleep either," he said.

"But still I had a terrible dream," she said.

Spurlock said nothing. It was his doing. He had handed it over to her in a thick packet.

"It's like he said," she continued at last, "it's like what Dad—like what David said: I am certain that on some level I always knew."

"What did you know?" asked Spurlock.

"Just that . . . just . . ." As she hesitated, Spurlock noticed for the first time that her hands were empty. She had not brought the heavy envelope with her. "Just that I knew. I knew ever since I knew anything that something wasn't right."

"What did you know?" asked Spurlock, unaware that he had just asked the same question.

"Which is absurd," she went on. "When did anyone, anywhere, ever feel that everything was exactly right?" She was looking down at her long shadow. "But I knew, and he knew I knew, that something wasn't right. What he didn't know was that it didn't matter. When I grew up, I was pissed off, like every other teenager. I know he thought I was angry because I suspected something. He thought that my anger would drive me to hunt for reasons, causes. But he was wrong about that. I was angry not because I didn't know something, I was furious because it didn't matter what I knew. It didn't matter what was fucked up in him or in his past or in Miriam. It didn't matter because they were the people I came from. They weren't even my parents, not my real parents, and still they were the people I came from. You can't choose the people you come from."

"He let your mother die," said Spurlock, the fact real to him as it had never been before. "Your mother, the girl who gave birth to you, she was younger than you are now."

"It didn't matter."

"He could have saved her, but he let her die instead." The fact faced him, in its horrid nakedness. "It was an inhuman act."

"Inhuman," she repeated, in neither agreement nor denial.

"I thought . . . ," she said after a pause, "I thought last night—or rather this morning, when I'd finished reading what he'd written—all of a sudden it all seemed just incredibly strange, being here, in Ohio, in Ohio of all places, for God's sake. Like I'd been dropped here by a freak waterspout. That I'd been abandoned."

"You were." Spurlock was aware that this expression of empathy concealed within it an insistence that she accept his conviction as her own.

"Yes, I know that. I believe I've always known that. And I was furious ever since I could remember. What is more natural? Inhuman, you say— which is strange, because what I thought last night, this morning, was that outrage is a human thing. But they aren't human anymore, Miriam, David, the girl who was my mother. They are all gone, and whatever they were, they aren't that any longer."

She said, "It's not that I'm trying to let him off the hook. It's that *I* am the hook. Once he had me, he couldn't let me go."

"But he did let you go. He left you an orphan."

"Like every parent does, sooner or later. And anyway, Reverend Father Nelson Spurlock, aren't you supposed to say something now about my being the child of God, about forgiveness?"

"Am I?" The very possibility of forgiveness struck him as obscene, an offense, in some literal way unthinkable. He wanted to say that forgiveness would be an outrage. But he said nothing, silenced by the thought that true forgiveness must always be an outrage, an affront to justice's imperious claims. In fact it was inescapably unjust.

"Anyway, if you had known him," she said, "you would have seen it, the sadness. You would have felt that something was off, that there was a sickness, that he knew—" She stopped.

"That he knew what he had done?"

"He knew one day it had to end. That made him vigilant. To keep it . . ." She paused again.

"To keep the lie hidden."

"No, not that, not that at all," she insisted with vehemence. "He just wanted to hold on to it while he could. That was the sadness in him. Because he knew he couldn't hold on to it forever."

"To hold on to you."

"To— Yes, no, you are right: to me," she said, as though she had never thought of it that way. "I was his reprieve, right? As his child, I was a reminder of the past—its embodiment, even, in the most literal way. He knew that one day there would have to be a reckoning. But I was his daughter, and that meant that the reckoning had to wait. He had to see me grown, to send me off. So as his child I represented . . ." She hesitated. "I was his crime, but at the same time, I was his reprieve."

"I see it," said Spurlock. "I see it now."

"Whatever his correspondent told him," she went on, "David knew already. It wasn't news. It was what he'd known all along."

Spurlock said nothing.

She continued: "Even last night, as I was reading it, I was convinced—at least, I tried to convince myself—that he'd just made it all up. I mean, he'd already made up my past, he'd made up all the whole elaborate story of how Miriam was my mother. Surely then he could have made up the story of the letters too, the postal box, the photographs, the correspondent. Page after page, I told myself that was what he'd done."

"Is it possible?" Hope surged up in Spurlock. The possibility that Oppen could have invented it all flared with the vividness of a hallucination. "Could he have done that? Could he have made them up, the letters, the photographs?"

"No—I mean, maybe I would have believed it, maybe I would have convinced myself, if it wasn't for the other letter you brought."

The other letter: Spurlock had been so preoccupied with whether to give her Oppen's confession that he had forgotten about the other letter, the one in the blue airmail envelope.

"What did it say?" he asked.

For several seconds she said nothing. Finally, she took the envelope from the pocket of her jeans. She tore open the flap, withdrew a sheaf of light pages, and began to read.

Mon cher enfant—

Why had he not considered that it would be in French? He remembered the day, years earlier, when she had appeared in the church and unfolded that first sheet of paper, the sheet on which he had seen his own name caught in the snare of a language he had never spoken.

"I'll translate as I go along," she said.

"'My dear child,'" she began.

I would spare you the story, but it is not fair that you remain uninformed, and I am a fair man. Do your hands tremble, holding these pages sent to you by a stranger? You see how mine tremble too, writing these words, and not only because I am an old man. I can feel how death grows impatient of my dawdling. You will understand how strange it is for me to address you in this manner, strange because you are in fact no stranger to me. After all, dear child, I have known you since the day you were born.

I say death grows impatient of my dawdling. Perhaps I am the impatient one. I have never feared death; indeed, he has been my faithful companion. He was my playmate, looking with me through the magnifying glass at the ants I burned up in the sun. He crouched with me beside the first hare I shot as the last flutter of life departed the small body. He was my steadfast comrade in the Algerian war, where I served in the Signal Corps. There we were inseparable, and he never faltered, never rested.

But then he took my young wife, the mother of my only child, and next, as though this too were his right, my daughter too, my Miriam.

You see, child, how age has taken from me any scruple for
what I say.

You never knew her, my Miriam. She drowned before you
were born. It was as though death were jealous that I should
presume to make a life for myself, for my little family, enraged that
after the obscenity of Algeria I should clothe myself in respectabil-
ity as Maître Levaux, solicitor, in the provincial city of Nevers. Me!
Maître Levaux, who had been death's agent and his entrepreneur,
all through the battle for Algiers, or in the CRA at Constantine,
who with the most rudimentary objects—a coil of wire, a bucket of
water—could anticipate and satisfy his most extravagant desires. It
was as though he was saying: I will not permit you to abandon me.

I did not ask why he chose me. He loved me, I thought, because I
loved justice, and I could not love justice without loving him as well. It
was as though he said: I made you; you cannot leave me.

"It is— He is Miriam's father," she said, looking at Spurlock in wonder before turning back to the pages.

My daughter, Miriam, you never knew her.

I kept asking her, is it someone, and she kept saying, it is everything. You are pregnant, I said, and she knew that I knew, but she
said no, no, no, no one, it was impossible. I said it must be someone:
you are carrying someone's child. She said that I must stop, that one
could not choose, that no one could choose who or what one loved.

This of course proved that she had been alienated from her
senses.

Did he abandon you, I asked, and she said, everyone abandons
everyone, and anyway it's not anyone, it's not anything, it is everything.

For a moment then I thought it would be all right, that it was
only one of her spells. She had always had spells. Her attempt
to kill herself, she had said it was an error, an accident, that it
could never happen again. She promised me it would never hap-

pen again. She said: I could not give it to you lightly, my word
of honor. And I who have never believed anyone believed her,
because she was my daughter. She embraced me and said she was
sorry and asked would I forgive her? Would I promise? I said—and
it was the last thing I ever said to her—there was nothing to forgive.

Then she had gone. In two days they found me and gave me
the news.

I went immediately to Nevers. My inquiries there were brief and
straightforward. Yes, said the shopkeeper at the hardware store in
Nevers, the girl had come in and purchased a great length of chain.
The police had inquired as well, and a tall Dutchman had come in
too, not long after, looking for chain, just like the girl had. Maybe he
had been English. Yes, he could have been American. He was drunk
and had frightened her. In the end, all he had bought was a hammer
and chisel.

Others had seen him too, I discovered, in the place Carnot, on
the rue Saint-Étienne. An American of his description had taken a
tent site at the campground across the river, a notable fact, because
the nights were still cold.

Within days I had learned all there was to learn. The man was
David Oppen, an American. It was not, as she had said, anyone
or everything, but a specific person, an American, a man named
David Oppen.

David Oppen. I say the name now, and it is just as intolerable as
it was a quarter century ago. But—I cannot deny it—that name was
a gift to me. Though grief had thrown my life into disarray, a new
purpose had driven out that darkness. I say new purpose, but in truth
it was none other than my old beloved, justice and justice alone. Its
light like a lantern flame had singled out the name of David Oppen
and had fastened an indelible shadow to his heel.

I became a foreigner, a sojourner in my hometown, pitching
an old army tent on the other side of the campground, disguising
myself as a tourist with camera and sunglasses, not so much to

conceal myself from Oppen but against chance encounters with
my own acquaintances. Dislodged from the groove of routine, how
abruptly one vanishes. . . .

I'd affected the camera merely as a component of my disguise, but
then it occurred to me that I could use it to take pictures. Soon each
click of the shutter afforded me an instant of relief, a flash of hope
that an explanation would be disclosed, a pattern revealed. This
hope grew. As for David Oppen, he leant each night against the
railing of the bridge, appeared daily at the shop where he bought his
liquor, nodded on park benches like a derelict, but mostly walked
and walked and walked.

I might have understood that his grief was a cousin of my grief.
I might have understood that he had lost a Miriam all his own. I
might have, but I did not. For me there was one fact and one fact
only: he was alive and Miriam was dead. Click went my camera,
and the lens snapped up image after image, as though it had been
starved. Knowledge or understanding could not satisfy this hunger.
Only justice could: justice, I knew, was the sustenance of the gods.

When I saw him outside the pharmacy, leaning over that
drugged-out Gypsy girl in the bushes, helping her to her feet—
when I saw that the girl was pregnant, that he was helping her
home, I saw no Good Samaritan. No: what I saw was an opportunity, an opening. I neither knew nor understood what I saw,
feeling only the first inkling of a conviction: justice had chosen
me and would show me the way. If I held fast, in time I would be
rewarded. What I was owed would be delivered into my hands.

Hanging a block behind them, I followed them on their slow
progress through the streets. I watched them disappear behind
the plywood sheet propped over the entrance to an abandoned
construction site out on the rue Saint-Saturnin. I returned to the
campground to wait.

I did not have to wait for long. That night, a young man appeared on a motorbike at the campground where David Oppen

had rented a tent site, the campground in whose opposite corner
I had pitched my own moth-eaten army tent. The young man was
shouting: Where was he, the American doctor? For God's sake,
where was he?

The American doctor? I said, emerging. You'll find him in his
campsite down by the water.

After they had left the campground on the young man's motorbike, I followed without haste, out to the unbuilt building on
the rue Saint-Saturnin. In the shadows of the rue Saint-Saturnin, I
waited.

Abruptly, the boy on his motorbike burst from the mouth of
the garage, skidding to a stop on the street, frozen in indecision.
For a moment he rested his forehead on his handlebars. Then
he lifted his head, and looking straight at me or through me, he
planted his heel on the pavement, wrenched his bike around, and
sped away in the direction of the ring-road and the autoroute.

Nothing happened. The sky stayed black. I waited. The plywood board hung open on its hinge as though inviting me to pass
through. I passed through.

From the edge of the ramp I could peer down into the garage.
They lay in the weak light of a candle or lantern. They did not
move, neither the girl nor David Oppen, nor the little shape between them, or the dog at their feet. It was as though they had been
carved on the lid of a tomb. I had to rest the camera on the railing:
the shutter hung open for what seemed like seconds, soaking the
film with that darkness. The shutter closed and the dog jerked. I
fought back the urge to retreat from my post. I waited until I was
satisfied I had escaped notice then slipped back out to the street.

Shortly after daybreak he emerged, torso bare in the cold
morning, in his arms a bundle wrapped in a bloody shirt. He
veered out into the street, bellowing for help. Then police cars
bumped up onto the curbs, their strobes reeling. At last the strobes
faded, and I was just another of the gathered passersby, the frowning, shrugging citizens of Nevers.

All day, from a chair in a waiting room in the Hôpital Colbert, I watched the nurses as they came and went. At last I approached one and explained how I happened to have been walking past when the man, the American, appeared in the street with the baby he had saved. Could she reassure me that the little one would be all right? No, no, I said, I did not need to visit! If she could just reassure me. Oh yes, she was happy to assure me how lucky the girl had been, how lucky that the American doctor had appeared, that she had been rescued from that basement from those filthy Gypsy kids. And had I heard? Why, the American doctor had arranged for the baby's transfer to Paris, to the Necker Pediatric Hospital, at his own expense. Was that so? Yes, it was so, and to the Hôpital Necker, no less!

In Paris, I took a room in a veterans' pension and joined the cadre of Necker volunteers. I assisted parents in their distress, accompanied them in their vigils, sat with them in their grief, all the while watching out for the bent silhouette of the American doctor in the waiting rooms. He was no longer intoxicated but alert, not reading, not watching the whispering televisions mounted on the walls. He merely stared at the floor as though waiting for it to open up. Nine weeks you were there, my child, until you were transferred to the Maison Nôtre Dame. It was from one of the nuns at the Maison that I learned the American doctor had filed for your adoption.

One day when you, my child, have a child of your own, you will learn what otherwise cannot be taught: that this tiny stranger was fated to appear here, to take its place in this world. This I learned staring at my daughter, Miriam, when she nursed in my wife's arms. She was frighteningly small, born almost two months early. How precarious she seemed, and yet she too had steered her way through all time to be here.

After he took you from the Maison Nôtre Dame, after he brought you to America, to New York, it took me a full year to catch up with him. During that year I traveled first to Canada, much easier to immigrate to than the States. In Québec I met some Basque shepherds from the Ossau Valley in the French Pyrénées, on their way back to ranches in Alberta. Their village in France would have been less than a day's drive from Nevers, but their dialect was incomprehensible to me. They were by nature suspicious of any non-Basque Frenchman, but in the end I earned their trust. They had cousins working in Wyoming, and so to Wyoming I went on a shepherding visa. Back then, such a thing was possible, encouraged even, and the pay was good. By the end of the second lambing season, I had learned a little English, a little Basque, even a little Spanish from the Mexican farmhands. I had learned enough to permit someone now answering to the Basque name Itzal Etxebarria to work his way into the confraternity of doormen back in New York. I started as a janitor, living at a YMCA, pitching in on garbage days up and down Oppen's block. I made it known I was always ready to perform odd handyman jobs in his building, always ready to step in when the other doormen were sick. I was ready when a position became available in the building. Why not Itzal? He knows us. He is a stable, trustworthy sort. So they said on the co-op board, agreeing to sponsor me for my green card.

You were three years old then, your father unchanged, save for hair now gray at the temples. He took great care that you would always greet me politely, and in French. Bonjour, Itsy! you would say. Such an agreeable little girl you were. Do you remember it, our little game? Bonjour, Amy! I would say, and you would say, I'm not Amy, Itsy! I'm Emmy! And I would be sure to make the same mistake again, knowing that for my part I would never say, I'm not Itzal Etxebarria, I'm Yves, Yves Levaux, the father of Miriam.

The girl, Jessica Burke, your father's patient: she was the key. A kind girl, but troubled. For her appointments with David Oppen she would often arrive early, and rather than waiting in the little seating area outside his office, she and I would smoke together on

the sidewalk. "Señor Itzal," she would say, accepting my light, "one
of the last smokers in New York." She said, "I want to be a Basque
shepherd in Wyoming. Make it happen for me, Itzal!" Because I was
a doorman and immigrant, I could ask her anything. Did she have
family? (Only her mother.) Did she have a boyfriend? (No. Love was
a lie. She lived alone.) What did she need an expensive head-doctor
for? "Oh, Itzal," she would say, "life is complicated, and I don't have
any sheep to talk to. Don't you miss home?"

It was much easier than it had been in Algeria, because the micro-
phones by then were so much smaller. All I had to do was drill a
little hole from the basement up through the floor under the couch
in David Oppen's ground-floor office. The tapes I made, I would
listen to them into the night, taking notes, erasing them before
morning. I began by recording all of his patients, but in time I taped
only Jessica Burke. I could not have said what I was listening for, but
I knew I had what I needed when she mentioned a poem, a poem
she described in detail to him. "The Stolen Child," it was called, by
William Yeats. As for David Oppen, he knew it well. So he said to
Jessica Burke. Of course he did. It had been one of Miriam's favorites; she had performed a setting of it the year before she died.

    It was only once I had learned how to wait without knowing
why, nor what for, nor for how long, that she was given into my
possession. I was working the night shift; it must have been midnight, or a little after. She was desperate, crying, hysterical, and her
breath bore a volatile odor. Itzal, she said, you have to help me.
At first I thought, insanely, that she had come for my aid, but of
course she had come for Dr. Oppen. Itzal, you have to make him.
You have to make him come down. You don't understand. He
doesn't understand.

    I said I could call him on the intercom, and she said she had
called him already on the telephone, that she had only reached
his answering machine. I told her to wait and I would get him. I
would go to his apartment. I told her to wait for me on the lobby

bench. That is what I said to her, but at his door—at your door—
I stopped. I did not knock. The little peephole in the door was
dark. I stood there and I waited. Minutes passed. Without knocking, I turned and went back downstairs. In the vestibule I told her
he was not at home.

He has to be home, Itzal, she said. We have a session tomorrow. He has a daughter.

I told her there had been no answer.

He needs to help me, she said. Itzal, he needs to help me.

Let me help you, I said, but she only repeated herself. He
needs to help me. He needs to help me.

You are tired. You are just very tired, Jessica. Everything will be
better in the morning, I said, aware only that these were the words
I had said, again and again, to Miriam, my daughter, when her
spells took hold of her.

Yes, she said finally. She made a little laugh. Everything will be
better in the morning. I'm sorry, Itzal. I'm going home now.

I followed her out, catching up to her a little way down the
sidewalk. I told her I was worried for her, that I would call her, that
if I didn't reach her I would come and check on her. I made her
tell me her address, and she watched me write it down.

At two in the morning, the night shift ended. Her building was
only six blocks away. It would have been about 2:10 or 2:15 when
I arrived. I rang her bell, but there was no response. I waited to see
if anyone arrived or left. No one came. Finally, I pressed my hand
along all the buttons on the panel. Someone, expecting someone
else, tripped the buzzer and I was inside.

I knocked on her door, though I knew she would not respond.
It was unlocked. I opened it and stepped into the darkness of her
apartment. From the bathroom came the sound of water. I sat
on the edge of her bed. Behind the closed door, the water kept
running, just a trickle, and that was the only noise. In the room I
breathed the smell of paint, of linseed oil and turpentine.

What looked like heavy blankets had been hung over the windows. When my vision adapted to the shadows I could make out sheets of paper or photographs clipped to a string stretched across the corner of the room, alongside thinner strips suspended like ribbons, negatives, I decided. Her apartment must also be her darkroom. How long did I wait there, and for what? I was aware that someone, anyone, having observed an intruder standing outside the apartment of a single woman, could have called the police. Perhaps I was waiting for the police. Perhaps, on the other hand, there would be the noise of splashing water, and Jessica Burke, having risen from her bath, would appear in the bathroom doorway, naked or wrapped in a towel. But no police arrived, and the only noise was the uninterrupted trickle from the bathroom.

The needle still hung from her vein. When I touched her fingers they were cold. Her pulse was nearly undetectable, and her skin had darkened as though tarnished. Beside the bathtub, a candle had burnt down nearly to the floor. Under her sink, I located a stash of plastic sacks stuffed into an emptied tin. I removed one, and after searching a little longer, found a roll of masking tape next to her developing chemicals. I had to hold her upright to keep her from slipping down into the bathwater as I positioned the sack over her head, drawing the edges down and securing them with tape around her neck. Where the sack molded to her face, two little patches of mist, no bigger than bee's wings, appeared against the plastic beneath her nostrils.

The camera I found was a Leica, with a flat lens and no flash. It was already loaded with slow film, so I pulled down the blanket from her bathroom window, hoping to bring in the glare of a streetlight. I was amazed to discover instead that day had broken. First light streamed through the window onto her body. The patches of mist inside the plastic bag had now disappeared. Click went the shutter. Then once, twice again. I shot the entire roll, then removed the plastic sack and put it along with the camera in

my pocket. I listened from behind her door for any sounds in the
hallway. Hearing none, I slipped out into the hallway, down the
stairs, and out onto the street.

Later, when I walked by on my lunch break, there were two
police cars and an ambulance outside the building, their strobe
lights off, some uniformed officers standing on the sidewalk, drink-
ing coffee. I waited until the paramedics had brought her down,
face covered, on a stretcher, and watched as they loaded her into a
low and windowless white van. The other vehicles dispersed. The
police did not notice me. No one asked what I was doing there.
Nothing happened.

I rented a darkroom by the hour downtown and developed roll
after roll of film—hundreds of pictures I had taken for practice of
the wall or the window—until I was confident enough to develop
the roll of film I had taken in Jessica Burke's bathroom. When I
saw it, finally, the image of her body in the bathtub, I knew what
I had and what in time I would do with it. Even before I sent it to
David Oppen, before I saw on his face what he had seen in the
envelope, I knew that the hook was set. From that moment on,
even when I was doing nothing but watching, standing behind the
grille of your building's door waiting for him to appear, I could feel
it, the weight and tension on my line, the force of his struggle, and
the strength with which he exhausted his strength.

For three years my only care was that the line would not break.
You grew into a teenager. Your beauty settled on you, whether you
liked it or not, and acceded to your womanhood. I watched you
make your peace with this, even as I sensed in you the infiltration
of a malaise. You no longer called me Itsy. You said you were leaving for France, as soon as you could. Through the line I felt the vi-
bration of your father's agony as though it were my own. You would
leave as soon as you could, and when you left, I would be ready.

More than fifteen years had passed since I had set foot in my country, or should I say, our country? You could have no memory of it,

and what I saw in Paris I hardly recognized: new heroic architecture crowding the Seine and the avenues, American coffee shops, Russians on the Faubourg Saint-Honoré, Senegalese priests in the pulpits. You were not, for all that, difficult to find, nor was it difficult for me to blend in—no longer Basque, no longer Itzal Etxebarria, just an aging Frenchman like so many others. You never noticed me. How could you have? You were not looking for Itzal the doorman, but for someone you had never seen. You were looking for Miriam's parents. How close I came to you that day in the café as you pored over that map of the Morvan, that range of black hills rising east of Nevers and the farmland of the Nivernais.

It was there, in the Morvan, you came looking for me. It was there, after my departure from New York, that I had broken open the door of my house—hardly a house, really a cabin—and swept away the cobwebs and accumulated dormouse droppings. The cabin is the only possession I had kept in France, paying the pittance of tax I owed with an American money order sent in once a year. The run-down structure had been my father's, and before that his great-uncle's. Originally it had been a tenant farmer's, one half for housing animals, the other for human habitation, a single room with an open hearth. My wife and I would bring Miriam there on the weekends; it is not far from Nevers. The land around it was sold long ago, so aside from the building itself, all I own is a little gravel court enclosed by a hedgerow on three sides and by the house on the fourth, the hillside sloping up behind it. My nearest neighbor lived almost a kilometer away, a spinster who had for reasons I never knew nursed a grudge against my father and all Levaux. She allowed the use of her telephone at the rate of one franc—now one euro—per call. When I took up occupancy again after my long absence, I undertook to cultivate her favor, clearing brush from her woods, and, on the morning you appeared, carting her garbage to the town dump in her old Renault sedan.

It had been in the same moldering sedan that I had made my final trip to the post office, to send my final letter to David Oppen.

Every New Year, David Oppen had given me a gratuity, two stiff new hundred-dollar bills folded in a card. You would sign the card too—just a little scribble at first. Naturally, receiving even a single cent from him would be intolerable, but the fact that he tipped me twice as much as any other resident was torture. Of course I could not spend the money, but I did force myself to keep it. I set it aside. The years went by. The stack of bills grew, folded over and stuffed in a bandage tin. A week or so before you appeared on my hillside, I had taken the money out of its tin. I counted it. A little over three thousand dollars. The sum no longer tormented me because I knew what I would do with it. I would prepare the last letter.

My last letter: it was smaller than some of the others had been, just a regular envelope in which I had placed the two tickets I had purchased with the folded bills, one for the flight from New York to Paris, the other for rail passage from Paris to Nevers.

Along with the tickets, I had sent a small photograph of some items I had assembled in the underbrush of the riverbank, just downstream of the Isle of Terns: a length of chain, purchased at the hardware store LaPorte, as well as a flywheel from an old steam pump, bought at a flea market. I placed this little sheaf of documents in an envelope addressed to David Oppen at his postal box, our little rendezvous. I had seen his face after I sent the photograph of Jessica Burke. I knew how deeply the hook was set in him, how inexorable the compulsion to return to the box, to learn what awaited him there.

The day you appeared at my house in the Morvan was only two or three days after I sent that letter. When I had returned my neighbor's Renault after carting her garbage to the dump, she said to me, "Your American granddaughter is coming to visit you." Of course I told her I had no granddaughter, American or otherwise. She said, "Monsieur, it is not impossible that you would have a granddaughter whom you do not know," then announced with evident pride that she had received a call from this person, not an hour earlier. My neighbor said that this person sounded Parisian but claimed she was American, and had stated that she hoped she could pay her grandfather a visit. She was to arrive in the afternoon.

I made it known to my neighbor that I had no intention of staying at home to receive a nonexistent granddaughter. Nevertheless I hurried back, and in great agitation contrived to spend the rest of the day on the far side of the hedgerow bordering my yard, pretending to trim the outer side even though the cows had already cropped it. When you arrived, you appeared alone, on foot, though you must have hitched a ride from the station in Luzy. Through a gap in the hedge, I watched you knock at my door, and knock again. Finally you tore off a corner of your map, took out a pen, and leaning against the jamb, began to write a note.

Even when I had seen you poring over maps of Nevers and its environs at that café in Paris, I had thought only of how David Oppen would respond if he learned you were planning such a trip. I had never considered it possible that you would in fact locate my little, hidden house. Yet there you were, leaning against the side of the door, scratching your pen against the paper, struggling to make it write. You shook it, touched the tip to your tongue, scratched it again—but nothing. You pried the little plug from the rear of the pen and blew into it. Finally you gave up, and after walking once around the house, hoisting yourself on tiptoe beneath the windows to peer inside, you stared for a long minute out over the valley before turning and walking down toward the main road.

What would you have said to old man Levaux, had he appeared from behind the hedgerow? What would you have done when you realized, as he approached, that the Yves Levaux you sought was none other than Itzal Etxebarria? And what would I have done? Watching you struggle with the pen, watching you hesitate before knocking a second time on the door, or standing on tiptoe, your hand cupped against the dark glass, I knew then that I could never touch a hair of your head.

I had climbed up behind the house so that I could watch you

as you departed. If you had looked up onto the hillside, I think
now that you would have seen me. But of course you did not look
up, and of course you did not see me. You did not see that I was
weeping. I know now that I would not see you again, the little
American girl who had called me Itsy, the little American girl who
was now a beautiful young woman who had come to find me,
out of the desire to know her past, out of love for the woman she
believed to be her mother—and had now disappeared forever. But
at that moment I believed I wept because I had released my grip
on the snare I had knotted and reknotted, night after night. I wept,
I thought, because I myself had been freed from the snare.

That was the moment, precisely, when it ended. The dream
had simply released me, the dream of revenge that had devoured
all the long years since Miriam took her life. When I reached the
house, there was no trace of you anywhere, no note, no exhausted
pen, not even a crumpled scrap of map. I knew then there was no
chain that could not be cut, no sentence that could not be com-
muted. I knew that there was no one who could not be freed, even
from such a snare as I had knotted—night after night, year after
year. I cannot explain the joy I felt when I thought: You are no kin
to me. No blood of mine flows in your veins. It was with an un-
speakable tenderness I thought: You, child, are a stranger to me.

On the heels of that recognition came another. I understood
that the letter I had sent, my final invitation to David Oppen,
would be the last contact between us. I knew that he would not
obey my summons and appear. I was not disappointed. In fact, this
realization seemed to restore me to a spotless innocence, accompanied by a surge of distilled contempt. Of course he would not appear. Holding those tickets, reading their dates and destinations, he
would see the path open before him, the path that justice required
him to take. He would see the path, he would hesitate, and in the
end he would turn away, his future a coward's future.

With what pleasure I envisioned for him the agony of the
following weeks, the wait between his refusing my summons and

the moment when finally after months of silence he would hear your voice again. You would tell him you were tired and penniless and done with traveling and wanted to come home. Without your knowing it, your voice would also inform him that I had released you. He would know then that perfect justice had tracked him down, had lain in wait, had breathed upon him, and with godly disdain had cast him aside.

It was not that my plan had failed, only that its fruition was utterly unlike what I had imagined. The moment had arrived, and the plan had been accomplished, but not in the service of revenge. Instead, the accomplishment was an intolerable mercy. My trap would shut, but not on a victim. It would instead shut like a book, a book of accounts zeroed out and closed forever.

Just as I had let you walk free, down the hill away from my house, I had let him free as well. No one would appear on the bank of the Loire at the appointed hour. I alone would be the one to finish it, carrying the weight of chain and the flywheel out into the channel. I would be the one to lay down the burden in the Loire, to cast it away and emerge again on the bank, alive, dripping, and released.

That is how it could have happened. That is how it should have happened. So you can imagine my astonishment when he did appear on the riverbank, at the appointed hour. What froze me was the realization that the net I had knotted night after night was not of my solitary handiwork, but that it had been a secret, silent collaboration. All along another set of hands had been just as busily knotting and reknotting the opposite edge of the net. His labor had been as dogged and intent as my own, though what his fingers fashioned was not a snare but a shroud.

"Etxebarria, Itzal," he said to me, and then, "Monsieur Levaux."

"Do you know how long I have waited for this rendezvous, Mr. Oppen?" I asked him.

"Yes," he said. "I do know how long."

"Out there, just beyond this little island, which is called the Isle of Terns. That is where she drowned."

"I know," he said. "With our child."

"Yes," I said, "with the child."

"I assume—you brought it with you, everything—" he said, "everything necessary." Without waiting for confirmation, he continued. "First, though, a request," he said, pressing into my hands something he had carried, a heavy package. "It is for a priest, in America. Please send it for me. It is, you could say, a sort of confession." The package was a block of unbound pages, wrapped in a heavier paper and tied with twine.

"It is not for the girl?" I asked.

"She does not know. She cannot," he said.

"She tried to find me—" I said, and sensed a chill pass through his body with this news, "but she did not. I saw to it. The girl is free."

"Free," he said, as though the word were strange to him. "She must learn that now. You know where she is. Let my lawyer know where he can find her. His name is Hale, Albert Hale. He will tell her what happened to me."

"As are you, Oppen," I said. "You are free. You are free to leave this place."

I spoke again: "I mean what I say, Oppen. It is over." I pressed the package back into his hands. "Go find the girl," I said. "She has no parent but you." It was only after speaking these last words that I understood how irreparably they had torn me. They had torn him too, I thought, because he grasped my shoulder and pressed his packet against my chest. I said, "Oppen, you must leave," trying to push him away and failing because he was at least a half head taller than I. I felt again the force of his struggle, but the force had become a sheer weight, bearing down on me, so that I was no longer trying to push him away or fend him off but to hold him up. The package fell with a thud at our feet. I braced myself against

his leaning bulk. I thought I would surely fall with him, but he
buckled, first to his knees, then toppled sidelong onto the sand at
the water's edge, lying where he fell, even though his head was
half-submerged in the water, and the river's froth collected in his
mouth. I moved to drag him back, but he was heavy, and I managed only to haul his head above the waterline before I slipped
back into a useless position against the bank.

Only then did I realize that something had fastened onto my
hand. Whatever it was had pierced the fleshy pad at the base of my
thumb and hung there like a scorpion or eel, refusing to let go. I
flailed my hand, trying to shake it free, but it held fast. Finally, I
mastered my revulsion enough to hold the thing up to the lights of
Nevers across the river. The part in my hand was a needle, connected by a short length of thin, flexible tubing to the cylinder of a
hypodermic, the bore large, the plunger pressed home. Breathing
deeply, I extracted the needle from my hand.

Though Oppen's head was no longer in the water, the froth,
pinkish, still trailed from his mouth. I pushed up his sleeve to
reveal the tape where he had affixed the hypodermic to his arm,
securing it in the vein, ready to be discharged when the moment
arrived. I knew then that no breath would clear the froth from his
throat, that my fingers, should I kneel beside him and press them
to his neck, would find no pulse.

If I waded into the water and crouched on the other side of his head,
I could get a better purchase on his body. At first I could not move
him and sat for an impotent moment in the shallows. In the end,
however, grabbing him beneath his armpits, I managed to haul
him down into the river, across the shoal downstream of the Isle of
Terns. Once past the shallows, the current took some of the weight
of his body, little by little, until finally it suspended him in perfect
equilibrium. A shift in the current lifted my feet from the sandy
floor, and I was forced to cling to his body because together we had
begun to move with the movement of the river. Seized with fear that

we would be drawn out together, I shoved myself back from him, back-paddling until my feet regained their purchase on the riverbed. By the time I had steadied myself, the combined force of my shove and the strength of the river itself had pulled his body out into the current. It turned once, then sank beneath the surface.

The water had closed over it all: their three lives, Miriam's, David Oppen's, their unborn child's. Somewhere else, far away, a lawyer would inform you—an orphaned girl—that your father had drowned in the Loire. With what sorrow or relief would you greet that news? Unbeknownst to you, you had been released from the lie that had made up your only reality. When you had heard the news, you would know only that you were alone—in reality no more alone than you had ever been, but now in possession of the fact.

As for me, standing on the riverbank, I was a shadow only—no, not even that. I was the shadow of something that had ceased to exist.

I returned to my house in the Morvan hills. Did I hope that you would try to find me again? Did I fear that others would now seek me out—detectives, investigators, officials bearing warrants? No one came up the road. You would not and neither would the law. Justice, I thought, had exhausted itself. It had no more use for me. It had spent me already.

For several days it rested on my table, the package he had consigned to me, addressed to a Reverend Nelson Spurlock, at the Church of the Incarnation. He had already affixed postage in the corner and had marked the package "Printed Material, Third Class Mail." Such a package would take a month to arrive. (I saw how in choosing to mail it from France, he had built in a delay, sufficient time for you to return home, to learn what you were to learn from the lawyer. He had also, I knew, made it possible for me to read it.) If I sent it first class instead (I thought to myself as I cut the twine), if I sent it first class after I read it, the package would arrive in New York no later than he had planned.

"Father, you will not remember me. My name is Daniel Abend."

So began his narrative. But that you know already. Along with this letter, has not the priest Nelson Spurlock brought it with him to give to you, the true testimony of that invented person, Daniel Abend? How queer it was to read it through, as though I too did not know how it would end. When I was finished, I sealed it in an envelope and sent it to the priest.

Soon after that, still unused to sleeping in this house, I had a dream. A week or two later, I had it again, exactly the same, just as I have had it ever since then, always the same. In it my daughter is alive again, still a child, and she and my wife have climbed the hill behind the house to look for blackberries in the clearings. From up on the hill they call to me. They want me to join them. Yves! cries my wife. Come look! And Miriam calls out, Papa! Papa!

I hear them, but I am detained below, though by what I do not know. When I do not answer, Miriam joins her mother in calling out my name: Yves! Yves! At first I am touched and mortified that she addresses me by name, but then I understand that my daughter alone is calling me, that she is alone, lost somewhere on the hillside. Papa! she cries out again, but I cannot answer her. Yves! she calls, but more weakly now, her voice the voice of someone who expects no response. I hear her but am paralyzed and cannot make a sound. Finally, despairingly, she calls out, Itzal! Itzal! Answer me! But she has already wandered to the other side of the hill, and Itzal cannot answer her. He is no longer here. Itzal has dissolved, as a shadow dissolves in darkness.

The years flowed past me, an old man and in time a sick one. Death, I believed, would be my next caller. I imagined him showing up, perhaps in the winter, out of breath, knocking the mud off his boots on my doorstep. "Yves, *mon vieux*," he would say, "better late than

never." He will be welcome when he arrives, but he has not found
his way yet. And so I wait for him. Each night now the dream returns
like an enormous black bird. It alights again on my chest. It feeds
once more on my heart.

No one visits, no one except the fat Moroccan curate from the
church in Préporché and the silent, whiskery woman (his girlfriend,
I assume) who prepares my meals, what little I can eat. The curate
drives me to my doctors in Decize, when he can persuade me to go,
or he comes on Sunday evenings, just to drink my gnôle and smoke
his disgusting Dutch tobacco. When the evening is mild, he brings
me out beneath the walnut tree. He calls me Old Goat and Infidel
and I call him Eunuch and the sun goes down. This past Sunday I
told him I would not be keeping my doctor's appointment this week,
and for once he did not argue. I asked instead if he could mail a
letter for me to the United States. "The old goat Levaux," he said,
"finally making amends to one of the women he ruined." One likes
to let the curate dream a little, no? The price of my gnôle, he knows,
is his promise to let me die in my house.

God will forgive us all, he says, even the old goat Levaux.

Sad God, I say, with no one to forgive Him in return.

Is that, my child, what I am asking you, your forgiveness? David Oppen was right: it is unforgivable that we should ask such a thing from our
children. And yet I have written you, knowing that the Reverend Nelson
Spurlock will find you. You are reading this, so I trust he is there with
you now. As for me, I must go. The night is far gone. My child, will you
permit an old ghost to address you as he always did, indeed, as he always
shall? Ma petite fille, ma Miriam à moi—adieu!

Yves Levaux

"Em," he said, and she looked at him for the first time, the nickel
gray of her eye bright with a suspended tear. "Em," he said. "Em is for
Miriam. Your name is Miriam."

"Yes," she said, "though no one calls me that." She smoothed the sheets and folded them back into the envelope, staring for a long moment at the patch of grass between her shoes. The dew was gone now, but her shoes were still wet.

"It's over. It is all over now," said Spurlock, because he did not know what to say. The words passed dry and comfortless from his lips. He had wanted them to convey, if nothing more, that she was not alone on this stone bench. Instead, they hung in the air as though they had been spoken by someone else, someone trying to wake him, trying to tell him it was late now and time to depart.

"It is strange—" she said at last, then paused and started again. "No. What I mean is, *nothing* is stranger—nothing is stranger than knowing that you've been allowed—that you've been permitted to live."

How inert it had lain, Oppen's testament, and for so long nearly forgotten on the top of the filing cabinet in his office. But maybe, thought Spurlock, its weight had served all along as a kind of mooring. It had anchored the tail end of a long string, a kite string stretching its curve to a minute fluttering at the edge of sight. But no, that wasn't right, not exactly, because when he had set out in search of that remote point, a point named Clementine Abend, he had discovered that Clementine Abend was not Clementine Abend. Cut free, the kite string had gone slack and laid itself down in illegible loops, tangled on the ground.

"A thread," she said.

"A thread?" said Spurlock, astonished that the kite string in his reverie might have been a shared apparition. She, however, had intended something else.

"That's what it was, a thread. The codicil to his will was a thread."

"The codicil—that paper you showed me?"

"The first document, the one I showed you—the codicil to my father's—to David Oppen's will. On the first day we met, at your church."

"The day I called you Clementine Abend and you vanished—"

"I vanished because I sensed it—how the codicil was a thread. It was handwritten, unwitnessed and unsigned, so it would have been useless as a legal document. And anyway, all it said was that correspondence addressed to his daughter, his only heir, would be addressed to you, Nelson Spurlock, at the Church of the Incarnation."

"Except—"

"Except the daughter was this Clementine Abend, this person I didn't know, a name I'd never heard."

"And you thought he must have had another daughter, that you weren't his daughter at all."

"No," she said, "I didn't think that. I never thought it, not for an instant. Because I was his only daughter. Everything else was impossible: that my father could have died, had in fact died, killed himself, and in France—a place he said he'd never go again. The apartment had been emptied and was under contract to be sold. It was like the whole world had been dismantled. But even then, even when the codicil appeared, with the strange names—this Clementine person, this Nelson Spurlock—I never doubted that I was his daughter, his only child. I bolted because I knew—knew and couldn't acknowledge—that Clementine Abend was me. For some reason, for some purpose, I was this person whose name I had never heard."

"But why would he send the codicil to you, especially after taking such pains to seal up his story, to disguise the names?"

"It would have been—yes, it must have been the last thing he did, the last thing before meeting Itzal at the riverbank. He'd sent the handwritten codicil knowing it would bring me to you, knowing you could put a face to the name he'd given me, even though that name—Clementine Abend—was one I didn't recognize. Don't you see? In the end, he blinked. He made it so that you could find me, if you saw fit—" For the first time, he felt the intensity in her voice turn to strain, and when she tried to speak again, it broke. He thought at first she had been seized by pain, so forcefully did she press the balls of her hands against her eyes, but after a moment, and a single shuddering breath, she wiped her hands on her jeans, her tears leaving two dark streaks on the fabric.

"It was done. It was over. He'd built his labyrinth and he'd hidden his secret inside it, but he'd built it around a thread, a thread for someone to discover and follow."

"For you to follow," he said, "back into it."

"Yes," she said, then, "No. Not back into it. Out of it. A thread to lead you to me, and the way out."

"But why would Itzal—why would Miriam's father send his letter to you in my care? Why wouldn't he send it to you directly? Surely he knew where you were."

"His letter wouldn't have made sense without the confession."

"But still, he could have told you what he needed you to know, then directed you to me, in New York, to learn more."

"There was too big a chance you wouldn't tell me anything. Maybe if he directed me to you in New York, if I just appeared, the seal on the confessional would oblige you to keep your peace."

"But isn't that all the more reason why he would contact you directly?" Spurlock heard the insistence in his own voice: how badly he wanted to believe his presence had not been required in the unfolding of this plan, that he was a peripheral figure, a bystander.

"And anyway," she said, "if he had told me to go find you, I wouldn't have gone. After Hale, the lawyer, told me my father had killed himself, I didn't want to know more. I wanted to unknow it all. Starting then, I was in flight. Itzal knew that if he told me outright, I just would have fled farther away. It's like I've been swimming like mad away from a sinking ship so I don't get sucked down behind it. The odds are bad, they say, for the children of suicides. . . ."

The odds were terrible, Spurlock knew, but what wasn't terrible in her story? "Why would Itzal have cared that you read the confession?" he asked.

She looked at Spurlock directly, and a glint, something like amusement, crimped the corner of her eye. "He did care."

She went on: "For Itzal, it was no longer a question of telling me what really happened."

"But isn't that just what he's done?"

"That's exactly what he *didn't* do. He sent his letter to you, trusting you would bring it, trusting you would bring David's confession too. Maybe he wasn't certain—maybe it was a gamble. What was certain was that he didn't want me to receive the news alone. He wanted someone else to be present. He trusted that you would be here with me when I read it, so that we could wonder about it, talk about it, like we're talking now. He could only send me the story if he sent me you as well."

For David Oppen, Spurlock realized, the confession had served its purpose, the unburdening of a soul. For himself and for the girl, however, the confession's purpose had become something wholly different, a purpose he could not have understood had she not appeared this morning in the arboretum. (He was aware now how much he had hoped she would appear, how this hope alone had steered him back to the bench where they had met the day before.) And appeared she had, just as she had years before in his church. Itzal's final act had been to place that confession between them. What had been the reckoning of a debt, a closing of accounts, was now something living and shared, entrusted to their care, something (as she had put it) they could wonder about, could speak about, could hope in time to comprehend.

"He loved me, but there was no way out. There was no way out," she repeated with a dry laugh, "and he took it. What am I supposed to feel about that?"

"Lost, for starters," said Spurlock.

"Maybe," she said.

"Maybe bereft, while you are at it."

"What I feel is maimed."

"Maimed?"

"Mutilated." The dryness in her voice, he thought, was a dryness beyond tears. "I loved him because he was my father. And he loved me. And now he is dead and I am disfigured."

Disfigured. The word, uttered flatly, seemed to Spurlock an emissary from a realm of irrevocable aftermath. Her expression too had taken on a flatness, and he remembered her profile on the day he first saw her, in silhouette against the limestone wall of the church as though cut there in bas-relief. What had struck him then as her otherworldly beauty, he understood now, had been in fact that mark of aftermath. He had recognized it because he had seen it before, in a thousand different inflections but always the same, in the faces of the drifters and the lost who had sheltered themselves in the Incarnation's unlicensed sanctuary.

"But isn't that what we all are," she said, "sooner or later, disfigured by love?"

"Are we?" The idea, alien to anything Spurlock knew of love, struck him suddenly as true.

"I believe we are," she said.

They were quiet for a long moment.

"Maybe—" said Spurlock at last, "maybe when we recognize our disfigurement, we get a glimpse—we see ourselves as God sees us, with love. In love."

"As love, even."

"Yes," said Spurlock. "As love."

Afterward, without intending to, without thinking, he had assumed his accustomed posture of prayer: elbows on knees, thumbs braced under chin, hands together, with his forehead pressed against the tips of his index fingers. He had not known he was praying, much less what he was praying for, until he felt her hand slip between his palms. The shock of it jolted him, but she did not pull away. After a moment of inner tumult— what did she want? what should he do? what comfort had he to offer?— all disquiet subsided, yielding itself to the current of an unfamiliar solace, the solace that merely being there together, in that instant, was enough. It flowed from her hand and circulated through him before flowing, changed, back into her. The silence, he understood, was hers to break, and for a long time she did not break it.

It was at that moment he noticed as though for the first time what he had noticed years ago, when she had first appeared at the church: the glint of gold about her face, a ring or rivet somewhere odd, piercing her brow or the hood of her ear. But what he saw was neither stud nor loop. It was in her eye, a foil-like flash or fleck in the nickel gray of her eye, struck (because her head was turned toward him) by the sun which had floated free of the horizon. The glint was just a feature of her face, un-chosen, and because unchosen, irreducibly alien and beautiful—alien and unchosen and beautiful, he thought, as every face is.

At last she said, "You will miss your plane, Nelson Spurlock."

"I will?" he said.

"Unless you let me take you, and we hurry."

"It's Sonny."

"So it seems, for once," she said, and smiled her downturned smile.

"No," he said, laughing, "my name. You should call me Sonny. Everyone else does."

"Well," she said, "it's settled. I promise. I'll call you Sonny."

"And I promise I won't call you Clementine."

"Why not call me Miriam? No one else does."

"Miriam, then," he said, and this time it was Spurlock who extended his hand and Miriam who took it between both palms.

"Sonny," she said. "*Enchantée.*"

Were you there, had you taken as I had the form of a crow in the crown of a yew tree—a crow hunched and inkily unkempt, hoarse from its dark, disconsolate colloquy—you would remark how they walk without haste, side by side, down the cinder path toward the sunrise and the eastern gate: my daughter, Miriam Oppen, and her kind companion, his head inclined toward her to listen.

ACKNOWLEDGMENTS

Bill Clegg, for your imagination, encouragement, and faith. Chris Clemans, Simon Toop, Jillian Buckley, Marion Duvert, Drew Zagami, David Kambhu, and Kirsten Wolf, for your exemplary competence, seriousness, goodwill, and good cheer. Kate Medina, for your trust and confidence and vision. Anna Pitoniak, for your patience, precision, friendship, diplomacy, and incisive husbanding of the manuscript. Erica Gonzalez, Derrill Hagood, Steve Messina, Robin Duchnowski, Joe Perez, Laura Klynstra, Susan Turner, Avideh Bashirrad, Andrea DeWerd, Sharon Propson, and Alena Jones, for steering the book with sure and light touch through each stage of its progress. Families Baudot, Harrison, Gillies-Lattman, Jennings, and Rogers, for your love and support. Ethan, Hugh, Thomas, and Phoebe, for choosing me to be your father. Laura, for the world.

ABOUT THE AUTHOR

DESALES HARRISON is an associate professor of modern poetry and acting director of the Creative Writing Program at Oberlin College. He earned his BA from Yale University, his MA from Johns Hopkins University, and his PhD from Harvard University. He studied psychoanalysis at the Institute for Psychoanalytic Training and Research in New York. He is married to the literary critic Laura Baudot, has four children, and spends part of the year near Nevers, France.

Twitter: @anotherdonkey

ABOUT THE TYPE

This book was set in Electra, a typeface designed for Linotype by renowned type designer W. A. Dwiggins (1880–1956). Electra is a fluid typeface, avoiding the contrasts of thick and thin strokes that are prevalent in most modern typefaces.